# NOTORIOUS

Mags McMillan

Cover created using Canva and Canva design elements. All credit to the original licensors and illustrators.

*This story was originally published on Wattpad in 2015 and amassed over 3 million reads. The story has since been edited, revised, and now includes a long-awaited epilogue. This new version is dedicated to those original fans that were so devoted and invested in Aspen's story. I hope these last 5 years have been kind to you and that this new version of Notorious brings you nostalgic joy. I'm so honored and grateful to have grown up alongside you all these years. Thank you for all your continued support.*

*CW: drug abuse, violence, sexual content.*

# CONTENTS

# OMINOUS

Ominous: giving the impression that something bad or unpleasant is going to happen; threatening; inauspicious.

Now, I don't know much about premonitions or superstitions, but what I do know, are definitions. By definition, the feeling I've had in my gut since this morning has proved to be very foreboding.

My eyes burn holes through the can as if somehow, my glare would make the magical brown powder appear. But, of course, the effort is fruitless and I'm left with the simple fact that I'm out of coffee. Aspen Marino is *actually* out of coffee... I must be dead. This has to be hell.

Aspen Marino *never* runs out of coffee.

Yet, somehow, when I opened the tin to feed my growing addiction to caffeine, all I was met with was air. *Air.* That never happens to me; as soon as the can even drops half-way I run to the store to buy more in order to avoid situations just like this. The time spent between work and rehearsals must have made me completely forget about my one true love: caffeine.

I set down the can with a resounding clank and rigidly step away from the monstrosity. The fact that I don't have coffee to start off my morning has my stomach in knots. It's just as angry as I am about not getting it's fix and this rare coffee shortage can only be considered a bad omen.

Already in a nasty mood, I set the burner on my tiny stove to boil water for tea. *Tea.* I shiver at the pathetic excuse for a placebo. It takes me almost an hour longer than it usually would to throw on some make-up and an old band shirt for multiple reasons:

1. I physically can't function without my morning coffee.
2. The Italian blood running through my veins has already caused my quick temper to spark at this inconvenience and I have to play with my corgi, Yoda, to cool down.
3. I'm drinking *bloody* tea, for goodness sake.

The whole coffee debacle has made me late and I have to toss aside the books, clothes, and shopping bags that litter the small hardwood floors of my London flat to find my favorite wooden guitar pick. Finally, I find it just under my blue tweed couch and sigh in relief.

Slinging my guitar case higher up my shoulder, I lock up and amble down the stairs of my complex. I receive a few 'good mornings' from the tenants and narrowly avoid another conversation with Betty about how her cats are feeling this morning. Living in the same building since I was eighteen comes with its perks: I'm invited to all the Christmas parties, free snacks and cookies whenever I'm ill, and people are surprisingly kind to a girl they've practically watched grow up the last four years.

However, things do get a bit awkward whenever I bring a boy home since the twelve people that live on my floor are basically like embarrassing chaperones. Which is exactly why I refrain from bringing members of the opposite sex over as much as possible.

The gust of cold I'm met with once exiting the swinging glass doors nearly knocks me back and I immediately regret wearing a leather skirt today. I know it's February, but you would think that London had been transported to Antarctica overnight.

I ignore the way my legs shake from the frigid air and that my hands are turning an alarming shade of blue and instead focus on the sound of my boots clicking on the busy sidewalk and keeping my chestnut tendrils out of my face as the wind picks up. The sky is as gloomy as I feel and a mist of chilling rain makes me pull my leather jacket tighter around my body as I trek through the streets. The walk isn't far, but by the time I make it to Jesse's loft I'm practically a popsicle. A very bitter popsicle that is dreaming of how warm it would feel back in California.

"Well, if it isn't Miss Sunshine herself." The red-headed Scot greets me as soon as he buzzes me up, but I shove right past him and head towards the brick fireplace facing the windows.

Jesse's apartment is fairly large, but rather sparse. He's a minimalist whose content with just the essentials, filling the space with friends instead of things. ¾ of the people that make up our band, Saints & Sinners, are already seated next to their respective instruments, spread out on the oak floor, and I take a moment to observe them while blowing hot air into my frozen palms.

The olive-skinned and tatted bass player, Enzo, already has his hazel eyes and amused smirk trained on me and my obvious distress. I promptly flip him off. My brother —and all-around puppy-dog— Marco, twirls a drumstick between his fingers, too oblivious to have noticed my entrance. And my best friend, Avery, watches Marco with her chin in her palm and a dazed look in her sunflower eyes.

*Subtle.*

"You're right on time," Jesse, our manager, claps me on the back and looks at his watch. "Which, for you, is actually twenty minutes late." He sends me a cheeky grin and I roll my eyes.

"Hey, Aspen, what's the word for someone who's never on time?" Enzo's voice drips with mock curiosity and I grit my teeth, but decide to humor him.

"Unpunctual?"

"No, that's not it… it was… Oh, yeah! A diva."

I laugh humorlessly and send Enzo a second bird for the day as I make my way to the stool centered between the other instruments. He's such a smart-ass, even more than I am. Always teasing me for my love of words and throwing the hobby in my face.

"You seem grumpy." Avery's light voice startles me and I glance up to find her fidgeting in front of my mic.

My brows furrow at her nervous state. Avery Forman may be a lot of things: kick-ass piano player, trust-fund kid, and a man-eater (metaphorically, of course... or, at least hoped). But, if there is one thing she isn't, it's *nervous.*

"Yeah, I ran out of coffee this morning. Why are you all... *jittery*?" I gesture at the way her fingers are pulling at each other and how her head keeps swiveling as if looking for someone.

As soon as the words leave my lips, Avery drops her hands and responds with an exaggerated shrug, "'mm not... Anyway, how could *you,* Aspen Marino, run out of coffee?"

Her blatant change of subject only makes me more bewildered, but I drop it. If she doesn't want to talk about what's bothering her, then I won't force it. She'll tell me when she's ready, she always does. "I don't know how I forgot to restock, it's truly a tragedy... I didn't think I could go on without it, but I know you all couldn't function without me," Avery rolls her eyes at my dramatics, a curve to her red lips. "But... seriously, since then, I've had a *bad* feeling in my stomach."

I laugh lightly because it sounds ridiculous said out loud, but Avery's dark eyes widen in distress under her bushy brows. She brings a manicured hand up to play with her wild curls and alarm bells immediately start going off in my head.

"What's up with you?" I don't mean to sound harsh, but my quick-temper is easily ignited —especially when my caffeine levels are dangerously low.

She gulps, glancing around us as the others start paying attention to our conversation. Taking a deep breath, she nods her head and begins toying with her fingers again.

"Don't be mad," she starts out pleadingly and I feel the boys gathering behind me. "But, you know how we talked about adding another singer to the group?"

I nod an affirmative, already seeing where this conversation is headed, but trying to keep my anger at bay. Jesse catches my eye, but quickly busies himself by checking his phone and whistling casually. *Coward.*

"Well, I kind of... maybe already hired someone."

"You *what?!*" I'm on my feet in a flash and Avery flinches at the harsh tone in my voice. It's not that I don't want another stranger joining our tightly knit-group, really, it's just that we'd already discussed that it would be a group decision. With the band competition coming up and so much on the line, we needed to find someone who could fit in with all of us.

I've been the lead singer since Marco and I started playing instruments in our garage when we were six to drown out our parent's fighting. We fell in love with the music and never stopped playing, adding more people to the band throughout the years like a makeshift family.

But, my last boyfriend absolutely obliterated any confidence I had in my abilities. Singing now makes me uncomfortable and anxious and I've been able to perform adequately less and less, nerves getting the better of me. So, the band decided that we would add another vocal until I could gain some of that confidence back and overcome my fear. I just never expected them to find someone so soon... and without even consulting the person the new member is meant to replace.

"Well, he kind of approached us about the job offer... and we all took a vote."

"I sure as hell didn't vote on this."

"We knew you wouldn't agree to it because it's a huge risk. But, I can't –*we* can't let you sing up there anymore. It doesn't make you happy like it used to, it just makes you miserable and stressed. I can't put you through it anymore until you gain back some of the confidence that asshole stole from you."

Marco's steps between Avery and I, tone soft, but barely veiled with an undercurrent of distaste for my ex. I know he's right, but it doesn't make the impact hurt any less.

I used to love singing. Even when Marco and I would pretend to be Salt and Peppa and put on performances for our parents, I would try to outshine him by singing louder and prouder. It's what I've always been best at, one thing I *knew* I could be proud of.

Pouring my heart into a song and being praised for it made me feel important, made me feel like I was worth *something* for the first time in my life. And I let some dumb *boy* rip that gift away from me.

He turned my greatest talent into a phobia. He mocked and belittled me and made it seem as if I was some American Idol reject and not a serious artist like I considered myself to be. He made me feel *worthless.*

You hear something long enough and you really start to believe it.

I know if I want the band to flourish, then I'll have to relinquish my dream to someone else. "Okay, *fine.* You're right. But, only until I can belt out the classics without flinching!"

They all give me enthusiastic thumbs-ups before informing me that the new singer has actually been waiting downstairs. I try not to let their secretiveness put me in a worse mood and shoo them away. As soon as they clamber out the doorway to greet our new member, I bend down to where I've placed my guitar case and rifle around until I find my pick.

My pick that has mysteriously broken in two.

I curse loudly as the bad feeling in my stomach grows: first the coffee, then the new singer, now my favorite pick. How could this day get any worse?

"Skirts a bit short, don't you think, Munchkin? Not that I mind, because I really, *really* don't mind."

*I spoke too soon.*

The familiar raspy voice causes the hairs on the back of my neck to rise and I snap up from my bent position, turning to face the pervert. Emerald eyes trailing down my figure, wild brown locks held back with a headband, and a cocky grin taking residence on full pink lips. All attributes I've come to associate with one person, if you could even call him that.

My so-called friends had chosen the most notorious man in London's underground music industry to be our lead singer.

Everett *Fucking* Fox.

Ominous has never sounded more right.

# LOTHARIO

When I started dating, my mother told me: "Aspen, never trust Prince Charming. A man who says and does all the right things knows the game too well. He is a method actor in the dating game and you are just another rehearsal."

Those are the words that I've lived my romantic life by. If a man never stumbles over his words or even pauses to think, he has said the same line one too many times.

Everett Fox is a *very* charming man.

I've concluded this just by being squished in a booth with him and the rest of the band for the last few hours. The way his tongue so easily articulates each syllable, how his hands accentuate what he's saying like they've memorized the story, and the arrogant grin that remains on his lips throughout his entire conversation with Avery are all tell-tale signs.

He is very well-rehearsed in *literally* charming the pants off people.

How easily he got everyone to agree to have drinks tonight to celebrate his welcome to the band is proof enough. Marco hates bars and Avery told me she wanted to cuddle up with a movie. But, Everett snapped his fingers, and it was decided.

Now I know how he weaseled his way into the band in the first place.

I'm sure his dimpled grin and seawater eyes helped a little too.

"Ask Aspen, she'll know the answer." Avery acknowledges

me for the first time since we sat down and I begrudgingly sit up in my seat as Everett turns to me with a stupid smirk.

"What's the card game that old people play where you're set up in pairs? Like, the more cards you have, the higher the points, and you play with tricks, I think? And each deal has—"

"Bridge?"

"That's it," he sends me a wolfish grin before turning back around to Avery. "So, the joke was: having sex is like playing bridge. If you don't have a good partner, you'd better have a good hand."

Avery immediately howls with laughter and Everett chuckles along with her and it takes everything in me not to roll my eyes.

"That was awful." I deadpan and Everett turns to me with a raised brow.

"Maybe because it hits too close to home?"

"Or because you had to ask me what the main punchline for the joke was called."

He rolls his eyes and I take a long swig from my bottle as Avery gets up to use the loo. Enzo has gone to talk to the DJ, Jesse is dancing by himself on the dancefloor, and Marco disappeared as soon as we walked in to our local pub. Now, I'm alone with my replacement. *Great.* Everett's grin has grown suspiciously mischievous by the time I bring the beer back down onto the sticky table.

Then I notice where his gaze is focused.

"Find anything interesting?" The slight buzz that courses through my veins helps control my temper because, otherwise, the neck of my bottle would be shoved somewhere he'd find rather unpleasant.

*I'm in an old t-shirt, for Fox sake.*

"Oh, you have no idea, Munchkin," his husky voice rasps and he finally raises his gaze to meet my unamused one. "So, tell me why I'm here."

"First of all, don't call me that. Secondly, because you forced everyone to come here?"

"First of all, I think the nickname fits the bill. Secondly, I meant, why am I the singer for the band, when your voice is obviously well enough to make smart-ass remarks?" His smirk widens and he leans back in the booth to swing an arm over the red leather.

I shift uncomfortably in my seat because I don't like how close he's gotten and also because I forgot we told people I had swollen lymph nodes as an excuse for my lack of performance. That was much easier to explain.

My silence spurs another chide remark, and even though the booming pop music and loud laughter from the crowded bar make it hard to hear, his smugness rings clear.

"Oh, so now that I've confronted you, your swollen nodes have suddenly acted up again?" Everett's voice drips with sarcasm and I resist the urge to use the headband wrapped around his head to choke him.

"I just don't want to sing anymore, alright? Just drop it." My irritation makes the truth slip out as a way to shut him up. I wince, wishing I could swallow the words back up.

Everett's smug grin is wiped off his face and replaced by furrowed brows and a slight frown. I'm surprised that I find the pouty look to actually be quite cute on him. I'm even more surprised when Everett actually does what I ask and drops the subject. The booth falls into a strained silence and I chug the rest of my beer, examining our new front man. I've never actually seen him up close, just far away at parties or up on a stage. The rumors had not done him justice.

Despite the boyish dimples and full lips that scream innocence, the rest of him conveys the exact opposite. Black button down that's open enough to allow a peek at the rustic rendition of a lighthouse tattooed across his chest and the scripted words displayed across his ribs, scruff that darkens his sharp jawline, and intense mossy-green eyes that hold many secrets.

It isn't just the lack of color in his wardrobe or the tattoos that litter his tanned skin that reveal his true attitude, but it's really the way he carries himself. Even now, he' slumped against the booth —one arm draped across the top and the other placed on the calf of his right leg that lays crossed on top of his left thigh.

He *exudes* confidence. His posture, the conviction in his voice, and how he can just waltz into a room and own it is something to be envious of.

Too bad he's infamous for being a Casanova. I've heard his name whispered in awe and anger through many years, always with some story about a groupie he took home and kicked out in the morning without even remembering their name. Hell, the reason he was fired from his old band was because he slept with the drummer's sister.

The boy could give Michelangelo a run for his money with the amount of time he's spent staring at a ceiling.

"See anything interesting?" His raspy voice pulls me out of my reverie and I flush at being caught staring at him, my own words thrown back in my face.

I snap my gaze away, begging for someone to come back to the booth and break this awkward silence, but it isn't long until my attention has circled back to Everett.

A large, tattooed hand somehow finds its home on my knee, sliding up my bare thigh until the pinky brushes the hem of my skirt. I try to ignore the fire his fingers leave in their wake and instead focus on the fact that this bastard actually has the nerve to feel me up.

"What's the word for a man who would love nothing more than to take you home tonight?" Everett's husky voice dominates my senses, his warm breath dancing across my ear.

I never paid much attention to those rumors, but their sheer volume and this offensive display tonight tell me everything I need to know. I've barely met the man, he's meant to replace me in *my* band, I clearly am not a huge fan of his, and he dares to make a move on me?

With fury and an overwhelming sense of competition running through my veins, I lean in, my own lips brushing his ear as I trail a finger up his chest. He visibly shivers at my feather-light touch and my red lips pull up into a smirk.

"A Lothario." I breathe.

"What?" Everett freezes.

"A man who behaves selfishly and irresponsibly in his sexual relationships with women."

"I know what the hell a Lothario is." Everett pulls away just as I do, anger barely veiled in his darkened eyes.

"I'm glad you're self-aware, then." I send him a condescending smile and pat his chest lightly before removing myself from his grasp and scooting out of the booth.

I try to keep my rage at bay, but it's boiling under the surface and grows with every step I take. I've only known him a few hours, but there's just something about Everett that sets off my temper like flint against steel. The boy has some nerve to think I would be willing to go home with him just because I was staring.

I do have *some* sense.

"Whoa, why do you have that murderous look on your face?" Avery bumps into me in the middle of the small dance floor and I can't help but chuckle at her words.

"No reason, but you better dance with me before I *do* end up poisoning Curly over there."

Avery's eyes widen at my words, but she laughs and assumes I'm joking. Little does she know I've already imagined the scene in my head too many times in the last few hours to still be considered sane.

But, if there's one thing that always calms me down, it's music. And as soon as we hit the dancefloor, my whole body relaxes and instinctively moves to the beat of the popular R&B song.

The subtle drop of the bass makes me run my hands down my body, thrumming with the vibrations from the shaking ground. Avery's hips sway, her dark skin glowing from the blue lights above us. I follow her lead, hands dipping into the curves of my figure before reaching my hair and mussing it up.

Avery flips me around so I can dance against her front, but I freeze.

Dark emerald eyes pierce through me from the back of the bar. They're hooded with lust and the irritation in his expression from before has vanished as he spreads across the booth lazily, watching me.

A smirk tugs at my lips as I continue dancing, skin heating at the intensity of his gaze and the unabashed way he's staring, but I ignore the pounding in my chest and keep moving against Avery, hands trailing slowly across my body.

As soon as my hands reach up to cup my breasts, Everett shifts uncomfortably in his seat, hand disappearing beneath the table, and that's enough satisfaction for me. I send him a smug grin before turning back around, satisfied at my teasing and swift rejection of the Big Bad Fox.

But, when the song ends and we head back to the table, I catch the familiar head of curly hair slipping out of the door with a blonde bombshell latched to his arm.

I guess some girls never learned not to trust a charming man.

# FAVORITISM

Marco Marino is the golden boy that has overshadowed me for my entire existence.

He was captain of his footy team, volunteered at the local soup kitchen, earned straight A's, and never *ever* got in trouble with our parents.

I, on the other hand, can barely run for two minutes without feeling like I'm going to die. I've never been involved in any charity work unless it benefited me, I would've failed my classes if it weren't for my smarter friends, and I got in so much trouble that my mother didn't even bat an eye the night she bailed me out of jail for public indecency.

From conception, we were different. Even in the womb, Marco was still and peaceful, while I was rambunctious and kicked my mother's bladder constantly.

My brother and I have always been complete opposites and it shows through our mother's preferential treatment. He is Ross and I am Monica. So, am I surprised that my mom calls Marco twice a week to chat, when she hasn't bothered to call me for a month? No. Does it hurt? More than I would care to admit.

"Yes, mom, I got the care package in the mail," Marco snickers at my offended expression. "I'll deposit the money when we're done with rehearsals."

*Care package? C'mon, I don't even have milk in my apartment right now.*

I childishly mock him behind his back and Enzo can barely contain his snorts of laughter. Marco turns to glare, but I drop my hands and flash an innocent smile before he notices. Jesse huffs, knocking Marco's combat boots off his glass table before handing me a coaster for my beer. Marco shoos Jesse away, continuing to talk into the phone as Jesse tidies up.

If he didn't want us in the nice, expensive apartment his parents bought him, he shouldn't hold rehearsals here. Or, entice us with free booze and food.

"Hi, mumsy!" I yell towards the phone, voice sickly sweet, and Marco cringes.

"Yeah, that was Aspen. She says hello... do you want to talk to her?"

I wait patiently next to Marco as he listens to our mom on the other line. His face falls slightly at whatever she's saying and avoids eye-contact. I suddenly take interest in the rips of my boyfriend jeans, perfectly aware of my mother's reply without having to hear it.

"Love you too. Bye." He hangs up and turns to me apologetically, "she had a meeting to go to. She said to tell you that she loves you, though. And that she'll call when—"

"Yeah, yeah. No need to lie on mother dearest's behalf." I grumble, the heels of my boots clicking against the floor as I make my way over to the mic.

"Don't be like that... you know she's just busy and loves you just as much as me."

My head immediately snaps to face my brother who is sporting puppy-dog eyes and pouted lips. The room fills with awkward tension as Enzo hums his way into the kitchen and Jesse leads Avery away from our confrontation. I think they can see the anger pulsating from me in waves.

"Favoritism: the practice of giving unfair preferential treatment to one person or group at the expense of another." Marco rolls his coffee colored irises in exasperation, but that doesn't stop me from continuing. "She always went to your games instead of my gigs and practically throws money at you, but won't even loan me twenty bucks. She calls you constantly when I haven't spoken to her for over a month. Admit you're the favorite already and move on... I have."

*Sorta.*

Marco is silent as my words sink in and his bushy eyebrows link together in pity, but I just shake my head. It bothers me, yeah, but I've lived my whole life knowing that if both of us were at the edge of a cliff, my mom would choose to save Marco every time.

I want to blame it on the fact that my honey eyes are a replica of my father's and that I get my plump lips and quick temper from the man that left my mother for some thirty-year-old child.

But, I know it's much more than that.

"It's fine, M. I don't blame her for favoring you. I've disappointed her more times than I can count." I muster up the best smile I can manage, but Marco has always been good at reading people and he's about to open his mouth to argue when Avery waltzes back in.

"Everett's on his way up." She can't even control her amusement as we lock eyes and she giggles at my pinched face, smoothing down her wild curls. I'm thankful for the change of subject, but her words bring a new irritation that makes my skin prickle.

It's only been a week since Everett joined our band and I'm really starting to question my sanity. He knows how to push my buttons in just the right ways to infuriate me: constantly mocking my American accent, calling me munchkin even though I'm not *that* short, and his eyes never trail far from my chest or ass.

Of course, I'm the only one that feels this way. He's already weaseled his way into Avery's good graces from just a few compliments and he bought the band some ritzy lunch the other day that practically made Jesse swoon. He's even got my brother stopping by his flat to play video games.

The only person who even slightly shares the same animosity towards the curly haired freak as I do is Enzo —who always glares at Everett when he bursts through the door all cocky and with a new joke that makes our skin crawl.

"Can't we just give him the boot already? The guy is an arrogant, crude, womanizing, talentless asshole. He never shuts up, his jokes are all stupid, and I really don't think..." My voice trails off as I notice the horrified expressions of my bandmates, stomach dropping, "he's right behind me, isn't he?"

"Careful, Munchkin. You're starting to sound like my mum." Everett's raspy voice is slightly amused and my ponytail whips me in the face from how fast I spin around to face him.

I curse under my breath, because of *fucking course,* he looks gorgeous adorned in a crisp white button-up, black jeans, and boots that —embarrassingly enough— match mine. His wild curls are slightly damp from the rain and his emerald eyes are even lighter than they were the day before.

*Fucking Everett and his stupid fucking face.*

"Whoops." I shrug it off even though my cheeks burn from embarrassment and my heart is thudding in my chest. His expression remains amused, but I don't miss the slightly offended look in his eyes.

"My jokes are *not* stupid."

"That's really all you got out of that?" I deadpan and he just lifts his shoulders with a smug smirk on his full lips. Avery and Marco watch the interaction in amusement, but don't come to my rescue. Enzo finally leaves the loo, freezing in the hallway as he appraises the uncomfortable situation before him.

"Oh, and we both know that I could sing circles around you." He struts towards the modern kitchen where I can hear Jesse banging around in. I grab onto his elbow and ignore the feeling of the firm muscle.

"*Excuse* me? That's bullshit."

"Then, why am I the one singing in your place?" He challenges, face way too close for comfort. His breath fans my lips and I get slightly distracted by the scent of tea and mangoes. He even *smells* good, that just isn't fair.

I open and close my mouth, taking a step back from him as I try to think of an answer. He kind of has me there. My face only grows hotter as I let him go, swallowing uncomfortably.

"No, *really*... can someone tell me why I'm the lead singer, when she can sing perfectly fine herself?" He stuffs his hands in his pockets casually, completely oblivious to the tension he's just caused.

Marco suddenly busies himself with setting up the drums and Avery just blatantly watches our exchange shamelessly. Enzo is the one that steps forward, sharp jaw locked, arms crossed, and bushy brows pulled together.

"That's none of your business, Fox." He grits out and I'm taken aback by the hardness in his tone. Everett raises his brows, gaze shifting between the two of us bewilderingly. A smirk suddenly lights up his face as his eyes clear in understanding. He nods and lets out a raspy chuckle before sidestepping Enzo. I breathe a sigh of relief when he raises his hands in surrender, clearly dropping it.

"Touchy subject. Got it." He eyes me curiously, before thankfully changing the subject, "so, Munchkin, anything else you hate about me that you'd like to share with the class?"

A small laugh escapes my lips before I notice the serious expression on Everett's face and realize that he does actually want to know. I stare a bit longer, contemplating if this is a trap or not. I don't notice that Enzo has walked off until I actually open my mouth, my tone half-joking, half-serious.

"Well, I hate that you call me Munchkin. So, stop. And you *exclusively* drink tea, so I'm a little suspicious of your character–"

Everett lets out an exaggerated gasp and I look up to catch his mouth agape, eyes wide, and a large hand placed on his chest as if clutching his nonexistent pearls. I try not to chuckle at his offended expression, but fail miserably. "You hate *tea?* We are in England you know? Time to acclimate, love."

I ignore the way heat rises up my chest at the nickname and

cross my arms in defiance, but I'm surprised to find that I'm not as irritated as I was before. "Yes, and the fact that you *only* drink tea means I like you even less."

"Oh c'mon, Munchkin... can't we all just get *oolong*?" His lips pull into a boyish grin at the joke, but my expression remains impassive. However, it doesn't take long for my stony composure to break, chuckling at the proud look on his face and ridiculousness of the joke. His smile only grows as he watches me laugh and I think for just a *second* that we *could* maybe get along.

That thought flies out the window pretty quickly though. I'm reminded why I dislike him so much when I and notice what his gaze is *really* focused on.

"Oh, for *Fox* sake. Stare at my chest one more time, and I *will* castrate you."

# MASOCHIST

If you want a simple, easy way to torture me physically and emotionally, I have just the solution for you: take me shopping.

Nothing will make me unhappier than spending hours traipsing around a mall behind slow-walkers and trying on clothes that wouldn't fit a Barbie. I love the results of shopping, but I hate the process.

I've been walking around this materialistic hell hole for almost three hours now and my back is aching, my patience is wearing thin, and my self-esteem has plummeted. And all I have to show for it is two dresses and a pair of heels I probably won't even like tomorrow. Avery, however, continues to tug me along to every shop known to man with a content smile, and I'm forced to wonder if she's actually Satan or just a sadist.

"We *have* to get some new lingerie while we're here! It will perk you right up."

*Both. She's definitely both.*

I grumble some more protests under my breath, but Avery pretends not to hear and grasps my hand to pull me though the throngs of people. Some of this trip is selfishly motivated for her, as she finally has a day off from band practice and her accounting job and wanted to splurge. But, I know that Avery is also dragging me around this kid-infested building for my benefit. The introduction of my replacement stirred up a lot of self-doubt and depression and Avery definitely noticed.

She always does.

I'm sure that, in her mind, spending an obnoxious amount of money on things I don't need will be therapeutic for me. Maybe it will, but it probably won't tomorrow when I check my bank balance. Regardless, I stick a sickly-sweet smile on my face for her sake.

Avery allows me to make a pit-stop for coffee and the first sip immediately puts me in a better mood and authenticates my grin. I swear I think my veins are running on this liquid drug from the amount I consume daily. No wonder I'm so short, they say coffee does stunt your growth. No wonder I'm a *munchkin.*

My face pulls into a grimace at the reminder of the nickname and the man who gave it to me. The exact man this shopping spree is aimed at helping me expunge from my thoughts. I grunt in frustration at his stupid pet name and his stupid face invading my Saturday morning without permission.

"We're just shopping! This is supposed to be fun. *Jeez*, you'd think I'm bloody torturing you." Avery laughs once she notices the disgruntled expression on my face and I shoot her an unamused look.

"I wasn't making that face at shopping."

"What else could make you scrunch up your face like you just ate month old ravioli?" Although her tone is interested, she becomes immediately distracted. An excited gleam shines in her chocolate irises as soon as we walk through the threshold of the lingerie store.

We make our way to the absurd amount of lace in the back of the dimly-lit store and it's just the distraction I need to ignore her question. Everett is the last person I want to discuss when shopping for lingerie. Avery turns to me with an eyebrow raised and I know she's trying to read me. She's so good at it that I sometimes think she can read minds and her next statement only adds to that suspicion.

"Everett?"

"How the hell do you do that?" I hiss, but Avery just flips her long, curly mane and shrugs. "Yes, unfortunately, I was thinking about him... can't we kick him out of the band yet?"

She laughs lightly, picking up a thong so thin it could be floss, "on what basis?"

"Bad jokes?" I offer and Avery grins at my suggestion before shaking her head and picking up the matching bralette.

"He's a little cocky, but you've got to admit that he isn't half bad to look at."

"Please, like you spare a look at anyone who isn't my brother." Avery immediately turns around to look at the garters lining the leopard print wall.

"I don't know what you're talking about." Her tone is defiant, but the red flush underneath her brown skin betrays her. Satisfied that she'll drop the topic, I peruse the table next to her.

When we recruited Avery into our band a few years back, she instantly became infatuated with Marco. He's so much kinder and more put-together than all the assholes she used to date, that it almost makes me want to root for them. He, of course, is too oblivious to notice her crush, despite the fact that she watches him like good TV, blushes whenever he talks to her, and has basically sworn off men since meeting him.

*Men. What are they good for?*

As if the thought summons him, I hear a slow and familiar drawl behind me, "I'd absolutely love to see you in this number."

I spin around to find Everett holding up a white bralette with embroidered flowers and matching high-hip panties. A dirty smirk is accompanied by darkened irises and I resist the urge to punch the look right off his face. Avery is watching from behind Everett and I silently beg her to step in and save me from committing murder. She shakes her head, grinning in amusement.

*Traitor.*

"I'd love to see you in a coffin, but ya know, we don't always get what we want."

I'm disappointed that his smirk only grows, "you wound me, Munchkin." He holds the two-piece in front of my figure and closes one eye in concentration. "Oh yeah, I can imagine it now. You in this, with that red lipstick you wore the other day, hair all messy and tangled, just *begging* me to tear apart this lace and—"

"Se dici un'altra parola ti uccido, stronzo pervertito." [If you say another word I'll kill you, perverted asshole.]

His already darkened eyes deepen, leer transforming into a delighted smile, "holy shit, you speak Italian? *Fuck.* That's hot." His eyes rake my figure like he wants to rip all my clothes off in the middle of this store. Avery is invested in our conversation, I imagine her shoving popcorn into her mouth behind him.

My skin heats up under his burning gaze and I curse myself for the bad habit of ranting in Italian when I'm angry.

I huff, crossing my arms, "I just *threatened* you... I wouldn't call that 'hot.'"

He tilts his head as if pretending to think, before that wolfish grin fills up his face again, "No, definitely still sexy."

"What are you, a masochist?" I'm really just trying to get him to stop flirting with me because it's doing something to my insides that I do *not* like. I know this is just who he is, a flirt, that he means nothing by it. That it's not serious. But, it's still extremely aggravating.

Everett only furrows his brows at my question and I meet his eyes, sighing, "Masochist: a person who is pleasured by pain, degradation, etc., that is self-imposed or imposed by others."

Everett's lustful expression briefly transforms into one of fondness, but it's gone in a flash. "I could be one for you, if you're into that kind of thing."

I scoff, about to mock him again, when a petite brunette suddenly appears behind Everett and places a quick peck on his cheek. The insult dies on my tongue as she turns to face Avery and I, a genuine smile digging dimples into her cheeks.

"Hi, I'm Marisol, a friend of Everett's." The girl holds a dainty, manicured hand out towards me and I take it in a firm shake, faltering slightly.

*Friend?* This isn't the same *friend* he left the bar with the other night?

"I'm Aspen, definitely *not* a friend of Everett's." To my shock, she laughs at my joke and Everett joins her, then her dark eyes suddenly widen in realization and her grip grows tighter.

"Oh, I know you! You used to date the lead singer of The Bloody Diamonds, right?"

The polite smile tightens on my face and I drop her hand as if she burnt me. It's an innocent inquiry that I get asked more than I would like, but it still doesn't stop my heart from sinking to the bottom of my stomach. Unfortunately, Sam's band has a pretty large following in the underground scene and his dark curls and piercing cerulean eyes have made him a fan favorite amongst all genders. Which means, his ex-girlfriend also developed quite a reputation.

*One I wish would simply die out already.*

I give her a curt nod, but keep my mouth shut because I'd rather throw myself into a volcano than ever have to talk about Sam again. I feel Avery's pitying gaze and only hope my face reflects the stony coldness I feel inside. Everett obviously notices my discomfort because he quickly swoops down to give Marisol a quick kiss to the corner of her lips that shuts her right up.

"Is that for me?" Blood rushes to her cheeks as she points to the set that Everett picked out for *me.*

I roll me eyes because, of course, Everett would take a girl to a lingerie shop as a date. He swings an arm around Marisol's shoulders and looks from me to the —actually really pretty— lingerie with a small smile on his face.

"No, no. This definitely isn't for you." His mossy green eyes meet my hazel ones, lingering there as if sharing a secret. He places the set back with a last look and my heart has the audacity to flutter at his longing expression. Thankfully, the feeling immediately fades when he turns to a different stack of push-up bras. "No, you would look much better in red."

I shake my head in disbelief and quickly stride away from the couple, back to a laughing Avery. I can't believe that he would hit on me in the same store that his fling—or whatever they are— is shopping in. Marisol seems like a sweet girl who deserves much better than that. He's either extremely ballsy or just a downright scumbag.

I'll go with the latter.

"Don't *even* say a word." I warn Avery as soon as I see her amused expression.

She pretends to lock her lips and throw away the key and the adorable gesture eases my irritation slightly. I help her pick out a few pieces to buy while trying to ignore the giggling I hear every once in a while, from either Everett or Marisol, even when we're at opposite ends of the store.

Luckily, they leave shortly, but not without Everett sending me a suggestive wink while resting his hand low on Marisol's hip.

*Gross.*

Thanks to my short fuse, I stew in anger the rest of the day, but despite my violent thoughts towards Everett, I find myself walking back towards the lace area of the shop. I pick up his selection—a delicate lace bralette that doesn't cover much and matching underwear that comes up to my hips, but the material is thin and see-through.

It's vintage, delicate, and just my style. I find myself walking up to the register before I can even question what I'm doing.

*It's only because it's pretty, not because Everett picked it out.*

I repeat that statement over and over in my head as the woman rings up my ridiculously expensive purchase. I avoid Avery's knowing stare as I stuff the red bag into my larger one, astonished that I actually bought the set and confident that Everett must *never* find out.

I'm really beginning to question my sanity.

Regardless, I take a peek into the bag and admire the fabric with a small smile on my face and briefly wonder if it's actually *me* who is the masochist.

# ABHORRENCE

Throughout my vast drinking experience, I've learned that there are five types of drunk people: the emotional, the happy, the flirty, and the philosophical. After another successful rehearsal that resulted in cracking open Jesse's extensive liquor collection, I can't help but place each one of my bandmates into these categories.

**Jesse:**

It's pretty humorous to see the burly, bearded, and broad-shouldered Scot brought to tears by a few shots of whiskey.

As soon as the bottle touches his lips, Jesse is struck by cupid. He clambers up to Everett as he comes out of the bathroom and practically tackles him to the ground. "You know, I don't get why Aspen hates you so much," he slurs and Everett raises his brows at me in amusement. "Well, you are a bit of a twat, but I quite like you! You're funny and you brought us cake, what more could we ask for?!

"It's so unfair that you've got the dimples, the voice, *and* the hair." His fingers reach up to tug on the wild curls and Everett winces. "How the *fuck* do you get your hair like that? You know what? I take it all back, I hate you. You steal all the good-looking birds."

Marco and Avery have to practically drag Jesse away from a laughing Everett after that.

In true Jesse fashion, though, he stumbles back around not five minutes later as Everett is telling me another dirty joke. Jesse looks down at his feet, playing with his fingers nervously.

When he glances up, he has tears swimming in his mossy eyes, "I'm surry, Fox. I act-actually do looove you, mate. I didn't mean it."

**Avery and Marco:**

It isn't surprising that both Avery and Marco end up being the overly giddy ones. They so graciously make the six of us Jell-O shots, and then so graciously proceed to eat them all themselves. They spend a majority of the night laughing hysterically at every joke Everett makes —much to his delight — and even come up with a few of their own that mostly go something like this:

"What do you get when you put a banana between two oranges? Genitalia!"

Even Everett cringed.

Most of the night is spent watching the two idiots dance to every song that comes up on my phone. I discover, much to my pleasure —and slight horror— that *both* Avery and Marco know the entire dance to 'Everybody' by The Backstreet Boys.

**Enzo and Everett:**

It will shock no one to discover that Everett and Enzo are flirty drunks.

Everett still manages to make my skin crawl every time he opens his mouth, but that doesn't stop him from spewing corny jokes and flirting with me at every opportunity. I've gotten drunk with Enzo enough times to know that alcohol tends to make him bold and suave, even throughout my relationship with Sam. In the three months since I broke up with Sam though, he's held himself back. Until tonight.

I'll chalk that up to my good friend: Jack Daniels.

Enzo holds a tattooed hand out, suave smirk on his full lips, as he motions for me to dance with him. The peach schnapps still tingling my tongue makes me clasp his hand and he pulls me into his chest, giggling. My gaze lands on Everett who is sitting on the leather couch, Jesse is passed out on his shoulder. Everett's burning gaze remains on me, a frown etched deeply onto his face. Childishly, I stick my tongue out at him before turning back to Enzo.

We spend a few songs swaying along to the soft jams of Don Hathaway, Enzo's hands on my hips and mine wrapped around his scruffy neck. It would be very romantic if the room wasn't spinning. When the song picks up tempo, Enzo pushes me away, only to spin me back in and I giggle at the silly move, curling back into his arms, my back to his front.

It's in this position that Everett stands and makes his way towards us, "can I step in?"

"No, fuck off."

I'm forced to stand between the two of them as I uncoil myself from a suddenly rigid Enzo. Their gazes lock, Everett's jaw clenching tightly and Enzo's fists trembling. In the few weeks since Everett has been in the band, they've already begun to have daily pissing contests. There just isn't room for two huge egos in this room.

"I think she would rather dance with me, mate."

Enzo scoffs and crosses his arms, "really? Because I'm pretty sure she can't stand you, *mate.*"

Normally, I might've made sure they didn't beat the shit out of each other, but my inebriated state has me easily distracted. When I lock eyes with Avery and see her making more Jell-O shots between the kitchen doors, I slip out from between the two of them unnoticed. I spend the next twenty minutes helping Avery make *and* eat more Jello-O shots, but as soon as I'm back in the den, I trip over someone's discarded shoe and a pair of ring-clad hands reach out to catch me.

"You fallin' for me, Munchkin?" To my own horror, I actually laugh at his joke. *Laugh.*

I'm drunker than I thought.

Everett pulls me up and lightly pushes me up against the nearest wall and I let him because I'm very drunk and he smells like mangoes and I'm hungry.

"Thank you." Everett chuckles and my brows draw together in confusion. *Did I say that out loud?*

"Yes, yes you did." I curse under my breath, but that doesn't stop the chuckles falling from my drunken lips.

Nothing is really funny, but for some reason, I can't stop my body from shaking, eyes from welling up, and laughter from filling the hallway. I barely notice Everett's grip on my hip and the other hand that twirls my hair, but I don't slap them away either.

His stare is so intense that blood instantly fills my cheeks and I'm thankful when he dips his head, breaking our eye contact. Though, I only grow more flustered when his curls tickle my jaw as his head lowers into the crook of my neck. "You smell bloody intoxicating too, like strawberries."

He inhales deeply and the hair on my neck raises as his warm breath caresses the flesh there, lips just grazing my skin. The combination of his husky voice and delicious scent makes me incredibly dizzy, but the trance is broken when a voice calls to us from the hallway.

"Jesse is crying because he dropped his Jell-O. He's callin' out for ya, Aspen, you should go check on him." Though Enzo is speaking to me, his hard gaze is set on Everett, who has now leaned far away from me. I shove him off me and make way down the hall, violently shaking my head to clear it.

I *am* way more drunk than I thought to allow Everett Fox so close to me.

**Me:**

After a couple of peach schnapps, I become a mini Aristotle with musings of love and peace and the fall of mankind. Though, much less profound.

I'm pretty sure at some point I said something like, "a day without sunshine is like night," and Jesse looked at me as if I was the second coming of Christ. If their attention wasn't easily swayed, I think my bandmates would've eventually built a shrine and treated me as their savior.

After my altercation in the hallway, I tried to start up some intellectual conversation with the Wonder Twins —Avery and Marco— with musings like:

*How do you describe color? What does water taste like? Who really* did *let the dogs out?*

Alas, none of these topics interest them for long and I find myself sitting alone on the couch as everyone starts to pass out. "Did your followers leave you?" Everett plops down next to me with an amused smile on his full lips.

"Yes, but they'll come around. I'm sure no one jumped on Plato's bandwagon, but look at him now! They named silly putty after him!"

"I'm not quite sure that's true." Everett barely bites out before he snorts with laughter, shaking the couch. I pout at him for laughing at me, but that soon turns into a few chuckles of my own because the booming and raspy sound of his laughter is practically contagious.

We sit for a while longer and watch as each of our friends pass out one-by-one in various positions and places. I find it increasingly difficult to keep my eyes open as the room continues to spin and the alcohol makes my brain all fuzzy. I yawn, feeling Everett's gaze trained on me, but I can't find the energy to turn my head.

The couch is very plushy and I find myself subconsciously inching closer to Everett's warmth, rational thought poisoned by the liquor. His thigh presses against mine as I lean my head back into the couch, listening to his low breaths and the deep sound of someone snoring in the distance. I want to find a comfortable place to sleep far from Everett, but my movements are just as sluggish as my mind.

"Munchkin?" I barely grunt a response, leaning closer in closer, craving his body heat in the frigid flat and not thinking of tomorrow's consequences. "Knock-Knock..." His words slur together, but I can hear the smile in his voice just as the room begins to fade to black.

"Shut up, Curly." A low rumble of his laughter carries me off to sleep.

* * *

The first thing I notice when I wake is that my body is covered in a thin layer of sweat and I feel slightly suffocated. It's then that I also account for my throbbing head and the fact that my throat is as dry as the Sahara. I manage to crack open my eyelids only to find myself practically on top of and wrapped around a very pleased looking bandmate. What's worse though? There's a trickle of obvious drool pooled on the black shirt clinging to his chest.

"Morning, Sleeping Beauty." He's way too smug for my liking and the deep, raspy tone of his morning voice has me practically jumping off of him.

The small couch we're on doesn't accommodate a lot of room for movement and I struggle to entangle my limbs from Everett's. He makes no effort to remove his arms from my waist and I'm grateful that everyone is still passed out from our night of drinking and won't witness the consequence of my brief lapse in judgment.

*I couldn't live down the shame.*

The thigh wrapped around his waist lowers back to my side, only stopping when it brushes over something hard and intrusive. The sharp intake of breath that comes from Everett confirms my suspicion and I grimace in disgust.

"It's biology, baby," he grins devilishly, shrugging without remorse.

"Firstly, don't call me baby. Secondly, remove those hands before I remove them for you." Groaning in revulsion, I use his chest as leverage to free my limbs from his hold. I stand on wobbly knees, mind still foggy from the alcohol and my own stupidity. I ignore Everett's pout and make my way to the kitchen to help myself to Jesse's coffee pot.

The rich smell of coffee quickly spreads throughout the trashed apartment and one by one, my friends wake from the dead to join me in the kitchen.

"The fact that we have to go to that mixer in a few hours has the whiskey in my stomach threatening to make a reappearance." Everyone dramatically takes a step back from a very queasy looking Jesse.

Marco and I groan in remembrance of the event being hosted for the bands participating in the competition a few months out. I send Jesse a vicious glare for making us "celebrate" last night when we have to drink and mingle tonight. I don't know how much more my liver can take.

I dread having to make small talk with a bunch of strangers that have surely heard the gossip about Sam and me. I used to love these events and meeting new people, but ever since Sam, I find it hard to maintain conversation with anyone, let alone a bunch of strangers.

After leaving Jesse's flat, I spend the rest of the day trying to talk myself up and gather the courage I need to get through tonight. When the clock finally strikes five, I slip on my navy jumpsuit and quickly apply my rogue lipstick before slipping out into the brisk winter evening.

The walk to the indie club isn't that far considering my apartment is smack-dab in the center of the city and I manage to make it through the glass doors just twenty minutes late. I slip through the throngs of people easily and try to find a familiar face between the flashing lights, music connoisseurs trying to schmooze me, and the champagne trays that fly by consistently.

Despite my hangover, I snatch a flute off of said tray just for something to do and head towards the buffet tables in the back. I catch sight of Enzo talking to an older woman in the corner and although I'm dying to find anyone to talk to, I decide to let him woo her in peace. Instead, I take residence between the cucumber sandwiches and cheese plates.

Furtively glancing around, I stuff some pigs in a blanket in my purse for later. I'm only *slightly* embarrassed because I make very little money in the band, and the guitar lessons I give at my local music store barely covers my rent. I think these snobby execs can deal with some missing finger-food. Before I can empty the tray, though, I'm interrupted by a scratchy voice that turns the blood in my veins to ice.

"Long time no see, Aspen."

I freeze, hands full of the glorified hot dogs, the elevator music playing through the large speakers seeming to quiet as the panic sets in. Heart thundering and breath caught in my lungs, I jerkily turn to face the man who broke my heart.

*How could I have forgotten he would be here?*

My stomach turns to concrete when I take in the familiar blue eyes that used to look at me with love, but now only detachment. He still has a crook in his nose from when he broke it in a fight, his scruff has grown into a full beard, and he has a new tattoo on at the base of his throat I can't make out. The brunette locks I used to mindlessly run my fingers through are gelled back and I hate how good he looks in a suit.

Abhorrence: a feeling of repulsion; disgusted loathing.

I'm pleased to find that the only emotion stirring in my belly is one of pure abhorrence and a faint sense of betrayal. No longer does this man fill me with warmth or devotion, but I still feel weak under his powerful gaze. Still feel small and insignificant.

"Not long enough, unfortunately." I'm surprised at the steadiness of my voice because I feel anything but.

Sam seems surprised by my response, eyebrows practically shooting up into his hairline. Unfortunately, it never takes him long to think of something clever to make you feel like an imbecile. "Don't be like that, baby. You know I've missed your fiery personality."

"What do you w-want, Sam?" I curse myself for stuttering, heart thrumming against my ribcage when his tattooed hand raises to tuck a loose strand of hair behind my ear.

"I just wanted to say hello to my girl." He coos and I shiver from his lowered tone and fingertips trailing my cheek. Sam is a master manipulator and he's more than aware of the effect he has on me. I could be livid with him for flirting with someone else one minute and the next he would have me screaming his name for an entirely different reason.

He was a puppet master and I was his marionette.

I'm more than disappointed in myself when I feel my resolve weakening at the softness of his voice and the gentle caress. But, I force myself to remember all the horrible names he called me and how he treated me like a clingy pest.

"I'm not your girl, Sam." I step away defiantly, slapping his hand away from my face.

"You'll always be my girl, Aspen... always."

"I stopped being your girl the second you started to insult me more than praise me." His nostrils flare and moves to grab my shoulder, but I'm pulled out of his reach by a firm arm around my waist.

"I don't think the lady wants your grubby hands on her." Everett pulls me into his side protectively and though my instinct is to shove him off, I'm actually thankful for the interruption. My hands won't stop trembling and my eyes begin to burn.

For once, Everett doesn't have a smirk on his face. Instead, there is a clench in his jaw and spark in his emerald eyes that almost frightens me. Sam clenches his fists as he squints between Everett and me. "I don't think that's any of your business, mate."

"Oh, but it is *mate.*" Everett snaps before purposefully leaning down to brush his soft lips against my temple, leaving a lingering kiss there.

I think my heart bruises my ribs from how hard it begins to beat.

Sam lets out a sharp, humorless laugh. "You and *Fox*? You've got to be kidding me."

He sneers, glancing between us and I open my mouth to correct him, but a gentle squeeze of my hip stops me.

"Wow, you sure did downgrade.... Although, maybe he is more on *your* level."

The scathing words barely slip past his lips before Everett releases his grip on me to charge towards Sam. Despite my own boiling anger, I reach out a hand to wrap around his arm and am shocked when Marco suddenly appears and pushes

Everett's shoulder back. This succeeds in stopping him, but leaves him practically seething next to me.

I glance around us briefly, horrified that almost the entire room is watching the altercation unfold. Part of me wants to flip them off, but the bigger part of me is still reeling by Sam's reemergence.

"I think it's best if you walk away, Jones, before *I* finish the job." Marco grits the threat out through his teeth and Sam rears back in shock.

Marco is basically a teddy bear —*I* was the one protecting *him* on the playground, not the other way around. Despite his mushy inside, he's quite burly on the outside and one threat from him has Sam turning away with a final glare in our direction. Marco follows him through the crowd to make sure he doesn't circle back and I watch until they fade into the mass of people.

"You alright?"

Everett is much calmer now, eyes dark with concern as they trace my expression. Warmth rises up my chest from the embarrassment of having Everett witness such a personal moment in my life. He brings a hand up to graze my cheek and it's then that I notice a few tears have slipped down my face. I let out a shaky breath and nod, wiping my face furiously as my humiliation only grows, but Everett doesn't buy it.

He mumbles an apology even though he has nothing to be sorry for and the coldness of his rings against my flushed skin sobers me. I hate crying in front of other people, even worse to cry in front of someone I barely know. Especially after everything he just witnessed.

"D'ya wanna hear a joke?" I let out a soft laugh at his question and can feel myself calming, nodding hesitantly. Nothing could make me feel worse than I do now, not even his bad one-liners.

"Why was Harry kicked out of Hogwarts?"

"I don't know... Why?"

"He was caught playing with his broomstick."

Even though the joke is absolutely awful, I find myself laughing anyway, scrunching my nose up in disdain. Everett flashes me a proud grin, swiping away the last of my tears. I don't recognize this gentle and serious Everett, but I'm extremely grateful for his interception.

My mood has lightened dramatically by the time Marco walks back over to take me home, face still pinched in rage. Everett and I nod at each other in an awkward goodbye and as Marco leads me towards the exit, I look over my shoulder to find Everett still glued to the same spot, watching us leave.

I'm thoroughly confused by his kind demeanor tonight and doubt it will carry into tomorrow. I also know I'll want forget this interaction ever occurred out of sheer mortification, but I still smile at him and mouth a genuine *thank you.*

He bows jokingly just as I turn back around and maybe it's because of the champagne, the fact that he saved me from Sam, or maybe because he cheered me up, but somehow, I actually feel quite fond of the curly haired freak.

But, I know this feeling and Everett's momentary lapse in personality won't last.

# TEMPTATION

Every member of Saints & Sinners has their own distinct pre-show ritual that they absolutely have to do before even stepping foot on stage. This is our first gig since Everett joined three weeks ago and we've been nervous wrecks all day, needing these comforts more than ever.

Avery has already gone off to a quiet corner to pray, Jesse is currently scarfing down nachos at the bar, Marco is on his 28th push up, and Enzo is napping in the dressing room. The only person besides me that isn't preparing is Everett. He remains seated on the couch, wearing a flannel unbuttoned just enough that his lighthouse tattoo is peaking out on his tanned chest.

I haven't really spoken to him since the incident with Sam the other night. Even though he was uncharacteristically caring and sincere that night, he's back to his regular old arrogant self today like I knew he would be. Striding into sound check 30 minutes late and refusing to apologize when I caught him ogling my ass. Though, I don't really mind it.

Despite my low self-esteem after Sam's reappearance, I do actually feel good about my appearance tonight. My legs are clad in leather pants, my black shirt has various sized holes torn into the fabric to tease my bare skin, and I'm wearing red boots that match my red lips. I feel powerful and assertive for the first time in a long time and it feels *good.*

"Don't you have a pre-show shtick, too?"

Everett's mossy eyes meet mine, but the rest of him stays slouched into the stained couch. "Already put it on," he points up to the navy headband that holds his wild curls back from his face. "Only wear this one during gigs. I haven't seen you do any sort of ritual though?"

I blush furiously because I have *two* habits that I've already partaken in. One similar to Jesse's, in that I eat one chocolate donut covered in sprinkles (it was my dad's favorite) and one similar to Everett's.

Except mine doesn't come in the form of cotton, but lace. There's something about wearing lingerie on stage that really empowers me. I did contemplate wearing the white set Everett picked out for me that's been stuffed in the recesses of my closet since. But, the thought alone had me both nauseous and red in the face. So, I opted for simple back instead.

"Already did mine too." I state confidently, but don't divulge anything more. Everett smirks and opens his mouth to reply, but a loud bang followed by a grunt catches our attention.

Enzo had somehow fallen off the adjacent velvet couch during his nap and grudgingly rubs his forehead in pain. I snort at his misfortune, helping him back up, but when I turn around to face Everett again, his attention is diverted elsewhere.

"Oh, for Fox sake." I groan and face him fully, so the object of his attention is hidden from view.

"Please, you wore those pants to torture me. I mean leather? *Seriously?* You're gonna send me to an early grave."

His husky voice and hooded eyes make my cheeks heat, not used to compliments. His bluntness is so... *refreshing* that it throws me off, but I hate that I lose my quick wit when he says stuff like that. Luckily, I don't have to think of a comeback because Jesse appears behind the door and informs us that the show is about to begin. A sigh of relief leaves my lips as I turn away from Everett's intense gaze and grab my old guitar.

Everett brushes my shoulder, standing next to me and brings his lips down to my ear. His voice is raspy and his breath warm as it dances across my flesh and causes my hair to rise.

"It's show time, Munchkin."

* * *

And what a show it was.

There is something so... *electric* about performing in front of people and this night was especially jam-packed for two reasons:

1. It's our first show in four months.
2. Everett.

I recognized a majority of the faces in the crowd, but there were definitely new fans. Since most of these newbies were of the female variety and screamed every time he opened his mouth, it's clear they showed up for the infamous Everett Fox.

His notoriety does partly come from his promiscuity, but also for his immense talent.

Everett transforms on stage. Instead of his usual irritating self, he becomes this carefree and mysterious enigma. Our sound is classic rock with a bit of pop, and *very* sexy. Everett embodies this vibe perfectly, singing my lyrics with such with passion and grit. Nobody could keep their eyes off him for long, not even me.

His performance, the flashing lights, and the adrenaline that made my flesh vibrate every strum of my guitar made the experience invigorating.

Despite this, I don't get the same rush playing guitar as I did when I was in Everett's position. Nothing compares to filling an entire room with your voice and having the room answer back by singing with you. It's the only time I've ever felt truly adored, truly liked.

But... being front-man is all over for me now and I don't think there's any going back.

We ended up doing two encores in the smoke-filled club and even stopped to sign a few shirts Jesse had printed with Everett front and center. I don't think I've ever seen someone so happy to sign a woman's chest than Marco was. That was definitely a first for him.

With the rush of performing warming our veins and the overall success of the night, we do what we do best.

*Celebrate.*

"Cheers!" We clink our glasses together, the alcohol sloshing over the sides, before we tip them back.

"That was bloody amazing! I don't think the crowd has ever been that big!" Avery squeals excitedly and Marco nods along with her.

"And the response! Hell, I almost lost my hearing!"

"I know! I think it has more to do with Everett's looks and reputation than anything. They were never that loud when Aspen performed. Even when—"

Jesse stops talking suddenly and shoots me an apologetic, guilty glance. Marco punches his shoulder in annoyance and everyone else coughs awkwardly, avoiding my gaze. I squirm in my seat at the uncomfortable silence, but I'm not angry because he's completely *right*. It does sting, but Everett is a very good singer, and more than that, he's a *performer*. It does bruise my already pummeled ego that the man I despise replaced me *and* does a better job than I ever did. But, it's just something I have to get over. It's for the good of the band.

"They were never that loud because I never showed as much chest as Curly does." I joke, and slap Everett's exposed skin playfully, trying to lighten the mood.

"True! You'd practically cause a riot if you did that."

I send Avery a grateful smile, her comment easily lifting the tension at the table. I sit back silently, the buzz from performing now long gone, and pick at the label on my beer as everyone in the booth continues their mindless chatter. Everett has been silent since the moment he walked off stage and I feel his gaze on me, but don't meet it.

Everett scoots closer, leg grazing mine, and breath warm on my cheek, "you did great tonight, Munchkin. Would've been better if you sang though." I assume he's teasing, but there's a rare seriousness in his eyes when I finally look up.

"Thanks, Curly. I would complement you, but 'mm afraid you might not be able hold up your giant head anymore." I expect him to make some snarky joke, but he just releases a low chuckle, shaking his head. This time, I don't shrink away from his intense stare as it roams my face. He begins to lean in and just when I think he's going to get a black eye for kissing me, he turns his head last minute to leave a lingering kiss on my warming cheeks.

I'm too dazed to respond, heart caught in my throat and skin hot with embarrassment, glancing around to ensure the band is too distracted to notice the interaction. I don't understand why he's being so kind lately and I'm even more dumbfounded by my body's response to it.

It's in my stunned silence that the band makes the executive decision to go home and change into nicer clothes so we can meet up at Club Essex for a real celebration. I almost contemplate blowing it off, but Avery insists we go to her tiny flat to get ready and she seems so excited that I can't turn her down.

Two hours, lots of hairspray, and a few more shots and we're finally pulling up outside the busy street and bright lights of the best club in London. Jesse talks to the bouncer while the rest of us gather together for warmth on the crowded sidewalk. They chat a little too long for this weather before the bouncer opens the ropes and lets us cut about 60 people in line.

I'm not sure how Jesse knows so many people or always manages to get his way, but I'm not complaining.

As soon as we step into the crowded club, the flashing purple and blue lights blind us and the thumping bass sends vibrations up our spines. Some heads turn in the busy club to appraise us and I have to stop myself from hiding behind the group. Avery is clad in a tight red ensemble that matches her lips, Enzo has his hair slicked back and a fitted blazer outlining his broad shoulders, and Marco and Jesse are wearing almost identical black button-ups. I borrowed Avery's light pink knee-length slip dress –the cowl neck so low I constantly have to adjust.

Everett waves eagerly from the bar having gotten here early to pre-game and we weave through the crowd to reach him. He greets Marco in a bro-hug before giving Jesse a sloppy kiss on the cheek. "Took you lot long enough! I had to start without ya!" His slurred speech and glazed over eyes tell me that he did more than just 'start.'

After shoving my way between a few girls at the neon bar I'm finally able to see Everett clearly and nearly choke when I do. Black boots and jeans that show off his fit legs, fitted blazer, and unbuttoned white blouse that showcases his tan skin and black ink.

It's so unfair that the worst kind of men are always the most good-looking.

I blame the vodka for the way I nearly start to salivate at the sight of him, my heart bruising my ribcage and skin growing hot. These feelings of attraction fade fast, though, when I see his arm draped around the girl he had with him at the lingerie shop. Not that I care.

As the band exchanges greetings, I take it upon myself to order a round of shots, having to yell over the thumping music and sound of the crowd. When I turn from my perch on the bar, I'm faced with a very drunk and very frazzled looking bandmate. His reddened eyes rake my figure, lingering at my hips and exposed breasts before continuing down my legs and darkening to a frightening degree. Usually I would call him a pig and walk away, but the shots I took before getting here have begun to cloud my judgement.

*Let him stare as much as he pleases, doesn't mean he gets to touch.*

Everett continues to leer as the bartender passes me the shots and I greedily grab two before holding one up to the curly-haired drunk in front of me. We clink glasses before downing the tequila, his hooded eyes locked on mine, heavy and dark as the lights flash behind him.

"I'm not quite sure if Munchkin is an appropriate nickname for you anymore." He breathes, gaze intense as I wipe my lips dry. The club is so loud that I have to lean closer to hear him, his scent sweet and intoxicating.

I fight my grin as I down the next shot, cringing as the burn slides down my throat. I notice Marisol talking to Jesse and Enzo at the end of the bar and that Marco and Avery have disappeared elsewhere. It's just Everett and I, surrounded by strangers in this hot and dark room.

I decide to play along. "Okay then, what would be a more appropriate nickname?"

"Sex kitten, maybe? Temptress? Siren? Shit, I can't think straight with you looking like that. Can't even think of a good joke." He seems genuinely upset at that, but the devilish grin on his face as his eyes travel down my body tells me otherwise. I swallow, throat suddenly dry, and try to ignore how my heart is almost thudding louder than the bass speakers.

"Well, Curly, at least *your* nickname still stands." I brush past him as I whisper the words, fingers tugging lightly on his long curls. I'm more than pleased when I hear his breath catch in his throat, feeling his eyes on me as I make my way towards our friends.

"Shots, anyone?" Jesse and Enzo jump at the chance and just as Marisol reaches for the last one, Everett swoops in and knocks it back before she can grab it. "Don't be a jackass, Everett." I shoot him a glare that only makes him grin in return.

"Oh, hey! It's Aspen, right? The one that was at the shop?" Marisol pipes up excitedly and I can't help but smile back. The girl practically radiates sunshine.

We chat over the loud music and I continue to drink until everything Jesse says is hilarious and I start seeing two of Enzo. Everett stays silent during our idle chatter and I glance up a few times to catch his gaze set on me, eyes dark and low. I don't know if it's the alcohol or the lustful way he keeps watching me, but a dull warmth spreads through my stomach. Just as Marisol starts talking about the children she tutors—of course— I catch Everett drinking in my figure again and have to excuse myself.

Everett has always flirted and ogled at me before, but tonight feels different. There's a hungry burn in his eyes that has my legs quivering and I don't like it one bit. For the first time, it seems less like an innocent flirtation and more like something serious and profound. What's more troubling though, is that I don't feel the usual repulsion towards him I used to.

Whether it's the loneliness or the tequila, I find myself liking his attentions. I'm in very dangerous territory.

Luckily, it doesn't take long to find Avery, who is absolutely livid that Marco left with someone else. We distract ourselves with quite a few more drinks and a lot of dancing.

It doesn't take long before I feel eyes on me again and search the club until I see the group has moved to a booth just across the dance floor. Even though he has a girl next to him talking his ear off, Everett's dark eyes watch as I sway to the beat.

The alcohol has made my blood warm, vision blurred, and inhibitions loose. My hands dance over my curves and his intense gaze follows my every move. His tongue slides out to wet his lips and my breathing falters when I see his hand disappear beneath the table.

Our gazes are locked and intense, the moment intimate and dangerous surrounded by dozens of people. The heat of the room, disorienting music, and dim light only add to the heavy tension that stretches between the booth and dancefloor. His arm tenses slightly beneath the table and I wonder if he's palming himself through his jeans. The idea does naughty things to my body; my legs beginning to shake as I falter slightly in my movements.

I just can't breathe when he looks at me like that.

Then, somebody walks in front of me and blocks my view of the tempting man and the spell seems to be broken. The first thing my eyes land on when my vision is clear is the sweet and innocent girl sitting next to him. My stomach twists with guilt and I'm immediately brought back down to Earth.

*This is so wrong.*

He's here with a date and I'm trying to *what*? Seduce him? Tease him? I'm not even sure. I let loneliness and tequila cloud my judgement. Fall prey to the allure of Everett Fox.

The alcohol I consumed begins to stir in my stomach and I feel physically sick. I don't bother explaining myself to Avery as I push through the hordes of people and into the empty restroom. I lean against the sink and try to calm my erratic heartbeat, but that proves futile when the door is pushed open again only seconds later.

"*Don't.*" I grit out and try to send Everett a cold glare through the mirror as he locks the door behind him. *Shit.* "I mean it, Fox. Stop it."

"Stop what?" I bite my lip to control myself, his voice dangerously low.

"You know what."

He stalks closer, tall figure looming and making my chest shudder. "I don't think I do."

"*Stop* looking at me like that!" I shout in frustration, meeting his gaze in the mirror, but refusing to face him. "Stop looking at me like that when there is a perfectly nice girl sitting next to you. It's not fair, to *anyone*."

"Looking at you like what, Aspen?" My heart bruises my ribs as it pounds against my chest, his voice eerily calm and jaw set.

This is the first time he's ever actually said my name. No Munchkin, just Aspen. My knees almost give out at the way it rolls off of his tongue so effortlessly, as if caressing each syllable. Almost sinful.

*Stop it, Aspen. You're just drunk and sad.*

A gasp leaves my lips when his hard body presses up against mine and his hands come around to cradle the sink, effectively trapping me between his arms. I glance into the mirror and am met with eyes so dark they're almost black.

Temptation: a desire to do something, especially something wrong or unwise.

Staring into his lustful gaze and feeling his erratic heartbeat against my back, I know that I'm in too deep. Everett is the ultimate temptation and even if I may not like him as a person, I can't deny that I'm unbelievably attracted to him. My inebriated mind smothers any logical reasoning as I watch Everett lowers his head, lips connecting with the base of my neck.

"Looking at you like I want to rip this dress off your body? Looking at you like I've dreamt of what it would feel like to be inside of you every night? Looking at you like I haven't imagined what you would look like naked, writhing, and *dripping* beneath me?"

His warm breath caresses the skin of my exposed neck with each syllable, the dirty words falling from his inviting lips making me dizzy. Each sentence slowly picks away at my resolve and the anger I felt towards him a minute ago is long forgotten.

My skin flushes violently at his confession and when he presses his body harder into mine, I can't suppress the moan that leaves my lips. The proof of his declaration digs into my spine and my knuckles turn white from their grip on the sink. I find myself craning my neck to allow him more access, the alcohol completely taking over.

"Because let me tell you, Aspen," he growls against my skin and I have to clench my thighs together as his warm tongue licks a stripe up my sensitive flesh. "Not looking at you like I haven't fantasized about doing this a million times is too fucking hard."

Before I can say another word, Everett squeezes my hips and spins me around to face him. The only thing I have time to register is the flush in his stubbly cheeks and wild look in his eyes before his head dips down and lips are on mine.

They spark together like flint against steel and the reaction is lethal. My mouth is kerosene and his full lips are an erect match that sets my skin ablaze. His fingers explode like fireworks against my hips, hot and desperate. We're a chemical reaction and although my first instinct is to pull away and stop us from combusting, I only end up melting against him.

He is a flame and I am on fire.

His hands grasp desperately at my hips as his tongue traces my bottom lip before delving inside and entangling my own. My hands move from his broad chest to clutch at his thick hair, seemingly on their own volition. He tastes like summer and tequila, and a hunger that hasn't been sated in months takes control of my actions. I teasingly bite down on his plump bottom lip, earning a wild groan from him. There's a tiny voice in my head that tells me this is wrong and demands I put a stop to it, but his hard body slots perfectly against my soft one and his tongue is warm and strong and I'm only human.

His hands explore my figure tantalizingly slow, as if engraining every dip and curve into his mind, wanting to imprint the feeling into his skin. His lips mold against mine and his calloused palms slide down to wrap around my backside. The ferocity of the moan that crawls up my throat as he squeezes the flesh there even has me surprised.

"*God*, Aspen," he groans, sliding his hands down further and wrapping them around my thighs, to slam me down on the cold counter.

The force of it makes me gasp and he takes the opportunity to slide his lips across my jaw and down my neck, peppering kisses along the flushed skin. A fog has settled over my mind and all I can concentrate on is just how *good* his lips feel as they suck on the sensitive skin under my ear and how *hot* it is when his hands slide up my thighs, taking my dress with it.

This is *so* wrong.

I hate Everett. I hate his flirty remarks, womanizing, and smug face. I hate his stupid curls that feel so good tangled between my fingers, his obnoxious rings that are so cold against my hot skin, and his petal-soft lips that pull back to bite down against the hollow of my neck...

*Oh, for* Fox *sake.*

I use my grip on his hair to yank his face towards mine,

slamming my lips back down on his. He moans as my tongue explores the mouth that made all those sinful confessions to me. My hands slide from his hair to explore the rigid planes of his chest before settling on his hips and using the flaps of his jacket to pull him closer. Everett's own hands leisurely move from my thighs, across my hips, and up to my petite breasts. His name is a sigh in my mouth as his fingers tease me through the thin material, my skin tingling and blood pumping in my ears.

"That's right, baby. Say my name." He groans into my mouth and I oblige him eagerly, locking my ankles together around his back. I languidly pepper kisses along his sharp jawline, sucking desperately on the skin that meets his neck. Everett hisses as my teeth nibble on the flesh there before my tongue slides out to soothe the sting.

We are desperate hands and needy tongues and I've never felt so on fire. My mind is hazy with lust and sound of his heavy breaths and all I want to do is rip his clothes off and let him take me on this bathroom counter. But, as soon as this thought crosses my mind I suddenly remember that we *are* in a bathroom. In a club. In a bathroom in a club where his date is no less than thirty feet away.

Just like that, the fog is lifted.

I fall back down to Earth and shove Everett away, our lips making a harsh popping noise as they disconnect. He stumbles back a few steps and if I wasn't suddenly so upset I would jump on him again. Flushed chest, swollen lips, tangled hair, and wildly dark eyes. Because of me. *I* did that to him.

"What the *hell,* Aspen?" He pants angrily and takes a step closer, but I hold up a palm to stop him. I adjust my dress and try to calm my erratic heartbeat as fire fuel my veins for a different reason.

Everett came here with another girl—not just any girl, but a genuinely kind and friendly person. Yet, here he is, practically dry humping me in some dingy bathroom at a club.

And here I am, letting him.

I suddenly feel dirty and… *used.* I know what it feels like to be cheated on, to find out that your significant other has been gallivanting with another woman while you remain obliviously happy. It doesn't matter what title Everett and Marisol have: boyfriend/girlfriend, friends with benefits, whatever. They are here together and are *something.* Obviously, that doesn't matter to Everett, but it does to me. What was he planning to do; hook up with me in the bathroom and then get back to his date?

I shouldn't be surprised, I've heard all about him for years and still let his flirtations and desire draw me under his spell. Desperate and lonely, I was easy prey.

"Fuck off, Everett." I spit angrily and hop down from the counter on slightly wobbly legs.

Just as I'm about to walk past him, he grabs my elbow and whips me around, "what are you on about?"

"This is wrong," Everett still looks confused and I rip my arm out of his grasp. "You're with another woman, asshole! Yet, here you are saying all these things and looking at me like that and trying to screw me on top of a counter like I'm some worthless tramp! And, I almost let you, which is just *so* much worse."

The alcohol is slowly seeping into my brain and I begin to see two very concerned looking Everetts. He tries to reach for me again, but I take a few more shaky steps backwards.

"Whoa, Aspen, you were literally all over me two minutes ago and now you're calling me an asshole? What the hell? I didn't… you're not a worthless tramp… what even…?" He's scrambling for something to say, looking completely disheveled. The sight of a red mark under his jaw already forming has my stomach twisting into knots.

"Go back to your date, Everett. *This,*" I gesture between our ruffled appearances, "Is *never* going to happen again." My words slur together, but I'm sure he gets the idea. That is, until, a sly smirk tilts up his lips and the confusion fades.

"Oh, it's not?" He takes a deliberate step towards me and I

gulp, frowning.

"No."

"You sure?" Another step.

"Yep." He hums in response, backing me up into the door and I let out a shaky exhale. "I'm serious, Everett. I don't-"

Before I can even finish my sentence, his soft lips brush against mine before applying pressure, causing me to gasp. My resolve snaps like a twig and I'm kissing him back fervently. His hands rest against either side of my head and mine dangle loosely by my sides as our mouths do all of the talking. The haze has settled again, but my mind tries to fight through the fog his lips seem to cause. I was mad at him... this isn't right...

As his tongue traces my lower lip, I break through the lustful haze and remember why. I shove him away again, this time much more harshly. I'm livid at him, but also at myself for succumbing to him and my foolish drunken desire. He's using me, treating me like every girl he humps and dumps, and I refuse to be the other woman.

"You're just like Sam."

The scathing words are out of my lips before I can stop them and even in my inebriated state, even in my anger, I know that I've gone too far. Everett knows enough about my past to know that Sam is the scum of the Earth, to know that I hate him. I might as well have just compared him to Satan himself. That actually may have been better.

Everett's jaw twitches and fists clench, eyes refusing to meet mine. I keep my mouth shut because despite my accusation, he's still in the wrong here. Or at least, I think he is. I might be too drunk to tell and will regret a lot of this interaction tomorrow.

"You're right."

My head snaps up at his words, shocked that he's agreeing with me and the coldness in his tone. He looks at me in a resigned distaste that has my gut plummeting.

"This *isn't* going to happen again." With that, he brushes past me and strides out the door. My eyes sting and throat closes and I'm so confused and angry that I just sit in the bathroom for a long time, hating myself and hating Everett.

When I finally gather up the courage to leave the bathroom, I catch sight of Everett walking out of the club with his arm around Marisol's waist and his lips at her ear.

# ANIMOSITY

"I can actually see the floor... have I stepped into The Twilight Zone?" Marco ogles my sparkling hardwood in mock amazement, earning a snort from me.

When I'm not at band practice, I'm giving guitar lessons, and I don't have time to clean. Even if that means having take-out boxes, clothes, and half-empty cans of beer littered around the loft. I'm sure if Mom didn't pay for Marco to have a maid, his place would be just as dirty as mine. I open the door wider to let him, but then I catch sight of the mop of curly hair standing behind him and almost slam the door in his face, "Curly can't come in. He wasn't invited."

It's been three days since that night in the club and I've been avoiding Everett. I can tell that he's just as mad as I am because I haven't received *one* measly bad joke text from him since. I finally got what I wanted: a life without Everett bothering me... So, why does it feel so bad?

"Well, I was hanging at his when you texted me. I couldn't just ditch him," Marco sighs, foot lodged in the door as Everett avoids my glare.

"Sorry, Marco. Everett is not allowed in my home. *Ever.*"

"He brought booze."

"On second thought, the more the merrier."

Marco rolls his eyes at my large grin before stepping into the foyer with the spawn of Satan hot on his heels.

"Wow, wonder what changed your mind?" Everett scoffs before practically shoving the bottle of whiskey into my hands.

I try to contain my eye roll as I watch him and my brother step into my shabby apartment. Marco heads straight into the connected living room, while Everett glances around curiously. I'm suddenly very conscious of the fact that I have a picture of Marco and I dressed as the red and pink Power Rangers for Halloween hanging up.

At least *I* wasn't dressed as the pink ranger.

"Pick up the pace, Fox, everyone is waiting." I mumble, shoving past him to lead the way towards the band stuffed into my small den. I hear his boots clicking behind me and try to steady my suddenly nervous heart. I'm still beyond pissed that he was such a skeeze, but there may be a teeny tiny, itsy bitsy chance that I feel bad for comparing him to Sam. Of course, I would never say that aloud. I'm much too prideful for my own good.

Regardless, I squeeze myself between Enzo and Avery on my tweed couch to avoid sitting next to Everett on my mismatched love seat. He obviously notices because he rolls his eyes, plops down, and rests his feet on my new glass coffee table.

"Get your disgusting feet off of my table, you prick."

"I'm sure you'd like to see my prick."

"Do you always have to revolve conversations around your micro-penis?" By now all conversations have stopped, the gang watching us warily.

"There isn't anything micro about me, Munchkin."

"Please, my eyeliner is thicker than your dick."

Everett's nostrils flare and Avery lets out a snort, while Jesse laughs nervously. "Jesus, what is up with you guys lately? If I didn't know any better, I would say that you two did the horizontal bop and it went horribly wrong." Avery cackles at her joke and I have a hard time controlling my heart rate, nearly choking on my own spit.

Everett's wolfish grin scares me, "Well, actually—"

"Actually, Everett has erectile dysfunction, so he won't be

doing that with anybody."

By now the rest of the band has focused their attention on the two of us and all laugh hysterically at my accusation. Everett's grin turns to a scowl and he leans forward to face me properly, "Or maybe my willy just shrivels up when you're around."

"Oh, please. I could easily prove that theory false."

"You would like that, wouldn't you? Any excuse to get near my dick."

"I wouldn't touch that thing with a ten-foot pole."

"Don't you mean 'I would touch your ten-foot pole'?"

"You're disgusting."

"And you're a bit—"

"Listen, stronzo [asshole]. I'm going to shave that stupid fucking hair of yours and–"

"Aspen!" Marco shouts angrily, "che diavolo c'è di sbagliato con te?" [What the hell's wrong with you?]

"Non c'è niente di sbagliato in me. Everett l'ha iniziato!" [Nothing is wrong with me. Everett started it!] I can feel the confused stares from our friends, but I promptly ignore them.

"What the fuck? Are you talking shit in another language? I hear my name." Everett accuses, glaring between the two of us. We flip him off simultaneously.

"Che cosa è successo tra voi due?" [What happened between you two?]

I tense up at Marco's question because there's no way I'm explaining to my brother that I almost did the naked tango with a friend of his in a club bathroom, while his date was right outside the door.

"Niente. Ho sempre odiato Everett." [Nothing. I've always hated Everett.]

"Seriously, guys! English, please. What are you guys saying about me?" Everett whines anxiously and Marco shoots me a look that screams this conversation isn't over. The room is silent again as everyone quite clearly knows Marco and I were just talking about Everett, despite it being in Italian.

I jerk slightly when I feel a hand clasp my legging-clad thigh, "Where's the cheap liquor you promised?" Enzo laughs lightly and I can tell he's trying to ease the tension in the room by changing the subject. I send him a grateful smile, excusing myself to the kitchen while conversation slowly picks back up again. I'm fully aware that I'll eventually have to make-up with Everett for the sake of the band, but he makes it so hard to be *civil* when all he does is brag about mini-Everett, make terrible jokes, and hit on anything with legs.

I think I'd rather pull all of my hair out than be friends with him.

Instead of thinking about a pesky tattooed singer, I go about grabbing some beers for Jesse and Enzo, and whiskey for everyone else. Of course, as I'm in search of a clean glass, I'm interrupted by the sound of boots scuffing on my tile and the smell of mangoes.

"I don't appreciate you talking about me in some alien language y'know."

"It's Italian, not alien, you uncultured swine." I spit and spin around to face him leaning against the doorway, jaw clenched. Though, I do notice his lips tugging up at my insult.

"You sure know how to sweet talk a man, don't you?"

I press a hand to my chest and glance around the kitchen in mock confusion, "I don't see any men here, do you?" He scoffs, but the smirk on his face remains as he eyes my figure.

Shocked by his lukewarm reaction, I sigh. "Do you enjoy women belittling you?"

"Yes, actually." He shrugs devilishly, moving to stand in front of me. Before I can step away, his arms trap me against the marble counter, "However, I don't enjoy being talked about right in front of me in a language I can't understand."

"Take Italian then."

"Munchkin," Everett warns, clearly done with our banter.

I don't even bother correcting him on the nickname because I'm too distracted by his close proximity, and frankly, very stubborn. Our position brings me right back to that night at the club and I battle between the feeling of disgust and lust. This cannot be healthy.

His breath fans my face and I have to stop myself from leaning into his inviting lips. It seems no matter how angry or annoyed I am by him, I can't deny the physical pull between us. My body aches for him even if my mind turns him away.

"Marco just wanted to know what was going on between us, that's all." I shrug, avoiding all eye contact.

"What *is* going on between us?"

His gaze has softened dramatically, look into my own hazel eyes with curiosity and confusion. The sincerity in his voice and gentleness in his eyes makes me wants to apologize for the harsh words I said. But, then I remember the reason I said those things.

I remember how he treats people —women, especially. I remember the stories I've heard over the years about him treating his bandmates like trash and using women like toys. How he showed no remorse for coming onto me with an unsuspecting Marisol a few feet away. How he acts like he's the greatest person to grace this planet. Like Sam.

Then I shove him away from me.

"As far as I'm concerned, there is *nothing* going on between us. I must have been *extremely* drunk to even allow you near me... You treat people like shit and have no regard for the feelings of others. The only person you care about is yourself and It's *toxic.*"

Everett immediately shuts down as soon as the scathing words fall from my lips. All the softness in his gaze is gone and replaced with what has been between us since he joined the band.

Animosity: strong hostility.

He takes a deep breath, stepping back, as his jaw tenses and hate clouds his irises. "I feel bad for you. It's *sad* how lonely and pitiful your life is, how bitter you are. You couldn't even keep *Sam Jones* interested, let alone anybody with standards. I may be toxic to others, but at least I'm wanted."

With that, he stomps out of my apartment and leaves my worst fears realized.

*At least I'm wanted.*

# AESTHETIC

I ignore Everett for a week.

I don't answer his texts or calls. I pretend I'm not home when he knocks on my door twice. I don't utter a single word to him during rehearsals and avoid any and all eye contact. But, I can feel him watching me. His emerald gaze burns a hole into my skin when he's singing or discussing gigs with Jesse. He tracks my every move when I set up my guitar and eavesdrops on my conversations with Enzo. It's petty and stubborn of me, but I pretend he doesn't exist because he might as well not.

My momentary lapse in judgement last week seems like a lifetime ago, like a different person made out with Everett in the bathroom. Now, I'm back to my senses and filled with animosity towards the pervert. I know I'm not innocent in our arguments, but he knew just how to hit me where it hurts, just what to say to crush my spirit. The words have been echoing in my mind and souring my mood and heart like poison ever since.

*At least I'm wanted.*

That simple sentence was certainly effective. It was like all my worst nightmares put into four words and laid bare at my feet. Being alone and unwanted is my greatest fear and it's consistently realized over and over. First with my father who left our family for another woman, then with my mother and her blatant preference for Marco, and finally with Sam and his proclivity for sleeping with other women. Being discarded is something I've grown used to.

However, I refuse to be sad. Rage is a much more tolerable emotion than misery.

Which, apparently, is pretty obvious.

"So, what's got your panties in a bunch recently?" Avery's tone is light, but I can tell she's genuinely concerned. We'd been chatting for the last half hour about her younger sister's recent move to the states and the family drama that decision spurred, but it's clear my mind had wandered elsewhere.

*God, I'm an awful friend.*

A heavy sigh escapes my lips and I switch the phone over to my other hand while I make myself a pot of coffee. This may or may not be my fifth cup today, but I'm finding it a better alternative to the whiskey I have stashed in my top cabinet that calls out to me. "I'm so sorry, Avery. I was listening, I swear." She brushes it off and inquiries about my worries again, but I can only grumble in response, "What else?"

"So, it is Everett then."

I hadn't told Avery all that went down in the last two weeks with Everett and me, but I know she's gathered enough evidence to come up with her own conclusion. She's too smart for her own good.

"Of course, it's Everett. It's always Everett." I decide to not drudge up the details –it would be complicated enough for a novel. "I've never daydreamed about slitting someone's throat more."

She chuckles, but the sound is strained, "should I be worried?"

"Hmm... no, all my knives are dirty at the moment, so I wouldn't worry just yet."

"It's oddly comforting that you would only want to use a clean one on him." We both laugh as I continue to fix my cup of coffee before grabbing a bowl of strawberries and plopping down on the couch Yoda is sleeping on. "Seriously, what is going on with you two?"

"Let's just say that we've both said some things we probably shouldn't have. I swear we can't be around each other for more than an hour without finding some way to get under each other's skin. He's just so... so *arrogant* and selfish and inconsiderate! Literally everything I hate wrapped up in one person." I'm almost out of breath and really wound up, but the rant doesn't make me feel better like I thought it might.

Avery falls silent for so long after that that I think she hung up, but it's when I'm absentmindedly running my fingers through Yoda's tan fur and eating my fourth strawberry that her voice carries through the line. Hesitant, sad, sympathetic.

"Aspen... I think... I think that Sam was the worst thing to happen to you, that he messed you up more than you let on and you can't let it go. Everett... he may not be the nicest guy in the world and he may play the field a bit, but please don't make him out to be another Sam. Don't let that asshole poison your mind any more than he already has."

My heart drops to the pit of my stomach at the mention of my ex and it falls even further at Avery's warning. She was my crutch after Sam and I ended things. She sat with me when all I did was stare at a wall for hours, picked up the pieces after I broke down, and was the one that told me to get my shit together when I finally dried my tears.

So, her opinion means everything to me and her words resonate deep down into my bones. I'm aware that I've been more cynical since the break-up, but maybe I *was* looking for Sam in Everett.

Images of Everett leaving the bars with different girls, of his neck covered in hickeys, of him staring down my top one second and then pretending he wasn't when Marisol nears are shadowed by much clearer images. Images of Everett making stupid puns and laughing at them by himself, of him genuinely concerned about why I stopped singing, of him standing up to Sam in my defense and then cheering me up with some stupid joke.

For a measly second, I think that Everett may be different,

that I may have I judged him too quickly.

*At least I'm wanted.*

And just like that, the thought is gone.

"I know Everett charmed his way into your hearts, but," before I can finish my sentence a loud pounding on my door nearly sends me to an early grave and Yoda yaps in response. "But, he has you all fooled into thinking he's some kind of god."

Yoda is hot on my heels as I make my way towards the foyer and the knocks don't let up. I have to restrain myself from screaming at whoever is behind my door.

"Aspen, please. Don't write him off on just a few bad traits–"

"A *few,*" I scoff as I swing the door open, only for the words to die in my throat. "Everett has more than a few—"

"More than a few what, Munchkin?"

*Speak of the devil and he shall appear in suede boots and a barely buttoned shirt.*

Everett's fist is raised mid-knock, trademark smirk curving dimples into his cheeks. Yoda tries to run towards him, but one stern look from me and he backs down. "I've got to deal with the trash, Avery. I'll call you later." She begins to protest, but I hang up on her and slide my phone into my vintage jeans.

"The trash? You wound me, Munchkin. I just—," I slam the door before he can finish his sentence. However, this doesn't derail him, "oh, come on, love! Please just let me say my peace and then you can slam the door in my face, kick me to the curb, curse me… I don't care! Just let me apologize. Please."

Reluctantly, I crack open my door and lean against the edge, leveling him with an unforgiving stare. His brows raise in shock and he fumbles a bit, not expecting me to actually hear him out. "Okay, so I'm a bloody arsehole. I could come up with some excuse as to why I said such a horrible thing to you, but my mum taught me better than that, so I'll just own up to it. What I said was not only completely uncalled for, but also undeserved and *untrue.*"

He fidgets slightly once he notices my expression remains

unchanged, scratching the back of his neck.

"I'm really shit at this. The only woman I've ever apologized to before was my mum and I reckon you're much more terrifying." That makes me smile a little, which eases his stress, "I just... I've felt like utter shit since last week and I'm... just really sorry, okay? I didn't mean any of it. Not a single word. Jones was a moron for letting you go and he—"

"Everett." I cut him off before he can continue because I've already heard enough about Sam today to last a lifetime and it's really off-putting to see Everett actually be sincere. His apology does strike a chord with me and I can tell he means it, but my heart doesn't budge.

"What?"

"I'm sure you're used to people falling at your feet and forgiving your every indiscretion, but I'm not one of them. I know I'm not blameless and I'm sorry for how I acted, but what you said was out of line and cruel. You have no idea how hard it was on me after him —how much I *did* feel unwanted —" to my horror, my throat closes up and I quickly curtail the conversation, "none of that matters anyway. I shouldn't care what you think about me because we're not friends. We're bandmates. For the sake of the band I'll tolerate you, but that's as far as our relationship will go."

My words linger in the air between us as Everett shakes his head slightly. This is how it should have been since the beginning. I never liked him much to begin with, but sometime in the last six weeks I'd begun to think that we could be friends.

Which honestly went straight down the toilet as soon as I stuck my tongue down his throat. But, it's more solidified now that I know how much he could hurt me with a few carefully chosen words. Just how easily he could make my worst fears come to light.

He chews on his lips, eyes scanning my expression as if trying to read it. Finally, he sighs, "If that's what you want, I'll take it. For now."

"For now?"

"Yes, for now. I've decided that we're going to be friends. I know I hurt you, so we can just be band mates for now, but I'll prove to you that I'm not the guy you think I am. I'm going to be your friend, I just have to prove to you that I can be."

"Everett, that's not what I—"

"It's decided, Munchkin." A determined grin lights up his face and I'm honestly too stunned at his confidence to speak. That whole speech I made... and he just disregards it.

"We're *never* going to be friends."

"Wait, is that the famous Yoda?" Everett points behind me in an obvious attempt at distraction and I turn to see my dog obediently sitting behind me, short tail wagging.

I nod in affirmation and nearly jump back at Everett's booming laughter as he doubles over and clutches his stomach. "Oh god. You really named him Yoda," Everett actually wipes a few tears from his eyes as he stands from his crouched position and looks between the two of us in disbelief, "Short legs, big ears –just like Yoda. And... and..."

"What, Everett?" I breathe a laugh at his amusement, confused at what exactly caused it.

"It's just... you know how people say dogs look like their owners?" I nod my head hesitantly as Everett tries to control himself. "Well, your dog is a munchkin just like you."

I slam the door in his face again.

"I'm still going to make you be my friend!" Is the last thing I hear through choked laughter before I make my way back to the couch and try to get his smile out of my head.

* * *

For the second time in two days, I open my door to find a curly haired brit.

For the second time in two days, I contemplate violence.

"What the hell are you doing here, Everett?" I snap, looking at the clock on the wall to find that it's barely nine in the morning. *He's a dead man.*

"We're going to the Japanese Gardens today."

"Were you dropped on your head as a child or are you really that dense? I specifically remember telling you yesterday that I wanted nothing to do with you. Yet, here you are." I didn't actually think he was serious about the whole friend thing. Clearly, I was wrong, but coming to my flat before I've even had a sip of coffee is not a healthy start to a friendship, regardless.

"I actually might have been dropped. Me mum was pretty clumsy," Everett muses, either obliviously unaware of my growing rage or choosing to ignore it. "Funny story, there was this one time when my mum—"

I slam the door in his face again.

"That's no way to treat someone that brought you coffee." Everett's teasing voice carries through the door and I tense instantly, cursing him silently. Not fully convinced of the truth of his statement, I glance through the peephole to see him holding up a carton of coffee like he knew I would check. Grudgingly, I swing the door open to reveal a very smug idiot.

"I knew you couldn't resist." He laughs as I snatch the mug from his grasp and take a sip, shocked to find that it's exactly how I take it: a dash of cream and two sugars. It instantly warms my body and lifts my mood, but my glare never falters.

"I'm not going anywhere with you, I think I've made that abundantly clear." He follows me inside and lovingly greets Yoda, who bounds up to him. "Why do you want to go to the Japanese Gardens, anyway?"

"Because I feel like a real jackass and Marco told me you've always wanted to see cherry blossom trees in bloom, so..." a faint blush creeps up his neck and he avoids eye contact with me. My jaw is practically polishing the floor by now.

"What the hell has been up with you lately? What happened to the apathetic and degenerate asshole we all loved to hate?"

"Trust me, he's still alive and kicking, but I've been a real tosser to you and I can't live with the guilt... So, will you please, please, *please* clear my annoying conscious and allow me to treat you to a day of pointless crap you love?"

*Ah,* it all makes sense now. The coffee, the heartfelt apologies, and the offer to take me to see my one childhood dream realized—all to clear the guilt eating away at him for making me feel worthless. "How can a girl say no?" I muse and he grins wildly, only for it to be wiped away by my next sentence. "Oh yeah, like this: hell to the fucking no."

I make my way back towards the door, intent on kicking him out, when he blocks my path. "I'll leave you alone," he blurts out, causing me to freeze, "If you let me take you out today and you still think I'm a dick by the end of the night I'll never bother you again."

"Do you mean that? Would you sign a blood oath?" My heart warms at the prospect.

He hesitates slightly at my suggestion before nodding his head slowly, unsure if I'm serious or not. "Yeah... sure?"

"Deal." I reluctantly take his outstretched hand and ignore how warm and firm it feels in my grasp, knowing I'll triumph over this agreement. There's no way I'll ever think that Everett isn't anything more than the absolute prick he is.

* * *

Soft rosy petals dance in the breeze: tangling into hair, latching onto clothing, and painting the cobblestone path in a river of pink. The whole street is lined with tall trees, branches intertwining over the path and acting as clouds that rain down the delicate petals every time the wind picks up. Children play on the walkway, kicking up petals with each jump while parents take pictures. I can only watch in awe, taking in a sight I've wished to see since I first learned about the beautiful trees. It's bittersweet because my dad promised he would take me to see them and then vanished before he could fulfill that promise. Still, the sight is one to behold.

Spring has come and the cherry blossoms have bloomed.

"I take it by the way your mouth hasn't shut since we got here that you like it?"

Everett's teasing tone in my ear makes me jump. I'd been so swept up in Mother Nature that I honestly forgot he was there. The reminder has my awestruck smile slipping into a frown. However, once I turn around to look at him, that grimace is replaced by uncontrollable laughter, "oh my god." I gasp out between giggles, the sight of him covered in pink flowers petals unbelievably humorous and, admittedly, adorable.

"What? Why are you laughing like a hyena?"

He pouts as I try to stifle my giggles and quietly reach up to pluck a single petal from his unruly hair. He groans in irritation, shaking out his head like a dog trying to dry. They fall from his hair in a flurry, but I decide not to tell him that three more immediately take their place —along with the ones tucked into his collar and on top of his shoulders.

"I don't know why you wanted to come here so badly, anyway. It's just a bunch of trees."

"*Just a bunch of trees?* Look around you, Everett. The petals falling, the branches linking together overhead and enclosing us in. *This* is Mother Nature at her finest." I try very hard not to smash his head into said trees. I'll just add his ungratefulness to my list of many reasons not to associate with Everett Fox.

"I still don't see all the hype," he grumbles, kicking fallen petals with the heel of his boot.

I sigh exaggeratedly, shaking my head in disappointment. "Aesthetic: concerned with beauty or the appreciation of beauty. This is *my* aesthetic and you need to appreciate it."

I manage to tear my eyes away from the pink rain just in time to catch Everett watching me with a small smile on his lips and dazed look in his eyes. "What?"

"Maybe I'll find my own aesthetic someday." He laughs lightly under his breath, looking away, and walking down the path. "You're somethin' else, Munchkin."

Deciding to ignore his statement, I follow behind him leisurely. Taking in the sights and listening to the distant laughter of children and our boots scuffing against the cobblestone, I feel light and relaxed. Everett keeps his eyes trained onto his feet —which annoys me to no end— while mine dart from the petals falling from above, to the ones painting the ground, and to the tall trees they're born from.

"You've got petals tucked in your cleavage." My eyes snap to Everett, only to find him staring at my chest and the low dip of my sundress with a slight smirk on his face, "let me get those for you."

Teasingly, he begins to reach for my exposed chest, but I smack his hand away and curse at him. Laughing, he shakes off his hand as if that actually hurt while I remove the petals. "You couldn't even last a few hours without finding some excuse to try to feel me up, huh?"

"I'm an opportunist, what can I say?" He grins proudly, but I only flash him a grimace.

"Well, looks like you've only confirmed that you're still an asshole. Which, according to your deal, means you have to leave me alone." I flash him a sickeningly sweet grin before turning away, but not before catching his boyish grin turn into a frown. I barely make it two steps before I feel his hand wrap around my elbow and spin me around.

"Wait, no," he runs a distraught hand through his hair, catching a few petals between his fingers before tossing them aside in annoyance. "Listen, I really am trying here. I can't... I'm not good at this whole... *thing.*"

"What thing?"

"Apologizing. For whatever reason, the idea that I made you so upset has me feeling like utter shit. You *have* to believe that I didn't mean what I said at all. I'm trying to make it up to you." His voice is desperate and pleading, but as much as I want to deny it, what he said was true. My mom didn't want me, my dad didn't either, and not even Sam wanted me.

It sucks, but it's something I've come to terms with. Or at least am trying to.

"No, really Aspen, you better not believe what came out of my stupid mouth. I wanted to hurt you like you hurt me when you compared me to Sam. It's the furthest thing from the truth, though... I know I'm an asshole, but I just... I just need to know that you forgive me."

Maybe it's because he took me to see cherry blossoms, or the coffee he brought, or the clear sincerity in his tone, but I find myself slumping in defeat and meeting his eyes. Hating him takes a lot of energy. Still, I want to make him work for it.

"Tell me five decent things about yourself and I might *consider* forgiving you."

Everett looks taken aback by my request, but nods his head eagerly at the opportunity.

"Five things. Okay, let's see..." oh boy, this could take all day. "I always tip waiters generously because my mum was a waitress to support us growing up and I know how shit that is... I once helped an old lady cross the street. She even gave me a kiss on the cheek after, but I think she had a crush on me. Understandably." I roll my eyes, chuckling lightly, and Everett grins in response, keen to elicit another laugh from me.

"Uh... oh, I give to charity. Don't tell anyone, but I donate to the children's hospital whenever I have some extra cash." The shock must be clear on my face because he mock scoffs, "oi, why so surprised? That wounds me, Munchkin. Fourthly, I bring the world joy and laughter with my amazing jokes and —"

"Doesn't count."

"What, why?" He pouts, surprised.

"Because they aren't funny." I deadpan, causing Everett to sigh dejectedly.

"Again, wounded... but, fine. After I shag a girl I always call her a cab so she doesn't have to walk home... lastly, I'm a good friend. Despite what you may think, I'm always there for the people I care about."

Rolling past the cab part, I begrudgingly note he might be right about being a good friend. I witnessed it first hand when he stood up for me in front of Sam. Even if he's a right prick half the time, he's there when he needs to be.

"So... do I pass the test?" He asks the question lightly, but he plays with the rings on his fingers and he bites his lip as he awaits my response. Even though I still think Everett is an asshole, even though he was extremely cruel to me, even though the boy still makes me want to scratch my eyes out, I find myself nodding. Maybe I judged him too harshly, maybe we both just have short-tempers and say things we don't mean. Maybe I'm just tired of hating him.

"You're on probation, though. I swear Everett, one more strike and you're out. Don't screw it up."

"Scouts honor." He salutes, a goofy grin on his lips and I roll my eyes before demanding that we find some food and spend the rest of the day underneath the cherry blossoms. Of course, he complains, but eventually caves to my powers of persuasion. It isn't until we're sat at a bench with dripping ice cream cones that I begin to regret my decision.

"Why couldn't the flower ride its bike?" He asks, licking his cone with a childish grin.

"No."

"Because it lost its petals!"

Definitely regretting my decision.

# INEVITABLE

Upon seeing the words, "The Mothership" light up my phone, my eyes nearly pop out of my skull from shock. I bet most of the population in their early twenties are probably annoyed at having their mother call so much, but that's not the case for me. I'm frankly lucky to hear from her on my birthday, let alone a random Thursday afternoon.

"To what do I this pleasure?" I ask as soon as I press accept and excuse myself from the rest of the band, making my way down Jesse's hall.

"That's no way to answer the phone, Aspen."

"I knew it was you, Mom," I roll my eyes, leg shaking violently as I lean against the wall. "Did you just call to criticize my phone manners?"

I hear her sigh and try not to let my nerves escalate as I wait for an answer. My mother *never* calls me, so this has to be extremely important. Or maybe, just *maybe,* she genuinely wants to chat and ask about my life in—

"Your brother hasn't been answering his phone. Can I speak to him?"

Of course, how could I possibly think she'd want to speak to me? I ignore the stinging in my eyes and try to play off the situation. "What about me? You haven't heard from me in two months." I joke lightly, but it's anything but.

"Of course, sweetie. How are you?" I can just imagine her flipping through files, sipping on her coffee, while blowing away her perfectly coiffed dark hair and pretending to listen.

"I'm good, actually. We had a really killer gig a few weeks ago that everyone freaked out about. We have a new band-mate that's sort of an asshole—"

"Language, Aspen. What about that boy you were dating? Seth something or other?"

I freeze at the mention of Sam, a hollow feeling filling my gut. Forget her messing up his name, we've been broken up for months. How could she not remember that? I barely made it to Christmas, I was so distraught, "we broke up a while ago, Mom."

"That's wonderful, honey. Now, can I speak to Marco? It's urgent." I know she wasn't listening, I just wish she was a better actress. The only thing that probably registered to her was my cussing. Scoffing at her indifference, I swallow down the lump in my throat and force myself off the wall, stomping down the hallway. When I re-enter the living room everyone notices my hurt expression, shooting me worried looks that I ignore. Marco's face twists into concern and even though this isn't his fault and I shouldn't be upset at him, I can't help but feel resentful.

"Mommy dearest wishes to speak to you," I spit, tossing the phone into his lap, his face instantly falling at my words. He gingerly picks it up and places a sympathetic hand on my shoulder as I plop down into the armchair, but I brush it off. I don't want or need his sympathy —I'm used to my mother's apathy by now. Breathing a resigned sigh, he slips into the kitchen and leaves me to answer the band's wary stares.

"Well, where's my beer?"

Jesse is quick to reach into the case next to him and pull out a bottle, hastily popping off the cap and passing it to me. I cheers him in thanks and down half the bottle's contents in one go, only setting it down when I hear Everett's familiar deep rumble. "I think that's enough, Munchkin. Don't want to pump your stomach tonight."

"Shut it, Curly. I can do what I want." I shoot him a glare, but he only rolls his eyes and grins in response. Ever since our little outing, Everett has been following me 'round like a puppy. I already told him I forgave him, but he took that as a sign to stick to me like a leech until I promise that we're BFFs and paint each other's toenails. It's unbelievably irritating.

Marco timidly rejoins us just after I've finished off my beer and he passes me my phone with an apologetic smile. "She said bye and that she'll call you later."

"Yeah, and I'm the Queen of England." I scoff, and Everett lets out a small snort. The room slowly falls into mindless chatter as more drinks are passed around and no one dares bring up my mother. But, after a few beers and some of Enzo's embarrassing stories being brought to light, I'm feeling much less angry. I even find myself laughing at Everett's horrible jokes.

*That's when you know you're really tipsy.*

It's only an hour later that we find ourselves sat at Jesse's large dining table with boxes of take-out being devoured and a very revealing game of never have I ever being played.

"Never have I ever... hooked up with someone in Jesse's bed." Enzo wiggles his eyebrows suggestively from my left and Jesse's face scrunches up in disgust.

"No one better drink to this."

However, Marco raises his beer with a guilty smile, and this time two more grimaces accompany Jesse's. Mine, at the idea of my brother hooking up *period,* and Avery at the idea of Marco hooking up with anyone but *her.*

That poor, poor, lovesick girl.

"Never have I ever... been arrested for public indecency." Marco sends me an accusatory grin and I whine as I take a long swig of my own beer.

"Whoa, Munchkin... how have I not heard of this?" Everett looks positively smug as he turns to face me from his seat at my right.

"Because it's none of your business... but, let's just say that people in a library apparently don't like being mooned."

As soon as the words are out of my mouth, the whole table falls into fits of laughter even though most of them have heard this story plenty of times.

"I think I would've quite liked it if I was in that library. Would've livened up my studies, that's for sure." Enzo jokes with a wink and I laugh heartily at his words. Marco groans at him to stop flirting with his sister and I feel Everett tense next to me.

"Never have I ever gone skinny dipping." Avery cuts into Marco's complaints and Enzo and I meet each other's eyes with secretive and guilty smiles as we bring our bottles to our lips and take large swigs.

"Both of you have gone skinny dipping?" Jesse's eyes nearly bulge out of his head as he looks between the two of us and then jumps out of his seat in realization. "Wait a second! That camping trip two years ago, when you two disappeared for hours and then came back soaking wet?! You told us it was a flash rain, but you went skinny dipping without us, didn't you?"

Enzo's mocha eyes catch mine again, his alight with humor at the memory and I find myself practically keeling over in laughter. "To be fair, we were both very drunk and very sweaty and the water was inviting!" I choke out in between fits of giggles. "Nothing else happened you guys!"

"So, you couldn't have went for a dip *with* your clothes on?" Marco groans, hiding his face in his hands.

"Now, where's the fun in that?"

"Yeah, it was quite fun. Maybe we should do that again, Aspen?" Enzo winks, and I laugh, punching his tanned armed teasingly. Our innocent flirting is cut short when I feel a familiar, warm hand clasp my knee. The fire it sends shooting through my veins causes me to jump slightly and I back away from Enzo to glance at Everett.

His jaw is set tightly, but he stares forward, face neutral as if he isn't invading my personal space right now. Marco continues to whine in the background, but I concentrate on Everett, who just innocently shovels noodles into his mouth with his free hand. He was awfully silent during my banter with Enzo and from the looks of it, he didn't like it very much. It isn't until I feel his thumb begin to trace circles onto my bare skin that my shock wears off. My hand drops down, dipping under the table cloth to grab his hand and fling it off my knee discreetly, so as not to draw attention. Everett concedes with a satisfied smirk, continuing to chew.

"Don't blame me, Marco. It was Aspen's idea —she was practically drooling at the idea of seeing me naked." Everett's advances are completely forgotten once I hear Enzo's accusation and I whip around to defend myself.

"Excuse you, I'm more than sure that it was *you* who whipped off your pants as soon as I even suggested swimming! You're the one that—"

I nearly choke on my sentence once I feel that same large hand on my leg again, but this time much higher up and more determined. He squeezes my thigh lightly as his fingers disappear beneath my plaid mini-skirt to trace the flesh of my inner thigh. Chow mein remains untouched on my plate as the cool rings on Everett's fingers send waves of heat traveling up my thigh.

"Are you okay, Aspen?"

"Y-Yeah. I... uh... I'm fine, Jesse. Just choked on a noodle is all." My skin heats, completely flustered, and my heart stutters in my chest at his touch.

I begin to drop my hand below the table again to remove this bastard's hand, when Avery's voice stops me in my tracks. "Aspen, can you pass the chow mein?"

Begrudgingly, I look at the rather large and heavy bowl sitting in front of me and practically growl at Everett's next words, "you're probably gonna need both hands for that." His voice is smug and husky and I squeeze my thighs together to stop his trek up the edge of my skirt. I pick up the bowl with both hands and nearly drop it at the feeling of his palm sliding dangerously close to my lace underwear, fingers tracing the edge.

I jolt slightly from the feeling of his fingers right where I'm aching for him, only separated by a thin barrier of lace. "I have one..." Everett trails off as his fingers lightly brush me through the lace, my thighs clenching at the tease and a small whimper slips past my lips. Everett smirks at the sound and I successfully pass Avery her noodles, not even caring that I'm now able to remove Everett's hand. Not even wanting to anymore.

"Never have I ever hooked up with someone in a club bathroom."

I freeze in my seat, still trembling and slightly out of breath as his fingers go back to massaging my thigh, knuckles brushing my underwear occasionally. He finally rests his eyes on me, the once light green now considerably darker, as his lips wrap around his bottle and he takes a long and deliberate slip, Adam's apple bobbing. My mind flits between desire for Everett's nimble fingers and confusion about what happened to him trying to be my "friend".

*Is this what he does with his* friends?

No one seems to notice or care about our exchange, all too tipsy to pay close attention. I'm thankful for it, because his knowing smirk and hooded eyes make my thighs tremble so hard I have to shovel noodles in my mouth to distract myself. Everett begins to tug at the side of my underwear when he whispers into my ear ever so lightly, "aren't you going to drink, Munchkin?"

His words and enthusiastic fingers seem to be the metaphorical bucket of water splashed over my head. I quickly rip his hand away from my thigh and shoot up from my chair on wobbly knees. "Sorry, I just remembered I needed to show Everett something in the kitchen. Please excuse us." I rush and grip his wandering hand, leading him out of the dining room and into Jesse's quiet kitchen, sliding the door closed.

I round on him immediately, my face still hot and chest still heaving. "What the hell was that, Fox?"

"What was what?" His question is innocent, but his darkened eyes and satisfied grin tell another story.

"Don't play dumb with me, Curly." I point an accusatory finger at him and back away just as he takes a step closer to me. "Didn't I tell you that you were on probation? What the hell was with your happy fingers all of a sudden?"

"All of a sudden? Do you not recall everything I said to you that night at the club? About how I think about fucking you all the time, how I want to bend you over—"

"*Okay! Okay!* Yes, I remember. But, just the other day you said you were going to prove to me that you could be a good *friend.* Friends don't try to feel each other up under tables where their other friends are sitting, no less!"

"Don't even try and tell me you didn't want it too." He all but growls and I shiver as he backs me into the counter, "I do intend on being your friend. But, I had an epiphany last night."

"What would that be?" I ask breathlessly, his hands coming to rest on either side of the counter, effectively trapping me in his arms.

"That some things are inevitable."

"Inevitable?"

"Inevitable: certain to happen; unavoidable." My jaw drops at the recited definition and I'm slightly concerned for my sanity when it actually turns me on even more. "What? I own a dictionary, too... You know what I realized?"

Everett's gaze is determined and passionate as his head ducks down to brush his lips against my own. They spark from the simple touch and I hold my breath in anticipation, knees shaking. I hate the man, then I think we can be friends, then I hate him again, and then I want to strip him down and sex him up. *What is he doing to me?*

"I've discovered that *we* are inevitable. Fight it all you want, but it won't take long until you find yourself in my bed, screaming my name. It's just written in the stars, baby."

With one last cheeky peck to my lips, Everett sends me a loaded wink and saunters out of the kitchen, leaving me a melted puddle at his feet.

* * *

If there's one thing I hate about living in London, it's the weather. If it's not ridiculously cold and gloomy, then it's so hot that you might as well be sipping tea in hell with Satan. So, when rare good weather comes along, I can't pass it up.

The sun kisses my skin, subtle wind blows through my wavy tendrils, and the earth is silent except for the chirping of birds and distant laughter from children enjoying the good weather. It's the perfect day.

"It's so hot outside that chickens are laying hard-boiled eggs!"

Never mind.

I don't even have to open my eyes to know that Everett has waltzed through the gate and into my brother's backyard. The joke and his own raspy guffaw that follows is proof enough of that. I peek one eye open anyway and instantly regret it.

*Damn him. Damn him and his stupid Tarzan hair and gorgeous body and hot tattoos. Damn those small yellow swim trunks that highlight his gorgeous tan. Damn him.*

"You invited Fox, Marco? *Traitor.*" I growl, sitting up on my elbows to catch his sheepish smile, slinging his arm around Everett's shoulders.

"Sorry, Aspen. The boy practically begged me when he heard you were gonna be here." Marco narrowly dodges an elbow to the side from Everett, who glowers at him. I feel heat crawl up my cheeks at his words and instantly look away from the duo. Memories of the dinner the other night flash through my head: Everett's skillful fingers on my thigh, the dirty words said in the kitchen, the fire felt from his kiss, the unspoken promise of more. Even though the sun warms my skin, I feel goosebumps rise on every inch of exposed flesh.

"I'm beginning to think you're trying to torture me." Everett's husky tone pulls me from my previous thoughts and plunges me into a whole set of new, naughtier ones. His mossy eyes darken as they trail over every inch of my bikini clad skin. I suddenly feel very exposed under his scrutiny and wrestle between covering myself up or straightening my posture in confidence.

"Dude, that's my sister." Marco groans and Everett teases him for the American slang, leaving me to ogle his physique in turn. Is it wrong that I want to trace every tattoo of his with my tongue? Even though I still don't particularly like Everett, I've been craving his skin against mine since that stunt at dinner. But, I made a promise to myself that I would try to resist his advances. Key word: *try*.

"You know, Aspen," Marco is stepping inside with a phone to his ear and Everett is sufficiently blocking the sun from shining on my lounge chair. "I couldn't stop thinking about your soft skin and little whimpers all night. Couldn't sleep a wink. What do you have to say for yourself?" I choke on my own spit, bronzed skin flushing at his boldness. I subtly squeeze my thighs together, heart fluttering at the reminder of his rough fingers.

*Resist Aspen. You* must *resist.*

"I don't know... Did you have fun touching yourself to that image, knowing my hand will never replace your own?"

Everett's dimples carve deeper into his cheeks as his smirk only grows, pleased by my response. I don't even have time to be irritated that my insults only amuse him before his strong arms wrap around my thighs and he lifts me from my chair, tosses me over his shoulder, and laughs manically.

"Everett!" I shriek as he carries me in the direction of the pool and it doesn't take a genius to figure out his intentions. "Fox, don't you dare! You put me down right now, or I'm going to take the rustiest knife I can find and—"

*Splash.*

As soon as the water engulfs us I detach myself from Everett's grip and break the surface, sputtering for air. He follows shortly after, a satisfied grin on his lips and I don't waste time in wiping it off his face by splashing him.

"What the hell, Fox?"

"You were obviously being delusional. I thought the refreshing water would clear your mind and help you see the truth." I scoff, clearing water from my eyes as I watch Everett run a hand through his hair, chest glistening in the sun.

"And what truth would that be?" Everett's signature grin is back, warm hands wrapping around my thighs. Although I know I should push him away, I allow him to pull my legs around his waist.

Listen, he's wet and glistening and smiling at me and I'm only human.

"The truth is that you want me just as much as I want you." He whispers and a small gasp slips past my lips as I feel the pool's edge hit my back. Everett's eyes have gone serious and dark as they trace every inch of my skin, lingering on my breasts before settling on my lips. His hands slide up the length of my thighs to cup my bum.

"Hmm... I don't think that's true at all. We're just meant to be *friends*, Curly, and we're hardly that." The wispiness of my voice is evidence enough that my statement is the furthest thing from the truth.

"We'll see about that, Munchkin." His voice is so confident and sure that I really start to believe him. He pulls me in until his hips slot into mine and I can feel his arousal against me.

My head tilts back slightly at the feeling and fire instantly courses through my veins when I hear Everett let out a small groan. My mind is way too foggy to pull away and when I feel the subtle thrust of his hips into mine I know that I'm in way over my head. My hands clasp around his shoulders as his head falls into my neck, lips gently grazing the skin there as his hips buck again, but harder. The moan that leaves my lips only causes Everett's grip to tighten and he lifts his head, pressing his forehead against mine, face pinched with pain. "*God*, Aspen. You have no idea—"

"Sorry about that, you guys. Jesse wouldn't shut up about

the rehearsal schedule."

The second I hear Marco's voice, I shove Everett away and fan my warm face. Marco glances between the two of us questioningly as he rounds the patio, but I avoid his eyes and lift myself out of the pool. I feel Everett watching me as I dry off and take a seat back on my lounger, acting like nothing happened, but internally freaking out. I can barely tolerate the kid, but I let him dry hump me in a pool? I think I need to get my head checked.

I spend the next hour scolding myself for succumbing to his advances and ignoring his watchful eyes as he and Marco goof off in the pool.

*If I hear one more Marco-Polo joke I swear I'm just going to jump off the deep end.*

But, it doesn't take long for Marco to leave Everett and me alone again so he can go pick up dinner, ignoring my protests. When I feel Everett sit down in the lounge chair next to me, I know his intentions are anything but innocent. They always are.

"You look quite hot."

"Is that a pickup line?" I quirk one eyebrow up and Everett looks confused for a second before chuckling and leaning his elbows onto his knees to look at me closer, totally shameless.

"I meant that you look flushed from the sun, but you do also look hot too." I close my eyes again, trying to ignore the rapid beat of my heart and his heavy gaze. However, my relaxation is cut short when I feel something cold and wet rest on my forehead. My eyes shoot open to find that Everett took one of the ice cubes from my lemonade and placed it onto my slightly sweaty forehead.

"What? Just thought you'd need to cool down from the sun and... *other* activities."

Everett's movements are slow as he drags the ice down my nose, cool water dripping down my cheeks before dragging it across my lips, wetting them. He continues his travels across my jaw, down the length of my neck, and into my collarbone. The cool sensation on my hot flesh makes me shiver, my breath picking up. I only open my eyes when Everett's hand reaches my breasts and I hold my breath as he traces the swell of each one, the cold droplets dipping into the valley between them. I revert my eyes back up to his face, his hooded eyes following the ice cube intently.

He lingers on my chest for a while before continuing his voyage to my stomach. Everett's lip turns white from his teeth biting down on it as he watches the dwindling cube circle the skin around my navel. His movements are achingly slow as they dance across my hips, the cool water dipping below the high waist of my bikini and sending shocks up my body and making me squirm.

Everett doesn't hesitate to drag the ice cube over my suit bottoms and my back arches, a soft mewl escaping my lips. He drags the freezing cube over my center twice, the ice seeping through the fabric and cooling my warm and aching flesh.

It's like nothing I've ever felt before and I'm a writhing mess from the conflicting sensations. Everett's name leaves my lips in a small moan as he circles the frozen water around me once more. My chest rises and falls rapidly and my skin tingles, but his hand suddenly disappears and the feeling vanishes.

I open my eyes and look down to see that the ice cube has finally melted against my heat and I can't help but feel disappointed in the absence of both the ice and Everett. My skin, although just cooled, feels much hotter than it did before his efforts.

I look up at Everett to find him tracing over every inch of my now slightly wet skin with dark eyes and flushed cheeks. He almost looks more hot and bothered than I am, chest rising and falling rapidly and tongue peeking out to lick his lips. When he finally meets my own lust-filled gaze, he shoots me a seductive grin. "You're welcome for cooling you off on such a hot day," I almost moan at the gruffness of his voice and obvious bulge in his trunks. "After all, what are *friends* for?"

That sentence alone has my body heating for an entirely

different reason and Everett shoots me a smug grin before getting up from his chair and slipping inside Marco's house. I'm left to gawk at the now closed door, body flushed, my core aching for relief, and my conscious scolding me for being so weak. I fell right into his trap, so easily, all for him to throw the term 'friends' right back in my face.

I stew in my rage and mortification, plotting my revenge, until Marco comes back with the pizza. Aspen never falls prey to a man, not anymore. He's obviously underestimated me if he thinks that I'll just let him get away with being such an arrogant, womanizing, *tease*. Well, Everett Fox is about to learn a very valuable lesson.

If this is how he planned to show me it's 'inevitable' that I'd end up in his bed, then I only have one thing to say:

Game on.

# FEMME FATALE

This is crazy. You're crazy. You're an insane, evil temptress, idiot. Take it off.

The minute I slipped on the white, lacy lingerie Everett picked out and my thumb hit 'send' on such a stupid message, I knew I was certifiable.

No one's here yet, but the door is unlocked. Let yourself in.

Yeah, no one else is here yet because I told Everett to come at an earlier time than everyone else. Again, seriously bat shit crazy.

Crazy for revenge.

I hear the doorknob twist and door squeak open and know it's too late to back out. Time to put on a confident façade, even though I have no idea what I'm doing. Marco informed me yesterday that my mother wants us over for dinner this weekend and I found myself desperate for a distraction. Desperate to feel wanted and desired for a brief time because I know my mother will squash that feeling like a bug.

Ever since the pool shenanigans, Everett has been relentless in his teasing: constantly finding excuses to touch me, whispering things in my ear that would make porn stars blush, and always watching me with such a heavy and lustful gaze that it makes my knees weak. I so desperately want to give him a taste of his own medicine and it might give me the confidence I need to make it through dinner.

"Munchkin?" Everett calls out, clicking of his boots getting closer to my room.

I quickly turn to face my closet, pretending I didn't hear him. I sort through my clothes to make it seem as if I was in the middle of changing and not just waiting for him to walk in on me in the lingerie he has no idea I bought. The sound of his footsteps comes to an abrupt halt in my doorway.

I feel his burning gaze scanning my figure, skin heating and heart practically jumping up my throat, but I swallow it down and spin to face him, feigning surprise.

You can do this, Aspen. You are a confident, sexy, clev—

"Oh, Everett. I-I didn't hear you come in."

Okay, maybe you can't do this.

The awkward laugh that escapes my lips is almost pitiful and the way I fumble around trying to act surprised to see him won't be winning me any awards. But, he doesn't seem to notice my unease, gawking at me with desire and awe. The once emerald green in his widened eyes has shifted into a dark abyss as they rake over my scantily clad figure. His jaw sweeps the hardwood until his teeth appear to capture his bottom lip, jeans noticeably tighter. He isn't sure where to look first, eyes jumping around every inch of my skin and lingering on the clothed bits. I can only stand and watch as he blows out a breath of air and finally meets my eyes.

"Jesus Christ," he seems so taken aback by my appearance – the one I had followed exactly as he described when he picked out the two-piece: red lips an tousled hair. "Is that... that's the... the—"

"The lingerie you picked out for me," I smirk and he nods eagerly as I saunter towards his still figure, "It was so pretty, I couldn't help myself... don't you think it's pretty, Everett?"

"I don't know if pretty is the right word for how you look right now."

"How do I look right now?" I pout innocently, running my fingers down the delicate strap of my bra, his eyes following the movement. I try to calm my erratic breaths, playing it cool.

He whimpers, actually whimpers at my question. His hands twitch by his sides, eyes lingering on my figure. "So fucking sexy that I'm having a hard time not ripping it off of you."

The air in my lungs leaves in a rush and his tempting words send shivers down my spine, but I fight how they make me feel. I refuse to give in this time, to let him have the upper hand.

"The fact," Everett shakes his head as if to clear it, "the fact that you actually bought this after I suggested it... God, you have no idea how hard I am right now." The intensity of his gaze, coupled with the honest words falling form those kissable lips does naughty things to me.

It's about time I do naughty things to him too.

I pray that he doesn't notice how my hands shake when I rest them against his chest, the simple touch causing his breaths to shallow. My lashes flutter and I step closer until we're almost chest-to-chest. My hand travels down, tracing his abdomen through his shirt, and making him shiver from my feather-light touch. His heart races underneath my palm, but I don't linger long before resting my hand against the front of his jeans. I feel him twitch under my palm, letting out an almost imperceptible moan. Glancing up at him from under my lashes, I stroke him lightly.

"I think I have a pretty good idea."

The growl that escapes Everett's lips at my whispered words is almost animalistic. I don't have time to think or even breathe before his palms are gripping either side of my face and his lips are slamming onto mine. His kiss is hungry and desperate and full of pent-up desire and I instantly drop my charade. Everett's full lips are relentless against my own, teeth gnawing on my bottom lip, and tongue dipping into my mouth.

I reach out to grip his hips and pull him against me. A guttural groan tears itself from Everett's throat as he grinds against me. My tongue glides against his as I tug desperately at his curls, his palms sliding down to skim my breasts, teasing me through the rough lace.

"Oh shit," he pants as I release his lips to trail kisses down his sharp jaw. "I want to rip this thing to shreds, but seeing you in it so unbelievably hot. You've no idea what you do to me."

Everett squeezes my breasts and I can't bite back the moan that escapes me. He walks forward, moving us back towards the bed and just as my knees hit the edge, I'm quick to turn us and shove him onto the mattress. The air leaves his lungs in a whoosh and he sits up on his elbows to gawk at me: flushed cheeks, swollen lips, hooded gaze, straining pants.

I slowly crawl onto the bed, swinging my legs over his hips so I'm straddling him, and brushing my lips against his once more. They melt together desperately and I try to control the fire in the pit of my stomach as I roll my hips against his, a simultaneous moan of satisfaction escaping both of us at the relieved pressure. His fingers bruise my hips as I move on top of him.

I know I need to stop this before it goes too far, but I'm afraid it already has. I find it impossible to stop: drunk on his petal-soft lips, on his warm tongue that teases mine, and his rough palms gliding over my sensitive flesh and tangling into my hair. However, the next words that come from his panting lips as I suck on his collarbone are all the motivation I need, "I knew you'd end up in my bed eventually. Inevitable."

I tear my mouth from his flushed skin, tracing them over his lips one last time, before pulling back to meet his dazed eyes. "But, you see, Everett," I whisper faintly, voice husky, and my fingers tracing his stained lips. "This is actually my bed."

I climb off his lap like I'm not affected at all and walk towards my closet. Everett just continues to lie there completely dumbfounded, the only sound in the room his harsh panting and hangers clanging together. He curses under his breath and I try not to laugh. "Do you know what a femme fatale is, Everett?" I try to keep the smugness from my voice, not waiting for him to answer, "femme fatale: a mysterious and seductive woman whose charms ensnare her lovers, often leading them into compromising situations."

He's silent, but I can practically feel his jaw dropping and anger building as he realizes this was a plot to get back at him for all of his stunts recently, "are you fucking kid—"

The lord is on my side today because I hear a faint knocking on my door and the chatter of our friends just as my hands find a tee-shirt dress. I slip it on over the sinful lingerie and face Everett. He's still laying on my wrinkled sheets and staring at me with a slightly infuriated, slightly confused, and very much still aroused look in his eyes.

"You might want to wipe my lipstick off your lips and start thinking about your nan or dead kittens." I smile innocently, motioning to both his stained lips and the tent in his pants as Everett's fury grows. Before I walk out the door to greet my friends, I look over my shoulder one more time, "you're welcome for the advice... after all, what are friends for?"

However, Everett doesn't yell at me for teasing him, nor does his face grow red with rage when I throw his words back in his face. Instead, his darkened eyes meet mine with a determined glint and his angry frown morphs into a mischievous smirk.

# DESIRE

Curly: Having sex in an elevator is wrong on so many levels.

I roll my eyes at yet another one of the jokes Everett has sent me in the last two days. All of them sexual and all of them making me blush harder than the last. Each one has me itching to block his number, but I never do. I've got issues.

**Curly:** *What's long and hard and has cum in it.*

**Me:** *No.*

**Curly:** *A cucumber!*

**Curly:** *You dirty girl, I know what you were thinking. You want my cucumber, don't you?*

I ignore Everett's texts and change his contact name while I wait in line to purchase my shoes. I've been shopping for my mom's dinner tomorrow for three hours straight and have only managed to snag jewelry. Although, I could show up in an outfit fit for the Met Gala and she would still find something complain about. It's incredibly frustrating.

Everett's inappropriate messages aren't exactly helping.

It's been a few days since I avenged my dignity by seducing Everett and leaving him unsatisfied as he did me. Of course, my victory was slightly hindered by that vengeful glint in his eyes. Something tells me he won't let me have the upper hand for long. He's very competitive.

**Horny Bastard:** *Wanna hear a joke about my dick? Never mind, it's too long.*

**Me:** *Wanna hear a joke about my pussy? Never mind, you won't get it.*

**Horny Bastard:** *You know, you shouldn't bend over in those tight jeans. Might give the grandpa behind you a heart attack. Might also make me bend you over that table. x*

My heart thrums in nervous excitement and I quickly scan the area, finding Everett next to the window of the shop with a goofy grin, pointing to a mannequin that's currently pantless. He lets out a sharp laugh and smacks the mannequin's plastic bum.

I pretend I don't know him.

"Munchkin!"

I shield my face, eyes peeking through my fingers to watch him saunter my way, dirty grin on his face and hands running through his long hair. I swear every girl in the shop follows his every move and although I would deny, deny, deny if anyone asked –I don't blame them. Flannel shirt buttoned half-way, tight black jeans, signature ankle boots. The boy looks like he waltzed straight out of a magazine. Though, that isn't the reason I gawk at him.

We match.

"I have to say, babe, you've got style." Everett eyes me appreciatively, dimples deep and eyes amused. I hope these strangers don't think we matched on purpose like some lovesick teens.

"What are you doing here, Fox? Stalking me?"

"You wish." He wiggles his brows teasingly and I bite back an involuntary smile, "just happened to be looking for a new watch. Saw you in here, wanted to come chat."

He sounds innocent enough, which is exactly why I don't buy it. Before I can question him the sales lady waves me forward. Everett is politely silent, but I feel his eyes burning holes into my skin not so politely. I ignore him and hurriedly pay for my strappy black, block heels.

"Where to next?"

"Excuse me? I'm not going anywhere with you."

"Don't be that way, Munchkin. Just tryin' to be friendly is all." His words are full of innuendos, accentuated by his lingering gaze, and sending tingles straight down my spine.

I have a feeling that if I let him tag along, he may very well try to get his revenge. The thought makes my skin prickle and heart knock at my ribs. So, I'm not quite sure why the next words fall from my lips, but they're impossible to stop.

"Well, we are friends after all."

* * *

If you ever want to feel bad about yourself, shopping is the way to go. The fabric is itchy, the plum color horrendous, and it's loose around my waist, but so tight on my bum I might rip it just by walking. Has my body always been this disproportional or is it the dress?

I tell myself it's the dress.

Regardless, I step out of the changing room and am instantly greeted by obnoxious laughter. I huff in annoyance as Everett throws his head back, giggles falling from those devilish lips. I curse him under my breath, which only makes him laugh even harder. "Ya look like a grape... a bloody grape, Munchkin!" He barely chokes out, eyeing the high collared, knee-length dress. I can't say I disagree.

"I give up. All these dresses make me look like some kind of fruit." We've been trying on dresses for almost an hour and either the price tag or the mirror has made me want to cry.

"Wait," Everett's finally able to catch his breath, reaching behind his position on the circular couch to grab a white dress hanging behind him, "try this one on."

I don't bother examining it before snatching it from his hands and stomping into the changing room. My hands can't move fast enough to remove the abomination and all I can think about is the tub of ice cream waiting for me back home. My bitter thoughts are halted, though, once I catch a glimpse of the dress in the mirror. It's a vintage piece with long, flared lace sleeves, a few inches above the knee to show off my tan skin, and a plunging neckline that stops in the middle of my chest.

It's somehow both innocent and wicked, and the combination almost revives some of my shattered self-esteem. When I step out of the dressing room I keep my eyes on my bare feet, but hear Everett let out a heavy gust of air. "I'm not sure if I want to pinch your cheeks or fuck you right now."

I cough, choking slightly, and watch as Everett leans forward on his knees to get a better look at me, my own knees growing weak. My throat runs dry when I see his pink tongue swipe along his lips, moistening them, like a predator about to feast on prey. I squirm under his observant and darkening eyes, imagining the dirty thoughts that must be running through his head. I'm suddenly glad that this store is so empty, so no one can see how Everett is looking me like I'm a tall glass of water and he's a man lost in the desert.

"Okay, I'll get this one. I'm gonna change now." The words fall from my lips in a jumbled mess, but I'm sure Everett doesn't hear me anyway.

I scurry back into the dressing room because I really can't handle it when he looks at me so heavily, so full of want. The tension that's between us has been building steadily over the last few weeks –like someone lit a match to a very long fuse. But, I think the fuse is nearing its end.

Before I can even unzip, I hear the door click open and Everett squeezes through quickly, his hooded eyes meeting mine through the mirror. "You can't be in here, Everett!"

He ignores me, eyes tracing my figure leisurely, before meeting my own. "You know, your little stunt the other day wasn't very nice."

The husky rasp of his voice is enough to have my palms sweating and stomach clenching, his words both a veiled threat and promise. Everett takes two deliberate steps towards me, chest flush against my back and eyes never leaving mine through the mirror. "Well, neither have the stunts you've been pulling on me," I choke out, voice breathy and face hot.

"Well, I'm done with that now, no more teasing. I want you, Aspen. I want you so bad that it's all I can think about. I can't live another minute without having you. I won't." His honest words and intense stare send shockwaves straight to my core and I barely choke out his name before he has one palm encircling my hip and the other brushing my hair over my shoulder. His jaw is set and his emerald eyes sincere as they hold mine in the mirror.

"It's game over, Aspen."

With that, he dips his head to lick a bold stripe up my neck, making my knees quiver and hair stand on end. A strangled gasp leaves my lips when his teeth nip my jaw. Encouraged by my reaction, he leaves a trail of wet, hot kisses down my flesh before connecting with my collarbone and sucking on the skin harshly. An involuntary moan slips past my lips and Everett smirks against my skin, curls tickling my cheek as he goes back to marking me.

"Everett, I—"

"Shh, let me show you. Let me show you how much I want you, Aspen."

I whimper at the need in his voice and Everett takes that as an invitation to run his palms up the length of my body. When his hands graze my breasts, I try to turn in his grasp to touch him or kiss him or do anything, but his grip only grows tighter.

"No, I want you to watch. I want you to watch what I can do to you. I want you to watch as I make you come."

Oh. My. God. I'm so fucked.

I'm complete putty in his hands, mind fogged over with desire, and I can only stand limply as his hands knead my breasts through the thin material. His lips continue the attack on my neck as his hands glide down my bum, giving it a firm squeeze before continuing their journey to the hem of my dress. My breath catches when I feel the expanse of his calloused palms run up and down my thighs. I reach around to wrap a hand in

Everett's hair as the other leans against the mirror in an effort to maintain my balance.

This is wrong and stupid and reckless. We're in a dressing room and I'm meant to hate him but, when his fingers reach my inner thigh, my dress rising with it, I find myself not caring. Two months ago, I never would've allowed Everett Fox near me, let alone touch me like this. I don't know what's come over me lately, but all I do know is that Everett's tongue is teasing my ear and his hands are inching their way up my legs and I never want him to stop. The moan that leaves my lips when his fingers run over the lace of my panties is shameful.

"Fuck, Aspen. You're soaked."

His hips buck forward and I can feel him against me, hard and straining in his jeans, and I can't help but push back into him. He pants against my skin and our eyes meet through the mirror. "You have no idea how long I've wanted to do this."

Those are the last words exchanged before his fingers tug my underwear aside and trace themselves up my slit slowly. I have to remind myself to keep quiet —that we're in a public place. But, that only makes my heart stutter and stomach clench from the riskiness of it all.

Desire: strong sexual feeling or appetite.

The feeling of finally succumbing to our desires after so long is overwhelming and I know Everett feels the same from the moan that slips out as his fingers slide up my folds again. His rings are cold against my flushed skin and the contradicting sensations nearly make me convulse. When his fingers finally find my sensitive nub, I swear I black out momentarily.

"Oh my god, Everett." I whine desperately as my head falls back onto his shoulder, hand tugging his hair harshly. He doesn't relent, fingers circling me and tongue continuing to lap at the hollow of my neck. His other hand trails up my waist before cupping my breast, gently kneading it in his palm and causing me to bite my lip to stop the moan that begs to escape.

I'm panting and breathless as his slender fingers tease me, the cold rings causing me to jerk my hips forward for more.

Suddenly, those expert fingers are trailing down towards my slick entrance, not even hesitating before sliding in. Everett curses under his breath as he slides another finger in, causing my knees to buckle from the sensation.

The sounds are shameful, even as we try to stifle ourselves. Everett panting against my neck, eyes never leaving where his hand disappeared under my dress, watching transfixed. And I watch him watching me, my moans barely muffled by my teeth. I swear I can hear my pounding heart echo off the walls. "You're gonna have to be quiet for me, baby."

I clench at the nickname and Everett groans, bucking his hips against my backside and moving his fingers at a harsher pace. His teeth nip my neck, thumb rubbing in faster circles. I can feel my orgasm building inside me as I watch him though the mirror: mouth ghosting across my neck, hand squeezing my breast, forearm flexing with each pump of his fingers.

It's all too much.

His fingers curl, reaching a spot I never even knew existed and my vision flashes a brilliant white. Everett's palm suddenly clasps around my mouth as a satisfied moan falls from my lips. I tug at his roots desperately, my back almost breaking as the pleasure ricochets through my body. My thighs shake uncontrollably and vision blurs as he rocks me through it.

The fuse has reached its end and I'm the one that combusts.

I slump against him, bones officially turned to jelly. My body shakes, aftershocks of the earthquake I just experienced. Our gazes lock as he pulls my underwear back into place and brings his fingers up to his mouth, slipping them inside. He sucks on them lightly and I flush even more from the sight. "So fucking sweet."

I physically cannot reply to his filthy words, only huffing in response as my lungs beg for air and Everett releases his hold on me. I stand shocked as he commands me to get dressed, making his way out of the room, and turning around one last time with a satisfied smirk.

"This is only the beginning, Munchkin."

# EPIPHANY

His hands look like they were sculpted by gods. Long, slender fingers clad in various silver rings that make him look sinful despite the small cross tattooed by his thumb. Hands lightly tanned and constantly moving as he speaks. I bet girls and guys alike wonder what those hands can do. But, I know.

I know and it's all I can think about. It haunted me all night.

The sound of his groans in my ear, full lips teasing my neck, and that tongue lapping at my collarbone replay in my brain even in my sleep. The feeling of his palm cradling my breast, hips thrusting desperately, and those fingers sending me to Heaven and Hell have taken up residence in my brain.

"What's got you spacing out, Munchkin?"

My eyes snap up to meet mischievous green ones, face warming at being caught. From the smug grin on his lips and the way he plays with a ring on his finger slowly, teasingly — I know that he knows exactly why I was spaced out. When I woke up this morning to two deep bruises on my neck, I wasn't even mad. No, I almost felt... aroused at the sight of them, *proud.* I can't even think of a clever reply, mind too full of Everett. I have no idea how to feel: my body craves his, but my mind urges me to jump off a cliff every time he opens his mouth.

"She's probably trying to figure out a way to get out of the dinner tonight."

An earth-shattering groan slips past my lips at the reminder and I instantly flop onto the couch face first, thoughts of Everett vanishing instantly. I hear Jesse whine after Avery socks him in the shoulder for bringing up to the touchy subject.

"If I suddenly turn up missing after tonight assume that I've either stabbed myself or my mother did it for me. Either way, it was nice knowing all of you."

"I'll pick out the flower arrangements for your funeral." Avery mock sympathizes, so I send her a mock-grateful smile.

"I'll make sure they play 'Highway to Hell' as they lower your casket." I bark out a short laugh at Jesse's suggestion and wait for Everett's inevitable input.

"I'll be the inappropriate one that hits on your cousins and talks about how fit you were."

I knew that the second I actually giggled at his horrible joke that any suspicions Avery may have had would be confirmed. To her knowledge, I never *ever* laugh at Everett's jokes and pride myself in the fact that I despise everything and anything about Everett.

Or at least, I *used* to.

"Can I talk to you for a minute, Aspen?"

I don't even respond to Avery, just simply follow her lead into the kitchen. I feel Everett's eyes on me the entire time, but keep my gaze trained on my feet until we stop in Jesse's modern kitchen, leaning against the island. "You wanna tell me what's going on between you and Everett, or shall I just draw my own dirty conclusions?"

I shrug innocently, but I avoid her inquisitive stare, looking out the small window above the sink, overlooking the park below. "Nothing's going on."

"So, what exactly is your definition of nothing? Because those poorly disguised hickeys on your neck don't exactly scream *nothing*." My hand immediately flies up to my throat, where I thought I'd successfully covered them with make-up. "So, you guys are hooking up?"

"No," I blurt, but sigh dejectedly when I realize that I actually don't know the answer. "I don't know *what* we're doing. I mean we've mostly been messing with each other, but..."

"But... you want more?"

Her question shocks me, but my hesitance shocks me even more. I've always found Everett irritating and womanizing and everything I stand against, but I crave his touch, his voice, his lips... the man has gotten under my skin.

And I'm not sure I want him out.

Noticing my trouble, Avery sighs and shoots me a sympathetic smile, "I'm glad that you're getting out there again. I know I told you not to write anyone off because you got burnt in the past, but... I just want you to be careful, Aspen."

"What do you mean?"

"You always end up giving flowers to people that never tend to them. Don't let Everett be one of those people. That's all I'm saying. You deserve someone that'll help you grow."

Her words resonate deep into my bones, my eyes stinging and skin paling. I know that Everett and I aren't serious. I'm probably something for him to pass the time and my appeal comes from the chase. Most of the time I hate the man, but Everett is the first person to show any interest in me since Sam and it does make my heart tender. I'm just not sure if it's just from the attention or the man giving it. I'm just so confused. Confused and scared.

Before I can even dwell on it, the sound of a throat clearing ends Avery and I's conversation and there's a sharp shift in the atmosphere of the room.

"Marco's here to pick up Aspen." Just like that, my main supporter forgets all about my dilemma. Avery's eyes literally light up just at the mention of my brother and I try not to gag when I tell her that she can go greet him. She's so whipped that it would be pretty cute how devoted she is, *if* Marco actually knew about her feelings.

As soon as she leaves the room I turn to face tangled hair, dirty grin, and mischievous green eyes. The room seems to be electrified, as if just reaching a hand out would send shockwaves through my entire system. Everett's intense gaze doesn't leave mine as he saunters over, cornering me into the counter. His chest brushes mine and I try to calm my breathing, watching in a trance as Everett reaches up to brush my hair over my shoulder. A shudder rips through me when his fingers ever so gently dance across the marks *he* made on my skin. "You tried to cover these up, Munchkin?"

The question is rhetorical, but I still nod feebly when his warm breath ghosts over my face. He tuts lightly, a disappointed pout on his face as he dips his head down to my neck. His lips trace my skin teasingly and I don't know what comes over me, but the words slip out of my mouth before I can stop them, "Avery knows something's going on between us."

Everett pauses briefly before planting a soft kiss near my ear, "oh?"

His tone implies that he isn't very interested in the topic at all, but Avery's warning is bouncing off the walls in my brain and I need answers. "What *is* going on between us?"

This makes Everett stop his movements and, this time, he doesn't continue. No, he removes his lips and body from me completely—taking one large step away and crossing his arms in front of his broad chest. "What?" He's confused and almost... *annoyed* that I asked.

"What's your endgame here, Fox? What do you want from me, exactly?" I don't know why, but his negative reaction has me on the defense instantly. I don't expect anything from him and I'm not sure what I want either, but *he's* the one that instigated this whole mess. *He* should be the one to clear it up.

"You know what I want from you. I've made it very clear."

"So, you just want to fuck me? Then what? Is that all you want? My body?"

"Where is this coming from?" Everett shakes his head, brows furrowed in confusion. He reaches a hand out, but I flinch from his touch, "you didn't seem to care about my intentions when I was making you come yesterday."

He's right —I didn't mind yesterday. I was somehow fine with being Everett's next target because I didn't want anything else from him. But, Avery's talk today has my thoughts jumbled. I would've been perfectly happy hating him forever, but he just had to flirt with me and touch me and make me want him. Now, I have no idea what I want.

"So, the plan is to hump and dump me, then? Just use me and go?" I hate the whine in my voice and the words coming out of my mouth, but I can't stop them.

"Don't put words in my mouth, Aspen," he spits and his tone is so venomous that I'm taken aback, recoiling as if he slapped me. This makes his expression fall and he looks away, rubbing a hand down his face and sighing tiredly. "I just don't want you to get the wrong idea."

Harsh reality hits me like a wave and I almost drown under its weight; Everett meant more to me than I'd originally thought. His statement shouldn't shock me and I don't know why I expected anything less, this is just who he is: aloof, indifferent, careless.

Epiphany: a moment of sudden revelation or insight.

Somewhere along the way, Everett had gotten under my skin. And not in the way either of us predicted. "No, I think I have just the right idea." I breathe, ignoring the ache in my chest and pushing past him to go to a dinner where the rejection I feel now will only grow.

* * *

Elizabeth Marino is a world-renowned lawyer. Cut-throat, cruel, and powerful when it comes to getting the job done and getting it done right. It never mattered whether the client was innocent or not; she would take defend them all and win.

Which explains the mini-mansion I grew up in, the bullying I received in school, and the cold-shoulder I got from her whenever I fell-short of expectations. Which was often. Every bad grade, every lie, and every hair out of place was met with derision. There were no mistakes allowed growing up —in whatever I did, I had to be the best and I didn't excel in most things, which certainly didn't help my chances for Best Child award.

I gave up trying a long time ago, anyway.

"What happened?" The car jerks slightly as Marco shifts into park in front of the obnoxiously large oak doors and I turn to face him hesitantly.

"What do you mean?"

"I know that you've been dreading this dinner, but you're acting like Yoda just died."

"Don't you even joke about that." I snap at him, but he just levels me with an unamused stare, knowing that I'm trying to change the subject. "Nothing is wrong besides the fact that I have to spend the night hearing about what a disappointment I am."

Marco sighs and opens his mouth —no doubt to spew some crap about our mom not thinking of me as a failure— but, I quickly exit the Porsche mommy dearest bought him. That's really only part of the reason I'm in such a sour mood, though.

I don't want to think or talk about Everett. The realization I had about my growing feelings is one thing, but hearing him confirm he was just trying to get into my pants is another. Both, equally as crushing. But, my foolishness in believing otherwise is more upsetting.

On some level, I thought Everett's fixation on me meant more than it did. That maybe, just *maybe*, someone could actually want *me*. All of me. And once again, I was wrong.

"Just please try not to cause a scene." Marco pleads as he races in front of me to greet our mother first. I clench my fists so I don't hit him and clear my mind, plastering on a sickeningly-sweet smile as the doors open to reveal the woman that scolds me even in my dreams.

"Marco, I've missed you!" Her petite frame is completely engulfed by his broadness and I awkwardly inspect my hands as I hear my mother dote on him. "You've grown a beard! I bet all the ladies love it, but none are good enough, ya hear me?"

Marco just laughs uncomfortably and pulls away to reveal me standing behind him. My mother's chocolate eyes flit to me and even though I would like to pretend I imagined it, I know the way her smile tightens slightly is all too real. "Aspen, darling," her tone is dramatically colder as she pulls me into a quick embrace, red lips attaching to my cheek before examining me. "Have you put on a bit of weight?"

Marco visibly pales and it takes everything in me to bite my tongue and not make some comment about how the orange dress she has on makes her look like a pumpkin.

She leads us through the large foyer like a tour guide even though the marble floors, grand staircase, and excessive amount of artwork are all too familiar. The house is filled with illusions of grandeur and wealth that most kids dream of, but only serve to remind me of the bitter resentment and cold affection of my childhood.

"Margo made us divine oysters for an appetizer and some lobster for dinner."

"Uh," Marco looks from our dark-haired mother to me multiple times, hoping that she's joking. "Aspen is allergic to shellfish..."

She spins around just as we enter the large dining room, "since when?"

"Since birth?" I retort in disbelief, ignoring the jab in the ribs from Marco. "Do you not remember when I ate oysters at the market when I was seven and had to be rushed to the hospital because I couldn't breathe? I almost died..."

The idea that a mother wouldn't remember a simple allergy that could kill her only daughter would seem unbelievable to some, but doesn't surprise me as much as it should. Maybe that's why it hurts so much, the predictability of it all. The outright blatancy of her disdain for my very existence.

"Oh, I'm sure it wasn't that bad," she trails off in thought and I scoff at her indifference to such a traumatizing moment in my life. "I guess you can have the salad. Probably best for your figure, anyway." She sighs disappointedly, as if it's *my* fault oysters could kill me.

*Just grin and bear it. Just grin and bear it. Just grin and bear it.*

The silence is tense as we sit at the mahogany table that is much too large for the three of us. Even though my mother doesn't deserve sympathy, I can't help but wonder how lonely she must get in this big house. I suppose her ego is large enough to take up a few rooms.

She strikes up a conversation with Marco while slurping oysters, ignoring me and my dry salad, and when she asks about any potential girlfriends, I tune them out. The buzzing of my phone is a welcome distraction and I pull it out of my clutch eagerly.

**Horny Bastard:** *I don't want to leave things how we did. Call me when you can.*

**Horny Bastard:** *I realized you probably can't call me for a while. Or maybe you can and are choosing not to. Whatever the case, I think we should talk about us.*

**Horny Bastard:** *Not that there is an 'us,' I just feel bad about how that sounded in the kitchen. I hope I didn't give you the wrong impression.*

**Horny Bastard:** *Aspen?*

His stupid texts make my skin flush with irritation and I have to grit my teeth in order to keep in the scream that has been clawing its way up my throat since I arrived at my mother's.

**Me:** *Vaffanculo.* [Fuck off.]

"Aspen, it's rude to be on your phone at the dinner table."

My bad mood has worsened considerably and suddenly, I don't want to bite my tongue anymore. I'm tired of being dragged through the mud and I'm tired of *letting* people drag me through the mud. I'm tired of giving flowers to people who don't tend to them.

"Yeah? Well, I think it's rude to ignore people at the dinner table." I snap, crossing my arms and ignoring Marco's pleading gaze. As far as I'm concerned, he's complicit in my mother's attitude towards me. He loves to soak up all her praise and doesn't care that I'm left out to dry and wither away without it.

"Excuse me?" Her crow's feet cracks as she squints her eyes and I take an odd satisfaction at the sight.

"Aren't you going to ask about my life? Or do you just care about Marco?"

Her manicured hand comes up to her chest, as if offended I would think such a thing. "Of course, I care about you, honey. What... what *have* you been up to?" Her mock enthusiasm makes me sick, but I still try to think of something to say. Surely telling her that I hooked up with some guy I can barely stand in a public dressing room or that I quit singing wouldn't be appropriate dinner conversation.

"Working on some music, teaching guitar, taking care of Yoda. I'm good."

"That's great, honey." Her napkin dabs at her lips and she seems to be searching for something to say. "How are you and that... that boy with the tattoos? Sean something or other?"

My blood runs cold, but my cheeks flare. I can tell from the way Marco slumps in his seat and shakes his head that even he knows this night is past salvation.

Six months. Six months since Sam and I broke up. Not only could she not remember the name of the man that was such an integral part of my life for two years, but she also couldn't remember what he did to me. She couldn't recall her daughter had been cheated on, manipulated, and pushed around by some man for two whole years. I gave up the one thing in my life that I loved because he constantly told me I was horrible at it and that continuing was useless.

She has no idea. She doesn't care.

She never did.

"Fuck you," I seethe, my hands shaking and eyes seeing red. She gasps dramatically as I point a finger in her made-up face. "Fuck you for making me feel worthless my whole life. Fuck you for not giving a damn about me because I couldn't live up to your standards —because I look like dad. Fuck you for favoring Marco, for not knowing I'm allergic to shellfish, and for not being there for me when I needed you the most. Just... just *fuck you* for not loving me as much as I loved you."

I can barely choke out the last few words and I'm not sure if it's because a lump has formed in my throat or because blind rage has made it hard for me to speak. Either way, the words come out shaky and emotional, but they have the intended effect.

My mother's eyes fill with shocked tears and Marco's face only reflects pity as they both sit speechless. All of that is barely registers over the ringing in my ears and the pounding of my heart from finally saying what has been bubbling under the surface for so long. I waste no time in grabbing my clutch and storming out of the room, heels clicking furiously on the polished marble. A distant chair screeches back, followed by quiet murmurs, but I drown it out.

No one comes after me. I don't expect them to.

I burst through the doors and trek down the long gravel drive, needing to get as far away as possible as soon as possible. I don't know if it's force of habit, desperation for familiarity, or just that I have no one else to call, but my thumbs tremble as they dial the only number I have memorized. It rings once, twice, three times before it's picked up with a distant click.

"Aspen?" The silky and familiar voice instantly soothes me and the next words leave my lips in a breathy and desperate plea.

"I need you, Sam."

# DESPERATION

Bright lights. Thumping base. Loud shouting. Endless shots. Glazed eyes. Sloppy movements. Pounding head. Scorching throat.

The familiar scene of the club has me feeling sick. The bar stool is uncomfortable and the bartender is way too flirty and I just want to leave, but I remember Everett's rejection and my mother's inability to care about any detail of my life and I stay exactly where I am.

"Can you stop ogling my breasts and bring me a shot of tequila?" I snap at the burly man, to which he smirks and quickly caters to my request despite the waiting people at the bar. "Keep 'em coming." I down my second shot for the night, welcoming the burn that slides down my throat and quickly taking the third from his grasp, tossing that one back just as quickly.

"Now, this is a sight I never thought I'd see again."

The silky voice instantly has me spinning in my stool to face the man who broke my heart, but the action dizzies me. I'm met with icy blue eyes, scruffy beard, messy brown locks pushed to the side, and an array of tattoos. My heart squeezes painfully at the sight of the man I once loved. "Took you long enough to get here. I had to start without you."

Sam's smirk grows and he easily slips onto the stool next to me. "Guess I should catch up then." He takes one of the shots from the sticky counter, clinks mine, and downs it. Just like that, it's like the last six months never happened as I drink with him, gossiping about old friends. In the back of my mind I know this is a mistake, that this will just set back my progress. I know that Sam doesn't deserve any of my time and that I should just throw my drink in his face and leave.

*I just don't want you to get the wrong idea.*

*How are you and that... that boy with the tattoos? Sean something or other?*

I toss back another shot, wiping my mouth with the back of my hand.

"Spill." Our easy banter halts and Sam's grin turns into a frown as he faces me. I'm taken aback by his somber attitude and avoid his intense stare as I play with the lace of my dress. The same dress that Everett touched me in. The thought makes my stomach churn.

"Spill what?"

"Don't play dumb. I can read you like a book —always could. You wouldn't just call me up here for fun, I know that. Something happened."

"Don't act like you care," I snap, watching his face fall at my words. He shakes his head furiously before grasping the small glass, bringing it to his lips, and downing the liquor —his Adam's apple bobbing with the gulp. It's oddly hot. He's hot. I'm really drunk.

"I dated you for two years, Aspen. I might have been an asshole, but I still cared. Still do." Usually any affection from him would seep into my bones and warm me, but the last few months have changed me. Hardened me. Now, his confession bounces off of me like rubber. "I'm guessing that it's either that Fox twat or your mum."

"Try both."

I laugh humorlessly, leaning over the bar to grasp the bottle of tequila —tired of waiting for the useless bartender to serve me when I'm capable of doing it myself. Sam eyes me worriedly as I fill my glass to the brim, the liquid sloshing over the sides from my unsteady hands. "Aspen, I don't think you should—"

"I didn't call you so you could tell me what to do, Sam," I snap, but my words have begun to slur and a fog has settled into my brain.

"Then why *did* you call me?"

I don't really know why; maybe it was desperation for familiarity, maybe I needed to be reminded what it felt like to feel loved, or maybe I had no one else to call... But, as my phone buzzes again in my clutch I know that's not true. I let it ring and turn to face my drinking partner.

"Just give me one night, Sam. Just you and me like old times. Let's forget everything, just have fun like we used to before everything went to shit. *Please.*" I know, even drunk I know, not to let Sam in again. That he ruined me and my calling him is so foolish and masochist. But, I'm hurt and angry and in desperate need of an escape, of familiarity.

And I know he'll concede to my request before he even grabs the bottle from my hands and places his lips on the rim, chugging straight from the source. "Just you and me, baby."

We spend a good hour drinking and ignoring my continuously vibrating cell phone. It doesn't take long for our flirty remarks and wandering hands to lead us to the dance floor. I let the alcohol lower my inhibitions and just allow myself to let loose —to forget everything that's happened today, to forget that the man I'm with is the same one that destroyed me. To just *forget.*

Our sweaty bodies find a rhythm we perfected over the years, one only the two of us know. His hands find home on my waist as I sway against him. My fingers reacquaint themselves with his soft locks and my head falls back onto his shoulder. I don't stop him when he peppers slow, open-mouthed kisses down my neck. It feels nice to be engulfed by his familiar cologne, to feel his familiar lips against my skin, his hands against my body.

"I've missed this." I've missed *this.* Not, I missed *you.*

The fog clears enough for me to remember that just like

Everett, my mother, and my father, he doesn't truly care and I suddenly feel sick. I was using him to fill a void, but he's just as empty as I am. I'm always a second choice, an afterthought, someone people can use and toss like a tissue and I don't want to feel that way anymore.

I make some feeble excuse and barely hear his reply before I'm jogging towards the bathrooms. My head spins as I push open the swinging door and ignore the two girls applying lipstick in the mirror. With shaky hands, I pull out my phone and squint in order to clearly see my screen lit up with notifications. Most are calls from Marco, a few voicemails, and apology texts. None from my mother, of course, but I only check the ones from Everett.

**Horny Bastard:** *Marco called me. Where are you?*

**Horny Bastard:** *You better call me right now, Aspen.*

**Horny Bastard:** *You aren't at home. Where the fuck are you?*

For some reason, I feel guilty for calling Sam instead of Everett. I have no reason to feel that way, my stomach plummets with the feeling. My head throbs violently as I sway on my feet and I miss the 'call' button twice before my thumb lands on it. I lean against the sticky wall and giggle as I watch more girls stumble through the doorway.

"Hello?"

My chuckles stop instantly at the voice that answers. A voice that *definitely* doesn't belong to Everett, "You're not Everett."

"Aspen? Hi, it's Marisol! How are you?"

The pain that shoots through me is unexpected: heart caving and throat closing. Our conversation earlier today makes sense now. Clearly, Everett didn't want to *be* with me because he's already with someone else. Someone I'd foolishly assumed he stopped seeing when we started whatever we started. I guess I was wrong. I guess I meant even less to him that I thought.

"Aspen? Are you there?"

I hang up.

Just like that, the momentary guilt I felt vanishes, only to be replaced with anger and disappointment. I don't know what I expected from someone with a reputation like Everett's, but I feel oddly betrayed, and yet a part of me knows I have no right to be. I don't know which feeling is worse. I'm just done being so weak and easily manipulated. I want to take control of my life and stop caring about others' opinions. I'm just so fucking done with *caring* in general when no one cares about me in return.

In record time, I make my way through the throng of dancing people until I spot a bored looking Sam at the bar, swaying along to the beat. It doesn't register, nothing really registers. My heart is pounding, hands are shaking, and mind determined. My phone vibrates in my hand and I barely glance down to see that it's Everett calling —or Marisol— before I shut off my phone completely. Sam looks up just as I stop in front of him, a lazy grin on his face. I waste no time in gripping his chin in my fingers and bringing him close, our lips crashing together.

It's no match to kerosene like it is with Everett, but maybe that's better. That way, I won't burn out.

Our lips meld together easily, like getting on a bike after not riding one for years or visiting home for the first time since moving away. His hands wrap around my waist to pull me between his legs and I slide my fingers through his hair. His tongue slides against mine with skill and precision and I pull away with swollen lips and hooded eyes. His own eyes are wild with lust and confusion and I bend down to peck his lips once more before grazing his cheek to whisper in his ear. "Take me home, Sam."

Desperation: a state of despair, typically one that results in rash or extreme behavior.

* * *

My aching head is slow to process much of anything as my eyes are blinded by the sunlight filtering through my curtains. I do manage to process three things, though:

1. I messed up big time.
2. I'm not alone.
3. I'm never drinking again.

The dip in the mattress alone is enough to tell me the second fact, but it's the warmth and familiar cologne I smell that brings back a flood of hazy memories. What's even more disconcerting are the lapses in between those memories that remain blank. Ignoring the fact that my throat is painfully dry and the drumming in my head makes me want to hurl, I turn around to confirm what I've already gathered.

There, a white sheet barely covering his tanned and naked flesh, is a snoring Sam.

I quickly look down at myself in realization that, I too, am very much naked. My dress is crumpled at the foot of the bed, Sam's pants are in the doorway next to my heels and my bra is flung onto a lamp. All I can drudge up are hazy memories of grabby hands in a cab and smudged lipstick. It was fumbling down my hallway, sloppy kisses, and trying not to laugh as Sam fell up the stairs in a failed attempt to slip his hand up my dress. Then there was unzipping and searching tongues and loud moans leading into the bedroom.

Then it was... *blank.* I'm gonna be sick.

I pop out of bed with the sheet wrapped around my body and ignore Sam's now bare bum. I spring towards the bathroom and make it just in time to lean over the bowl and purge the poison from my body. As I'm bent over the bowl, the inevitable regret I knew I would feel begins to seep in. I was weak to call my ex, even though last night was fun and it felt nice to feel wanted. But, Sam didn't really *want* me. He wanted what I could offer him. Just like Everett.

*Oh god, Everett.*

Then I'm retching again, eyes watering. This time, when I empty my stomach, I feel a pair of familiar hands holding my snarled locks back. "Please tell me we didn't sleep together?"

"First time I've heard that from a woman."

I groan as I wipe the corners of my lips with the sheet, "Sam."

He sighs exasperatedly and I turn around, only to come face-to-face with little Sam. I instantly shield my eyes and groan in annoyance. "Jesus, Sam. Put on some pants."

"Again, first time hearing that." Tired of him skirting around my question, I swing my fist back and make it look as if I'm about to take a shot at his goods. He instantly backs away and cups himself with a horrified expression.

"*No*, you violent woman. We didn't have sex," I sigh in relief, which makes Sam scowl immediately, "don't sound too relieved because we might not have gone full coital, but we did plenty else until we passed out." Then it comes back in flashes; dropping to my knees in front of a very eager Sam, who later reciprocates with his head between my thighs and my fingers clawing his hair.

My skin flushes at the memories and I tighten the sheet around me. "Don't bother covering up, babe. You and I both know I practically have your body memorized." The snarl that slips past my lips only makes him chuckle as he leaves me on the cold tile. The door shuts behind him and I'm left alone with my shame. It's with great effort that I lift myself up from the tile, joints aching and head throbbing, as I step in front of the sink. I let the sheet fall from my chest and cringe at the sight of my tanned flesh marred by hickeys of various sizes and colors. The fresher ones are a rosy color peppered along my chest, collarbones, and hips. It's the fading purple ones in the hollow of my throat that make my heart sink.

What is *wrong* with me?

Just three days ago I was in a changing room with Everett, who was knuckle deep inside me and sucking these marks onto my skin. Then, last night I was wrinkling my sheets with my horrible ex. I let my emotions and the liquor control my actions and it landed me right back where I was just a few months ago. Drinking myself into a stupor, wallowing in self-pity, and making reckless decisions.

"Are you just going to stand there and admire yourself all day?" I nearly jump out of my skin when I hear Sam's amused voice behind me, having reappeared in the bathroom dressed. "I wouldn't blame you... You're something to be admired."

I quickly snatch the sheet from the ground, wrapping it around myself, and giving Sam a suspicious look. When I saw him just a month ago, he was the same familiar jackass that he's always been. But, last night he was nice and gentle and caring and so very, very unlike himself.

"Shouldn't you have snuck out in the dead of night before I woke up?"

Sam's face falls at my words, "Why would I do that?"

"Because that's what you do?" I scoff, as if the statement should be obvious, "you get what you want and then you leave. It's who you are." I push past his still figure in the doorway, tired of standing in front of him fully naked when he's changed into his black jeans and shirt. I hear his boots thudding against the hardwood as he follows me, throat clearing.

"I actually wanted to talk to you... was going to call this weekend to meet up, but you beat me to the punch. Before I say anything, I need to ask you a question." He bites his lip and I hesitantly nod, surprised and distrustful "Did you... are you and that Fox kid actually together?"

He cringes as he speaks, my own shocked expression falling into a grimace. Any reminder of Everett causes my heart to squeeze painfully in my chest and I turn from Sam to rummage through my closet. I stall for time by pulling an oversized sweater over my head. I see Everett's grin flit behind my eyes, hear his raspy laugh, and fight off the ache in my chest.

I answer Sam the only way I can. "Never have been. Never will be."

"Good, you deserve better." I spin around, scoffing at the irony of the statement. He's quick to correct himself as I pull on a pair of ripped jeans, "I know how surprising that is to hear from me. But, it's the truth, Aspen. One that I've come to realize after the most agonizing six months of my life."

I know exactly what he's getting at and the thought makes my stomach churn and heart pound against my ribs. I'm quick to shake my head to stop him, turning around to snatch the phone from my dresser. I'm way too hungover for this. "Sam—"

"Please. Please, let me say this, Aspen." I reluctantly nod, unable to resist the desperate look in his ocean eyes, powerless against him. I eyes glance down at my phone, but instantly toss it on my bed when I see how many missed calls and texts light up the screen.

"When we started dating, it was like all the puzzle pieces in my life finally fit together. You were everything I wanted and I was *so* in love with you... but, your band was getting more attention while I was stuck playing open-mic nights." He chuckles humorlessly, shaking his head, "God, when I say this now it all seems so *petty*. But, you were all anyone could talk about and I was jealous...Jealous of your success and incredibly insecure. I was scared you were gonna leave me behind. So, I guess I made you feel like shit to boost my own ego.

"I didn't even realize then how much of an asshole I was to you —I had drilled it into my head that you were going to become successful and leave me and I let that resentment fester... I didn't even notice that you stopped going out, stopped singing in the car, completely lost yourself. Because of *me*."

"Sam, stop."

He continues as if I didn't speak, pacing the floor while Yoda watches him warily. "Then... my band started getting recognition... I had easier access to drugs and... girls." The mention makes me flinch, achingly familiar images flashing through my brain. Sam notices my distress and takes a step forward, but I back away. This is all too much. This is all too late.

"I won't rehash the details, but I was so far gone by then. So arrogant about my growing success that I didn't think about repercussions... didn't think about you or what I did. I used to —"

"Stop! Sam, *stop*!" I interrupt, my breaths shallow and voice cracking, "I know all of this already, it's all I could think about every damn day! You ruined me, Sam. You made me feel worthless... you—" I have to stop because my voice begins to wobble and a lump forms in my throat and I refuse to cry in front of him. I should've never called him.

"I know, Aspen. I know. That's what I'm trying to say!" He takes a deep breath, eyes full of regret, "that night... that night that you caught me with someone in our bed ... It *haunts* me. The second you walked out the door... I knew I made the biggest mistake of my life and I tried to push that feeling away, deny it. But, when I heard you quit singing I knew I was absolute scum. You were the best thing that ever happened to me and letting you go was the worst."

I fight against my sympathy, against his pleading eyes. "You didn't let me go, Sam. You were the one that walked away, long before we ever broke up."

He nods and has the decency to look ashamed. "I know you may not forgive me yet, or *ever.* I don't blame you, but I... I want to be with you, Aspen. I miss you. Last month, all I wanted was to kiss you and instead, I was a massive ass. I'm sorry, for it all."

Did I just step into the fucking Twilight Zone?

His words stun me into silence and my immediate reaction is to laugh, but then I look up from the floor and into his eyes and see the sadness, the guilt, the regret. I see the love and it kills me. Call it petty or pathetic, but how can I possibly forgive someone who caused me so much pain? How could I give them another chance when they received so many?

Where is the line between being the bigger person and being a doormat?

"This is too much. This is all too much. I can't... I just can't do this right now. Last night... it wasn't supposed to happen. I was sad and drunk and you were there... it was a *mistake.*"

"Don't say that. Don't... don't say that, Aspen." The vulnerability in his eyes is overwhelming and it's as if I'm looking at a completely different person.

"I can't deal with this right now, Sam."

The finality in my voice reaches him, and he concedes. "I'll be here. When you can deal with this, I'll be here."

My thoughts are racing, completely jumbled, as I lead Sam out of my room and towards the foyer. I just need to be alone... so much has happened in the last few days that I can barely wrap my mind around one problem before I'm thrown into another. I'm a mess.

But, before I can reach for the knob there's a loud and urgent knock on my door. My eyes fall from Sam's, to the clock on the wall to see that it's only seven in the morning. Whoever's at my door must have a death wish.

I swing it open, fully prepared to give them a piece of mind, only for the words to die in my throat once I see who's on the other side. His emerald eyes fill with relief as soon as he catches a glimpse of my face, shoulders visibly relaxing. Dark bags line his eyes and I'm more than sure that the wrinkled clothing adorning his body is the same outfit he wore yesterday.

Everett opens his mouth, but it quickly snaps shut as soon as he looks beyond my shoulder. This time, he tenses and his jaw sets, gaze growing cold. It's then, I realize a little too late, that Sam is still behind me. A mixture between a scoff and humorless laugh leaves his throat, head tilting back as he looks up at the ceiling. "Of course. Of course, he's here."

That's all that's said before Everett brings his fist back and slams it straight into Sam's nose. There's a crunch followed by a loud yelp as Sam staggers backward in shock and agony as Everett charges forward. Thick, ruby blood trickles down his lips and Everett's fist winds back again without hesitation.

*"Stop, Everett!"*

I hurriedly step in between the duo. "Get out of the way, Aspen." Everett grits, speaking to me, but not even looking at me.

"Don't tell her what to do, you twat!" Sam barks, gently pushing me to the side so he faces Everett, whose neck flushes red in anger.

"That's rich coming from you."

"Guys, stop." I weakly cut in, completely baffled about what to do in this situation.

My plea goes unnoticed as they try to assert dominance over the other. Sam's nose is still bleeding, but he doesn't bother to wipe it away. Yoda yaps crazily, bouncing around the scene. "I think you should leave, mate," Sam speaks condescendingly, making Everett ball his fists.

"I think *you* should leave, *mate*. She doesn't want you here."

"That's funny," Sam smirks, tilting his head to the side in mock confusion. "Last night she seemed to want me here *very* much." Everett has his fists tightened in Sam's collar and has him slammed up against the wall so fast I don't even have time to blink. He's shaking with rage and Sam looks all too pleased with himself. As of now, I'm pleased with neither.

"Don't you *ever* come near her *again*, Jones. I swear to God, if I see you so much as *glance* her way your nose won't be the only thing bleeding."

"Don't think that's for you to decide. If she wants to see me, then she'll see me."

The words barely leave Sam's lips before Everett is slamming him into the wall again, this time, with so much force that the picture hanging up next to them falls to the ground and shatters the frame, "I'll fucking kill you if—"

"*Stop!*" I scream so loud that both boys snap their gazes to me, Everett's grip on Sam's shirt loosening at the sight of my distress. "Both of you stop right now and get the *fuck* out of my house." My tone is eerily calm and it causes them to separate with guilty looks. Sam sends a lethal glare at his attacker before taking a step towards me. He swipes the blood from his nose with the back of his hand, smearing it across his lip, "Aspen, I—"

"Just go, Sam."

He nods solemnly, stepping towards the door, but turns to face me once more, "just tell me you'll think about what I said." Even though I really don't want to think about it, even though I just want to forget last night ever happened, I nod anyway. Sam's cerulean eyes brighten in hope before he steps outside and leaves me with a fuming Everett.

"Think about what?" He demands, jaw clenched and fists locked and I try really hard not to sock him in the face as he just did to Sam.

"When I told you both to leave, I did mean *both* of you."

"Did you fuck him?"

"What?!" I shout in disbelief and Everett takes a step closer to me. The nerve of him to ask me that —the damn hypocrite. "Did. You. Fuck. Him?" He annunciates every word, face screwed up in disgust as if not even wanting to ask.

"Why do you even care?"

"Are you kidding me?" He practically shouts, looking at me as if I'm crazy, "I was looking for you all night!"

"Really? I thought you were too busy with Marisol?"

He clenches his jaw even tighter, remaining silent. "That's what I thought." I nod, trying to ignore the ache in my chest at the confirmation. I disregard him, thinking he'll get bored and leave soon if I ignore him. My knees pop as I squat down to pick up the some of the larger pieces of broken glass from the picture Everett knocked down in his brawl with Sam. I hear him shuffle quietly, boots coming into view as he stands next to me.

"Just leave it. You're going to hurt yourself."

"I can't just leave it," I snap, not even looking his way as I gather the glass in my hand. "I think this conversation is over. You can go now."

"Here, let me clean it up." Everett's trying not to sound angry, but failing.

"I don't need your help. I don't need anything from you." A low growl escapes his throat and his hand wraps around my elbow, yanking me up abruptly and causing the glass to fall..

"Dammit, Aspen. Do you ever listen to me?" I rip myself out of his grasp, but this causes me to stumble backwards and I feel a sharp pinch on my heel —a searing pain traveling up my whole right leg. I yelp loudly, reaching down to cradle my foot and seeing a jagged shard of glass lodged into my skin. Everett instantly reaches out to me, brows furrowed in concern, but I shove him away harshly.

"Fanculo!" [Fuck!] I yelp, clutching onto my foot as it begins to throb, blood already dripping onto my newly polished floor. "Questa è tutta colpa tua, Everett. Dannazione, questo fa così male. Dio mio!" [This is all your fault, Everett. Dammit, this hurts so bad. Oh my god!"

"Okay, stop yelling gibberish and let me help you sit down." He insists, eyes trained on the thick blood dripping down my heel. I really, *really* don't want his help, but I was never good with pain and I find myself feeling faint at the sight of blood. So, I allow my arm to wrap around his neck for leverage, but gasp when he wraps a hand around my knees to hoist me into his arms.

"I'm not dying, Everett." I sigh at his dramatics, but he only tightens his grip as he carries me over to the kitchen and sets me onto the faux marble countertop.

"Oh, shut it." I don't miss how his hand lingers on my waist a bit longer than necessary. "I told you to leave it." He scolds, grabbing a washcloth next to the sink and dabbing it around the glass to clear some of the blood.

"Oh, shut it." I retort and he chuckles under his breath as if we hadn't just fought.

All I can think about is Marisol's voice answering his phone last night. What they may have done before I called... what they may have done after I called. I know it's none of my concern, Everett made that perfectly clear. He remains silent as he cleans the wound, only speaking to warn me when he's about to pull out the shard. It's a continuous pinch and I grit my teeth, whimpering when it finally dislodges. Everett holds it up to the light, my blood dripping onto the white tile.

"Luckily it's not deep enough to need stitches. Probably won't be able to put any pressure on it for the rest of the day, though." Everett works diligently, grabbing the hydrogen peroxide to dab it against the cut —and letting me squeeze the life out of his bicep as it sets my wound ablaze— then wiping the excess blood. He rubs in some anti-infection cream on the cut and places a bandage on the wound. I can only watch in awe as he works smoothly, as if well versed in the healing of wounds, "where'd you learn to do that?"

Everett freezes slightly as he tosses the trash in the bin before shaking his head, "nowhere. Just know it."

When I don't meet his eyes, he places his palms on either of my knees before squeezing in between them. "I would thank you, but it was your fault I got hurt anyway."

Everett snorts, eyes tracing every inch of my face with a soft smile. It fades quickly, though, "I can't believe that fucker was here." He shakes his head in disbelief, all gentleness gone. "After everything he's done, you go crawling back to him."

"I don't want to talk about this, Everett." I shove him off me and hop down from the counter, balancing on one foot.

"You deserve better, Aspen." *How many men are going to say this to me, without actually being the better man?*

"Better like you?" I snap, but Everett's gaze saddens and he shakes his head slowly.

"No, not me either," he whispers softly and then blurts out his next words as if they'd been on the tip of his tongue all along. "Nothing happened with Marisol last night, Aspen. She came over because I was worried you disappeared —she just wanted to help."

It's scary how much that simple sentence can lift the heavy weight on my chest, can ease my fears. If he *is* telling the truth, though, then I feel even stupider for running into Sam's arms. "I think you should leave now." His shoulders slump in defeat, but he doesn't argue.

"This conversation isn't over." He tries to sound threatening, but the mood has shifted... now he just sounds sad. I'm hurt and confused and overwhelmed by everything that's happened in the past twenty-four hours and I just need a little bit of time to let everything settle. I can't discuss my relationship with Everett when I'm not even sure we have one.

He steps towards me, reaching out as if about to take my hand or kiss my cheek, but stops. A tired sigh leaves his lips and I watch as he makes his way towards my door, "put on slippers or shoes with soft soles and then sweep the glass into a bin —don't pick it up with your hands." He advises without looking at me, gripping the doorknob. He turns around one last time, eyes hesitant and fearful, "you didn't... did you actually sleep with him? With Sam?"

I sigh, chest heavy. "No, Everett. I didn't."

He tries to remain unaffected, but I don't miss the faint relaxing of his shoulders. He nods and slips out the door, leaving me with an aching foot and aching heart.

# VACILLATE

Nothing can possibly describe the feeling of performing on a stage: adrenaline pumping through your veins, a sea of people singing along to your songs, bright lights shining in your eyes, and the base vibrating your body like a second heartbeat. It's a feeling I've always loved and one I wish I could take full advantage of by being up front —by reclaiming Everett's spot.

Everett —who is wearing his ritualistic navy headband and a shirt that may as well just be off since it's hanging on by two buttons— takes his last bow on stage. He blows a kiss as the rest of us bow humbly, ignoring the screaming girls shouting his name.

No wonder his ego is so big.

He waves one last time before turning around with a large grin and sweaty face, those emerald eyes locking onto my own almost instantly. My own gaze drops to my beat-up guitar as I set it down on the stand, but I don't miss Everett's face falling at my obvious avoidance. It's been a week since the dinner, since Everett punched Sam, since Everett left me confused and hurt. He hasn't tried to speak to me yet. But, that doesn't stop him from staring.

A lot.

Which he continues to do as we exit through the curtains and into the back. I should confront him, but I just haven't gathered up the courage. In the last two months, the boy grew on me in ways I didn't think possible. I had, idiotically, developed some kind of feelings for the twat. So, being curved by him hurt a lot more than I had anticipated.

"Has Mom called you?"

I nearly jump out of my skin as Marco creeps behind me, but I recover quickly, groaning. I debate whether or not to ignore his question, but I catch Everett watching me again and I would rather discuss my mother than deal with him. "No, she hasn't and she won't, so stop asking," I deadpan, grabbing a water from the stagehand and avoiding his puppy-dog eyes. Marco tends to stay out of my business and conflicts with our mother, but even this one is too big for him to ignore. My mother made her feelings for me clear and so did I. That's that.

"C'mon, Aspen," Marco pleads, trailing behind as I walk past the others and towards the couch. "You know she's too busy to keep track of everything in your life and—"

"What did she get you for your birthday, Marco?" I interrupt, voice completely void of emotion as the others try not to make it obvious that they're eavesdropping.

"What?"

"Your birthday. What did Mom get you?"

"Uh, my Porsche..." He trails off guiltily, knowing where I'm headed with that question.

"Right. You know what I got from mommy dearest?" The question is rhetorical, but Marco shakes his head anyway. "Nothing. I literally got nothing: no phone call, no card, not even a quick text. So, don't you dare tell me she's too busy to keep track of my life when she can buy you a new car for your birthday, but not even remember my own."

Marco falls silent, shaking his head and glancing around awkwardly. I slump into the couch and close my eyes as he walks away dejectedly. The others send me sympathetic looks, but go off towards the bar. All, but one. As soon as I feel the couch dip, I know exactly who sits without even looking. He remains silent, though I can feel his leg bouncing nervously.

"Can you not do that? Thanks." I snap and the shaking instantly stops.

"Someone's a grumpy goose." Everett jokes and I whip my head around to face him, sending him the nastiest glare I can muster and reveling in the way his face pales.

"I would tread very lightly, Fox. I'm not in the mood."

He nods his head understandingly and mirrors my position on the couch. My eyelid cracks open to take a peek at his relaxed form: the white shirt clinging to his slightly sweaty body, curls barely tamed by the headband sticking to his forehead, long and slender fingers nervously twiddling together.

God, I hate him.

"Listen, Munchkin..." I quickly avert my eyes as Everett straightens up with a sigh, "I'm sorry for barging into your house the other day, that was a bit rude... but, I can't say I'm sorry for punching that twat in the face."

"Seriously?"

"What do you expect, Aspen? Jones is an asshole and the fact that he was at your house so early in the morning..." he trails off and I catch his fists tightening and jaw clenching.

"So, what? It's none of your business who I spend my time with, we're not together. I don't see why you care, anyway. It's obvious you only talk to me because you just want to sleep with me." His jaw drops and eyes flash in anger, gaping at me. I'm not sure why he seems baffled when he was the one that told me 'not to get the wrong idea'. I deluded myself into thinking he wanted anything more.

"I... you... what?" He sputters, at a loss for words and I try to ignore the ache in my chest.

"It's fine, Everett. I'm not angry —don't want you *getting the wrong idea.*"

Now, he truly looks shocked. His own words thrown back in his face has cleared up some confusion and Everett shakes his head in disbelief, almost scoffing. "So, this is what this whole thing is about?"

"What whole thing?"

"You ignoring my calls and texts, going off with Sam that

night, being so pissed at me? All because of what I said last week?"

I flush instantly, not appreciating his condescending tone, "don't flatter yourself, Curly."

Everett just shakes his head again, groaning in frustration and running his hands through his hair. He stays silent for a few minutes before finally turning to face me, "Jesus, Aspen. I know I can be a right arse, but I'm not... I don't just talk to you because I want to get in your pants... God." He huffs in frustration, pulling his lip between his teeth, "I mean, of course I *do* want that, but I would never *use* you. I'm not that guy anymore... you confuse the shit out of me and you can be a right judgmental bitch sometimes, but I—"

Unfortunately, Everett's speech is cut off by the sound of the heavy metal door screeching open, allowing the thumping base to travel through the room, and revealing a very upset Jesse. Even though all I want to do is shut the door again and hear what Everett has to say, the person standing behind Jesse with a large bouquet of daisies causes me to shoot up from the couch in a flash.

"I told him that you wouldn't want to see him, but—"

"Sam?" I cut Jesse off quickly, my voice a breathless whisper as I hurry towards the pair. Avery and Marco trail past Sam and into the room, sending him glares so fierce I'm surprised he doesn't spontaneously combust. I ignore the three sets of eyes burning into my back as he holds the flowers out to me with a timid smile. He's still sporting a yellow bruise on the side of his jaw and his nose looks slightly swollen, but he still manages to look fit as hell.

"Heard you were playing here tonight, thought I'd drop by considering you haven't called me since last week."

"*Last week?!*"

"What the hell is he doing here?"

"Should I kick him out?

Marco, Avery, and Jesse shout at once in indignation and disbelief, only Everett keeping quiet, though I can feel his presence behind me. Sam ignores them, as do I. The man I once loved stands in front of me and the man I might have unrequited feelings for is behind me. This couldn't be more uncomfortable. "Thanks, Sam... you really didn't have to. I still haven't... I haven't really had time to process everything."

Which, is true. Sam's confession couldn't have been more horribly timed, and it hasn't been a top priority as of late. I try to feel bad seeing Sam's hopeful face fall, but I'm still resentful and take an odd satisfaction in his pain.

"*Process everything*?" Marco demands angrily, grasping my elbow. "What the fuck is Jones doing here?" I fumble for something to say, but Everett beats me to it.

"Oh, you didn't hear?" He taunts, voice full of barely repressed rage, "Sam here spent the night at Aspen's after your dinner and can't seem to take a hint." The bouquet in my hands suddenly feels too heavy and I avoid Everett's gaze, though I feel him glaring at me. Avery lets out a small gasp at the confession and Marco's grip grows tighter on my arm.

"Please tell me you aren't considering getting back with this moron?" Marco demands and the room falls silent in anticipation of my answer. Sam nervously shifts in front of me and Everett moves to stand next to my side, but I still don't look at them. I'd never once contemplated getting back with Sam. I'm still recovering from what he did to me. But, I can't deny I still have residual feelings for him, even if it's wrong.

Vacillate: alternate or waver between different opinions or actions; be indecisive.

After a solid minute of my silence, I hear Everett let out an angry huff and glance up just in time to catch him storming out, bumping his shoulder into Sam's on the way. He doesn't look back, but instead shouts one last scathing sentence before slamming the door shut.

"Get back to me when you finally gain some self-respect, Aspen."

* * *

"I can't be with you, Sam."

His once vibrant smile is wiped away almost instantly, but I can't possibly bring myself to feel bad. His eyes drop to the table and mine scan the small restaurant partly as a distraction, but also to make sure Marco is still at his post by the bar. His enthusiastic wave and thumbs up are all the assurance I need.

I brought him along as moral support and an anti-Sam barrier, because knowing me and knowing Sam and knowing *us*, I would not be strong enough to resist him by myself.

"But, why?" He pleads, hands clasping mine across the table.

I almost scoff at the question because shouldn't it be obvious? Despite my momentary lapse in judgment, these nostalgic flashbacks need to end before I get hurt. Again.

I sigh and shake my head to clear it, "you *ruined* me, Sam. You manipulated, degraded, and cheated on me repeatedly with no remorse until I left you. What kind of person would I be if I just went back to you after all of that? I'm sure you have changed, you do seem different, but it changes nothing... I deserve better."

*Get back to me when you gain some self-respect.*

Sam hangs his head in shame when my voice cracks, but I let no sympathy show. I should've done this a long time ago. I should've laughed in his face when he first suggested we get back together. I was so easily persuaded to give him a second chance *just* because he offered me something no one had before; he offered me love.

But, Everett's words yesterday resonated with me and snapped me back to reality. It also may have been Avery's scolding after the band forced Sam to go home. I may still love Sam, but I'm no longer *in* love with him and don't think I could ever be again after the way he treated me. I'm about to say this, but my buzzing phone stops me and I roll my eyes at the message.

**The Devil's Spawn:** *Is it done yet? Is he crying? God, please tell me he's crying. Should I come over and kick him in the cajones for* *good measure?*

I glance up to catch Marco staring at us very seriously, assuring me that he would follow through if I did say yes. I shake my head slowly and almost laugh as his shoulders deflate in disappointment.

Sam, on the other hand, is far from laughing.

"I could be better for you, Aspen. I could be the man you deserve if you just gave me another chance."

I'm shaking my head before he even finishes speaking. "That ship has sailed, Sam. I can't... I won't be with someone who made me feel unwanted. I've done it my whole life and I refuse to do it anymore." He was the one I ran to when my mother didn't come to an open mic night. He was there when my father screened my calls. He was there every time my parents left me in the dust, until he followed their lead.

"I'm sorry for everything I ever did to you." He whispers sadly, hands squeezing my own.

"I'm sorry I gave you everything I had without making sure you wanted it first."

"I want it now." He pleads, in a final attempt to win me over, but my mind is set.

"Now is too late."

His shoulders deflate and I scoot over in the booth to wrap my arm around him, petting his soft locks like I used to. "Can we still be friends?" He mumbles tentatively, warm breath tickling my neck, "I won't ask for much, but I miss having you in my life."

I just place a kiss on top of his head in answer because the scars he gave me may never heal, but his friendship might soothe the ache. He was my friend before he was anything else and if he needs me, then I'm here. It may not be the best idea, but I'm not sure I can cut all ties either. This was the man I wanted to marry once upon a time, after all.

It's only a few minutes later that Sam speaks up once again, tone barely restrained with irritation, "So, it's Fox, then?"

My fingers pause in his hair as the question settles, but the answer is one I've formulated after speaking to Avery and tossing and turning all night over it. I don't want to be with someone who doesn't want me and Everett may *want* me, but not in the same ways that I want him. And it's too painfully confusing to be anything else.

"No, not him either."

Sam lifts his head, brows furrowed in confusion, "why not?"

"Everett doesn't like me like that, Sam... and I don't like him very much either."

"That's bullshit," he almost laughs before observing my face and letting out a sad sigh. "Everett probably hasn't committed to anything in his life besides a gym membership, but that... *that* is bullshit."

"No, it's not, Sam. He doesn't want to be with me, he basically told me so himself."

Sam cringes and runs a hand down his face, as if even having this conversation is paining him. "He may have said that, but anyone with eyes can see the way he looks at you. It's sickening, actually. He's like a totally different person and people have started to notice."

"What the hell are you talking about?"

"Fox is infamous for getting in trouble with the cops, getting kicked out of bands, sleeping with groupies, and basically being an overall prick. But, since he joined your band, I don't hear nearly as many stories as I used to; nothing about girls or illegal activities. He's a changed man apparently... and you're telling me you had *nothing* to do with that?"

Everett and I were at each other's throats up until a few weeks ago, and even a few times since then. There's no way I had anything to do with his transformation. If he even had one. He's still as arrogant and short-tempered as he was before. He still pursued me while fooling around with Marisol. I may not have known him before and sometimes he can be gentle and kind, but his behavior as of late contradicts that.

"You're delusional, Sam. Everett hasn't changed that much and he certainly wouldn't change because of *me*." I force a laugh, shaking my head, but Sam's face only grows more solemn and his cerulean eyes bore into mine with regret and shame.

"You just don't see it... I made you not see it."

"See what?" Instead of answering, he tucks a hair behind my ear, an apology in his eyes that makes my chest hurt. He closes the distance between us, lips grazing my cheek, a little longer than necessary. I still, allowing the kiss, knowing it's one of the last for us. It's a painfully beautiful moment, but one that is soon ruined by the bell chiming above the door, signaling someone's entrance.

The sound of my heart sinking to the floor of the restaurant is clear as I pull away and lock eyes on a scene I'm sure Marco had been trying to prevent as he talks to the duo heatedly and quietly. I feel Sam's hand squeezing mine softly in reassurance, but I don't pay any mind to him or Marco or Marisol or even her hand locked around Everett's.

All I can concentrate on are the emerald eyes ablaze in anger, trained on Sam and I in what appears to be a compromising lack of distance. Maybe I should jump away from him or try to quell the fire in Everett's eyes, but I don't. I don't because his hand is wrapped around Marisol's and she is nuzzling into his shoulder. Sam couldn't have been more wrong.

Everett doesn't want me and I certainly don't want him.

I've made my choice and I choose me.

# LA DOULEUR EXQUISE

Two pearl necklaces, a workout dvd, Chanel perfume, a pair of Louboutins, and an old copy of Pride & Prejudice. Everything my mother ever gave me inside one cardboard box.

"How can you do this to your Lous? What have they ever done to you?" Avery practically whimpers, clutching onto the red-bottomed black heels desperately.

"They were bought by my mother." I yank them grip and toss them in a box marked CHARITY for the auction we all have to attend in a few days.

"I know you're trying to *cleanse* yourself of our mother, but giving away everything shes ever given you? *Really*? It's a tad dramatic."

I ignore Marco, choosing instead to knock Enzo's feet off my glass coffee table and scold Jesse for getting crumbs on my rug. *This* is why I never invite the band over. Let them tear up Jesse's suave apartment and keep my small one safe and clean. Even though Everett is currently nearly spilling his full mug of tea on my rug, I ignore him. Just as I've been doing all week since he walked into that bar with Marisol and I stormed out. I know I'll have to talk to him eventually, but I'll avoid it for however long I can.

Even at the sacrifice of my vintage rug.

With my new-found resolution to not rely on others for happiness, I felt an innate need to rid my apartment of my mother. I could never dream of affording some of these things working as a guitar teacher, but I don't need their lavishness either. Not when it's all tainted. So, I called the band over for moral support, the purge still painful. However, they brought one uninvited guest I would've kicked out, if not for the fact I'm refusing to speak to him.

"It's not dramatic, Marco. I just don't want anything to do with a woman that doesn't want anything to do with me."

"I'm sure if you just sat down and—"

"She hasn't even tried to call me since dinner. Almost two weeks and not a word." He doesn't say anything more after that and I'm glad. I'd rather not discuss my neglectful mother in front of my very nosy bandmates. I can tell Everett wants to say something because he can't stop fidgeting around me: playing with his hands, running them through his hair, fumbling with things around him. His lips remain sealed, though.

For that, I'm grateful.

I'm getting my life in order: ignoring Everett, making amends with Sam, writing songs for the band, ignoring Everett, purging myself of my mom, ignoring Everett.

I'm better. I'm trying to be more mature and kind and level-headed and—

"I swear to god, Enzo, if that's my last cup of coffee I'm going to take your beloved bass and shove it somewhere the sun doesn't shine."

Okay, so maybe not *totally* level-headed.

Enzo just shakes his head, eyes wide, and mouth full of shortbread as he joins the others in my living room to play their videogame.

"We Europeans prefer tea, not your overpriced jitter juice, Munchkin." I can feel Everett's smirk all the way from my position in the foyer, but I will myself to ignore him. *I'm the bigger person here. I'm not a child.*

"Better than your leaf juice." I mumble under my breath because turning over a new leaf is harder than I thought and I just really, *really* dislike Everett.

"What was that, Munchkin?" This time, I succeed in ignoring him, dropping my box in front of the door, and heading back towards the couch. I barely escape with my life, though, when I block the TV and am assaulted by popcorn. Marco sits at the end, next to Jesse and his deadly popcorn, Enzo is sat next to him, and Avery is happy on the ground, petting Yoda.

Which leaves me with two options: the floor or next to Everett on the loveseat.

Naturally, I choose the floor. Which, in turn, makes Everett want to pester me further.

"Would you like to hear a joke, Munchkin?" He leans forward, elbows on his knees, mouth too close to my ear. I grit my teeth and focus on the little men on the screen, but Everett continues anyway. "What does the sign on an out-of-business brothel say? Beat it. We're closed."

I'm proud of myself when I don't even *twitch* at his stupid joke even though the boys let out weak chuckles. I know he's just itching to get a rise out of me, but I refuse to indulge him. Instead, I focus my attention to the TV as Avery scores a goal and laughs in Jesse's face, Enzo yelling at them to shut up. Though, it's not even five minutes later that familiar fingers tangle themselves in my hair. They pull on it and twist it and comb through it, and I swear he even brings a few strands up to his nose to sniff, but I still ignore him. I have amazing willpower.

That is, until he grabs a fistful and yanks so hard that my head snaps back

"Oh, for Fox sake! Why are you such a child?!" I snap, pulling out of his grip and confronting his not-so-innocent pout, the others watching us warily.

"Whoa, calm down—"

"Don't you *dare* tell me to calm down," I grit out, standing to my feet and pointing towards the kitchen, "you want attention? You want to talk, Everett? Then let's go. Let's talk and get this over with."

I don't wait for his reply before I'm storming out of the living room and into the kitchen. The clicking of Everett's boots against the hardwood tell me he's quick to follow and I glance over my shoulder in time to catch Marco shooting him a loaded glare over the couch.

"What can I do for you, Everett?" I turn towards him as soon as we cross the threshold into my barren kitchen, but stagger backwards, somehow forgetting just how tall he really is. He towers over me, emerald gaze troubled and stormy.

"How's Sam?"

I scoff, crossing my arms, "really, Everett?"

"Yes, Aspen," he crosses his own arms, defensive and annoyed. "Has he degraded you recently? Shacked up with some bird in your bed again?" His words are scathing, but not unwarranted. Though, the patronizing way they roll off his tongue rubs me the wrong way.

"How's Marisol, Everett? You tell her you tried to fuck me in a bathroom while on a date with her? That you don't actually care about her, about *anyone,* but yourself?"

"I'm not *with* Marisol, Aspen. I've told you this."

"And I'm not *with* Sam, so you can stop your snide remarks." That succeeds in shutting him up, brows furrowing in confusion, as drops his arms to the side. There's suddenly a softness in his eyes that I don't want to see.

"I'm proud of you, Aspen." His raspy voice rings with sincerity and my chest aches, but I'm stubborn and hurt. Much too hurt. He's so confusing and I hate how much I care about his opinion.

"I don't need you to be proud of me." I spit out, sending him the most malicious glare I can muster, causing Everett to clench his jaw and roll his eyes.

"Why are you still so bitter? This whole fight between us started because of him, but he's out of the picture now, so..."

"So, what? So now I can go back to being your little play thing? No thanks, Everett. This fight didn't start because of

Sam. You and I both know that."

He takes a step towards me, shaking his head, but I walk back until I hit the counter. "Why do you always assume the worst of me? I would never use you like that."

"You could've fooled me! All your flirting and touching and caring was only so you could sleep with me... You practically said so yourself. You played me."

"*Played* you?"

"You've spent the last few weeks shoving Marisol in my face, even though you hit on me whenever you get a chance. You claim you aren't using me, yet harbor no real feelings for me. You're either ridiculing me or seducing me...you're a child, Everett." He kicks —actually kicks— my cupboard before running his fingers through his hair, yanking on the strands. He paces my small kitchen, chest heaving, as if having some great internal debate.

He turns to me twice before shaking his head and continuing his pacing and I'm just about to leave when he finally turns to me and stays put. His eyes are blazing a deep forest green and his hands are fidgeting next to him, "I've never done anything like this before, Aspen."

"I find that hard to believe." I scoff and Everett just shakes his head in exasperation.

"No, it's always been one night stands or short-lived flings. But... this... this is new to me. I don't know how to handle it, and it terrifies me. *You* terrify me."

His voice pleads with me, trembling ever so slightly. My resolve crumbles with a few measly words from him and I hate it, I really do. The hold this boy has on me is damning. I tried so hard to fight against my feelings, but there's no denying them anymore.

"So, tell me then. Tell me right now how you actually feel and I'll about the last few weeks. Just say what you really want, how you *really* feel, and I'm yours." His eyes widen and he opens his mouth, a small breath of air escaping. My heart beats erratically in my chest, breath held in anticipation. Anxious and afraid, I wait. I wait for whatever he's about to say to finally slip past his lips, but it never does.

"That's what I thought."

I nod in defeat, any hope I had that he might've felt the way I do is completely demolished. Swallowing the lump in my throat, and hiding my burning cheeks behind my hair, I shove past him, but his voice stops me in my tracks.

"Aspen!" He's standing there, fists clenched and lip between his teeth, chest flushed, and eyes hesitant. He takes one step forward before faltering, mouth agape.

*Say something, Everett. Say* anything.

But, his gaze falls to the floor and his mouth closes and I shake my head in disappointment. I don't know why I tried, why I thought we could be more than we are. This is who he is, and it's my fault for falling. "It's okay, Everett... I know when I'm not wanted."

I barely have time to catch his face falling before I'm turning on my heel and walking back into the living room with a heavy mind and an even heavier heart.

La douleur exquise: the exquisite pain of wanting the affection of someone you can never have.

# CATHARSIS

"Everett is staring at you again."

I don't even acknowledge Avery's statement because of course Everett is watching me. He always is. Usually I'd turn around and flip him off or make some cheeky comment, but this time, I don't acknowledge his presence or the intense stare I feel through my matching black crop-top and mini-skirt. My pride has taken a vicious punch to the gut and I've been too mortified to meet his eyes or talk to him since our conversation. I put myself out there and I got rejected. The fact that I still have to see him all the time is like rubbing salt in my wounds. I just need time to get over this hurt.

"What's new?" I sigh and order a new cocktail, completely taking advantage of the open bar. Who new charity auctions would accommodate us drunks so kindly?

"The guy is love-sick."

I choke on my drink, the liquid burning my throat and causing me to splutter. Avery laughs lightly, tossing her hair over her skin-tight leather dress and passing me a napkin.

"Just look at him, Aspen. It's so obvious it's almost pathetic. You can't possibly believe he doesn't have feelings for you." Avery waves her hand towards our large table in the center of the ballroom and I turn slightly to peek at him.

He is indeed staring at me, but as soon as our eyes meet he drops his gaze to the ground, cheeks flushing. His bashfulness would tug at my heartstrings if he wasn't being coddled by practically every person in the room. As soon as we walked through the doors of the crowded ballroom, Everett was whisked away by some rich producer and then flaunted around the room for the last hour. He's finally had a chance to sit down, only to be surrounded by female executives and investors, hanging on his every word.

"Yeah, he sure seems love-sick flirting with all his groupies." I roll my eyes and Avery can't contain her scoff as she orders another drink.

"God, who made you this cynical?" I shoot her an unamused look because that answer is obvious and is also sauntering towards us now.

As soon as Avery spots Sam's mussed up brown locks she rolls her eyes and treks back towards our table. Sam slides into her spot with a timid smile and glass of scotch, "you look lovely tonight."

"You clean up nice too, Jones."

His shoots me a cheeky wink before chatting up the bartender and my eyes lazily trace over all of the nicely dressed music biz professionals, the candle-lit tables, and the displays set around the room showcasing the items for auction, including my own. These events typically bore me, but they usually don't serve booze either. My eyes land on Everett, who's still staring at me, but this time with an angry scowl. And, this time, he doesn't look away. I narrow my eyes at his obvious distaste, looping my arm through Sam's and leading him towards our table. Everett has no right to be mad that I'm talking to Sam. Not when he's rejected me twice now.

"Hey guys, hope you don't mind if Sam joins us."

"I mind." Everett snaps, but I don't acknowledge him, smile tight.

"Okay, great."

Marco turns the corner then with two bottles of beer in hand, stopping short when he sees Sam and me. "This shouldn't be uncomfortable at all," he mutters under his breath and hands Everett a beer before sliding into a seat next to a blonde older woman. "So, what'd I miss?"

"We were in the middle of never have I ever... and Tiffany here, was losing. Horribly." The younger woman with short hair on Everett's right giggles and I take a seat next to Marco, Sam on my left.

"What are we, twelve?" I laugh incredulously and I see Everett's lips twitch, though he's still scowling at the arm Sam has slung around my shoulder.

"Aspen's just scared because she knows she'll lose, isn't that right?" Everett muses with a smug grin and I seriously want to punch the stupid dimples right off his face.

I send him a vicious glare, my competitive spirit kicking in and my resentment towards Everett encouraging me to accept the challenge, "Game on."

It turns out everyone at this table is a little wild and promiscuous because it only takes a few minutes for us to empty our drinks and order another round.

"Never have I ever had secret feelings for a friend." Tiffany laughs and almost everyone at the table takes a sip of their drink. I avoid Everett's eyes as I sip at my cocktail, though I do catch the look shared between Marco and Avery as they both guzzle their beers.

"Never have I ever... sent someone a nude." Sam smirks, the statement obviously meant for me and the one very tasteful picture I sent him while we were dating. I give him a light elbow to the ribs, gingerly take a sip of my drink, and notice Everett's knuckles go white against his glass. Avery and the woman with short hair also take sips of their drinks with guilty smiles.

"Never have I ever had an orgasm in a dressing room."

This makes all chatter stop, Everett's eyes hooded and grin cocky. I practically shake with rage at his audacity, downing the rest of my drink before shooting him a victorious smirk as the rest of the table watches on with worried expressions.

"Never have I ever been too much of a coward to say how I

really feel."

Everett's grin falls right off his face as he takes a sip from his bottle and leans forward over the table. Marco tries to cut in, but Everett quickly holds his hand up to stop him. Marco shakes his head, sitting back to watch our showdown silently. If our bandmates had any suspicions about us before, I think this little game confirms them.

Everett's eyes travel from Sam to me and to Sam's arm around my shoulder. A darkness flashes in his eyes, "never have I ever lied about sleeping with an ex."

I know he's referring to the morning he caught Sam leaving my apartment. I told him then that we didn't have sex, so I don't understand why he's asking again as if he didn't trust me. It's childish and petty, but I feel foolish. Foolish for having feelings for Everett, for believing that he would ever want me the way I want him, for letting him play with my feelings. So, I grab Sam's scotch and boldly take a gulp from it, watching Everett's face fall at my confirmation.

"Aspen..." Sam whispers next to me, but I raise a hand to stop him from talking. Everett's hurt expression has morphed back into a scowl and I take this opportunity to confirm my suspicions once and for all. "Never have I ever befriended someone just to use them."

I watch with bated breath and fearful heart as Everett chews on his cheek, face passive as he raises the bottle to his lips. The rim rests on his lips, before he finally tilts the bottle back and takes a sip. The others shift uncomfortably in their chairs, uncomfortable and tipsy. I know he could by lying to me just as I had to him, but my insecurities run deep. My heart falls to the pit of my stomach and I can feel my eyes sting, but I don't give him the satisfaction of seeing me cry.

We're just trying to hurt each other at this point.

"Never have I ever had my own mother hate me."

As soon as I process those scathing words, the air in my lungs leaves in a rush, the lump in my throat suffocating. Sam and Avery gasp at his scornful words, but it barely registers over my pounding head and aching heart. Everett's satisfied smirk quickly falls when he registers my pained, shocked expression. We may have been trying to hurt each other, but Everett just obliterated me.

"Everett!" Marco shouts indignantly, toppling over his chair as he shoots out of his seat.

"Aspen, I didn't—" Everett's eyes are wide with fear and regret, but I shut him down.

"No, don't," I shake my head, eyes watering and heart twisting at the pain his words bring, "I mean, it's true, right?" I weakly shrug, bringing Sam's glass to my lips and downing the rest of its contents, clambering away from the table without so much as a goodbye. My friends call after me, but I weave my way through the tables and throngs of people. I nearly run into Jesse and Enzo who both try to stop me upon seeing my crestfallen expression, but I shove past them.

I burst through the tall glass doors and into the brisk London night just as it begins to drizzle, a heavy mist that makes my hair stick to my cheeks and skirt mold to my body. I don't mind it, though. I always loved the rain. It could turn the sky from a cloudless blue into a mass of gray gloom in a second flat. It could be calming and sure, wild and ferocious, or as light as a breeze; so unobtrusive you almost don't realize it's there. A drumline to mundane life.

Rain is supposed to be a symbol of rebirth —of sins beings cleansed and washed away and starting anew.

But, I don't feel refreshed or calm as the rain softly pelts my skin and makes passerby duck for cover. No, it just becomes the background noise to my rage as I hear footsteps echoing behind me.

"Aspen!"

My heels click against the cobblestone as I fasten my pace, trembling from the cold and my own sense of betrayal from Everett's scathing words. I know we're both to blame for what just happened. We'd both been childish and cruel, but Everett took it too far. He always takes it too far, always knows how to hit me where it hurts, where I'm most insecure.

"Aspen, stop running from me!"

Maybe it's because I forgot my coat and am turning blue or because the liquor running through my veins is blurring the sidewalk in front of me, but I finally whip around to face him.

"God, Everett, *what*?! What more could you possibly want from me?!" I'm practically screaming and Everett stumbles back a few steps at my sudden outburst, but that does little to deter me. "Do you want to humiliate me some more? Maybe make fun of my appearance or, I don't know, laugh at the fact that my father left us when I was twelve?! Go right ahead and bring up another one of my insecurities because the damage has already been done."

A few people walking by eye us warily, but we ignore them. My breaths are labored as I watch him tug at his unruly hair and begin to pace the sidewalk. I have no idea where I am or where I'm going and the rain paired with the frigid night air has begun to chill me to the bone and Everett's words seem to be on replay in my head—mocking me.

*Never have I ever had my own mother hate me.*

"I shouldn't have said that, okay? I didn't mean it, I'm sorry."

"Yeah, you seem to not mean a lot of the things you say." I scoff and turn on my heel to continue aimlessly walking the streets, hoping that he'll leave me be, to no avail.

"So do you! I'm not the only one to blame here!" His breaths are ragged, words slightly slurred, but he still continues to follow me when I make a sharp left. "Did you lie about Sam?"

I laugh. I actually whip around to laugh in his face because this has to be a joke. How toxic is this relationship that we're yelling at each other in the street over lies we told to hurt the other? Even now though, with the rain making his blouse stick to his skin and eyes wild, he still manages to make me weak in the knees. I hate him for it.

"Why do you even care, Everett?! *God*, you are just so... so..."

"So, *what,* Aspen? What am I?" His emerald eyes are ablaze, cheeks flushed, and curls are sticking to his face and I hate this.

I'm tired, I'm just so tired.

"So *infuriating!* Jealous one second, insulting me the next. Yet, you claim to have no feelings for me? I'm not your little toy to play with when you feel like it and then toss aside and treat like shit when you don't." I feel like I'm choking, my eyes stinging painfully, and I will myself not to cry in front of him. Everett is practically ripping out his hair and he kicks —actually kicks— the brick wall of the building next to us. A group of drunk girls walk by and whisper to themselves, but when I promptly flip them off they scurry away.

"It's not like that, Aspen! How many times do I have to tell you I'm not using you?!"

"You haven't told me *anything,*" the words echo around the small side street, but it doesn't stop me. "You claim to not be using me, but can't tell me how you actually feel! You're with Marisol all the time, but get jealous of Sam? You act like you want me and then gaslight me when I think you might have feelings for me. So, yeah, can you see how I'm slightly confused? How I can't fully believe it when you say you're not using me? You're cruel and careless and... I mean, just *fuck you.* I'm worth it... and fuck you for making me believe otherwise."

The rain falls softly around us, the only sound besides our thrumming hearts and labored breaths. I'm hurt and I'm confused and I'm tired, but it feels good. It feels so good to finally say what's been eating me alive since I met this boy.

Catharsis: the process of releasing, and thereby providing relief from, strong or repressed emotions.

Even though I'm yelling at him, practically red in the face and fuming, just being in his vicinity still makes my knees weak and heart bruise my ribs. I simultaneously want to kill him and kiss him and I know my feelings are deeper than I believed, they snuck up on me like a riptide and now I feel like I'm drowning.

I know that in this torrential downpour, rain isn't the only thing falling.

I wait for him to say something to explain his behavior, his feelings. I wait for him to say anything of substance, of truth. But, he only stands, the rain sliding down his red cheeks and closed, pouting lips. His expression is stoic and eyes unreadable. I wait and wait, but he remains silent and I can't say I'm surprised. By this point, it's expected.

"Thanks for proving my point."

I shake my head dejectedly and barely make it five steps before I his hand wraps around my elbow, dragging me across the street. Everett is wild-eyed and frustrated and he doesn't falter his steps even when I begin to squirm.

"Let go of me," I hiss through clenched teeth, trying to rip my arm from his grasp, but he's strong. Much stronger than I would've guessed and I'm much too tipsy to put up any semblance of a fight. "God, why can't you just leave me *alone?!*" I shout as he continues up the street, past the curious bystanders, and stops at a large building with a doorman out front.

"That's exactly the point, isn't it?!" He faces me now and the desperation in his eyes halts me in my tracks, "I can't!"

His words stun me into silence and I let him pull me through the glass doors and into a small lobby. His strides are long and I struggle to keep up without stumbling. I'm soaked to the bone and I know if I look behind me there will be a trail of water following us.

"We can't be in here," I hiss, realizing this is some kind of hotel or apartment building from the man at the front desk and mailboxes tucked into the corner.

"I live here." Is all he offers me as he drags me towards the elevators.

Oh.

*Oh.*

"I'm not going home with you, you asshole. Who the hell do you think you are to—"

He cuts off my indignant whispering just as we step into the elevators, "It's raining, you're drunk, and we both need to cool down before we do something stupid. You're coming up and that's final."

I bite my tongue because I'll end up either yelling at him or kissing him, his assertiveness frustratingly attractive. The ride up the elevator is filled with quiet music and tension, the air charged with a current so dangerous, I'm sure if I reached out I could feel it. We're silent —caught up in our own thoughts and probably afraid to say the wrong thing... again. As soon as the doors slide open, Everett strides out and down the dark hallway and I reluctantly follow him to the farthest door at the end. I really should leave and move on with my life but, there's something that keeps tugging me back to Everett, no matter how hard I fight it.

As soon as the door clicks shut behind us I'm pushed up against the wood, the air knocked out of me. Everett has his arms on either side of my head and his damp forehead resting against my own. His breath fans against my lips and I feel light-headed at the sudden shift. In a swift motion, he swoops down and brushes his soft lips against my own. I jolt in surprise, both from the spark it causes and the rage it fuels. I groan, shoving him off of me so hard that he stumbles back into the parallel wall.

He balances against it, struggling to stand upright. His hurt expression morphs into one of utter frustration and he is turning from me, storming out into the darkness of his flat.

"Maybe I should have just left you outside." He snaps, back turned, and I growl in rage. If he thinks he can just try to kiss me after everything that's happened and get angry for rejecting his advances, he's delusional. Before I can process my childish actions, I'm grabbing my shoe by its heel and flinging it across the room and into the darkness, watching as it just barely grazes Everett's broad shoulder. I don't actually mean to hit him, just want to get him to stop walking away from me, but Everett sure doesn't take it that way.

He halts in his retreat and slowly spins to face me, the impassive look on his face fading to reveal underlying annoyance. His sinful lips contort into a malicious grin and he cocks an eyebrow at me, flinging his blazer off his shoulders, face as hard as stone. As soon as the damp piece of clothing is freed, he furiously tosses it aside, the material hitting the wall with a dull thud before sliding to the floor, leaving a wet patch on the beige paint.

"So, that's how you want to play? And you call *me* a child." He scoffs, trekking towards me like a cheetah hunting an elk, chest rising and falling rapidly.

"You don't just get to *do* this, Everett! You're so hot and cold and I'm so confused! You barged into my life with your stupid dimples and stupid jokes and you make me feel wanted for *once* in my life, but then treat me like I'm *nothing*?! You flirt with me and touch me and then you're jealous and cruel... I can't... I don't understand—"

He takes one determined step forward and cups my wet cheeks more forcefully than before, slamming his lips onto mine with a furious passion. His lips are so desperate and hungry that it clouds my judgment momentarily, only clearing when I feel a salty tear roll down my cheek. I shove him away again and I'm just so frustrated with him not using his words that I spit out the most spiteful thing I can think of, "I hate you."

His expression twists with hurt and he clutches his chest as if my words have physically wounded him before letting out a frustrated groan. He storms towards me once again and doesn't stop until I'm pressed against the door —chest to heaving chest.

"Damnit, don't *ever* say that to me again, Aspen," he grits out through clenched teeth, eyes flashing in agony. Our heated breaths mingle in the space between us and our soaking clothes create a pool of water at our feet. "You can't ever say that to me again."

His breath catches in his throat and he looks so pained, so afraid as his eyes search my face. When he speaks again his voice is so quiet I almost don't hear it.

"Not when... not when I'm falling for you this hard. Not

when I can't fucking *breathe* when I see you with him. Not when I don't know how to act or what to say because you scare the shit out of me. Not when I'm falling in love with you and it's terrifying."

This time, it's me who grabs his cheeks between my palms and slams my lips against his.

# INSATIABLE

Insatiable: (of a person) having an unquenchable appetite or desire for something, especially sex.

There's a fire on my lips and a hunger in my veins.

It's anger and frustration and lust and passion and finally, *finally* succumbing to our desires. It doesn't matter how long Everett's tongue caresses mine or how hard his hands grip the flesh of my hips or how loudly he groans against my mouth.

It's not enough.

*Not when I'm falling in love with you and it's fucking terrifying.*

His desperate revelation won't stop replaying in my head like a broken record. The vulnerable look in his eyes flashes behind my eyelids as I tangle my fingers in his damp hair, tugging on it frantically when he captures my bottom lip between his teeth. He tastes like whiskey and winter and I explore every crevice of his mouth to paint the taste onto my tongue. His movements are rough and fueled by the fury produced from our argument.

I know there's still so much to discuss, so much unspoken hurt feelings between us that need to be sorted through, but all I can focus on is the way Everett's hands are sliding up my waist, exploring the dips in my ribs, until finally tracing the outline of my breasts over the thick velvet material of my top.

"God, Everett."

It's a soft, desperate moan that awakens a beast, a low growl resonating deep within Everett's chest, palms sliding down to grasp my bottom harshly. He picks me up effortlessly, our lips separating as I wrap my legs around his waist, skirt rising with the movement.

Swollen pink lips, flushed chest, tangled curly locks, and wild stormy eyes. The sight stirs a heat deep in my belly and I waste no time in connecting our lips together again. They spark like flint against steel and I let out a sigh of relief as Everett's hands slide slowly up my thighs and under my skirt to grasp my bare flesh.

"Fuck," he groans lowly as I pepper hot, open-mouthed kisses down his neck. "You feel so good, so soft... you're gonna send me to an early grave."

I smile against the skin of his flushed neck and daringly glide my tongue up the expanse before trapping his earlobe between my teeth, tugging lightly. He jerks against me from the action and the moan that escapes me is much too loud and much too whiny. I can feel him there: hot and unbearably hard, straining against his skin-tight jeans. He continues to knead the thick flesh of my ass, circling around to caress my hips, my thighs, my—

"Oh my god." I writhe against him as soon as I feel his palm cupping me through my lace underwear and I buck up into him as my mouth sucks and nips at the skin below his jaw.

"Keep doing that and I'm going to fuck you up against this door."

I groan at the concept, fingernails raking down his still damp shirt. The wall I was pushed against disappears as Everett carries me through the darkness of his flat. We step through a doorway and it slams shut just as he flips a light on, blinding me momentarily. I squint at Everett from the sudden brightness to see his pupils blown out and eyes wild with desire.

"I want to be able to see every second of this. I want to memorize every face you make, every freckle in every crevice of your beautiful body, every inch of you while I'm fucking you."

I barely have time to moan at his words before he's tossing

me onto his white bedsheets, instantly dampening them with my wet clothes. He remains at the foot of the bed, drinking in my flushed expression and wild hair before he grips my remaining heel, rips it off my foot, and throws it behind him — probably making a hole in his wall from the force.

"Don't *ever* throw something at me again, understand Aspen?"

His voice is low, demanding, and it knocks me breathless with desire. My chest shudders with a gasp, thighs clenching. When I don't answer him, Everett grips the hem of my skirt and yanks so hard I swear the zipper snaps as he jerks it off my legs and tosses it behind him also.

"I asked if you understood me." His tone is guttural and dangerous and I want to answer him, I really do. But, he crawls towards me, lips slowly gliding up my thighs, and I don't even think I could recite my name if asked. Suddenly, his breath fans over the part of my body that is aching for him and I jerk my hips up violently in surprise. Everett sits up and pins my hips down to the bed, and I try to swallow but my throat is much too dry.

"Answer me, Aspen."

His calloused fingers leisurely dance up my bare stomach, goosebumps rising in their wake, before they reach the soft material of my top and he ever so slowly peels it from my body. A low groan rumbles up his throat at the sight of braless chest. Flushing under his scrutinizing gaze, my back arches off the bed when his palms slide up to grasp my breasts. He kneads them roughly, thumbs brushing my nipples and sending shockwaves to my core.

"Aspen," he warns, and though I'm not sure what the threat is, I'm quick to succumb. I'll say whatever the hell he wants me to say if it means he'll continue to touch me like this.

"I won't," I gasp as he lightly traces my nipples. "I won't ever throw something at you ever again."

"Good girl."

The smug, satisfied grin would've made me want to punch

him a few weeks ago, but now it only makes me moan in pleasure and lock my legs around his waist. His cocky expression morphs into one of shock when I spin us around and push him so he falls onto the mattress, knocking the air out of his lungs.

I lean down, capturing his lips, and beginning to undo the buttons of his silk shirt. He rises to a sitting position so I can glide the shirt down his shoulders and toss it aside. I lock eyes with him then; hazel against a darkened emerald, his hands placed on my waist and mine looped around his neck. He looks breathless and dazed and his eyes fall from my face to trail down my body. "You've no idea how long I've dreamt of this."

The anger and frustration in our movements seems to fizzle in that moment, replaced by a yearning passion.

It's gentle caresses, lapping tongues, tangling hair, and soft moans. I grind down on his lap slowly and he nips at the skin where my neck meets my shoulder. My hands trail down his toned stomach, tracing his tattoos, before sliding down and palming him through his jeans. It's then that he flips us over again so I'm underneath him, my control relinquished.

"You're so beautiful," he whispers, both his hands and eyes tracing every inch of my skin as if to memorize it. "I'm so sorry for how I've treated you. I just... I've never—"

I lean up to place a chaste kiss against his lips, knowing we should have a conversation about everything, but wanting and *needing* him tonight. "Let's leave the talking for tomorrow."

He looks like he wants to protest, but as soon as my hand trails down and slips into his jeans, he's silenced. I grip him in my hand and keen against him when I feel how hard and ready he is for me. I'm quick to unzip his jeans and he's even faster in shimmying them down his legs and kicking them off. I grip his stubbly cheeks, bringing his lips to mine again. They're no longer angry kisses, but are still full of urgent desire. His tongue slides against my own as his hand travels from my breast, down my stomach, and slips into my thong.

I instantly jerk when his cold rings graze my clit and Everett lets out a shuddering breath against my lips. "Always so wet for me. Just for me, right?" He rubs that ring clad finger against me and I hurry in sliding his underwear down his legs, freeing him.

"Only you," I moan and his fingers grip the hem of my underwear, *ripping* it in his haste. I want to scold him for ruining my very expensive panties, but the way he's drinking in my bare body like he wants to devour it has me speechless.

"So beautiful," he breathes, astonished, and I instantly flush at the foreign words. "All the nights I've spent fucking my fist, imagining you naked and writhing in my bed... it doesn't even compare." His hands are tracing over my hot flesh as he says the words and my whole body is aching for him, for his filthy mouth.

"Everett, *please.*"

The desperation in my voice seems to be a trigger because he leans over to reach into his dresser and pulls out a foil packet. He rips it open with his teeth and I wait with bated breath as he slips the condom on much too slow for my liking. Then, his mouth begins its assault on my body as my legs wrap around his waist: nipping at my neck, sucking at the swells of each breast, lapping his tongue around my nipples. He brands himself into my skin: *I was here, I was here, I was here.*

"Remember what I told you, baby?" He whispers against the skin of my neck, his tongue gliding up until his lips are brushing against my ear. "We're inevitable."

With those final words, Everett thrusts into me with one rough, sharp movement. A loud cry is silenced by his lips as my back arches off the bed from the force of it. He buries his face into my neck, both of us breathing heavily and reveling in the moment we've wanted for so long.

He's big, bigger than I've ever had and it feels heavy and slightly uncomfortable considering how long it's been since I've been intimate with someone. I quickly adjust as Everett slowly glides out of me, eyes trained on our connection. I release a loud moan when he abruptly slams into me again, nails marking his skin.

He finds an agonizing rhythm then, slow and deep and so, *so* good. I'm a writhing mess beneath him and I can tell by his contorted expression that he's trying to hold on. He props himself up with one hand as the other slides down my body to our connection, rubbing me there, and causing me to thrash wildly. I yank on his hair and meet his thrusts with equal fervor, clenching around him desperately.

"*Shit*, don't do that," he strains against my lips. "I won't last."

He runs a hand down the thigh that's wrapped around his waist and brings it up onto his shoulder, allowing him a deeper angle. My leg burns with the stretch, but it only adds to my pleasure as his thrusts grow rougher and I'm the one that isn't going to last with that angle and position. I feel his heartbeat hammer against my skin and soon I can't tell the difference between the rain and our sweat.

I kiss him then the way the sun kisses the water of the ocean just as it begins its descent; tenderly and warm. He kisses me like a man in love; quivering lips and passionate tongue. Each caress, each thrust, each kiss is full of all the words left unsaid and all the emotions we could never express verbally.

"Everett," I moan loudly, nails scratching down his back as he continues to push me over the edge with every movement and gentle nip at my neck. His hand moves to squeeze the flesh of my hip, holding me down to the mattress and creating marks in the shape of his fingers. He pounds into me, relentless and frenzied and my moans become erratic, biting down on his shoulder to control myself.

A growl rumbles from his throat and his pace quickens, lips meeting mine again. I yank at his hair eagerly, feeling myself building with each thrust, and his fingers release my hip to brush my nipple. "I'm going to—" I barely pant, Everett's husky, low voice interrupting me through his groans.

"Come for me."

It's dizzying stars and bright white light and a loud cry of his name. I arch off the mattress, nearly blacking out as my neurons short-circuit and whole body shivers in pleasure. One hand claws at the sheets and the other at Everett's hair and as soon as I let go, so does he —as if waiting for me to finish so he could.

He tenses above me, shoulders tight and veins straining against his flesh as he groans deep and low into my neck. My name is a moan on his lips as I clench around him, nails marking me onto his skin. I'm a quivering mess as my vision clears, Everett's face contorted above me before he collapses onto jelly limbs. We lay like that as we both calm down: our sweaty bodies tangled together, panting, and stroking each other's skin absentmindedly.

Everett rests his head against my chest and slowly pulls out of me, leaving me empty and aching. Unsurprisingly, it doesn't take long for my eyelids to begin to flutter from exhaustion. "Aspen?" His voice is tentative and almost scared – a stark contrast to how it sounded when he was screwing the living daylights out of me. "Do you... you don't really hate me... do you?"

My heart swells inside my chest at his shaky voice and question—so vulnerable and so unlike him— and I smooth the hair back from his forehead as I softly respond, the answer frightening me with its truthfulness.

"Far from it, Everett."

# REVITALIZE

It's a soft morning glow filtering in through the curtains that wakes me and its tan skin and a tattooed chest that brings a dopey grin to my face. I don't bother lifting my head for a while, just tracing the dove tattoos etched on the swells of his muscular chest. I shift my legs under the sheets and grimace at the slight ache between my thighs. When I do lift my head and place my chin on his chest, I can barely contain myself. His pink lips are popped open with soft snores falling from his mouth and long curls are bunched up on one side, head tilted down as if he was watching me before he fell asleep.

I hate him because I don't hate him and I really, *really*-should.

Regardless, I find myself pulling away from his vice-like grip and scrambling from the bed. In the light of day, I'm able to asses Everett's room and how immaculate it is —modern black and white furniture, floor-to-ceiling windows that reveal the city below, and clothes scattered on every surface. I blush immensely when I see my clothes strewn along the hardwood and debate putting them back on. But, they didn't dry properly and probably smell like wet dog, so I grab one of Everett's many button-up shirts from the desk in the corner.

However, bending over proves to be quite painful, my lower half very sore from last night. I glance over my shoulder to see Everett's white sheets hung dangerously low on his hips, and have to hurry from the room in fear of repeating last night.

His flat is almost exactly like mine layout-wise, except... colder and barren. The hallway empties out into a small den that's only occupied by a black couch, glass coffee table, and television hung on the exposed brick. It's a nice apartment and cleaner than I thought it'd be, but it just makes me... *sad.* He only has the bare necessities—no pictures, no artwork, no personal belongings of any kind and I realize that I know almost nothing about his personal life.

I step into the black-and-white kitchen and am both overjoyed and confused to see a coffee pot on the island. While waiting for the coffee to brew, my mind wanders to the events of last night and I berate myself for sleeping with him so easily. I'm a weak human. Weak when it comes to him at least. After everything that's happened, I caved after *one* honest conversation. The bar is so low and I'm so screwed.

Even though he was so vulnerable and open last night, how will he act today? Will he cast me aside? Pretend his confession never happened?

I hear a door open in the distance and know I'm about to get my answer.

Everett comes fumbling down the hallway, dressed only in briefs, whipping his head side to side, eyes frantic. It's only when he peeps around the corner and sees me that he lets out a relieved sigh. A shaky hand runs through his mussed hair as he tries to appear nonchalant, "I thought you'd left."

I try to hide my smile at his obvious panic, deciding to be honest, "I thought about it."

The coffee pot beeps in the silence and I see hurt flash in his tired eyes before he turns around to open a cupboard and pass me a mug with music notes on it.

"I wouldn't blame you," he whispers under his breath, leaning against the counter and crossing his feet at the ankles. I ignore him as I pour my coffee, watching as he leers at my scantily-clad figure. "I don't know what's more arousing—the fact that you're wearing one of my shirts or that I know you aren't wearing anything underneath."

Even though that one sentence makes me want to drop to my knees, I control myself. "Don't even think about it, Everett. We have a lot to talk about."

He holds his hands up in surrender, but the dirty smirk and darkened eyes suggest otherwise. I glance at him briefly as I take a sip, catching sight of a purple bruise on his neck. Knowing I have a matching one at the base of my throat stokes the fire in my belly and makes my cheeks heat.

"Alright... we'll talk, but at least let me eat breakfast first." Everett takes a deliberate step forward, tongue moistening his lips. I swallow, but it's suddenly very hot in this kitchen.

"Do you want me to go out and get something?"

"No, what I want to eat is right here."

When my back hits the edge of the counter and Everett places his hands on either side of me, I know exactly what his intentions are. The idea has my thighs clenching and mind grasping at any sense of reason I have left. "Everett," I warn, although it comes out shaky and weak. "I don't think that's a very good idea—"

"Oh, I think it's a *very* good idea." He gingerly takes the mug from my hands and sets it down on the counter next to him and I'm finding it very hard to keep my resolve.

"We have so much to talk about..." I trail off when his lips graze the flesh of my neck and I involuntarily shiver when he bites down gently.

"We will," he whispers huskily, hands trailing down to lift me up on the counter effortlessly. "But, how can I possibly hold a conversation with you when you're in my shirt, hair all mussed up, the hickeys I gave you last night on full display and *not* touch you?" His words are accentuated by his tongue tracing the fresh bruise on my collarbone. My resolve slowly chips away with each deep kiss, each hot lick...

*Ah, fuck it.*

I bring my hands up to fist his hair and kiss him fervently. He moans against my lips and traces them with his tongue before delving between the creases and caressing my own. I kiss him until my lungs burn and Everett breaks away to send me a devilish smirk. "If you'll excuse me, I'm positively parched."

I let out a light-hearted laugh even though I'm burning for him. He dips his head again to press hot, open-mouthed kisses down my neck, nipping the skin until he reaches the first button of my shirt. Everett's fingers are deliberately slow in unbuttoning the blouse, paying utmost attention to the flesh revealed by the release of each button. Each kiss, each touch, is like exploding fireworks against my skin.

*Pop.* He nips at the swells of my breasts and traces over the hickeys he marked onto my skin as I quiver before him. His tongue circles each of my nipples before gently biting down and causing me to cry out.

*Pop.* He dips his tongue into my navel, my head hitting the cupboard behind me.

*Pop.* He sucks at my hipbones eagerly, moaning against my skin when I pull on his hair, nose brushing my lower stomach and driving me absolutely mad.

*Pop.*

Except I don't feel him where I expect to —no, he skips right over that area to place hot kisses along my thighs. He sucks and licks the skin there, going up and down each leg, but never close enough. "*God,* Everett. *Please,*" I whine desperately and feel him smirk against my skin.

"As you wish, princess."

Finally, *finally* I feel his hot breath against my core and it makes me squirm in anticipation. This time, Everett wastes no time in flattening his tongue and licking up my slit. The action alone causes me to fall back on one hand, the other tightening its grip in his hair. The tip of his hot tongue traces my bundle of nerves and a whimper slips past my lips.

"Always so wet, so sweet for me." The words groaned against my heat send a vibration up my spine, my eyes practically rolling back in my head. "I know you love my filthy mouth, naughty girl."

By now his shirt has fallen to my elbows and I'm completely

naked on the counter. When I look down to see his blazing emerald eyes trained on my face in desire and awe I moan his name and he groans against me. His mouth closes around my clit, sucking wildly and causing me to yank on his hair, the pressure inside of me building up at an alarming pace.

His thumb takes over in circling my bundle of nerves, causing me to fall back against the cupboard as my chest concaves and eyes shut tightly. His tongue delves into me suddenly and I lock my legs around his neck, jolting in surprise. He alternates between tracing my folds with his expert tongue and delving in and out of me, all while his thumb never ceases its assault. It doesn't take long for me to begin to quiver against him —my moans uncontrollable and my breathing so harsh I'm sure I'll pass out.

"Dio mio. Please, Everett. Di Più. Ho bisogno more. Per favore, baby." [My God. Please, Everett. More. I need more. Please, baby.]

Everett groans at my mixture of Italian and English —my mind too muddled to make any coherent sentences in either language. "So fucking hot," he moans, his tongue never ceasing.

His hand slides up to my breast, fingers tweaking my nipple, just as his lips close around my clit, causing my orgasm to come crashing over me violently and suddenly. My back arches and eyes squeeze shut and all I can see is white as I writhe against him, desperate shouts of his name falling from my lips. Pleasure shoots up my spine, my climax overwhelming and so powerful I can barely even breathe.

"That's it baby, that's it," Everett coaxes gently, continuing to lap me up until I'm gasping for air and trembling. When I finally go limp against him, chest heaving and knees weak, Everett is watching with a fond smile and straining underwear.

"I love watching you finish —all flushed and sweaty, full lips popped open, panting wildly, eyes squeezed shut— because of *me.* I could get off just watching you."

He rises from his knees and licks his lips, pupils blown out and grin smug. Too exhausted to do it myself, Everett buttons my shirt, making me tremble every time his fingers graze my sensitive flesh.

"You play dirty, Curly." I scold and Everett bites back a laugh, shrugging innocently. I grab my long-forgotten mug to re-hydrate, but shoot him a glare when I realize how cold my coffee got. He shows no signs of remorse, a dirty smirk matching his proud expression.

"Best breakfast I ever had, Munchkin."

* * *

It's the kind of silence that is deafening.

Full of unsaid words that have been bubbling at the surface for much too long and thick with tension for what's to come. A silence that is much too loud to bear, but neither of us is sure how to break it or who should speak first.

"Wanna hear a joke?" Although he was looking at me with dark eyes and moistened lips from in between my thighs just ten minutes ago, he sits across from me now with a goofy grin and nervous eyes.

"Never from you."

"How do you make Holy Water?"

"Please, no."

"You boil the hell out of it!" The punchline is accompanied by an elevated voice, sharp bark of laughter, and —dear god— an actual knee slap. Except his laugh actually makes my chest warm and I really know I'm screwed when an actual chuckle falls from my lips at the joke. What have I become?

"That was *so* bad."

He wipes a tear from his eye, bicep flexing, and I thank the lord he decided to put a shirt on. "C'mon, I know you secretly like my jokes."

I decide to be as blunt as possible, tired of dancing around it. "No, I don't like your jokes. I like *you."* The smile is instantly wiped from his lips and the fluttery feeling I had in my stomach now feels like daggers. "Well, maybe not so much after that terrible joke."

Everett's face twists into pure confusion and hope, which really freaks me out. This morning has definitely not gone according to plan. Everett was supposed to come in here and lay everything out onto the table —good or bad— and we'd move on from there. Instead, with a wolfish grin and dirty words and fingers like Indiana freaking Jones, Everett seduced me. *Again.*

Now we're dancing around each other because Everett is terrified for some inexplicable reason and I'm even more confused by the past 24 hours because all I can recall is Everett getting jealous over Sam, then him being a dick during never have I ever, que screaming match in the street, Everett's confession out of nowhere, and then me somehow ending up in his bed.

Never a dull day here in London.

"You do? Even after everything that's happened?" He sounds astonished and completely baffled, but the smile growing on his lips is contagious.

"No, I slept with you last night because I hate you." Okay, I've really got to tone down the attitude if I want this conversation to go anywhere. "Yes, Everett... I like you, *way* too much if I'm being honest... considering everything."

The once child-like wonder fades into guilty pouting, "I don't even know where to start... do I apologize again or explain?"

"I'd rather slit my own throat than hear you apologize again. I just need an explanation before I can even start to believe anything out of your mouth. You say one thing, then do the complete opposite. Or, *worse*, you don't say anything at all."

He stares at me like I grew a second head, "you don't believe me?" I scoff at that because how can I trust in his words when his actions have proven the exact opposite? The boy is a walking contradiction and my head might explode if I don't get some answers fast.

"How can I when you admitted last night that you were using me?"

"When in the hell did I admit that?"

"Playing never have I ever!" And okay, saying that out loud actually makes me cringe and flush in embarrassment.

"We were lying, *obviously*!" He shouts as if it's the most apparent thing in the world, but then he falters, leaning back in the chair, expression turning grave. "We were lying, right? You told me you didn't sleep with Sam?"

Now it's my turn to feel guilty for acting so childish. "No! I'm also sorry for lying and how I acted last night, it was immature. Sam and I didn't have sex that night, but you don't want any details either." I could've left that last part out, but if we're trying to clear the air and be honest, omitting that detail would be a half-lie and I'm really tired of being deceitful. But, Everett's jaw clenches and eyes flash with rage. "You have no right to get mad at me for that, when *you* were stringing both Marisol and I along for months."

"I wasn't... I... Marisol and I fooled around a few times when I first joined the band, but... I cut it off after that night in the club when I first kissed you, because it just didn't feel right... It wasn't the same." He's fumbling with his words and his cheeks burn, and although I love to see him squirm, I'm more confused than ever.

"But, I've seen you with her so many times, she picked up your phone... you were all over her in the bar when I was there with Sam... I don't...?"

The tips of his ears turn pink and he refuses to meet my eyes, "we're just friends, Aspen. I may have noticed how jealous you were when she was around... and may have started bringing her along to things more often because of it... I know, I know how immature that is. I'm a dick."

The wave of relief I feel that he's just friends with her is shocking and overwhelming. But, the nights I spent tossing and turning because he led me to believe otherwise has left a bitter taste in my mouth. *Unbelievable.*

"So, let me get this straight: you said you were using me just to hurt me, shoved my bad relationship with my mother in my face, lead me on, acted like a jealous prick about Sam, and used Marisol to make *me* jealous?" One night of really hot, emotional, and passionate sex doesn't erase the months of torment and torture. I'm also guilty of some questionable behavior regarding Everett, but that was only the effect of the cause.

Everett groans, rubbing a hand down his face, "It wasn't supposed to be like this."

"Be like what?"

He lifts his head, elbows on his knees, hands clasped together, and gaze burning with troubled intensity. After a few agonizing minutes, he stands from the tweed arm chair and comes around the table to sit next to me. He resumes the same position as before, but this time his gaze is focused on the floor. "I joined the band because of you, y'know?"

And he says it so nonchalantly, so blasé, that I'm sure I'm imagining things. I didn't even really meet him until he joined, just heard rumors about him because we ran in the same circles. So, this confession makes no sense and only confuses me further. "Care to elaborate?"

"Two years ago, I was in a pretty dark place mentally and I just wanted to give up... on *everything*. I didn't care about anything or anyone, even myself. I was fucking any girl that offered, getting hammered every night, doing drugs... Until, one night I did something I shouldn't have —something seriously fucked up." He clears his throat, voice trembling, and expression pained. "I ran away from the problem, like always, and ended up at an overcrowded, dingy bar."

His somber tone shifts and a small smile flits up his face, "and when the band came on—I wasn't even listening, just hitting on some random— but... but, when the girl started to sing, it was like everything fell away. Everyone in the crowd went silent, the random bird disappeared, and I swear the whole world stopped to listen. It was soulful and clear, resonating throughout the pub. The chilling lyrics and angelic voice... it was aching, tragically so. I'd never heard anything like it before... It expressed something I thought I'd lost the ability to feel."

He looks at me then, cheeks flushed deeply and gaze nervous and hesitant. I suddenly find it hard to breathe because he could be talking about anyone, any girl in a band, but the way he's looking at me; I already know.

"That girl was you."

The confession is like a shot to my heart and I feel tears sting the back of my eyes, "I don't... I don't understand."

"I can't explain it, but seeing you up there like that... it made me realize how far I'd strayed from who I used to be, what I'd given up. You were so passionate about the music, so focused. I used to have that drive and love for what I did and I'd fallen *so* far... I vowed right then and there to get my act together and really focus on the music. I stopped with the drugs and *most* of the girls and I joined a band again... I didn't even know your name yet, but you changed my life. It was like you... you..." Everett stops and flails his arms around with pursed lips, "what's the word? Like... you brought me to life?"

"Revitalize: to make someone active, healthy, or energetic again. To bring new life and vitality." Everett nods eagerly at my help and I'm stunned into silence after that.

I expected to talk about why he wouldn't admit his feelings or where we stand now, but this sudden confession? Not what I had in mind. I made him have some kind of life-altering epiphany just because of some song at some gross bar? The idea is absurd and shocking and my brain throbs at the thought of it. I did not *revitalize* Everett Fox, how could I?

I'm not sure if he wants me to reply because I'm positive that I physically can't. My heart is lodged in my throat as I process this information, not meeting his burning gaze. The revelation is a shocking one, one I would've never even thought possible. Everett has kept this to himself this whole time — that I changed him, that he joined the band for *me*?

*Impossible.*

"So, that was the reason you joined our band?

"Not exactly," he shakes his head, fumbling with his rings. "I heard this crazy rumor that the same girl whose voice basically brought me back to life suddenly decided to stop singing because of *swollen lymph nodes*? The idea seemed crazy to me so I went to a show and it was like... like you were a completely different person. You'd faded into the back of the stage —much too thin, pale, dark eyes... you didn't interact with the audience, your voice was small and weak and numb to the lyrics and the crowd. So very unlike the girl from before."

"So, it was pity then? Pity that had you joining our band?" I grit out, eyes glistening from the reminder of my stolen passion. The swollen lymph nodes was just a ruse to cover up the real reason; that I just didn't want to sing anymore. *Couldn't* sing anymore. Everett's eyes widen and he reaches for my hand, gripping it tightly.

"No! I don't know... I thought that maybe, I could help you? Like how you helped me?" He scoffs, shaking his head and gesturing between us, "I just wasn't counting on *this*. You hated me from the *jump* and, I have to admit, I loved teasing you... you were all harsh words and witty comebacks and sexy as hell. Next thing I know, I'm lying awake every night waiting for you to text me like some love-sick pre-teen."

I fall back against the couch because this is way too much for me to even begin to comprehend. The idea that my singing had inspired Everett to turn his life around is flattering and terrifying all at once. He asked me all the time why I stopped singing, but I assumed it was just a general curiosity or a need for gossip like everyone else. I had no idea that it was so personal to him.

But, then I remember *his* attitude from the very start and it just doesn't add up in my head. "I don't get it... you've been nothing but an ass to me recently... how in the hell is that *helping* me?"

"It's not, I know it's not. But, I'm an idiot and when you

didn't want anything to do with me before you even really knew me, it hurt. I'd had this idea of you in my head, of how we'd be friends and I'd help you find your love for music like you did for me, but you wanted nothing to do with me... So, instead, I just started to tease you and pick on you and kept doing it because I like seeing your face pinch up when you're mad...

"I didn't realize I had feelings for you until that day we saw the cherry blossoms. It freaked me out so much that I tried to play it off... that's when I told you I didn't want you getting the wrong idea. Which was total bullshit. I didn't mean to hurt you, but you just kept coming back 'round and being, well, *you.* I really did try to tell you how I felt, but every time I opened my mouth, I choked. Until, I couldn't take it anymore.

"I was a coward for not owing up to it sooner. But, you scare the hell out of me." He laughs lightly, gesturing between us, "*this* scares the hell out of me... but, I'm tired of running."

It scares the hell out of me too, because he's Everett Fox and that is dangerous territory. And I'm frankly unsure if I should be flattered or pissed that this relationship started because Everett was trying to repay me. His confession, though, releases a cage of butterflies in my chest and I try to steady my racing heart. I'm still trying to wrap my mind around his story, the idea of him turning his life around because he saw me sing making my eyes burn and chest ache.

"Did you mean what you said before?" My voice is quiet and hesitant, though it's a question I've been dying to ask since last night.

"Which part?"

"About you falling in love with me?"

There's a long pause where the only sounds in the room are his shallow breaths and my erratic heartbeat. A traumatized part of me fears he'll laugh and say he was playing me the entire time, but then I feel a lone finger brush back a strand of my hair and I'm instantly calmed.

"It's more like crashing and burning rather than falling."

I feel like there's a double meaning in there somewhere, but my mind is much too jumbled with this new information to make sense of it. A smile fights its way up my lips, but my mind still replays his words from last night. "You really hurt me, Everett."

He grimaces, hanging his head in shame, "I know. I know I did and all I can ask is that you let me make it up to you."

I give his hand a squeeze to let him know that I'm here, that he hasn't lost me. "How?"

"By doing what I set out to do: helping you get over your fear of singing."

# DECEIVE

"You look absolutely stunning tonight," a light tug on my earlobe follows the whispered words and I desperately try to repress the shiver running down my spine. "Bloody torturing me, you are." His palm runs up my tanned thigh, wraps around my waist, before continuing their journey underneath the mesh of my white dress. A pleasurable sigh leaves my lips when he nips at my jaw, the idea of being caught only stoking the fire in my belly.

And the chance of us being exposed is high considering we're supposed to be on stage in the next fifteen minutes. "That wasn't my intention."

Everett lifts his head with a dirty smile, lips ghosting against my own. "Liar."

He presses against me harder, bulge hitting me right where I want him and causing me to groan and slam my head into the wall behind me, "God, I want you. I want you all the time."

This seems to please him because he jerks his hips up, a low growl resonating in his throat. "God, what're you doing to me, Aspen?"

And I know that anyone could walk through the door at any moment, to fix their hair or change their clothes for the show, but I don't care. It's only been a few days since Everett confessed his feelings to me, since we finally succumbed to our desires, and we've barely been able to keep our hands off each other since. We've been messaging nonstop, meeting up for drinks, and going on hikes. And even though I'm not exactly sure what we are, it's nice to spend time with someone. Someone you know likes you just as much as you like them.

When we're not chatting about our childhoods, when Everett's not telling awful jokes, and when I'm not teaching him guitar, we spend our time in bed. Or in the car, or the tub, or bent over a table. I spend more time wrapped in his arms than I do asleep and the result has my body constantly sore, but always ready.

It's addictive and secretive and so, *so* hot.

Before I can think of the consequences, I'm shoving Everett back so he lands on the tattered sofa behind us with an 'oompf'. His chest is already flushed and eyes almost black with lust as they ravish my body draped in a white mesh dress that would be completely see-through had it not been for the bralette and high-waisted underwear underneath.

It had the intended effect because one second I was warming up with the rest of the band and the next I was being pulled into the changing room, Everett ravishing my body with his lips.

"Why did you stop me?" He all but chokes on his spit when I drop to my knees in front of him, eyes bulging out of his head, and plaid pants straining.

"I don't care for this shirt you're wearing."

His eyebrows furrow in confusion, "okay? What do you—"

But, he goes silent, hissing through his teeth when my nimble fingers slide up his thighs and graze over his bulge. When they reach the hem of his black nylon button-down, I waste no time in tearing it open.

"Holy shit," he breathes when my palms slide up his defined torso and down again before my lips follow suit. They cover every line on his stomach and my tongue peaks out to trace over the lighthouse tattooed on his abdomen and roses at his hips. This causes him to jerk violently and I instantly halt my movements.

"None of that," I scold, heart skipping and skin hot to the touch. "If you're bad, you don't get your reward."

Everett lets out a breathy laugh in disbelief, "Jesus Christ, Aspen."

The awe in his voice is enough fuel for me to grip the top of his trousers, "these aren't good, either."

He's practically twitching with anticipation, but he's sure to be patient, chest heaving desperately and dark eyes boring into my own. "No?"

"No." I whisper, popping the button open and yanking the zipper down in one swift movement. Contrary to my quick actions, I slide his trousers down his legs deliberately slow, making sure to caress the fabric of his briefs he strains against as I go. My lashes flutter as I look up into his eyes; wild and blazing and filled with desire.

"Please tell me you don't like my pants either," he breathes, chest heaving rapidly and body thrumming with anticipation.

I almost laugh at this, *almost,* but my burning hunger has me shaking my head, fingers dipping into his waistband unabashedly. With my hooded eyes never leaving his, I leisurely slide his briefs down his thighs until they pool around his ankles, exposing him to me. Everett practically slumps over from the relief of being freed from his restraints and his darkened gaze is almost animalistic as he watches me watch him, a smug smile on my lips.

Our eyes hold steady contact, expressing our desire for each other's body and soul and it would bring me to my knees if I wasn't already on them. Finally, I break the contact as I trace light, teasing kisses up his thighs. They tense slightly as my breath washes over his tip, making him jerk underneath me. "Fuck... please, baby. *Please.*"

"I told you to be good, Everett." Even I'm surprised at my assertiveness, but it only turns Everett on more as he whimpers and tosses his head back on the couch.

"I will, I promise, I will. I'll be good, just please. Baby—"

He chokes on his words when I flatten my tongue and drag it up the length of him before focusing my attention on the head.

He jerks slightly and I take my time there, gripping him with one hand, while the other slides up his abdomen. My lips enclose around his head and Everett lets out a shaky groan when I hollow out my cheeks and suck lightly just at the tip.

"Fuck..." he twitches, eyes never leaving mine between his legs. "Can I... *shit*... Can I touch you?" He stutters and I bob my head lightly in confirmation. His hands wrap in my hair, yanking gently when my hands trail up his thighs and mouth descends down his shaft.

My tongue smooths around the silky skin as he slides down my throat. I go slow, taking deep breaths with every inch I manage to cover. Everett's low groans and whispers of my name are the only encouragement I need as I hollow out my throat until he touches the back of it. When the tip of my nose touches his lower abdomen and I've successfully swallowed him whole, he tugs on my hair harshly. The rough pulling stings my scalp, but the pain is pleasure and a low moan crawls from my throat, vibrating through him.

"Oh, *fuck*, baby. D-Don't do that again. As humiliating as it is, I'm already so close."

My chest swells with pride and I want to get him there as quickly as possible, so I suck more intensely, bob my head slowly, and swirl my tongue around him. I pay special attention to his tip —licking and slurping there before descending down him again. The rhythm seems to be too much for Everett because it doesn't take long for his abs to begin to tighten. At every slightest movement, his hips shift from beneath my palms and his breath hitches as if holding himself back from finishing too quickly. For whatever reason, the chemistry between us is unlike anyone or anything else I've ever experienced.

One touch is like a spark that burns down an entire forest.

It's when my hand slides from his hip to cup him that he moans deep in his chest, whole body quivering. "Shit, baby, stop. S-Stop... I'm gonna come."

Instead, I bob my head at a faster pace, massaging him and

continuously tracing my tongue around his skin as his groans become more frequent and hips less controllable. I glance at him from under my eyelashes and as soon as he catches my lusty gaze he's done for.

His stomach tightens and fingers yank at my hair as he groans deep in his throat. I have no choice but to swallow as he trembles uncontrollably, calling out my name in desperation. His chest and neck are flushed a deep pink and his eyes are squeezed shut in pleasure as he comes down, hand letting go of his grip on my hair to stroke it in an affectionate manner. I pull away from him, wiping my swollen mouth with the back of my hand as his head lulls forward, lazy grin sliding up his lips. "Where have you been all my life?"

The confidence that soared through my body before is nowhere in sight as I send him a shy smile, helping him put his pants back on, "Was it... was I okay?"

He pauses just as he begins to do up his zipper, face dropping in disbelief. "Are you kidding—" but, before he can finish his sentence, a thick Scottish brogue calls out our names from just beyond the door. Everett and I glance at each other in panic as we hurriedly fix ourselves just in time for Jesse to open the door.

"Where have you lot been? It's show time!" He exclaims, ushering us forward. Before we're fully out of the room, I feel curls tickling my neck and a low voice whispering in my ear.

"You were way beyond 'okay.' That blowjob had me writing my wedding vows."

* * *

The show only lasts an hour because we were opening for a bigger band at the small venue, but it seemed to last forever because Everett kept sending me dirty glances during the performance. All I could think about was him coming undone before me and his stupid mouth and getting him home quickly to do it all over again.

For the first time in a long time, I feel good. I feel happy and content and like maybe I can restore my confidence. Maybe, with Everett's help, I could get my voice back. He's been itching to get me to go to a karaoke club for days. Although I vehemently denied this request at first, the more he asks, the more I'm willing to give it a try. He makes everything quiet, he makes the voices of doubt in my head fall silent. He makes me want to try again, to find my voice. It's exhilarating *and* frightening all at once.

I'm practically skipping back to the greenroom after chatting with a fan and my excitement to see Everett almost disgusts me. But, when I reach the door, I hear familiar voices just beyond it. I'd assumed most of the band already left and I know I shouldn't eavesdrop, but the tone of those voices make my hand freeze on the knob and heart leap to my throat.

"... what you were told." It's Marco and he sounds angry, *very* angry.

"It's not what you think, okay? I'm not doing anything wrong." Everett. He sounds distressed and also irritated and I'm about to interrupt when Marco's next words stop me.

"I saw the looks you two were giving each other on stage! It better not be more than an innocent flirtation, Everett." They're arguing about *me?*

"I told you it's not what it looks like!" A loud thud comes from the other side of the door, no doubt something being thrown against it and I jump back, knowing this is a conversation I'm definitely not supposed to hear. "Marco, I swear to you. Her and I... there's nothing between us, okay? There never will be. I have no romantic feelings for her."

Deceive: cause (someone) to believe something that's not true, typically in order to gain some personal advantage.

# PETRICHOR

I am constantly trying to fight off my own insecurities and trauma, trying to pull myself out of the quicksand of my mind. But, it seems the more I struggle to free myself, the quicker I sink. I've been fighting against myself my whole life and my limbs are beginning to ache.

I want to believe the conversation I heard between Everett and Marco wasn't what I thought. Maybe Everett's harsh words were meant to keep our relationship private, maybe he lied to appease Marco. Maybe he hadn't meant what he said —he'd told me the exact opposite just a few days ago, after all.

But, the alternative won't leave my thoughts. That darkness is sucking me deeper into the quicksand and it's beginning to squeeze my lungs. Everett *could* be playing me, like I originally thought.

When I remember his honest confession of almost-love and the way he held me all night after we slept together, I know that those actions were genuine. But, I also remember Marisol and his cruel words and I can't distinguish what is real and what is a lie. I should've announced myself when I heard Everett and my brother talking. I should've demanded an explanation right there and then, but his words stung. It's what I've been afraid of all along and I can't stop replaying his dismissal in my head.

So, I left. I left and I met the band at a nearby pub to forget the conversation. I didn't meet Everett after the show like I said I would and he may still be waiting for me there. Though,

Marco did join us about ten minutes ago, much to my disdain.

"Why the hell does Everett keep ringing me?" Jesse groans, eyes squinting at his phone and I'm quick to snatch it from his hands.

"It's rude to be on your phone when you're out with friends."

"Well, now he's calling me." Marco, the only sober one at the table, pulls his phone out and goes to answer, but I interrupt him.

"Weird, didn't you just speak to him?"

His brows furrow at first, face contorted into confusion, but then this look crosses his face —something between fear and panic and it twists the knife further into my gut. Enzo suddenly lets out a bark of laughter, glancing at his phone. "Now, the bloke is calling *me*! He must either be really bored or really pissed."

"What the hell," Avery pouts, slumping into her seat. "He hasn't called me! I thought we were friends... I'm feeling left out." She sniffs, crossing her arms, and I shoot to my feet, tired of this discussion and its subject.

"Listen, no one talk to Everett. Don't invite him over here, okay? He's an ass."

Avery points a finger up in the air, a serious expression in her brown eyes, "a nice ass, though." I roll my eyes and walk away from the rowdy table. Peanut shells crunch under my heels as I weave between drunk dancers and desperate guys trying to hit on women way out of their league. I nearly knock into a waitress carrying a tray of pink shots and pick one up, downing it in one go, my body instantly warming. I rush to the bathroom, my bladder nearly bursting with all the alcohol I've consumed tonight. My head is cloudy and I'm at the stage of drunkenness where I find everything funny and my mind is completely free of all thoughts of a certain curly-haired brit.

But, that doesn't last long.

Because I'm washing my hands when the door bursts open and in walks said curly-haired brit with his black shirt half-way done, cheeks flushed, and face pinched in anger.

"Hey, you can't go in there." A random red-head tries to come in and stop him, but he slams the door in her face and I start laughing, though I don't find the situation all that funny.

I'm really not all that surprised to see him. In a bathroom. Again.

"We really have to stop meeting like this—it's unsanitary."

And there seems to be two of him as he makes his way over to me, face twisting in concern, but a fire still burning in his emerald eyes.

"Where the hell have you been? You don't meet me backstage and your phone is off and the only one who fucking answered was Enzo and," he stops when I begin to giggle, though I'm not sure why I do because I'm actually angry, *really* angry. "Are you drunk?"

"No," I protest, followed by a hiccup and guilty smile. "Okay, maybe a little."

He observes my flushed face and dazed eyes before running a hand through his hair in frustration. "That's just great, Aspen."

Suddenly, I don't feel so giddy anymore. "I don't see why you care anyway, Everett."

"Are you kidding me?" He shouts and I wince at the volume of his voice, my stomach twisting at the venom in his tone. "I've been calling you, calling the band, I even went to your apartment! Only to find out that you've been here, at a bar, getting plastered this whole time!"

And okay, when he puts it like that, it sounds really bad.

Maybe, if I was more sober or lucid I would be able to explain myself in a calm manner and confront him about the conversation I eavesdropped on, but that pink drink did me right in and I let the alcohol swimming in my veins control me. I let the hurt and betrayal I feel fuel the fire in my belly.

"Why go through all that trouble, Everett?" I shout back and he instantly opens his mouth to say something, but I cut him off. "Why go through all that trouble for someone you have *no romantic feelings for*?!"

He looks even more dumbfounded than before, brows furrowing and mouth hanging open. I practically see the wheels turning in his head and I know the moment it clicks because his eyes widen in panic and face pales dramatically. "H-How much of that did you hear exactly?"

"Enough," I spit, even more incensed that he doesn't deny it. "I had the pleasure of walking by when you were discussing us, but maybe there is no *us*. Maybe—"

"Fucking hell, Aspen!" He slams him palm down onto the counter, "that's why you did all of this? Because you heard part of a conversation and jumped to conclusions?"

"I think I heard enough to jump to conclusions! You—"

"No, you didn't! And you didn't even *ask* me about it!" His voice lowers and there's a dark hurt in his eyes and frustration in his voice. "How can you think that I've been using you? After all this time, after denying it time and time again? After telling you that I'm falling in love with you? How can you *still* not believe me? How fucked is it that you assume the worst of everyone? Is that all you've been shown that now you just expect it?"

I swallow harshly, suddenly sobered up with images of my father and mother and Sam and every shit thing in my life and my eyes sting. Had I really fucked this up? Had I let the quicksand swallow me whole? I did hear him... he said that to Marco... what else am I to think?

"Then why did you say that, Everett?"

There is something in his eyes then, a desperate battle of wits —of what he wants to say and what he should— before his shoulders sag and he sighs in defeat. It's like he wants to be angry, wants to yell and accuse me of things, but something is stopping him.

"Because I'm afraid." He can't meet my eyes, keeping them trained on his shoes, cheeks tinted pink, "I've never had a real relationship. I don't know how this works and I'm scared that once the band knows they'll muck it up or I'll muck it up from the pressure. Marco's already threatened me multiple times about it and I was trying to protect what we have."

The wave of guilt that overcomes me is crushing and my stomach instantly turns at this information. Because of course, I jumped to the worst possible scenario. No one has ever proven me otherwise and I pushed that expectation onto Everett.

"Everett, I—"

He shakes his head then, finally meeting my eyes with a somber expression, "No, it makes sense for you to assume the worst... I'm Everett Fox, right? Player extraordinaire. I mean, I haven't really proved the contrary." He trails off then, sad smile on his face, "I just thought... I thought that you of all people would have given me the benefit of the doubt."

I rack my foggy brain for something, anything to say because this unbelievable shame overcomes me for thinking of him in that light. Maybe he was a womanizer, but wasn't he trying to turn his life around? He was an idiot before with Marisol, but he apologized profusely and has been trying to make up for it and I haven't been letting him.

I open my mouth to say something, but in a split second I'm running to the toilet and falling to my knees. The contents of my stomach end up in the bowl, my mind replaying Everett's sad eyes and hurt words. I heave until there's nothing left, stomach still swimming. I'm completely mortified to be *this* hammered considering the situation.

"Shh, you're okay," a gentle voice whispers in my ear, making me whimper with guilt as fingers gently gather my hair. "You're okay."

And he strokes my back as I continue to vomit, holding my hair selflessly and breaking my heart all at once. It's only when I'm done and my throat has stopped burning that he speaks again, voice full of resignation and I know that this conversation is nowhere near over.

"C'mon. Let's get you home, Munchkin."

✻ ✻ ✻

It isn't the incessant chirping of birds that wake me from my deep slumber, or the man snoring like a train next to me, or even the alarm clock screeching some TLC classic. None of these things cause me to jump out of bed like my life depends on it.

No, it's vomit.

My stomach churns and on instinct I'm jolting from the warm bed, crashing into walls, and covering my mouth as I burst into the bathroom and fall to my knees on the cold tile floor. And the pink drink I found so delicious just a few hours prior suddenly makes me want to confront the inventor of that stupid drink and push him off a cliff.

I smell him before I see him; mangoes and a woodsy pine scent. And then just like the night prior, I feel a warm body saddle up behind me —smoothing down my hair and rubbing my back in circles, cooing in my ear.

And it just makes me sicker.

I wretch and I wretch and I wretch until nothing else could possibly come out of my stomach. I feel Everett move from behind me, the pitter-patter of his footsteps on the tile, a clinking, and then he's back. My world is spinning along with my stomach, but I still manage to grab the toothbrush he holds out as he helps me to my feet.

"C'mon, Munchkin. Let's get you all cleaned up —you're smelling up my apartment."

And he really wouldn't be Everett if he didn't comment on it, so I permit him to lead me to the sink and watch as he places a drop of toothpaste on my brush. Once I'm done cleaning up, he leads me to his bed and the humiliation continues when I look down to see that I'm dressed in one of his shirts, a bucket on my side of the bed.

I find little relief in the fact that the bucket is empty.

"Oh god," I groan, flopping onto his feather duvet and avoiding his stare. "I'm so humiliated." Embarrassed about getting black-out drunk, about the fight in the bathroom, about jumping to conclusions, about my entire life honestly.

"Yeah, I don't know how you're ever going to show your face in the light of day again." Despite his teasing tone, I still pick up a pillow and toss it at his face, my breathy chuckles muffled by the blanket. He laughs along with me, though I don't know why. He was upset last night and not the kind of angry upset that I'd witnessed from him before, but more a resigned hurt. Sad, yes, but like he was used to people assuming the worst of him.

Of me assuming the worst of him. Again.

And he would be correct.

The second Everett stepped into Jesse's apartment that first day, I'd already written him off. The rumors, the gossip blogs, the small amounts I saw of him in person all convinced me that he was some heartless philanderer. I held that against him, and clearly still do. Because when I heard that snippet of argument between him and my brother, I instantly convinced myself that Everett was the kind of guy to play me all along. Sam taught me that people can't be trusted, that they're just out for themselves. I'm still trying to shake off that mentality.

"I'm sorry, Everett," I whisper, words still muffled into the blanket, but I hear him sigh next to me, fingers mindlessly playing with my hair.

"I know... this just proves I have a lot to make up for. I have to make you trust me and I will." My heart clenches at his words and I can't even begin to understand how this is the same guy that made out with me in a dingy bathroom while his date was outside just a month ago.

He's changing. For me, for himself. Everett knows women in bars and backstage and storage closets. He doesn't know me and feelings and scary words like 'commitment' and 'relationship.'

His vehement denial stung, but what did I expect? We haven't set any rules or defined our relationship. We're just hanging in relationship limbo and I've no doubts that telling the band would ruin everything.

They're way too fucking nosey.

"I'm still sorry for standing you up and making you feel like shit."

He sends me a sad smile, "yeah, that part kind of sucked. But, I understand where you were coming from." I sit up in a flash, but instantly regret it when the world blurs and my head throbs viciously —punishing me for drinking, for being a bitch. I grasp my head in my hands and Everett tries to comfort me, but I shake him off.

"I was wrong though. You aren't that same careless fuckboy that waltzed into the bar that night you saw me singing, you aren't even the same perverted ass you were a few months ago. You still have your ass-ish moments—"

"Very inspiring, truly. You should be a motivational speaker."

"Oh, shut up, will you?" I groan, but chuckle at his deadpan expression, "I mean to say that you're trying. You're trying to be better and that's all that counts and I should've asked you about it first, that's all."

He doesn't respond, eyes searching my face and I use the time do the same. His long hair is matted down on one side and sticking up on the other from sleep, his cheeks are flushed slightly, and his eyes are a lighter shade of green —like the color of flower stems. And he's shirtless, small purple love bites dancing across his hips and v-lines and all I can think about is his head tossing back, my name falling from his lips, and his hands gripping my hair.

"God, what are you doing to me?"

And he sounds so perplexed and tired and full of emotion that my head snaps up instantly. I barely see the fire in his eyes before his lips are on mine, soft and longing.

His hands cup my cheeks and mine rest against his chest as his mouth molds against mine, all the frustration and misunderstandings on our tongues as they intermingle and our teeth as they nip the flesh of our lips. It's when he moans deep in his throat that I muster the strength to pull away. Because it seems I have this serious condition where I can't think about anything else but his conversation with Marco and what it really meant.

"So, this," I pant slightly, out of breath from our excursion and gesturing between us. "This is a secret? Whatever *this* is?"

He licks his lips and nods slowly, "for now... yeah. What we have is obviously fragile and I don't want to mess it up or have everyone in our business until we're ready."

The idea of not being able to kiss him or hold his hand in public makes my stomach lurch, but then I see us sneaking into dressing rooms backstage and explorative hands under the table and flirty texts and the idea doesn't seem so bad. We've been sneaking around for a few days already and it's been exhilarating so far. What's a little while longer?

"So... what now?"

"Now..." He trails off slowly, eyes light and playful, shoving at my shoulder lightly. "You go take a shower because you really do smell."

I gasp in horror and I guess my expression is hilarious because he keels over in laughter and I bite back a smile, standing up. Everything is back to normal and the relief is overwhelming and I think we both could use a little release. He reaches for me with a grin, but I pull away, "sorry, sorry. Just takin the piss. I could come with you, if you'd like?"

And I can tell by his darkening irises and the way he shifts in his seat that he's thinking of all the possibilities of his suggestion. Too bad I'm about to shut them right down. "Sorry, Curly, I don't think so. Since I'm just *so* smelly, I wouldn't want to make you suffer any more than you have to."

I smile evilly, overly pleased with myself as I watch his shoulders fall before turning on my heel and walking towards the connected bathroom. Before I'm out of sight, I lift his shirt from my skin, sliding it off my bare body teasingly, and tossing it behind me.

It takes less than ten seconds before he's following me into the bathroom, a devilish grin on his face and glint in his eyes. "I'll plug my nose."

"Hmmm," I act as if I'm contemplating it, turning the knob on the shower, and relishing in the groan that rumbles in his chest when I bend over. "No, it seems cruel to make you stand in an enclosed space with my *disgusting self* as the water slides down my skin... the steam fogs up the room... hands lather soap all over my body..."

I trail off, watching his eyes grow darker with my every word, pants tighter, and teasing expression turning into a serious one. It takes him two strides to stand in front of me, "I lied. You smell lovely... like, like roses and uh... peaches and rain."

"Rain?" I try not to laugh at his efforts and although he's beyond desperate to get into this shower with me, he's chuckling also.

"Yes, like the smell of the first rain."

He's trying so hard and I love the playfulness between us after feeling so shitty last night that I can't help but give in. "You've just won yourself a one-way ticket into my shower. Use it wisely," I tease as I step in, still facing him. He follows with a wolfish grin on his lips and promise in his eyes.

"Oh, I plan to."

And he does.

Twice.

The first time is animalistic. It's yanking hair and scratching skin. Loud moans and growls and sounds that would terrify anyone walking by. It's heated and full of passion and so intense that it leaves me quivering in the knees after. The second time is slow. It's stroking of the face, and kissing the neck, and quiet whimpers with teasing thrusts. But, it's also fumbling around from being so tired from the first time and laughing about it. It's fun and passionate and has me biting into his neck to keep quiet, leaving my heart swollen in my chest when it's over.

And it's when we're *actually* washing ourselves that I speak again.

"Petrichor."

"What?" He turns to face me, hair piled on his head with shampoo and water droplets sliding down his tanned, tattooed chest.

"Petrichor: a pleasant smell that frequently accompanies the first rain after a long period of warm, dry weather." For the first time, I feel sheepish about my hobby, "It's what you said I smelled like, though I'm sure you were joking. Regardless, that's the word for it... that's—"

He cuts me off with a swift kiss to my forehead, "I love that about you, ya know. So, smart, so cute. 'Mm a lucky guy."

He says it nonchalantly, turning away to wash the soap out of his hair right after. But, it gives me pause. Because no one's ever said they liked my love for words before. My mom thought it was annoying, Marco teased me for being a know-it-all (even though he always got better grades), and Sam used to call me a nerd anytime I'd talk about a word I loved or define a tricky one we heard on TV.

Hell, *I* don't even like the odd habit. It brings up memories of my dad that fill me with rage and pain. But, Everett loves it and suddenly... it doesn't seem so bad.

Impulsively, I press a light kiss to his shoulder, a smile on my lips.

"What was that for?"

"Nothing," I give his arm a light squeeze before pouring conditioner in my palm, mind and heart on over-drive, with one thought in my mind.

That maybe, just *maybe*, this could work.

# PHOBIA

It's grabby hands and quick movements and hair pulling and shaky limbs and whispers of, 'fuck' and moans of 'please' and Everett is relentless. I can barely keep up with his movements in this cramped space.

"Fuck, baby, just like that. God, you feel so good," he groans out, voice husky and out of breath. I raise my hips back up, lowering them down again in a small circle, slowly. The windows have fogged up, concealing our identity, but not what we're obviously doing inside. The rocking we're creating probably doesn't help either, but all I can think about is Everett driving his hips up to meet mine and how he tastes like toothpaste and coffee.

"Why do you taste like coffee?" I breathe, though it turns into a moan when Everett's fingers glide up my body to fondle my breasts.

My fingernails scratch down his chest as I disconnect my lips from his, sitting up to continue circling my hips and lifting them up, up, up, and then down, down, down, in varying speeds. A low groan rattles Everett's chest and he slides my leather skirt up higher to bunch around my waist so he can grip my bare flesh in his hands. I lean into him, tugging on his hair with one hand and gripping the collar of his shirt with the other, the heat in my belly growing.

"Do you," he pauses to drive up into me harshly, hitting that sweet spot of mine and causing me to writhe on top of him, "really want to talk about coffee right now?"

And the way he says it —underneath the lust and urgency in his tone— makes it obvious he's hiding something. He leans up to connect our mouths, but as soon as his breath hits my nose and it's plainly the smell of coffee beans wafting around me, I shove him back down by the chest, a winning grin on my lips.

"Have you been drinking coffee?" I ask, still moving against him, but overly giddy at the prospect of this avid tea-drinker coming to the dark side. Everett rolls his eyes dramatically, chest flushed, and hairline glistening with sweat as he grunts impatiently. He tries to lean up in the reclined seat again, lips aching to touch my own, but I stop my movements altogether, slamming him back against the leather. I raise my brows, making it clear I'm not backing down.

"Imighthavestartedtodrinksomeofthestuffyouleftatmy-housepossibly," he mumbles under his breath in a rush, trying to conceal his answer. I grin with devilish delight.

"I'm sorry, what was that? I couldn't quite hear you."

"I might have started to drink some of the stuff you left at my house the last time you were over, okay?" He slowly rises again and I'm too shocked to stop him as he nibbles on my neck and shifts his hips. "Now... can we get back to shagging, please? You look way too sexy all hot and sweaty on my lap like this."

Although his words stir the beast inside me, I can't let this go just yet. "I can't believe Everett Fox, tea enthusiast, has been drinking 'jitter juice'? Where's your loyalty, mister?"

"It smelled like you, okay? The tin was sitting on my counter and it smelled like you and tasted like you, so I wanted to try it, alright?" He clears his throat awkwardly and I shut up instantly, cheeks flushed and heart full. "Now, do you really want to discuss coffee or would you rather...?"

And to finish his sentence, he slides into me fully and roughly, fingers resting at our connection and causing my whole body to quake with need, a loud moan clawing up my throat.

I suppose my teasing can wait.

He starts up a rhythm then, fast and hard and pornographic and I'm clutching at his shoulders to relieve some of the pressure. I know the tight grip he has on my ass is going to leave marks, but I don't care. His tongue is lapping at my own and he's swallowing my moans and it's hot and in the middle of a parking lot and I can feel my orgasm building rapidly.

And from the way Everett begins to thrust wildly, I can tell he's close too.

"God, baby, you're so hot... feels so fucking good." He can barely speak between his groans, but his dirty mouth drives me crazy.

We're thrusting in harmony now, even our sounds of pleasure seem to be synchronized, both of us mewling unabashedly. I lean back against the steering wheel as he ravishes my chest and my hand slams against the window. Our bodies slide together and apart with ease, like they were built for each other and I really don't think I can keep this up without combusting. Just when I think I can't take much more, his hand comes down sharply on the plump flesh of my right butt cheek, the slap echoing through his car and setting me off.

My moan is vulgar and loud as my vision goes black, sparks of light bursting behind my eyelids as I continue to ride him. He meets his own end shortly after, a load groan rattling his chest as he stills inside me. We both tremble from the massive release, fire licking up our veins and bodies raw from the excursion. We hold onto each other like we might fall apart if we let go.

I sink into him when the sparks fade, shaking slightly, and trying to catch my breath in the over-heated, fogged up car.

He tucks my hair behind my ear, smiling softly, before planting a sweet kiss onto my sweaty forehead. He helps me slide off of him, making me wince at the sudden emptiness before plopping down in the passenger seat, not quite sure how I got on the driver's side in the first place. Or on the driver.

My movements are slow and disoriented as I grab my halter

top, fitting it over my body and readjusting my skirt before pulling my discarded thong up my thighs. I watch as Everett rebuttons his shirt and buckles his belt before leaning into the seat we just defiled, a dopey grin on his flushed face. As soon as we meet the other's eyes we burst into giddy laughter, not sure how we started to have rough sex in his car, but not complaining about it either. Recently we can't go five minutes without ripping each other's clothes off.

But, it's the post-coital I prefer. The talking, the laughing, the joking around. I've learned more about Everett than I ever thought he'd share, like:

1. He's deathly afraid of getting shots, avoiding them unless it's necessary. If it is, he needs his sister to go with him to hold his hand. I try really hard not to laugh when he tells me this. I fail.

2. He once tried to take his sister's fish for a walk when he was five. He used all the savings in his piggy bank to buy her a new one the next day.

3. I'm the only person he's ever allowed to sleep in his bed. The only one he's ever wanted to stay the night.

Each one of these things has me falling harder for him. Each one has me more fucked if he breaks my heart.

"We should head inside. They might already be suspicious." I attempt to fix my hair in the mirror, but all of the pulling and yanking has made it beyond repair. When Everett doesn't respond right away, I glance over to see his hand raised in the air and I really hope it isn't for what I think it is. "Please tell me you aren't trying to high five me for having sex in your car?"

He shrugs innocently, hand still raised, "what? That was hot, we deserve a high-five!"

*I'm so screwed.*

"You're such a dork." I snort, but relent in smacking my palm against his, pointing towards his wrist. "Now hand me your hair tie so I can fix the mess you created."

He places it in my hand silently, though I can feel his eyes on me as I tug my hair back into a ponytail, hoping the band won't suspect what we've been up to for the last half hour. When his gaze on me grows too heavy, I turn towards him and the look I see there steals my breath away. It's so full of emotion that I want to look away, but so soft and loving that I can't.

"What?"

There are so many words in his eyes, but none on his lips. "nothing," he shakes his head, a fond smile tugging up his lips. "Nothing."

I drop it because the car is much too hot and smells like sex and I may end up saying something I'll regret later, "c'mon let's go."

But, I don't even put my hand on the handle before he's stopping me, "we shouldn't go in together. They'll know right away—walking in all giddy and leaking pheromones."

He has a point, I know he does, but it's this part of the agreement that makes me feel dirty and used: walking from our rendezvous point freshly fucked and alone. It makes this feel cheap and meaningless and that's the last thing it is to me.

I nod anyway, a tight-lipped smile on my face as I open the door, turning around one last time to press a quick kiss to lips before heading up to Jesse's apartment.

I'm attacked by a very irritated Scotsman as soon as I walk through the door.

"You're almost an hour late, Aspen! Everett isn't even here yet, it's ridiculous. You both really need to get it together, I can't take much more than this."

I just flip him off in response and I know I shouldn't take my frustration out on the lad, but my ass is sore and my hair is matted and I feel gross in more ways than one.

"Sod off, Aspen." Jesse storms off, though I know he'll come back in about ten minutes, all smiles and hugs because Jesse forgives easily and we take advantage of it.

"Where've you been?" Both Marco and Avery saddle up to me with parental concern on their faces, looking at the other in shock of their mirrored actions and I can't help but laugh along with Enzo.

"Don't worry, mom and dad. I promise to call next time."

This seems to embarrass both of them because Marco stalks off, mumbling under his breath and Avery smirks, going back to clean her keyboard. And because he has the best (or worst) timing, Everett slams the door open and saunters into the room like he owns the place —fresh hickies on full display. I try my best to look nonchalant as he's scolded by Jesse, playing on my phone and pretending to listen to whatever Avery is saying. But, even I can't hide the goosebumps that dot my skin when his arm brushes mine on his way to the couch.

And I also can't hide the flush of my cheeks at my incoming text.

**Curly:** *Put some ice on that beautiful bum of yours... it's got a long road ahead of it.*

Everett is rubbing at his hickeys with a stupid grin on his face when his phone begins to ring. He pulls it out of his pocket and his face instantly pales, eyes meeting mine before looking away in a flash, ignoring the call. I eye him warily, but he doesn't meet my eyes again.

* * *

The one mystery in life that still intrigues me and that I may never be able to solve is how someone can so wholly believe that they can actually sing. They could sound like a dying whale, like nails on a chalkboard, like they need to be put out of their misery and they'll still be convinced they're the next Mariah Carey.

The man on stage right now is taking "karaoke night" to a new extreme.

Gold-studded blazer, tight (much too tight) black jeans, creepers, sunglasses, and fingerless gloves for the attire. Gyrating hips, flipping non-existent hair, crotch grabbing, and pointing to random people in the audience for the moves. Justin Timberlake's, "Sexy Back" for the song of choice.

This forty something year old man is living out his wildest fantasies in the cramped stage of the crowded pub so appropriately named, "The Mid-Life Crisis."

I refrain from laughing at the man despite the fact that he hasn't hit a single note, despite the outfit, despite the moves, despite the irony of the bar's name. I don't laugh because I'm actually envious of him. Because he's up there. He's on that stage belting out a song no one should ever sing in front of a group of thirty people, mostly in their twenties, and mostly assholes.

I can't even sing in the fucking shower.

Enzo is cracking jokes about his clothes and Jesse and Marco are laughing much too loudly at them and Everett has this smirk on his face that is so condescending I want to smack it off him. Hell, even Avery has her head down, shoulders shaking as she tries to contain her amusement.

Maybe a year ago I would've been laughing along with them, but now I wish I had half his courage. Now, I just sit back in the booth with my arms crossed and beer untouched. Everett expects me to sing tonight. But, there's no way I'm going up on that stage if they're laughing at some stranger like this.

The uppity twats.

Everett must notice my sour expression because I feel a foot connect with mine, curling around my ankle. I catch his eyes to find a concerned frown on his face and an unspoken question on his lips. He rubs my leg with his lightly —his way of soothing me without the others noticing and I want to reassure him, but Enzo cracks another joke and Everett snorts.

I pull my leg away.

And when that man belts out the last note of the song horribly off-key, I'm the only one that stands up to clap for him. In the midst of boos and laughter I holler out encouragement and the smile that lights up his face at my applause is one for the books.

When I sit back down I'm faced with six confused faces. I ignore them.

"That was awfully enthusiastic. I never pegged you for a karaoke fan." Enzo throws his arm over my shoulder casually and Everett's eyes instantly fall to it.

"I'm not," I take a sip of my drink, still slightly annoyed at their attitudes. "Just a fan of people being brave enough to do that."

Enzo barks out an incredulous laugh, "you do that—" he cuts himself off suddenly, shifting uncomfortably. "You *used* to do that all the time."

The table falls silent.

Everett is still glowering at Enzo, but I can't tell if it's because he still has his arm around me or because of what he just said. The rest of the table has the decency to look busy and I desperately want everyone to stop talking about my singing.

"So, Marco, have you talked to Satan's Mistress lately?" It's an odd subject change, but it's the first thing that pops into my mind. He glowers at me, halting conversation with Jesse.

"You mean Mom?"

"As she's sometimes called."

Marco shakes his head in disapproval, but I don't miss his amused smirk. He glances around the table warily, probably wondering why I'm bringing up a subject I normally avoid. "Well, she still wants you to get in touch with her."

I snort, "please, it's just to keep up appearances. She's only called me once and texted me to call her. She doesn't care."

"Always have to play the victim, huh?" His words make my jaw drop and Everett squirms in his seat, Avery choking on her drink. The words sting, but only slightly. I don't let them settle in me. I can't or I may end up launching myself across the table to strangle him.

"Only when everyone in my life turns out to be the villain." The table falls into awkward silence and I wish I hadn't brought up my mom. I wish I wasn't such a bummer all the time. "I'm getting another drink."

"You haven't finished that one." Enzo. Again. He really needs to stop talking.

I chug the rest of it down in one go, "happy now?"

I rise from the table, Enzo's arm falling from my shoulder and Everett's eyes following me as I go. I don't know what's gotten into me tonight, but all I want to do is go home and sleep and get far, far away from that stage. I'm sure the bartender can tell because he passes me a shot on the house.

"That was some performance, huh?"

The voice behind me is instantly familiar: raspy, harsh accent, slightly cocky. I turn around immediately, "Sam."

He pulls me into a hug and even though I haven't spoken to him since I rejected him, even though he broke my heart long before that, and even though he's the cause of many of my issues today, I let him. His hair is shaggier, sweeping across his forehead and falling into his eyes and his beard has grown tremendously.

"I've missed you, Aspen," he pulls away, the smile slipping slightly. "Why haven't you returned my calls?"

Guilt twists my stomach, "It's still... hard. I'm getting used to the idea of speaking to you again, but I'm happy to see you. You look... good."

His smile is back and what a smile it is, "I'm working on it. On myself. Writing more, drinking less. I'm working on it." It seems like he wants to say more, but thinks better of it. I place my hand on his arm, genuinely pleased at the statement.

"I'm happy for you, Sam."

"Am I interrupting something?"

I snap my hand off his arm at that familiar voice, so different from Sam's: slow, raspy, calculated. *Angry.* Emerald eyes flit between the two of us and our lack of distance before landing on Sam. Sam backs away slightly and crosses his arms, "yeah, actually. You are."

Everett's eyes flare at his words and he takes a protective step towards me, obvious animosity present between the boys. You can feel it in the tension that rolls off of them — whether it's jealousy or general dislike is unclear. I have a feeling it's both.

Sam's nose crinkles in distaste, "so, you two did end up together, huh?"

The assumption has my cheeks flaring and I'm about to deny, deny, deny like Everett told me to, when I feel an arm sling around my shoulders, tugging me into Everett's side possessively, "yeah, actually. We are together."

My head instantly snaps up to look at him, but his gaze is still set on Sam in an irate glare. Hope swells in my chest at his words, only to deflate the longer I appraise the situation. The only reason he admitted it to Sam is because he's jealous. Barbaric.

He can tell Sam we're together, but doesn't want to tell our friends? Okay.

I remain silent, spinning around to grab the bartender's attention as the two have their pissing contest.

"Well, don't fuck it up, Fox." The warning surprises me enough to turn slightly, seeing Everett's staggered expression morph into a serious one.

"Not planning on it."

The slight irritation I'd been feeling all night fades as I glance between the two of them. Sam's face contorted into remorse and Everett's expression one of serious determination. Sam glances at me with a small smile and wave before stepping into the crowd, disappearing.

"I mean it, Aspen." Everett turns to me, face hard as stone, but eyes soft as the sea. "You mean too much to me. I won't — I *can't* mess this up. Just... be patient with me. Please."

He tucks a stray hair behind my ear and his words seep past my skin, settling into my bones. I have a feeling that he's sensed my frustration all night and knows how everything is weighing on me. I'm a patient person, always. I never yell at red lights or sigh at slow walkers or grumble about long lines. I wait because I have to and I never complain or kick up a fuss.

But, when it comes to Everett, I want all of him. All at once. *Always.*

However, the affection in his eyes and fond smile on his lips stops me from voicing my impatience. "I'm here, Everett. For however long you'll allow me to be. I'm here."

My words seem to strike a chord with him because his smile slips and the affection in his eyes grows into something a lot less innocent. His hand slips to my thigh from beneath the bar and he squeezes tightly, releasing a long sigh.

"*God,* Aspen. You're making this so hard. I really want to kiss you right now."

Of all the foul things Everett has whispered or moaned into my ear in the heat of passion, this one makes me blush the hardest. It's so earnest, so pained.

"Then kiss me." My breath fans across his ear and he shivers before leaning in, our faces a breath away. He seems to be debating whether or not he should cave and risk getting caught or if he should tamp down his desire. But, my lips are already aching for his and this bar is crowded and dark and I have no patience for *this.*

So, when his eyes fall to my lips, I pull the bottom one between my teeth and his reaction is immediate.

"Fuck it."

His hand cups my jaw and he pulls me into a kiss so hungry and passionate that it sends shockwaves through my system. His tongue traces my lips before dipping between them, tasting like whiskey and lust. I turn to liquid from his kiss, my body melting into a puddle as his thumb caresses my cheek. He kisses me like he's waited all night to kiss me.

Just as my hand tangles into his hair and chest presses against his, he bites down on my lip, pulling away. I'm out of breath and moderately disappointed and he laughs at my pout. "There's plenty of time for that later. You have a song to sing."

And the puddle I melted into freezes, making me solid again and filled with fear. The remnants of the kiss are forgotten. My eyes slide over to the stage; small and black, one stool and a mic on top, and a spotlight shining down, beckoning me.

Mocking me.

Just looking at it has my palms sweating and throat drying and Everett can see the fear in my eyes because he begins to caress my thigh to calm me, but I'm inconsolable. I want to try, I want to sing again, but I'm filled with panic —the stage seeming much too daunting to approach. "I'm not going up there, Everett. It's too soon."

"Just one song... In front of strangers you'll never see again."

"Everett, I can't." I rip my thigh from his touch, irritated and panicked. He holds his palms up in surrender, but he doesn't.

"It's not that big of a deal, Aspen. You used to—"

"Yes, I *used* to! I used to sing in front of crowds all the time, but I don't do that anymore for a reason." I try to stop my voice from raising, "phobia: an extreme or irrational fear of or aversion to something... It's not something I can just get over in one night. It's a big deal to *me,* Everett."

"Okay, okay," he sighs, glancing from the stage and back to me in defeat. The look has my heart stinging, "do you want to go?"

I nod my head, "we can try again later, with baby steps... I'm just, I'm not ready." He forces a smile, telling me he'll bring the car around and leaving me to say goodbye to the rest of the band. I hate myself for being this weak, for disappointing him. But, I need time. I need to ease into singing again. Not get up on a stage in a bar full of people.

The band whines about me being no fun, but no one questions it when I tell them Everett is giving me a ride home. They're much too drunk to care by now.

When I make it back outside he's waiting out front and through the tinted windows I see him talking on the phone. He's running a hand through his hair and making hand gestures that suggest he isn't happy at the person on the other line. I knock on the window and he hangs up as soon as he lays eyes on me. He looks slightly stricken as he unlocks the doors, "you ready?"

I nod and he eagerly shifts into drive with a smile, but it

seems forced. "Who was that?" He clears his throat, pausing, and the longer he takes to answer, the more worried I become.

"My mum checking up on me. Asking if I've been eating, doing my laundry. The usual."

His nervous behavior doesn't sit well in my stomach and I remember the call he received the other day that he quickly ignored. The drive is silent, Everett still fidgeting nervously in his seat from my inquiry or his conversation, I'm not sure. I want nothing more than to pry, to ask him again what exactly that call was about.

But, then I remember his plea the other night to trust him, believe in him. My stomach twists at the reminder and I bite my tongue to stop the words from coming out. I need to put Sam behind me, I need to start trusting others again. I need to believe in Everett and his feelings for me. Still, there's a voice in my mind that won't quiet down. A voice reminding me of the calls Sam used to get when he was cheating on me.

It's this voice that speaks for me, "Everett... I change my mind."

His head whips towards me, eyes wide in panic and he nearly jerks the car in his alarm, "What? Changed your mind about *what?!*"

The meaning behind his sudden panic is clear and I'm quick to place a steady palm on his arm to calm him, heart hammering my ribs. "I mean about keeping us a secret... I thought that's what I wanted, but I don't think I can handle it. I don't want to hide anymore. I like you too much for that... It's either you have all of me or none of me."

He freezes, eyes tracing the planes of my face desperately. He turns his attention back to the road, knuckles turning white against the steering wheel. His jaw works and his shoulders tense and I suddenly wish I could swallow those words back up.

The car is silent as he winds through the dark streets and I try not to jump out of the car in my embarrassment and panic. The only sounds are my raging heart and heavy breaths.

Just when I'm about to lose all hope, his car swerves into my lot and jerks into park. I swallow harshly as he turns to face me, jaw set and eyes dark. In a flash, his palms are gripping my face, slamming his lips onto mine with such fervor and passion I feel as if I may pass out. It's desperate and terrifying and when he pulls away I'm gasping for breath. He lays his forehead on mine, eyes pleading with me, and holding on like I might flee if he lets go.

"I'm yours, Aspen. I've been yours since that first day you told me off, the first time I heard you recite a definition, the first time we kissed. Honestly, I was yours the first time I heard you sing all those years ago. If you want to go public, then we'll go public. I'll tell Marco and the band, I'll change my Facebook status, I'll shout it from the rooftops if that's what it takes. So, please, Aspen... are you mine?"

I've never been surer of anything. I sold my soul to him long ago.

"I'm all yours, Everett."

# ECSTASY

Sleeping with Everett is like drinking saltwater —it doesn't matter how often we find ourselves tangled in sheets together— nothing can slake my thirst.

His hands are everywhere: unzipping my dress, kneading the flesh of my bum, teasing my nipples, caressing the fabric of my underwear. Relentless, hungry, and anything but gentle.

Every touch short circuits the nerves in my body.

His lips are sure to follow his fingers on their voyage around my body and it's with trembling hands and blurred vision that I manage to unbutton his shirt, sliding it off his shoulders, before dropping his jeans to the floor. We stumble down the hallway leading to his bedroom, leaving a trail of breadcrumbs in the form of clothes along the way.

I'm not exactly sure what set us off, but as soon as the elevator doors closed, his hands were on me like they'd been waiting all night to touch me. I'm sure it has something to do with the fact that we've committed to each other. That we know where we stand. That we're official.

Every breath feels like were saying *I'm yours, I'm yours, I'm yours*.

By the time we stumble into his room we're both completely naked and unable to break eye-contact. Unable to stop touching each other. His fingers move deftly from my breasts, teasing my nipples there, and down to the area of my body that craves him the most. He traces one finger down my slit, causing me to mewl and buck slightly. However, just as I reach out to kiss Everett, he pulls away, flopping onto the mattress and scooting towards the headboard. I stand at the end of the bed, brows furrowed in confusion and cheeks warming as his eyes trace every inch of exposed flesh.

"Sit on my face."

I almost choke, "sit —*what?*"

A devilish smirk curls at the ends of his lips as he drinks in my body greedily. "I want you," his tone is confident and husky as he leans forward enough to grab my hand, "to sit on my face."

I'm sure that my soul leaves my body in that moment, mouth agape in shock and hair rising on the back of my neck from the image that flits across my brain. He tugs me forward until we fall back on the bed, my legs straddling his waist. I'm completely flustered, my face heated to an embarrassing degree as I try to think of something, anything, to say. He must notice my hesitation because his hands massage my thighs and a reassuring smile takes up his lips.

"Don't be shy, doll. I just want to taste you."

With flaming cheeks and thrumming heart, I slide up his chest slowly and watch as Everett tracks my every move, eyes darkening. I stop just short of the doves on his collarbones and Everett nods in reassurance. I can't help but worry that this night might end with a call to the police explaining that I suffocated my boyfriend by sitting on his face. But, when Everett nibbles on my thigh enticingly, I know it's a risk I am willing to take.

With great hesitance, I bring my knees on either side of Everett's head, still raised above him. His tongue slides out to moisten his lips as his emerald eyes, darkened by a lust I haven't seen before, glint hungrily. When Everett realizes that I'm essentially frozen in place above him, he tilts his head in order to nibble on the flesh of my inner thigh, sucking there gently before pulling away to blow on the sensitive skin. I shiver from the sensation, my knees almost giving out and Everett turns to blow on my hot sex, making me whine desperately.

I buck down onto him with a gasp and Everett chuckles deeply, sliding his tongue out to lap one long stripe up my slit.

"Oh," the syllable is stretched out and shaky and I instantly grip onto the headboard to keep my balance.

It's so dirty, so primal, so *needy.* And Everett shows no mercy.

He's relentless as his tongue teases my entrance before dipping inside and exploring, climbing back up to circle my hyper-sensitive bundle of nerves and causing my trembling thighs to collapse beneath me. I try desperately not to buck my hips, but when his sinful mouth encloses around my clit and begins to suck, my hips involuntarily grind into him.

"Shit, sorry," I breathe, using the headboard to pull myself back up, only to have his arm shoot up to stop me. I glance down at him through blurred vision and swear I almost finish right there and then. Because he drags his eyes up my body slowly, a hazy arousal clouding almost blackened irises. His lips are trained onto my sex dedicatedly, and he meets my gaze, the stare so intense and hungry that I might faint. That look is all the communication I need.

He wants me to not only sit on his face, but to ride it.

"Jesus, Everett," I moan when his tongue flicks my bundle of nerves, my hips moving unabashedly against his face. One hand remains planted on the headboard for leverage as I use the other to lean back, trying to splay it against the mattress behind me, only for another warm arm to stop me. I glance backward in confusion only to see Everett's arm that is trapped underneath me tensing and relaxing as his hand jerks his pulsing cock.

The sight alone has my orgasm coiling inside me like a spring and I can't stop the moans that fall from my lips at the sight of him touching himself, the way his tongue attentively laps me up. Curses fall from my mouth desperately when he hums against my flesh, causing me to keen against him, a low rumble of pleasure sounding from Everett's throat. My hands go back to the headboard, knuckles turning white from my grip. My eyes fall down to Everett, his arm still moving beneath me to jerk himself off as he watches me with those darkened hungry eyes. The stare is so intense and hot and he groans against my sex, tongue warm and eager, and I just lose it.

Like flicking a lighter into kerosene, my whole body is aflame.

A breathy moan falls from my lips as I toss my head back, thighs quivering on either side of his head as my orgasm rips through me, so powerful I'm sure I actually black out for a few seconds. Everett brings one hand up to massage my hip through it, his lips lapping me up entirely before pressing gentle kisses to my thighs. By the time my legs have stopped shaking and I can somewhat catch my breath, I collapse to the side of his body in exhaustion.

"Thank... you."

I crack my eyes open to catch the proud glint in Everett's gaze and his glistening mouth and chin. With a sheepish smile, I reach over to wipe the excess from his face, only for him to catch my fingers, dip them into his mouth, and suck them clean. I bite my lip, cheeks burning as his tongue curls around my fingers to lap up every drop. I can't help but laugh breathlessly at how ridiculous we are. Like two sexed-up teenagers.

"Liked that, did you?" His voice is gravelly and dark, cocky smirk carving dimples into his cheeks.

"Maybe."

He tries to look offended, but fails. "Well, judging by how loud you were, I'm going to go with '*Oh God, Everett, yes!*'"

I can't help but laugh as he mocks me, voice high pitched and head thrown back in mock ecstasy. He's right, of course. I mean, I'm pretty sure I just took a trip to heaven, but I'm not about to admit that. His ego can already barely fit in this room.

"I could've faked it."

He narrows his eyes playfully, lunging at me and tickling my ribs, a goofy grin on his lips at my squeals of laughter. I shove his arms to his sides to stop him, climbing up to straddle him once more, trapping his arms underneath me and laughing breathlessly. Coincidentally, I feel him between my legs—still hard, still ready. Everett seems to realize this at the same time I do because his goofy grin is replaced by a wolfish one. "Well, maybe it's time we test that theory once and for all."

And so we do.

I grip him in my hands and sink onto him with a patience I didn't know I had, filling me up achingly slow. Everett groans as soon as I've taken him fully, stretching me and warming me. I still, adjusting slightly, before I swivel my hips and rise slowly before sinking back down again. I set a pace that teases, makes him ache for more. Slowly, he begins to raise his hips up to meet my thrusts, our skin slapping methodically. I close my eyes and let my head fall back to focus on the feeling of him.

"I love to watch you like this... falling apart because of me," he breathes, hands sliding down to circle my clit, sucking in a harsh breath when I change angles. "You're so beautiful."

I moan a garbled version of his name, placing my palms against his chest for better leverage. He plants his feet on the bed and brings his knees up, causing me to fall onto his chest and surrender full control to Everett, allowing him to thrust up into me deeper than ever before.

"Fuck, Everett."

His hands wrap around my backside, kneading the flesh in his palm and using it as the leverage he needs to reach a place inside of me I didn't even know existed. He's relentless and unforgiving and our bodies slide against each other: sweaty, flushed, hot, and needy. The moans that fall past my lips are uncontrollable and Everett is almost as loud as me. I place one hand on the side of his head and use the other to tangle into his hair, bringing his lips to mine.

A guttural moan claws up his throat when I delve my tongue into his mouth, his palm coming down hard and swift on my ass. The shock of it travels all the way up my spine and makes me keen against him, gasping in the pleasure and pain. I feel him smirk into my mouth as I tug on his damp hair.

"I knew you'd like getting spanked, naughty girl. So dirty," he grunts, biting down on the pulse of my neck as he drives into me sharply.

Those filthy words make my toes curl and the coil inside of me tighten. "Oh god, I'm gonna come."

Then, suddenly, his thrusts slow and his mouth stops moving against mine. "No. you're not. Not yet."

I'm shocked by his refusal and that he suddenly slows his thrusts, the movement tortuous. I swivel my hips in a silent plea, but Everett slides his hands away from my bum to still them. His lips meet mine again, though we don't kiss —they just rest against each other as our bodies move. He continues to drive up into me deep and slow and the pace is maddening. I feel as if I've been put on pause, standing on a cliff and staring over the edge at my orgasm, but unable to jump. It's both incredibly pleasurable *and* painful. I tremble above him, head cloudy and breaths labored.

I bite down onto his shoulder and Everett curses, hips bucking suddenly and sharply. Moaning, I yank onto his hair, silently pleading with him to continue that movement. "Please, Everett," I rub my breasts against his chest and he hisses through his teeth. "Please, *please*, Everett."

My begging seems to please him greatly because he shoots me a wolfish grin, dipping his tongue into my mouth, and quickening his pace. "Good girl," I can feel him beginning to tense beneath me. "Come with me."

For the second time that night, I come ferociously, shouting Everett's name. The veins pop out in his neck as his body strains against mine, cock pulsating inside me. The orgasm rocks through me like an earthquake and I cling to Everett for balance as my legs quiver and skin prickles. We groan into each other's mouth as we still, the orgasms rocking through our bodies and short-circuiting our nerves.

Ecstasy: a feeling of great happiness and pleasure, often sexual pleasure.

When we come down from our highs, Everett wraps his arms around my limp body, turning us to the side so we're facing each other. He presses a quick kiss to my forehead, eyes slightly dazed, and a dopey grin on his lips.

"I... I think I just saw the Eighth Wonder" He whispers in awe and I can't stop the flush that rises to my cheeks or the giggles falling past my lips.

"Shut up, you big dork."

I slap him lightly on the chest, only causing his grin to grow, but the film of arousal fades from his eyes as he focuses on my face. They trace every feature of mine before landing on my own tired eyes and lingering there. His cheeks are flushed and lips stained pink and my heart thuds dully in my chest. We don't say anything more, just lay in each other's embrace in comfortable silence.

"I'm beginning to get addicted to you, I think."

I don't say anything because I can't. Because the words die in my throat —too frightened to really say what I feel, to admit to myself and him that I couldn't agree more. That if he ever leaves me, the withdrawals would be so intense I wouldn't be able to recover.

His eyes bore into mine, though he remains silent. The lust in them has faded to affection, thumb reaching out to trace my lips before sliding to caress my cheek gently, a stark contrast to his aggression mere minutes ago.

It's in the comfortable silence a few minutes later that Everett speaks again, his voice slightly shaky in the dark, but his words sure.

"I love you, Aspen."

# INEFFABLE

I can count on one hand the number of people who've ever told me they loved me.

That list includes: my dad (left me) and Sam (destroyed me and *then* left).

So, when those three beautiful words slip from Everett's lips, a dull shock runs through my body, followed by a crippling fear that can only stem from abandonment. The only sound in the room is our shallow breaths and even those seem much too loud. The longer I'm silent —frozen in a petrified, shocked state— the wearier Everett grows. His palm has gone still against my cheek, though I'm sure I can feel it shaking.

"W-What?" The word comes out unsteady and it's the only one I can muster as those eight letters settle deep down into my bones.

Everett gulps nervously, though a glint of determination flashes in his murky iris'. He sits up in bed, the sheet falling to his waist, but I remain lying on my side, staring up at him.

"I'm in love with you, Aspen. I think I have been for a long time. Maybe since the first night I saw you sing all those years ago. Maybe when I kissed you in that bathroom and you told me off. Maybe when I told you I was falling for you I'd already fell. You were so brazen and no-nonsense and intelligent and caring and so *fucking* beautiful. I found myself wanting to see you, to hear your voice every second of every day. And I don't know much, but I do know that I'm so in love with you it's almost excruciating and I don't want to deny it anymore. I love you, but it's more than that. I can't even... I don't even know how to express how you make me feel it's, it's..."

"Ineffable: too great or extreme to be expressed or described in words."

It's the first time I've spoken since he started his speech and I'm shocked to even hear my own voice —the words just slipping out on impulse. Everett seems shocked as well, like he almost forgot I was here. Then, his dimples dig in his cheeks and a grin so boyish lights up his face I'm sure my heart stops working.

"God, *see,* it's shit like that that makes it so hard not to love you. You're just... I don't know what I did to deserve you... no, I don't even deserve you, but you choose to be with me anyway and I love you more for it. You're... you're just *it* for me, Aspen."

My heart swells in my chest and I feel *full.* My head and my heart are full for the first time in a long time and although I can feel the fear of being hurt settle into my heart, it's overpowered by my affection for this rambling mess.

It's only when he falls silent that I feel the dampness on my pillow. That I realize I'm crying and once I do, I can't stop.

"Shit, are you... are you crying?" His face pales and jaw drops, "please don't cry. Please. You don't have to say it back, I don't —"

"Everett."

"I didn't say it so that you would say it back, I said it so that you knew because it was eating away at me and—"

"Everett."

"Just please stop crying. I won't—"

"Everett!"

Finally, *finally* he stops rambling and looks down at me with wild eyes and flushed cheeks, brows furrowed in concern. "What? What is it?"

"I love you."

His thumbs that were furiously wiping away my tears freeze on my cheeks and his eyes grow wide. His mouth opens and closes like a gaping fish and I'm sure he doesn't hear me so, with a growing smile, I whisper it again. "I love you, Everett."

And ever so slowly, a grin so large that it must hurt, curls up his lips. I'm sure his dimples must be permanently embedded there, cheeks pink and eyes glistening. "You do?"

"I do. Of course, I do. How... how can I *not* love you?"

He leans in and plants those petal-soft lips over every inch of my face. I giggle quietly when he gently kisses my eyelids, lips barely grazing there before forming back into a smile. "Say it again," he mumbles against my lips, pecking me again and again and again.

"I love you," I laugh as he trails his lips down my neck.

"Again."

"I love you," I gasp when he sucks on my collarbone. I latch my fingers onto his broad shoulders as his tongue traces my flesh, still giddy from the profession and even giddier when he slides himself between my legs.

I say it ten more times while his fingers dance across my skin, brushing against my breasts, and teasing where I need him the most. It's on the eleventh time those words slip past my lips in a moan when he slips inside of me.

Every kiss sears an 'I love you' onto my lips, the skin that connects my neck to my shoulder, the swell of my breast. Every moan and sigh and plea for more is another 'I love you' whispered into my ear. Every slow, deep thrust inside me is Everett assuring me of his love.

Every move, every touch, every kiss is an 'I love you.'

It's slow and deep and fills me with an ache only Everett can sate. Our moans are long and drawn out and he doesn't relent even when I beg him to, only pushing into me harder, pulling away slower. His eyes never leave mine once we both reach our highs—usually clouded by lust, but this time so clear I can almost see right through them. I see the love in them and any previous doubts I had fall away.

He fills me, hands holding my hips and lips hovering above mine. I take all of him, back arched and whispers of 'I love you' moaned into each other's mouths.

* * *

"So, how do you know so many words? Did you memorize the dictionary?"

We moved from Everett's bedroom to the bathtub, playing in the suds and feeling each other up. The relaxation I felt upon entering the bath is quickly replaced by tension once Everett utters the question I expected, but didn't prepare for. I distract myself by scooping more bubbles towards me, coating my body with them and also acting as some kind of barrier between him and I as I gather my thoughts. I can feel those emerald eyes boring into my cheek, though I don't meet his gaze.

"My dad," I trail off, noticing Everett freeze as he reaches for the wine bottle we brought with us. "My dad was an English Literature professor at the university we lived near and had a deep love for language. He'd come home every day with a new word he learned... My mother was never really interested in his passion or anything he had to say really, and Marco was a momma's boy. He worshipped the ground she walked on, so if she wasn't interested, then neither was he. So, all dad had was me... Every day he would tell me a new word and its definition. If, by the end of the week, I used all the words in sentences, then he would take me out for ice cream that Sunday."

"Let me guess," Everett cuts in, eyes alight with amusement and smile soft, "you always got ice cream, didn't you?"

Even though there are bees stinging inside my chest, I manage a smile. "Let's just say, I was a chubby ten-year-old."

Laughter rattles our chests, but it dies quickly because we both know this story doesn't have a happy ending. "He was my best friend... Mom dragged Marco along to all of her book clubs and dinners and brunches and my dad took me to guitar lessons and ice cream parlors and Shakespeare in the park. We were a team, him and I. Inseparable."

My eyes fall from his, though I can feel him watching me as I dip my fingers in the bubbles to aimlessly draw shapes and figures. My hand only stills when I feel a calloused one slide up my leg to caress my knee.

"What happened?" His voice is timid and unsure, knowing he's treading on the very thin ice of my heart.

Like a bum knee that still aches before it rains, this wound on my heart still manages to sting. "He was having an affair with his assistant and up and left us for her one morning when I was thirteen. All he left was a measly note on my bedside table with one last word on it."

"What was the word?"

A wry smile curls up my lips as I remember opening that note and my heart falling to the pit of my stomach at that one sentence, "sorry."

Everett's face crinkles in sympathy, but I look away.

"He tried to contact Marco and I a few times, but I was so angry, I always hung up as soon as I heard his voice... It only took him a few months to stop trying and move on with his new family."

It hurts to talk about, though I don't let it show. Don't talk about what happened after he left —how I was left alone while my mom consoled Marco, while she carried on being his rock and left me anchorless.

How I was abandoned all over again.

Everett is silent for a while, though I can almost hear the gears in his head turning, "you don't want to get in touch with him now?"

"I don't want someone that doesn't want me." I hope that he'll leave it at that, hope I've said enough about the matter, but I don't get my wish.

"But, he did want you.... that's why he still tried to get into touch. Maybe now—"

"Everett!" I cut him off abruptly, my chest pinching at the old trauma. "I won't be contacting my father. He left me and that's all I need to know."

Everett bites his lip, eyes falling to the murky water around us as he contemplates whether he should continue to push the subject. With slumped shoulders and a defeated sigh, he meets my eyes again, soft and sad, "you deserve so much better than what has been handed to you. Don't forget that."

I have to drop his gaze because a lump forms in my throat and his words settle under my skin and it physically pains me how much I love him and how scared I am that something will tear us apart. That I'll be alone. Again.

"What about your family, Everett? You don't talk much about them."

He sinks lower into the bubbles, pulling the suds towards him to make a beard on his chin. I laugh heartily and he grins, pleased at my amusement. Shrugging, he blows bubbles towards me and I fling them away. "Not much to say, actually. My parents divorced before I hit puberty, but it was amicable. I get along with my dad fine, though I don't see him very much. My mum... well, I've disappointed her a lot in the past, but she still supports me. More than I deserve, probably."

I rub my foot against his calf when I hear the sad lilt to his voice. "I'm sure that's not true. A mother's love is unconditional... supposedly." He grins at that, relaxing against the bath, and we enjoy the warm water and each other's company. Everett passes me the pink moscato, bicep flexing, and I notice —not for the first time— a jagged, pink scar slashed over an undecipherable tattoo there. I've never asked about it before, but I've noticed him rubbing at it absentmindedly every now and then. Sometimes, I'll even catch him staring down at it, the dark look in his eyes frightening.

My palms begin to sweat and heart pounds in my chest and I'm dying to know, but can't bring myself to ask about it directly. "I shared mine, but you've been cryptic. Any dirty laundry in your past I should know about?"

Everett freezes, skin paling and eyes widening slightly as he searches my expression in distressed confusion. His reaction alarms me slightly and my gut twists with foreboding, skin growing cold. My mind flashes with the memories of his mysterious phone calls and I briefly wonder if his reaction has something do with them or the scar on his arm or something more sinister.

*What could he possibly be hiding that could conjure that kind of reaction?*

Before I can further contemplate this thought and his panicked reaction to my innocent question, he regains his composure. "Besides a few adolescent mistakes, I'm as boring as they come." But, his eyes are like a tinted window; he can see out, but I can't see in.

And when he's quick to change the subject by slipping his hand underneath the water and sliding it up my leg, I try to shake off my suspicion. Try not to let the quicksand suffocate me, try to trust him like he asked. But, I still can't help but worry that my worst fears may come to fruition.

Can't help but worry that this might be the calm before the storm.

# ACQUIESCENT

Marco and I haven't always been the closest of siblings. He was haughty, distant, and competitive for the better half of our lives. Always trying —and succeeding— to one up me. So, he couldn't be bothered to threaten bullies or play dolls or give advice. That's how mom raised him.

But, then our dad left.

Whether it was sympathy or a change of heart, he started to treat me more like a sister and less like an intruder in his home. He brought me ice cream when I was sad and indulged my fascination with definitions. He beat up boys that broke my heart, covered for me when I was out too late, apologized on my mom's behalf... He was the protective brother I'd always wanted.

But, now that wish is coming back to bite me in the ass.

"What the *fuck* did you just say?"

The table jostles slightly as Marco shoots out of his seat, jaw clenched and fists curled as he faces Everett with a snarl. Everett's words were very clear and strong —still echoing around the room— and Marco heard him just fine. Everett gulps nervously at Marco's reaction and I make a statement by clasping my hand around his own, four pairs of eyes snapping to the movement.

"Aspen and I... we're dating."

Marco lets out a bark of humorless laughter, "I'm sure I heard you wrong."

I can tell Everett is getting agitated by how tightly he clenches his jaw. "Aspen is my girlfriend and I'm her boyfriend... that's what *dating* means." It's the first time he's called me his girlfriend and my stomach does this weird somersault thing and my heart is singing and I really, *really* love him.

Marco doesn't feel the same way.

Everett's condescending tone sets him off and he's quick to jump forward, rounding the couch, and lunging towards him. Jesse jumps up to stop the brewing fight, but I'm faster in stepping between the two boys. I place both palms on Marco's broad chest, but his fiery gaze is set on his friend. I could understand if he felt slightly protective and maybe even peeved that we kept it from him, but *this*? This is too much.

"Marco, what the *hell* is your problem?"

He doesn't hesitate, "Everett is my problem."

Everett's chest rises and falls rapidly with every shallow breath and the other bandmates watch the confrontation nervously, but I'm too busy holding Marco back to reassure them. "Why are you being like this? I can take care of myself."

"Oh, it's not you I'm worried about. Right, Everett?"

And maybe it's paranoia or the double meaning clear in his phrase, but I feel like there's more to this story than they're letting on. Everett tenses behind me and it's like I can practically feel the rage rolling off both of them. Looking back at Everett, my heart freezes at the wide-eyed panic that has become way too familiar on his face.

And it suddenly feels like I'm missing a vital component to this particular anger.

Everett gently moves me out of the line of fire, grabbing onto Marco's shoulder, though he quickly shrugs it off. "Let me talk to him, Aspen."

He doesn't even wait for my answer before he's kissing my forehead and leading the way down the hall with a very reluctant brother of mine. I watch them enter Jesse's room with an uneasy feeling in my stomach, running a hand down my face and letting out an exhausted sigh.

"Why is no one else surprised by this?"

I nearly jump out of my skin from Jesse's surprised and slightly frantic voice, turning around to find his eyes as wide as his grin. Enzo is leaning on his elbows, eyes set to the floor, and Avery is reclined into the couch with a bored look on her face. She leans forward at Jesse's question, voice monotonously faux surprised, "oh my god, I had no idea. This is so surprising."

I laugh at her terrible acting and she shoots me a wicked grin. A warmth creeps up my neck when I glance over to Enzo and see his head up and eyes on me, looking like he swallowed a sour lemon. Bitter and disappointed. "I can't believe *you* of all people fell for his tricks."

"Excuse me?" My veins turn to ice at his words, though my cheeks flush with anger, "I didn't fall for anything, Enzo."

He scoffs, shaking his head in displeasure, "well, you fell for him and God knows how he made that happen... he's playing you."

"Enzo!" Avery hisses, slapping his arm and glaring at him, but it's too late.

Normally, I'd brush off his words, maybe laugh or call him an idiot and declare that Everett wouldn't hurt me. But, I'm paranoid and suspicious and his words strike a chord. "Why do you think that?"

"*What?* That wanker is infamous for sleeping around and treating women like garbage! And what about Marisol? Wasn't he messing around with both of you at the same time? Going from Sam to *Everett?* Not the smartest decision."

"Everett is *nothing* like Sam." My eyes sting and voice wavers because Enzo just voiced my worst fears, but I know they're not true. They can't be. "He's not that person anymore."

Enzo opens his mouth to reply, but a door slams in the distance and Everett barrels down the hallway towards us. Except, it's not the sudden noise that makes my heart skip a beat. "Oh my god, Everett! Are you all right? What the hell happened?"

His posture is tense and head is down, but that doesn't mean I can't see the dark red blood trailing from his nostril, onto his lips. His nose is already starting to swell and I can almost see a bruise forming. My blood boils and mortification heats my cheeks at how poorly my brother is acting. "I'm gonna kill him," I mutter angrily just as Everett grabs for my elbow, "Marco!"

He tugs my arm, emerald gaze stormy and face grim, "C'mon, leave him. Let's just go."

"No, I'm not fucking going! If anyone should leave it's him... Marco!"

But, Marco still hasn't made a reappearance and Everett cups my face in his palm, his stern frown replaced with a soft smile. "Calm down, Cujo," he laughs, but his expression quickly turns somber, "can we just go? Please?"

And maybe it's because his voice cracks slightly or because I'm practically shaking with rage or because I really need to treat his wound, but I find myself nodding and muttering a quick goodbye to our friends.

This is not how I expected today to go. I expected confusion and maybe a bit of anger from Marco, but not him punching my boyfriend in the face and Enzo accusing him of playing me. Yesterday, Everett and I spent all day lying in bed and watching movies and talking about life and messing around. It was peaceful and light and fun.

Now, that bliss is gone.

I'm silent as we walk down the hallway, but I can feel Everett behind me, antsy and nervous. He's shaking slightly and refuses to let go of my hand and I really need to know what the hell went down. It's when the elevator doors begin to close that I pull Everett towards me, unwrapping my scarf from around my neck and using it to dab just under his nose where the blood has dried.

I have twelve floors to rant. And I'm going to make full use of them.

Everett winces from my touch, eyes sad, but he doesn't pull away. He just watches me as I clean his wound and keep myself from screaming. "What is Marco's problem? Why the hell did he punch you? Talk about overreacting! Did you say something to make him hit you? This is going to swell so much... I just don't—"

But, my angry ramblings are cut off when Everett gently wraps his hand around my wrist, pulling it down to stop my movements. I glance up to find his eyes set on my face, sadder than I've ever seen them and filled with a kind of fear that confuses me. My heart lurches and I want to ask him what's wrong, but his heavy breathing and the dull elevator music keep me silent. He eases me backwards until I hit the wall of the elevator and his forehead comes to rest against mine, "It's worth it. As long as I have you."

I swear my knees almost give out.

Everett wraps my face in his trembling palms, but all I can do is bunch his shirt at the waist, my heart hammering and mind reeling. "Don't leave me." His voice is gravelly and low and the way his voice cracks makes my heart ache. His eyes squeeze shut and I try to move so I can face him fully, but his grip is a vice.

"What... Everett? What are you—"

"Just, please," there's a quiet desperation in his gaze, this voice. "Please promise you won't leave. No matter what happens, you'll stay with me.... You won't leave me."

And his eyes are tracing every inch of my face like he's memorizing it; like he never wants to forget any detail. I'm trying not to whimper at his words because he doesn't sound like he's asking me to stay, asking me to never leave.

He sounds like I've already left.

"Aspen," his voice grows more frantic the longer I'm silent, thumbs tracing my cheeks. "Aspen, please. You can't leave me, you can't. I don't want to live without you... I love you."

He's ruined me.

"Shh, shh," I coo, trying to calm him, maneuvering around his arms to pat down his hair and lightly kiss his lips despite the dried blood there. "I'm right here, okay? I'm right here, Everett. I'm not going anywhere."

His shoulders slump with relief and I can see the storm in his eyes beginning to clear. "No matter what?"

My chest clenches and I know I shouldn't, but comforting this broken boy has taken precedent over my paranoia. The way he's acting now... I know that something much deeper is going on, that this isn't just about me. I know I need to ask about his strange behavior, have to find out if he is keeping something from me. But, staring into his desperate eyes and hearing his longing plea, I know that'll have to wait. Even if the lie is thick on my tongue and the promise makes my stomach churn, I know I would do anything for him.

Acquiescent: accept something without protest, or to do or say what someone else wants.

"No matter what."

# DISINGENUOUS

Everything is calm.

It's almost *too* calm. The last few days since Everett and I told the others about our relationship we've been in a state of bliss: holding hands in public and giving each other light pecks and not caring that anyone can see. Since the dust settled, everyone's been relatively supportive apart from Enzo and Marco —who still hasn't spoken to me.

Still, It's almost as if we're in a bubble. A bubble of peace and love and trust, but I'm afraid of this bubble's inevitable burst. Nothing can stay perfect for long and I'm suspicious that this bubble may be made of lies that will tear us apart. Yet... the last few days have been calm and I've never been happier. And maybe that's why I'm scared, because everything good in my life eventually turns sour and all I can do is wait for the doom and hope that I'm wrong.

That's why Marco's sudden, unannounced appearance at my flat doesn't faze me.

"To what do I owe this displeasure?" My burly brother shoves past me, only stopping to pet Yoda before rounding on me. My distaste for him at the moment only rises when I notice that he's uninjured and Everett is still trying to heal his nose that is slightly swollen, very purple, and a little crooked. "Sure, come in, Marco. Why don't you have a seat? Eat my food? Hit my boyfriend some more?"

He makes a disgusted face, "Is that wanker here?"

"No, he's not. If he was, trust me, you'd know." He nods in approval and paces back and forth against my hardwood, Yoda following his every move and yelping when he's repeatedly ignored.

Marco's phone lets out a shrill ring, but he's quick to silence it and stuff it back into his pocket. Noticing my curious stare, he answers my unspoken question, "that was mom."

"Wow, momma's boy is ignoring her calls... I'm *shocked*."

Marco only shakes his head at me, chewing on his lip, and continuing to pace the floor. This action only twists the knife in my stomach deeper because Marco never, *ever* ignores her calls. He might miss them when he's at dinner or his phone died. But, to actually decline her call? This must be bad.

When I fear he'll burn a path into the floor, I press my hand against the sleeve of his sweater, "Marco, what is going on with you?"

His reply is instantaneous, "you need to break up with Everett."

I pull away as if he scalded me, knowing this is why he came, but hoping for another reason. "Can you enlighten me please? Maybe tell me why you're so against us being together?"

And just like I thought he would, his gaze falls to the floor and he becomes uncomfortably quiet. I groan exasperatedly, running a hand down my face and trying not to throw something at him. He and Everett are one in the same really; always evading my questions and expecting me to do what they ask.

"I love him, Marco." He freezes in place, face paling, and expression so horrified you would've thought I told him I murdered a village of puppies.

"You... you *what*?"

"I love him."

He shakes his head furiously, "no. No, you can't." He strides toward me, gripping my shoulders tightly, coffee eyes scanning my face. "Please tell me you're lying. Tell me you're not... in love with him."

The desperate words strike fear in my heart and I can

feel myself being dragged deeper into the sea of doubt. This is different than simply disapproving Everett because of his past, this is something much deeper. I cling onto his forearms, my body beginning to thrum with dread.

"You would tell me, Marco," I choke on my words, fingernails digging into his flesh, "you would tell me if there was something going on, right? If there was something I needed to know, you would tell me?"

And I can almost see it: the exact moment Marco's resolve cracks. His shoulders droop and eyes fall and I know my trust, my desperate plea has broken him. When his eyes meet mine again, they're filled with remorse and it makes my stomach fill with trepidation, "Aspen, I—"

But, we're interrupted by a knock on the door and I feel my chance slipping away as Marco steps back, face stony. He's already built up that wall again, glaring at the door as if wishing he could burn a hole into it.

"That's him, isn't it?" He doesn't even wait for my reply before he's heading towards the door, "I should go. Just... be careful, okay?" I latch onto his arm in a pathetic attempt to stop him, but he's much stronger than I am and just drags me along as he wrenches open the door.

The grin that was on Everett's face falls instantly at the sight of my brother and I only let go of his arm to watch the standoff between the two boys. The boys that mean so much to me, that I love in entirely different ways, but seem to be hiding something perilous from me. Marco squares up to Everett with a threat in his eyes and Everett's gaze is full of desperation. I don't know which one is worse.

"Marco."

"Everett."

Marco lets out a harsh huff and pushes past Everett, knocking into his shoulder aggressively and continuing down the hall without another word. Everett clears his throat, pushing his hair back and taking a calming breath. "What was Marco here for?"

And the question would have seemed innocent under any other circumstances, but considering what Marco just said — and didn't say— it's anything, but innocent. "Nothing much, just asking me to break up with you."

Everett whips around, eyes blazing, "he *what?*"

I eye him suspiciously, looking for any trace of panic or shame, but find none. I battle with my desire to know what's going on and my fear that he will be hurt again if I don't trust him. I test the waters, "any idea why he wants us to break up so badly?"

He clears his throat, bending to accommodate Yoda's jumping and yelping for attention. He focuses on him, not meeting my eyes, "I'm sure there are a few reasons... I don't have the best track record, do I?"

"That's true," I sigh and he sounds so confident I want to believe that's all it is. "He seemed pretty angry for it just to be that, though."

Everett's hands freeze on Yoda's tan fur for a split second, before he stands up with a cheeky grin. "Aww, big brother wants to protect his sissy."

I roll my eyes at his teasing tone, shoving him playfully in the chest. Of course, his explanation doesn't justify their sketchy behavior, but I choose to believe him. Maybe I was reading too much into Marco's reaction. I don't want to let my fears, my trauma from past relationships, get in the way of something so good. Everett asked me to trust him and I am. If there was something more going on, he would tell me. I'm sure of it.

At least, I think I am.

"Well, I have an idea," he holds up a brown paper bag as if I'm supposed to know what that means and grins at me like he knows something I don't.

"Those don't come along very often."

"Ha ha, very funny," he deadpans, walking to the coffee table and setting the bag down on it. "We're behind in our quest to overcome your fears."

The knot in my stomach grows tighter.

"And whatever's in there is supposed to help?"

"Well, the karaoke bar might have been pushing you in the deep end. Wading in the kiddie pool might be safest for now." I stand off to the side with Yoda as Everett begins pulling out clear plastic casings with dvds in them from the bag. I'm confused for only a split second before I read the titles on the spines of the casings. Then, my blood runs cold.

"Everett, no."

He pauses his movements to glance up at me, a reassuring smile on his lips. He saddles up next to me, one hand cupping my cheek and the other tucking a strand of hair that fell from my bun behind my ear. "Don't be scared. I think seeing these tapes will help bring you back to a time where singing was your true love. They'll make you realize how hypnotizing you were on stage, I guarantee it."

His soft, comforting voice pulls at my heartstrings and though I can feel the anxiety weighing down on me, I nod my head in consent.

I lean up on my tip-toes to place a chaste kiss on his lips, but my nose accidentally bumps into his. He pulls away hissing, face crumpled in pain as he brings a hand up to his nose. "Oh, sorry! I forgot," I laugh as Everett releases the swollen flesh, a soft smile on his face despite the pain. He runs his thumb along my bottom lip, his lips following suit.

They capture mine in a sweet and achingly long kiss that makes my knees weak. I'm careful not to bump into his nose as I tilt my head, tongue dipping out to trace the plump flesh of his lips and hands bunching the soft sweater at his waist. Everett lets out a low groan when I bite his bottom lip, pulling away and panting, his face and chest flushed.

"Stop trying to distract me with sex, you vixen."

I giggle at his words, rubbing my tingling lips together and trying to quell the butterflies wreaking havoc in my stomach. I plop down next to Yoda on the couch and watch as Everett pops in the first dvd. "Where did you even get these?"

Everett fumbles with the TV a bit more before sitting down next to me, thigh against thigh. "Jesse, of course. He's all on board with our version of singing rehab."

Normally, I'd at least pity-laugh at his quip, but I'm too nervous now. Nervous to see myself up on that stage, singing my heart out, and scared that I won't like what I hear. Nervous to see just how far I've fallen. Nervous because maybe, just *maybe* this will actually work. That watching me doing what I used to love might defeat my fears and I'll be able to sing with the band and Everett will have no reason to stay.

I push that thought down because It's seriously irrational.

"Hey," Everett's husky whisper snaps me out of my reverie and he grabs my hand, thumb tracing over the knuckles. "If you really don't want to watch, we don't have to. But, I think this might help you see what the rest of us see."

So, I let him put it on.

The first disc is one I instantly recognize: bar clouded with cigarette smoke, neon signs hanging on every wall, and full crowd dancing. It was our first gig after being featured at a festival, when our popularity reached its peak. Right after Sam and I's one year anniversary.

Jesse practically skips onto stage to introduce the band, the crowd beginning to stomp their feet and chant. Enzo steps up first, picking up a guitar and reveling in the crowd's screams, Avery following him to the keyboard, earning her own hoots and hollers. Marco pretends not to even glance at the crowd as he sits down at the drum set, though anyone can tell he's absolutely buzzing at the turnout. And finally, one for dramatic entrances, I walk out on stage in my leather pants and curled locks I'd grown out to my hips, greeting the horde of fans.

The crowd goes wild.

Hearing them screaming my name again, even if just through a screen does unbelievable things to my heart. I have to close my eyes and take in deep breaths to calm the adrenaline, the pride that courses through my veins.

Because this is the past. My life isn't like this anymore.

Everett squeezes my hand as Avery plays the first few notes of *Addict*, a song I wrote when Sam and I first started dating. When the chorus kicks in —a slow melody transitioning to a heavy bass line— it's like I'm actually back up on that stage.

I can feel my body shaking with the music, the crowd cheering with every note I hit, the giddy feeling from being up on that stage with my friends, from having strangers love my voice. Our music. Every single sense is alive, almost as if I've been transported to that day.

"Please, turn it off."

The choked whisper shocks even me, having slipped out of my mouth without permission. But, Everett doesn't even listen, he just turns it up louder. The sound of my voice; lilting, haunting, and confident fills the room and even Yoda perks up his ears to listen. No fears, no doubts. Just strong and powerful and *beautiful.*

It's only when the music pauses and Everett cups my cheeks that I realize I'd started to cry. His brows rise in panic, thumbs trying to brush away my tears, "shit, okay. I didn't mean for you to cry. This was supposed to make you happy, nostalgic... God, I'm such an idiot. I'm so—"

"Everett," I laugh, even though it sounds like I'm underwater, "stop apologizing. I'm crying because I miss it, because it's hard. It's the first time in so long I've heard my own voice and *you* gave that to me... I should be thanking you, Everett. Truly."

He visibly relaxes at my reassurance, a dubious smile on his lips. I wipe away my tears, eyes fixated on the girl on the screen. A girl I can barely recognize.

A girl I want to learn from. To not go back to, but grow from.

"I love you," Everett whispers, lips pressing against my forehead. I close my eyes, exhaling and letting the words sink down into my bones. I want to respond with an 'I love you.' I should, but somehow the question that's been bubbling underneath has decided to surface. Like it clawed its way up and refuses to be tamped down any longer. Maybe it drew inspiration from my old self or maybe it's just *time*. But, either way, the words slip out before I can catch them.

"Are you hiding something from me, Everett?"

His body's reaction is the only answer I need. He tries to play it off, but his tanned cheeks pale and eyes go wide and my chest hollows at as he looks like he's been caught red handed and I can already feel our bubble beginning to release air.

"W-What do you," he stops suddenly, clearing his throat and dropping his hands from my face. He pushes his hair back and relaxes back into the couch, trying to seem nonchalant. "What do you mean? What would I have to hide?"

"You tell me."

He laughs then, and the sound cuts right through me, "Munchkin, I'm not hiding anything from you. Why would you think that?"

Yoda whines from next to me and I focus my attention on giving him some, though I feel as if I've just been sucker punched.

Disingenuous: not candid or sincere, typically by pretending that one knows less about something than one really does.

I don't want him to think I'm crazy or distrustful, but I can *feel* something isn't right. "I don't know... just a feeling. You've been acting a little strange lately... I don't know, maybe I'm just paranoid because of my past."

That last sentence cracks his façade slightly, shoulders drooping, though his face remains stoic. "I would never lie to you, Aspen. Or intentionally hurt you. You know that, right?"

I thought I knew that, but with the phone calls and Marco and Everett's sketchy behavior, I'm beginning to rethink everything I know. Everything I thought I knew.

The words burn on my tongue, but if he's telling me he's not lying, I trust him. At least until I figure out if it's all in my head or if he's actually hiding something, I'll believe in him. "Yes, I know that."

The bubble has burst.

# PASSION

"Aspen, I'll die if you don't let me."

I bite back my laughter as I try to walk into his sleek bathroom, but am pulled backwards once again. "And how will you supposedly die if I don't let you in the shower with me?"

Everett pauses, thinking for a bit before a devilish smile curls up his lips, "blue balls?"

A half-laugh, half-gasp escapes my lips before I place my hand on his shirtless chest and shove him. I stride into the bathroom and nearly shut the door before he wedges his foot in. "I knew it! You just want to sex me up! Every time I let you shower with me it always ends up with the water running cold and hickies all over my neck!"

He peeks his head in between the door, shooting me puppy dog eyes and pouting his lips, "I'll be good, I promise. Scouts honor."

I narrow my eyes at him, "Were you even a Boy Scout?"

"*Nope.*"

My chest shakes with laughter as I push all my weight against the door to close it, but Everett manages to slip in before I get the chance. "Everett, no! We don't have time to fool around! We have rehearsal in an hour!"

And this man actually falls to his knees in front of me, palms clasped together. "Please, Aspen. I won't try a thing, I promise! Please, please, *please!*"

So, that's how I end up in the shower with Everett... *again.*

"Oh, stop pouting. Be happy you get to gaze upon this glorious, glistening body," he grins, stepping into the shower after me and closing the glass door behind him. It's a tad crowded and the steam makes it extra suffocating, but I don't mind.

"I'm only disappointed in myself. You always get your way, don't you?"

He shrugs, reaching for his loofah, "when you're this good looking, it's hard not to."

"And so modest," I mumble under my breath, grabbing the razor I left here.

"What was that?"

"Nothing."

We're at this odd place in our relationship where Everett is possibly hiding something from me and I know he might be, but he doesn't know I know. And he won't know until I know if and what he's keeping from me.

Even I'm a tad confused.

I've called Marco a few times in the hopes of finishing our talk from the other day. Alas, he's not answered a single one of them and I can't help but feel that Everett is to blame for that. The guilt that stirs in my stomach over my secretive suspicions is warranted, but I tamp it down. I do trust Everett, *really.* I just want to be totally sure I'm overthinking this.

"Will you sing for me, Aspen?"

Having momentarily forgotten where I am and who I'm with, I nearly jump out of my skin at the reminder. When I turn around to face him, Everett is washing the suds off his body, the lighthouse on his stomach becoming clearer as the bubbles are wiped clean. When my eyes travel up to meet his emerald ones they are darkened slightly, focused on my breasts.

I gulp harshly, "I'm sorry, what?" He closes his eyes and shakes his head to refocus on the task at hand, repeating himself one more time. "Everett, no. You know I can't."

Gently, he cups my cheeks and presses a light kiss against

my lips, "you can, but you won't."

My eyes squeeze shut at the thought of singing again, even if in front of just one person.

He seems to notice my panic, "you're ready. It's just you and me and you know how much I love your voice. Let me hear it again, it's so lovely. *You* are so lovely."

"Everett—" I begin to protest, but he shakes his head, hands smoothing down my wet hair. His eyes are light and open, smile fond, and dimples deep.

"It's just you and me, Aspen. You and me. One song and I'll shut up about it."

Even though my heart is beating erratically and my palms are sweating, I can't deny that the offer does entice me. I haven't sung a single note in over eight months, but who better to hear it than Everett, the man I love? I loved Sam once, but he smothered my voice by constantly insulting it. Everett, on the other hand, has vowed to heal me and has made it known he's my biggest fan. Since watching the old tape of the band Everett brought over, the tickle in my throat has only grown. The want to sing again, to feel the way I felt that day. Free, happy, confident...

"You really do always get what you want, huh?"

As soon as the words leave my lips, Everett smiles so wide that I fear his dimples may be imbedded in his cheeks permanently. "Really? You're okay with it?"

I roll my eyes because he knows I couldn't possibly say no with him looking at me like that. I grab his shampoo off the ledge and shove it at his chest, "yes, but you can't watch, it'll just make me more nervous. Turn around and wash your hair. No peeking."

Once he's fully turned, shampoo poured into his palm, I gear myself up. Slow breaths in and heavy breaths out, shaking out my hands and clearing my throat.

*I can do this. I can do this. I can do this.*

Still, my mouth doesn't open. Everett sighs the longer I'm silent and begins to turn to face me. "Aspen—"

I grab his face, turning it away, and shoving it under the stream so the shampoo washes from his hair. I squeeze my eyes shut, take a deep breath, and for the first time in a long time, I sing *Blackbird* by The Beatles.

The slow, haunting melody fills the stall, the acoustics reverberating around us and making my soft voice sound loud and strong. Even if it's quivering slightly from nerves. Everett stills under my hands as the lyrics fall from my lips, my throat vibrating with the throaty tone of my voice. It's uncomfortable and foreign at first, but gets easier quickly, just like riding a bike. It's lilting, emotional, and smooth and it sends a chill through my spine, my voice growing louder with every line, though no more confident.

My voice shakes and I'm losing momentum quickly, the fear settling back into my bones. By the time I hit the last note my voice is dying off. Everett turns when I finish, a proud smile on his face. I, on the other hand, am trembling unbelievably.

He's silent for a while, just simply looking into my eyes as my face heats and throat closes. He grabs the shampoo bottle and pours some in his palm, massaging it into my hair. I close my eyes at the feeling, my chest swelling once Everett speaks again, "It's just like I remembered."

It's only then that it hits me; I sang. I finally sang again and it's all because of Everett. If he hadn't have pushed me, I probably would've never tried again –never seen the point. I'm nowhere near back to normal and I know that it'll be quite a while before I'm singing in bars and in front of others again. But... I sang. For the first time in eight months, I sang. My eyes sting with the realization and I have to bite my lip to stop a cry from escaping. It's so... *freeing.*

I was a prisoner of my own fear, my own insecurity. I'm not completely free yet, but I can see the escape now, can see the light at the tunnel, and I want to race towards it.

"How did it feel?" He asks, turning us so that my head can run under the water and wash the suds out of my hair.

"Terrifying," I laugh, opening my eyes and meeting his soft

green ones with a growing smile, "and liberating."

"God, that voice... It's so ethereal, so hypnotizing... how did you ever doubt yourself?"

Even the mention is like a knife in my chest and I think I've had enough progress for today, don't want to overwhelm myself. I grab the bottle of conditioner, pouring enough in both of our palms. "I don't want to talk about it anymore... We have to hurry or we'll be late."

We're silent as we rub the conditioner into our hair, eyes never leaving the other. Everett washes his out and I follow his lead, dipping my hair beneath the stream and closing my eyes.

"Do you remember the day I took you to see the cherry blossoms?"

A smile instantly lights up my face at the memory, "you mean the day you promised to be my '*friend*'? That didn't last very long," I snort and peak open my eyes to see him roll his.

"I was thinking more about the part where you told me what an aesthetic was. You told me that I would find my aesthetic someday, do you recall?" But he doesn't give me a chance to answer before he begins lathering soap around my shoulders and up my neck.

"You're it for me, Aspen. You're my aesthetic," he whispers, voice gravelly, but eyes clear as he brings his palms down the length of my arms. "You're the one thing I find most beautiful in the world. Your laughter, kindness, and wit..." My chest swells and goosebumps rise on every inch of skin as Everett speaks again, every word enunciated with a kiss against my collarbone, my neck, my jaw, and finally, my lips. "You. Are. So. Beautiful."

Gentle, calloused hands slide down my chest to rub my breasts, thumbs grazing my nipples and making me moan into his mouth. I wrap my arms around his neck as his hands travel down my stomach lower, lower, lower...

I gasp against his lips just as his tongue sweeps in, tasting like the tea he had for breakfast and the love he has for me. His hands leave me and slide around to my back, grasping the flesh of my behind roughly, a deep groan rattling his chest.

"How is it," he pants, releasing my lips to kiss down my neck, "that no matter how many times I fuck you, how many positions I have you in, my hunger is never satisfied?"

A low moan slips past my lips at his words and he licks a stripe up my neck before sucking on the flesh at the base of my throat. My fingernails scratch down his chest and Everett shivers in response, our desire growing, quite literally, between us. "Just touch me, Everett."

I can feel him smirk against my neck. "What's the magic word?"

I groan in frustration and decide to take matters into my own hands. I drop my hands from his chest, sliding them down my stomach to where I'm burning the most. As soon as I make contact, Everett pulls away in shock, eyes dropping to where my fingers have disappeared between my thighs. The water cascades down my body and I lean into it, enjoying the pressure and Everett's burning gaze. I'm anything but quiet as I to tease myself, chest rising and falling rapidly and fingers slipping inside.

A guttural moan makes my eyes snap open to see Everett stroking himself slowly with one hand, the other leaning against the wall to steady himself. But, his eyes... his eyes are trained on me; dark and hooded and like he's never seen anything so enchanting.

Water droplets trail down his body, glistening against his array of tattoos. His hair sticks to his face, chest is flushed, and lips are popped open, low groans emitting through it. His eyes trail up my body, lingering on my heaving breasts, my lips, before latching onto my eyes. We both freeze once they meet, but only for a second.

And then we lunge for each other.

Passion: strong and barely controllable emotion.

His mouth is everywhere: tracing my neck, sucking my jaw, and pressed up against my lips. His hands don't know what to do with themselves as they tangle into my hair, knead my breasts, and then grip my thighs and lift me up so my legs wrap around his waist. He swings me around until I'm pressed against the shower wall, slick and slippery. So many things are uncertain with us, but this physical intimacy is so very, *very* sure and stable.

I'll never want anyone else as much as I want him.

I grip him, heavy and thick in my palm and pump him slowly. He bites down onto my bottom lip, pulling it taught. "No, s-stop," he hisses, squeezing his eyes shut and taking deep breaths. "You know I won't last if you do that. I need you now."

He replaces my hand with his and leisurely guides himself into me until I'm full to the hilt. His breath fans my neck as the water falls onto his back, beginning to thrust. It's deep and slow and then hard and harsh, alternating so often that I'm close to the brink a dozen of times, about to fall off the edge of the cliff... before I'm pulled back again. My nails carve into his skin and he throws his head back in a desperate moan. My breasts are flush against him and I'm pressed against the wall by his body so his hands can roam freely.

First, he grips my hair; yanking my head back and lapping his tongue up my neck, hot and wet, before capturing my mouth. Then, they trail to my bum and sends a harsh slap to where the curve of my ass ends and the flesh of my thigh begins.

"Fuck, Everett." I nearly come then, moaning into his mouth and meeting his powerful thrusts. It's so warm and foggy and he's so rough and hungry, that I feel like I may faint.

One hand splays against my hip as he rams into me, while the other travels down to my clit and rubs harshly. I begin to shake in his hold, the relentless thrusts and forceful fingers bringing me to the brink once again and I know this time I'll take the plunge. I detach my lips from his to attach them to his clavicle, marking myself into his skin and causing him to growl. This spurs him on faster, harder than ever before and I can barely contain myself.

"Everett, I'm gonna—"

"Come for me."

And I do. Violently.

I'm a trembling mess in his arms; my vision blurring and words I never knew existed falling from my lips in between screams of his name. My legs pull him tighter into me before almost loosening completely, my bones liquefying.

But, Everett isn't done with me yet.

I can tell he's ready to come and has been since nearly the beginning, but this doesn't stop his pushing and pulling, twisting and teasing until I've come twice more. Then he releases inside of me with a moan of my name. When he places me back on my feet, I can barely stand, completely disoriented. He shuts off the water once his body has calmed and I regain enough strength to slap him on the chest sharply. "I told you! Every time I shower with you it ends up like this! There's no way we won't be late now!"

He laughs at my pouting, claiming that he *does* always get what he wants, and I leave so I can get dressed without another distraction. I'm so giddy and disoriented that when a phone rings I answer without hesitation and without checking the caller ID. "Hello?"

"Aspen?" I freeze, the post-coital bliss fading at the sound of my mother's shrill voice. "I wasn't expecting you to answer the phone." She sounds genuinely surprised and I don't blame her, considering that I haven't talked to her in over a month.

"Can you blame me?"

She's much more timid when she speaks again, "how are you?"

"I'm... better. Much better actually."

"That's good. Very good." And she genuinely sounds like she means it, but she's always been a good liar. I hear Everett rustling in the bathroom and I really do need to get ready.

"I really have to go, but... I'll talk to you later." I'm not sure if I will, but I don't know how else to end the conversation.

"Yes, of course." She doesn't sound like she believes me, but doesn't press it either, "and dear?" I hum in response, bending down to grab my jeans from the floor.

"Can you tell Everett I called? It's urgent."

Her words nearly make me choke, but she hangs up before I can question her. Everett? How does she even know who that is and why would she possibly need to talk to him? Why would she call *me* to say that, in the first place?

But, when I pull the phone away, I realize that it's not mine I'm holding. It's Everett's.

# REPRESSED

The day my father left home was the first time I ever tasted betrayal.

I won the spelling bee that day and came home with a ribbon I was going to show my dad, knowing he would hang it on the fridge proudly. Next to Marco's school portraits and drawings and report cards. But, I knew before I was even inside the house that something was wrong because my mother was on the porch with my brother, consoling him. When I asked her what was wrong, she just bluntly told me that he was gone. Cold, concise, and straight to the point with no cushioning for me to land on.

I ran up to their room to see his clothes gone and the study to see it devoid of his books. It was like he vanished, like he was never there to begin with.

I found the note he left for me in my room and brought it out to my mother. But, there was no comforting embrace for me. She let me break down in front of her with only a sigh in response. It didn't take long before she took Marco inside and made him dinner while I stayed on the porch and waited for my father's car to roll up the driveway as I believed it would.

But, the stars came out and the night turned cold and he never came home.

My mother didn't check on me once and I only went inside once evening had fallen.

The ribbon I won lost in the gravel driveway.

I don't know why I remember this scene now. Maybe because I've tasted betrayal once again or maybe because I'm sitting on that same porch now —building up the courage to go back inside the house I was raised in. Because this was never really my home. Just a place I was allowed to stay at.

Eventually, I raise my hand and use the brass knocker against the large oak doors. With bated breath, I wait the 27 seconds —yes, I counted— it takes for the door to swing open.

"Miss Aspen!" I'm granted slight relief upon seeing our stout Italian housekeeper answer the door with a shocked look on her round face.

"Ciao Adelina. Come stai?"

Adelina always treated me like the daughter she was never able to have, especially after my father left. He hired her just after I was born, ecstatic to have another Italian speaker in the family to chat with in his first language. I think that's why my mother always hated her. Because they both spoke Italian to one another and she never bothered to learn it.

Her warm hazel eyes turn glassy and she grasps my hands in hers, giving them a light kiss. In her native tongue, she ushers me inside and informs me that my mother is in her home office. With a light kiss on the cheek and deep breath, I head down the familiar hallway.

A hallway once filled with pictures of my father, now stands bare.

When I reach the doors that have been shut my entire childhood I almost turn around. What am I even going to do? Ask my mom point blank why she called Everett? Look through her texts, her emails maybe? This is a stupid idea. I'm either going to find nothing and feel like an idiot or uncover something I really wish had stayed buried.

*Curiosity killed the cat.*

And yet, it's that exact curiosity that has me twisting the doorknob and walking right in. I've seen my mom's office all of three times in my life —once during hide and seek and twice to be punished— but, it looks exactly the same. No paintings or personal affects, just bookshelves lining the walls, only law books residing in them. A large oak desk sits in the very center and my mother's topknot peeks over the computer. The same pine scent, the same clicking of keys, the same cold atmosphere I grew up in.

It makes me sick.

"Aspen," the clicking stops and my mother peeks her head over the computer to face me, eyes wide in shock. "I didn't hear you knock."

"Because I didn't."

My heels click on the hardwood as I plop down in the leather chair across from her. She's frozen with her hand over the mouse, "what are you...? You haven't been answering my calls?"

"For good reason."

She bites her lip, no doubt to bite her tongue. "So then, why are you here?"

Do I lie? Or do I come right out and ask her how she knows Everett? But, will she tell him I asked? I wanted to ask *him*, but I fear he'll be angry since he already said he wasn't hiding anything, fear he'll be hurt for not trusting him. But, what does this say about our relationship? It feels like we're both sneaking around and I just want someone to tell me the truth.

The longer I'm silent the more my mother looks bothered and I really should've thought this through before just waltzing in here. I'm fumbling for something, anything to say until I can get a game plan together and then—

"Why do you hate me?"

It slips out of my mouth without permission and my face heats from embarrassment, though I don't take it back. I panicked and It's not what I came here for, but it's something I've wanted to know my whole life.

Repressed: (a thought, feeling, or desire) kept suppressed and unconscious in one's mind.

My mother just laughs, a trill and condescending guffaw of hers that drives me insane like this is some kind of joke. Like

I'm a joke. "Honey, what?" She plays with the pearls at her neck and scoffs as if it's the most ridiculous thing she's ever heard. "Don't be dramatic."

And I balk in response to her blasé attitude, her indifference. She actually believes I'm being dramatic, when her obvious distaste has hung over me my entire life. My face heats with rage and I try to calm myself down because this wasn't even my reason for coming here, but I've never really been good with my temper. "*Dramatic?* Dramatic is stubbing your toe and demanding an amputation, going without water and then drinking an entire reservoir. The fact that you've ignored me, belittled me, and treated me like an intruder my entire life and thinking you hate me... that isn't dramatic. That's logical."

She's stunned into silence, eyes the color of the center of a sunflower—and exactly the same shade of Marco's— widen in shock and offense. Her thin lips pop agape and the color drains from her face and it's so comical I almost laugh. But, really, nothing is funny.

"I can't believe after all I've done for you—"

"Done for me?! What have *you* done for me?"

Her face is just as red as mine, though she keeps her composure, "I gave birth to you!"

"Oh, please, stop. You can't hold that over my head my entire life. I didn't ask you to give birth to me and even if that made you a mother you sure as hell haven't been a mom."

Her nostrils flare and her right eye does this odd twitchy thing that Marco's does when he's angry and their similarities remind me of one reason she probably resents me so much, "Is this because I look like dad? You resent me for looking so much like the man that left us?"

She truly does look flabbergasted as the words leave my mouth and she shakes her head, leaning back in the chair and turning towards the window. The sunlight hits her face, highlighting every feature, and she looks... old and *tired*. The lines in her skin have never been more prominent, the sadness in her eyes never so apparent.

"I don't... resent you because you look like your father, Aspen."

"Then why—"

But, a knock on the door interrupts us and Adelina peeks her head in, the tension in the room releasing through the cracked door. "The contractor is here, Ms. Marino."

She dismisses Adelina with a wave of her hand before standing, brushing off her pantsuit, and clearing her throat, "I'm putting a gazebo in the back next to the flower bed. I need to give them a rundown, but I'll be back in a few minutes." She practically runs out of the room, relieved for an escape from this uncomfortable conversation.

As soon as I hear the door clicking shut I'm shooting out of my seat and rounding her desk without a second thought. It's impulsive and something that only crossed my mind when she shut off her screen before leaving.

I press the power button, unsurprised when I see the screensaver is one of her and Marco. This is stupid and reckless and like something I've seen in a movie, but I need to know why she called him and I need to know the truth. I check her inbox, junk, sent, deleted, and yet nothing comes up having to do with Everett. But, this fact doesn't stop me from heading over to her computer files. I'm seriously wondering if I need a psych evaluation, but I think I've learned by now that love will make you do crazy things. And the fact that I've been betrayed so horribly in the past left a scar on my heart that aches every time someone I love does anything suspicious. So, even though the guilt creeps in, I still click on her folders anyway.

Except, when I get to her client files it demands a password.

Here's the turning point. Do I try to hack into my mother's private files to prove a hunch or do I walk away and just wait for everything to unravel around me?

And really, both options don't seem rational, but I'm not a rational person. I've already come this far and it would be a crime —okay, it's a crime anyway— to do something this idiotic without gaining something from it, right?

So, I only hesitate for a second before typing in my first guess.

*Marco*

**Access Denied**

*Marco Marino*

**Access Denied**

I try three more variations of his name, including his initials and middle name. I try the year he was born, his exact birthday, the hospital, hell even his favorite color.

But, nothing works.

It's already been a good five minutes and I maybe have five more before she comes back, if I'm lucky. So, I start typing in anything I can think of: my father's name, their anniversary, the place my mom was born. The time is winding down and I'm getting more desperate and nothing is working and on whim I type my name.

*Aspen*

**Access Denied**

I scoff because I really shouldn't be surprised, but then I start typing in anything that might work because I have maybe two minutes left and it's basically just gibberish until —

*94Marco96Aspen*

**Access Granted**

I barely have time to balk at the right password, how it involves me, and how I actually managed to hack into anything at all before I'm racing through the file names. By the time I reach the F's my hands are shaking and my heart is pounding because I'm hoping more than anything that Everett's name isn't here. That he isn't a client for whatever reason, that he hasn't been lying to me, that I was wrong all along. That everything has just been warped in my mind and my mom was contacting him for innocent reasons.

*Fairfield, B.*

*Feinstein, P.*

*Fox, E.*

Instantly, it's like shards of glass in my chest and a tsunami in my stomach and I keep blinking at the screen like that name might disappear. But, it doesn't. It's right there in plain black and white —glaring at me, mocking me, pulsating out of the screen and making me sick. Everett *is* hiding something. Something that involves my mother and Marco and the fact that he did something bad enough to warrant him needing one of the best defense barristers in the country.

And suddenly, a memory that was buried underneath so many seemingly more significant ones resurfaces. One of Everett and I —of Everett telling me about the first time he ever heard me sing... the memory is unfocused and blurred and I don't remember exactly what he said, but I do remember...

*"...Hammered every night, doing drugs... did something I shouldn't have —something seriously fucked up..."*

It feels like claws are squeezing at my throat and bile rises as his raspy voice floats through my mind and I hadn't really been too concerned about it at the time, but now...

Now I know that he's a client of my mother's and everything he's ever said needs to be analyzed and picked at... is he a drug addict? A dealer? Is that the big secret? The phone calls... maybe he was caught and that's why he needs my mom's help? Then why wouldn't he just tell me that? My mind is whirling with all the different scenarios and now I'm not only dealing with the fact that he lied to my face, but I'm also worried for him.

I shake my head to clear it because I'm just going to drive myself crazy with all these questions, when I really just need some answers. So, with bated breath and racing heart I click on the file.

As soon as I do, another password entry comes up and when I type in the previous one, it doesn't work this time around. My fingers shake against the keys as I retry all the previous passwords, but I soon hear the telltale sound of heels against hardwood. And that's when true panic sets in because I know an opportunity like this won't come around again.

I'm typing in everything to do with anything, but the footsteps keep getting louder and all I want to know is why my boyfriend's name is in my mom's client files, but the steps are just outside the door and I'm forced to hurry and exit out of the tabs, turn off the screen, and round the desk before my mother steps back in.

Without being able to open the file.

"I have to go."

She pauses, hand on the doorknob, and I try not to look like I'm panicking when I brush past her, "but you just got here."

"Yeah, I have a guitar lesson I forgot about. Sorry."

And I'm sure she can tell my hands are shaking and can hear the quiver in my voice, but she doesn't comment. I'm slightly sweaty and my face must look as green as I feel, but all I can do is take deep breaths and try not to drive myself crazy with theories. I got one question answered, only to have a thousand more surface.

Maybe it's not as bad as I think it is... a parking ticket gone wrong, perhaps? Maybe he went streaking and was charged with public indecency like I was once upon a time? Maybe he was a client before I even knew him? But, *why*? Why wouldn't he just tell me that and why wouldn't my *mom* tell me? Is it client confidentiality or something more?

"Aspen!"

I turn jerkily to face her in the foyer, but all I really want to do is scream and ask her why she hadn't said anything, but I can't yet. I need to get my head together first, gather some more intel before I start throwing around accusations and sounding like a crazy person. I'm also pretty sure I just broke a law and don't want to confess that to her. If anything, I should ask Everett, but I'm scared for his reaction. I just went behind his back to hack into some files to find out if he was lying to me. Turns out, he was... So, now what?

My mother rings her hands together, eyes on the floor, "I don't hate you, Aspen."

*Just go, Aspen. You got what you came for. Just leave. Do not start this with your mother.*

But, I can't because I'm hot-blooded or frustrated or maybe just an idiot. "So, then why? Why treat me so horribly all these years?"

"I haven't—"

I scoff, though my throat burns and eyes sting and my emotions are all over the place and I already know I'm going to say something I regret because all I can see is Everett's name in her client folder and her voice on his phone.

They're all liars.

"You haven't treated me like shit? Is that what you were going to say? Because not showing up to a spelling bee I *won*, not comforting me when my dad left, criticizing my weight, my grades, my goals, not knowing anything about my personal life or why I stopped singing, not remembering my birthday or even my allergy to shellfish... that to me? That's pretty horrible considering you're supposed to be my mom."

I want to say more. I want to say so much more about every neglectful wrong doing she's done and the trauma her absence in my life has caused, but my sentence ends with a cracked voice and glazed eyes and I know there's no point.

I can't turn back time.

I don't know what I expect her to say, but my disappointment almost crushes me when she refuses to comment. She just continues to play with the ring she still wears to this day, face pinched. She can't deny it because she knows I'm right. She knows she ruined my childhood.

"Yeah, that's what I thought." I continue my trek towards the door, heart heavy, but I barely make it three steps before my mother's frantic voice calls out to me.

"Your father wasn't leaving *us*. He was leaving Marco and me."

All the breath leaves my lungs at once, her words hitting me like a freight train and I stop at her words, not saying anything, but making it clear that I want —that I *need*— to hear the rest.

"Imagine my surprise when your father told me he fell in love with a woman half my age," she laughs bitterly, voice filled with years of pain. "And *then*, imagine my rage when he told me he wanted to take you with him. I assume he wanted to take Marco as well, but thought he had a better chance stealing one child from me. I couldn't let him take my daughter when he'd already taken so much from me. My dignity, my love, half of my money... the rejection," though I'm not facing her I can imagine her trying to remain composed though her voice keeps wobbling. "The rejection brought me pain I can't even describe.

"But, he wanted you, just *you*... like he got to pick and choose whom he called family. I know it's wrong, but I suppose I did resent you for that. You were always more his child than mine, but I've never regretted my decision in denying him your custody. I've always wanted you, Aspen. Even if I don't show it, even if I unintentionally favored Marco. The fact that he wanted to leave the rest of us behind and just take you... the fact that I know you would've chosen him in a heartbeat... that stung the most. I know I did nothing to change it, that's my fault. I let it fester and resented you for something you hadn't even done."

The revelation hurts in so many different ways, but there's too much information in my head now to fully process it. I can't think about my mother's jealousy or my father's selfishness in the past when so much is going on now. Her issues are very similar to my own: being rejected by the one person you thought loved you more than anything. But, we both handled those situations very differently and hers just so happened to break me.

She's always seemed so composed, so indifferent about everything. Never emotional or unsure, but now... It's clear that that was all a facade.

She's just as sensitive and human as the rest of us.

Although he gave up on me easily, I can't help but wonder how differently I would've turned out had I lived with my father. Would I be happier? Would I have been with Sam? Met Everett? Even be in the band? I wouldn't be going through *this* that's for sure.

And she ripped those opportunities away from me.

I've long harbored rage towards both parents, only magnified now. But, my mother's confession tinges that anger with sadness and hurt. I feel pity for my her and for myself over all that we've lost. But, these feelings are still clouded by the recent shocking discovery of my boyfriend's involvement with my mother. I can't handle much else and feel too overwhelmed to acknowledge this new parental discovery. My eyes burn and my throat aches and its just... *sad.*

And then I hear something I never thought I would. Something no one has probably ever heard my mother say.

"I'm so sorry, Aspen."

I'm just afraid it's too late.

A part of me wants to turn around and allow myself to rebuild a relationship with my neglectful mother, to forget her mistakes and transgressions and start anew. But, my head is too full and I'm so confused and I just need some time to let this all sink in and decide what the hell I'm to do with any of this information or the people in my life.

So, without saying a word, I walk out of my childhood home and don't look back.

In one day, I've discovered that Everett and my mother know each other, that he's a client of hers, and that he lied to me about it. Shockingly, I also found out that my father *didn't* want to leave me behind and that's the reason my mother has hated me all this time...

*Curiosity killed the cat, but satisfaction brought it back.*

Back to what, though? What's there to come back to when everything is falling apart?

# FOREBODING

Foreboding: fearful apprehension; a sensation that something bad will happen.

I've had this feeling once before. Just six months ago on a morning without coffee, I woke up with the gut instinct that something terrible would happen. Six months ago, to the day, that Everett joined the band. Six months later and that same ominous feeling is stirring in my belly and rearing its ugly head to the forefront of my attention. It's been right underneath the surface, like a predator lying in wait, and waiting for its opportunity to strike.

Now, I can feel it looming behind me, claws already catching on my flesh.

I try to convince myself that it's just nerves. That the bees in my chest and the waves in my stomach are all because of the banquet tonight. The banquet that's hosting the four bands that are playing at the Manchester Music Festival in the hopes of being signed to a label. Tonight, we meet those bands, the judges, and the executives of the record company, and it is quite possibly the second most important day in our careers (right after the actual festival night) and maybe that's the reason I feel like this.

But, I know better.

Because it's only been a few days since I found out that Everett is my mother's client. Days I've spent googling his name and only coming up with videos of his old bands and stan accounts dedicated to him on social media. Days I've spent trying to gain enough courage to ruin everything by finally confronting him about his lie.

Which I plan to do tonight, after the event.

I try to quell the storm inside me, but that ominous feeling is still there. It's there when I curl my hair, when I put on my red matte lipstick, when I slip on my navy dress with the slit up to my hip, when I buckle the strap of my heels around my ankle.

It's even alive and well when I answer the door to Everett's persistent knocking.

His eyes trace my figure ever so slowly, drinking me in and darkening at my tanned legs and rouge lips. I can't help my eyes from wandering down his frame either —I love him in suits. Especially velvet ones with the shirt half buttoned and his tanned, inked skin poking through.

"You are so dangerous to my health," he breathes in awe, shaking his head.

I want to laugh at the comment, but before I can even take another breath he's stepping through the threshold, closing the door with his foot, and gripping my hips in his palms. He places a light kiss to my lips before dipping his head down to my neck, brushing against the sensitive flesh and making me shiver. It's ridiculous how he can barely touch me and still manage to short-circuit every single nerve in my body.

It's when he begins to place open, wet kisses to my clavicle and his hands travel to my bum that I speak, "no, Everett. We're going to be late. We can wait till after the dinner."

But, after the dinner everything is going to change. After the dinner, we may never get another chance to do this again. There may be no 'us' after the dinner. Everything will come out: why Everett is a client of my mom's, why he never told me, why I went behind his back to snoop. This could be it for us if the lie is so significant as to destroy our relationship or if it's so insignificant that Everett is devastated I didn't trust him... *I feel ill.*

"I can't wait till after dinner."

I'm not sure if it's the words themselves or the growl they come out in that make me cave, but either way, I'm grabbing his face between my palms and slamming his lips down to my own in a second flat. He licks into my mouth, hungry and desperate, and I bite his lip, ready and willing. He's quick to use the hands on my bum to lift me up and I'm even faster in wrapping my legs around his waist.

One last time, one last moment of intimacy before everything changes. Before the truth.

His tongue flicks my ear and my hands are yanking on his hair, and he walks us backward, dropping me onto my wooden dining table. "Can't even make it to the bedroom?"

It comes out as a breathy laugh and it makes Everett pull away from my neck with a soft smile, eyes filled with awe as they trace my face again. "Not when you look this beautiful."

And before I can even register what's happening in my lust filled brain, Everett is pulling me to the end of the table and flipping me over so that my feet are on the ground and my stomach is flat on the wood. He runs his palms down my back: tugging on my hair, tracing my sides, and grazing my breasts, before he slips his hand into the slit on my right hip and trails down until he finds his destination. And then he stops.

"You're not wearing panties?"

His fingers are frozen against me and I wriggle slightly against them, "kind of impossible to when my whole right side is exposed up to my hip."

He slams his palm against the table and begins to lift my dress up, "oh, *fuck.* You're such a bad girl."

His husky voice and sultry words make me shiver and I grip the sides of the table when my dress bunches at my hips—only wishing I could see his face. His hands waste no time in gripping my exposed ass lightly slapping the skin there. "Oh, yes, I quite like this view."

"Everett," I whine, desperate for his touch, and glancing over my shoulder to catch his smug grin. I yelp when I feel a sharp sting on my right butt cheek, jerking against the table and swallowing a moan. He unbuckles his pants with one hand and caresses my stinging flesh with the other.

"Patience, Munchkin." It doesn't take much longer for him to slide against my aching flesh, teasing my entrance. There's no foreplay and it isn't really needed, I'm ready for him as soon as he opens his mouth. It's a blessing and a curse.

He's my oxygen, yet I'm constantly drowning.

A strangled gasp leaves my lips when he slides in fast and deep and I stand back up, leaning against his frame, and gripping his hair as he slides out inch by inch, tortuously slow. His hands find my breasts, kneading and teasing as he plunges into me unforgivingly, making me cry out in pleasure and pain. His lips find the pulsing point of my neck and licks and sucks at that flesh and it's all too much. He's meticulous in his torture: warm tongue never ceasing, pinching fingers never stopping, and thrusts never slowing.

"Always feel so... good around me," he grunts lowly when he pushes in again and I turn my head to find his lips and lick into his mouth, panting and wet.

We continue this pattern, each movement rougher than the last and I can't stand up straight anymore —causing me to fall back against the table again. My back arches with each thrust, always so deep and unrelenting that the table screeches against the wood floors.

I meet his thrusts as best as I can and Everett leans over my frame, calling out my name in a groan when I clench around him. The sounds are almost pornographic: my loud moans, his low grunts, skin slapping, and table shaking all heightening my arousal. Everett tangles his hand into my hair and pulls on it to keep me steady as he pounds into me fast and pulls out slow. It's a tortuous process that he's perfected and it makes my knuckles turn white against the edges of the table. I'm sure I'll have bruises on my hip bones from how hard they're slamming into the edge of the table, but the pain only increases my pleasure.

I'm clenching around him, unable to handle his expert movement, and when his palm comes down on my sensitive, plump cheek I lose all sense of reason. I black out as my orgasm rips through me, skin hot and thighs trembling A guttural moan rattles in my chest and my heart bursts at the seams as I come undone, calling out his name, cheek resting on the cool wood.

But, he doesn't stop.

In fact, he grows more fervent. Each stroke is deeper and sharper and I don't even see the second orgasm coming until I'm yelling out his name again, arching back into him as he comes, my name the only word on his lips. I'm a quivering, exhausted mess —mind foggy and body exhausted when I come down from my second orgasm. He stops shaking, falling on top of me in a panting, sweaty mess and I'll be damned surprised if I can even walk straight after this.

We stay like that for a while —pressed together and heaving and the only sound I can hear is Everett's breath and his heart racing against my back. He brushes the hair from my face and places a delicate kiss on my cheek before getting up. All I can do is turn around so I'm lying face up against the table, trying to catch my breath and watching as Everett adjusts himself. His wild hair has matted to his face, shirt sticks to his skin, and chest is flushed a deep red. I'm sure I look exactly the same, but I still take pride in being the one to make him look so unkempt.

"You made us late, you know?"

His lips curl up into a dirty smirk skin as he helps me up from the table, "It was worth it."

* * *

I really wish we'd just stayed on that table.

Each second that ticks by has my stomach churning and head dizzy with anxiety. The hall is busy with finely dressed strangers kissing each other's asses and soft jazz music that's in tempo with my racing heart. Marco and Avery escaped to the bar, Enzo is talking to some girl in another band, Jesse is chatting up all the producers, and Everett is nowhere to be found. Besides giving me a peck on the cheek and telling me he had to use the loo twenty minutes ago —I haven't seen him at all. I have a feeling that has less to do with a full bladder and more to with the fact that someone kept calling him on the way here. The fact that his face grew paler with every missed call tells me it wasn't his mom ringing to check in this time. If that was even true.

"Surprised Fox left you alone dressed like that. You know I love you in blue." I turn with a relieved smile, just thankful to not be left alone in this intimidating environment anymore.

"You don't look so bad yourself, Sam." He always did know how to rock a suit, even if he wore his Vans with it. He grins at me before popping a grape into his mouth and looking around at the decked-out dance hall with disgust.

"Can you believe this shit? 'S all just for show, it's pathetic how these stuck up pricks want us to kiss their ass just to record some auto-tuned, pop crock of shit for them."

"Surprised you showed. This scene was never really your thing."

Eyes soft, smile small, "well, besides it being mandatory, I did want to see you."

My chest stings, "Sam... I'm glad you're here, but I'm with Everett. You—"

"I know, I know." He shakes his head, looking into the crowd and trying to hide his disappointment before facing me again, "about that... how are you handling everything?"

"What do you mean?"

"Aspen, there you are... we need to go. Can we go?" I nearly jump out of my skin when I hear Everett's voice behind me, slightly panicked and hushed. I turn, my gaze drifting from his antsy expression to Sam's unamused one, not quite sure how to handle the situation or Everett's request. He keeps fidgeting from foot to foot and glancing around the room with wide eyes. His knuckles are white from the grip around his phone and his jaw ticks impatiently.

"You want to leave? We've only been here for half an hour?"

He licks his lips, eyes flashing to Sam before focusing on me, "I just don't want to be here anymore, can we please leave?"

I look to Sam for help, but he simply shakes his head and shrugs in confusion. I can tell Everett is growing more anxious as the seconds tick by and I have no idea what's spurred on this sudden urgency, but I feel the ominous cloud above us darken.

"Okay," I drag out, not wanting Everett to have a meltdown right here. "Let me just say goodbye to—"

"Aspen, please. Can we go right now? *Please.*"

And he grips onto my hand for dear life, eyes wide and terrified and I want to say no and demand he explain everything right this damn second, but when I feel his hand trembling against mine, I cave.

I always cave when it comes to him.

I say a quick goodbye to Sam before grabbing my clutch and letting Everett lead me into the crowded lobby. He doesn't look at me once, but his phone pings as we turn a corner and his head snaps right to it, eyebrows furrowing and face turning an alarming shade of green.

"Everett, what's going on? Is this about Sam, because you have—"

"This isn't about that bastard."

And that's all he says by means of explanation and I'm starting to feel sick as he leads us through the lobby. His grip is so tight on my wrist that it begins to hurt. I try to yank it out of his grasp as we push through the double doors, but Everett freezes in his tracks and I practically slam into his back from the sudden halt. I hear a faint shouting and see odd flashing lights and my heart thunders in my chest because that bad feeling is all that I can sense now. The predator has lunged.

When I look up, I see the flashes of light and a large group of people holding cameras and microphones. The lights nearly blind me and, in my confusion, I grip onto Everett's coat for support, but he's grown rigid. All I can hear is a dull shout of Everett's name through the second pair of double doors and the thick glass that separates them from us.

Everett turns to face me, eyes wide and full of fear, two words slipping out of his mouth before the madness begins, "I'm sorry."

I should have trusted my gut.

# TREACHERY

When I was younger, before my dad left, I used to have Marco and him pretend to take photos of me with a Barbie camera I got for Christmas. Marco would be the photographer and my dad would be the interviewer.

*"Aspen, who are you dating now? Leonardo DiCaprio or Johnny Depp?"*

*"Aspen, Aspen! How do you feel about being number #1 in the charts for six months straight?"*

*"Ms. Marino, who are you wearing?"*

I dreamed of living in the spotlight, of hearing questions shouted at me and lights of a camera blinding me.

But, I never wanted it like this.

The flashes disorient me as I try to balance on the cobblestone, my head pounding, and eyes straining against the bright lights. All I can do is grip onto Everett's hand tighter as we make our way to his car. I have no idea what's happening; why these people are taking our photo or why they're shouting Everett's name. I don't know why he apologized before leading me out into the masses, but I know *this* is the moment.

This is the domino effect that will cause everything to come crashing down around us.

"Mr. Fox, how do you feel about the allegations made against you? About CPS deciding to press charges?"

"Everett, are you still in contact with David McCain?"

The questions don't make any sense to me, but Everett's

grip grows tighter with each one hurled at him and I'm beginning to feel panic claw up my throat as the questions become more frequent, the flashes brighter, and the people more aggressive. His car is just in sight and we're so close to it, but of all the questions in the crowd, only one can be head above the rest, only one has me wanting to vomit up everything I just ate.

"How can you live with yourself after what you did to Leo Solis?"

*Leo Solis.*

Why did that name sound familiar?

I don't even remember the rest of the walk to the car, blocking out all the chaos around me until the passenger door is closed and I'm engulfed in silence. Everett climbs in and snaps his head towards me like he expects me to bombard him with questions and I should. But, my throat is suddenly too dry and my head is pounding and the people have their cameras shoved up against the window and I think I'm going to be sick. I keep my eyes on my lap because I don't know where I can look as Everett revs the engine and speeds off into the night.

The silence is deafening.

Everett keeps glancing over to me every few seconds as if to check that I'm still breathing and I can't even be sure that I am anymore. Even though Everett is sitting right next to me, I've never felt more distant.

*Leo Solis.*

My mind races, body still frozen in shock as I try to make sense of the cameras and the questions and then his file in my mom's computer pops into my mind and oh god—

"Everett..." I don't even know what to say. Where do I begin? How should I react to this?

"I'll explain everything, okay? I promise. I just... let's just get to my place first, okay?"

I don't respond, mostly because my heart is beating too loud, and also because his hands are shaking on the wheel and his voice is garbled with panic. He reaches for my hand, but

I pull it away almost instantly. I don't want him to touch me right now. Not when I'm left in the dark.

He pulls it back slowly and I can see his shoulders slump from my peripheral, but then his phone rings between us and we both glance at it at the same time.

**Marco**

I lunge for it.

Everett jolts in his seat when I grab the phone, looking between the street and me as if deciding if he would rather fight me for the phone or try not to kill us.

He chooses the latter.

"Everett, where the fuck are you? Did you take Aspen with you? I swear to God—"

"Marco."

A short pause, a sigh of relief, and then, "where are you? Where's Everett?"

"We're on the way to his flat. He's driving." My voice sounds eerily calm and maybe that's why Marco sounds so confused. I'm not sure why I'm acting like this; so composed and cool when all I want to do is stop the car and demand answers. Or throw up. Or both.

"Do you... know what's happening?" He says it like he knows something I don't. I know he does. He always has. It explains his anger and protective behavior the two months.

"Apparently Everett's a criminal."

Everett's head whips around to look at me and though I don't face him, I can see how his skin has paled and eyes have grown wide in alarm, but I ignore him. I think I'm in shock.

"Jesus Christ," Marco sighs at my words and the blasé way I say them. I hear chatter around him and more cursing and I'm pretty sure he just left the banquet. "Listen, whatever he says, don't believe him, okay? We'll explain everything—no, *I* will explain everything. I'm on my way."

I hang up then, not because I don't have anything to say, but because his words are making the bile rise up my throat and I really can't listen anymore. They're in on it —whatever it is—

*together.* I knew it, I always knew it. But, having him confirm it aloud... the betrayal stings.

What this all means, I'm still so lost and confused, but I know it can't be good. I know whatever they're going to tell me is going to destroy me. I already know this is going to be one of the worst nights of my life.

Like being tied to tracks and watching, helpless, as the train barrels towards you.

"What did Marco say?" He tries to sound casual, but can't mask the panic in his voice.

"Just not to trust you."

He slams his palm down onto the steering wheel lightning fast, "If there's anyone you shouldn't trust it's him, okay?" But, I know that's not true now. I shouldn't trust anyone; not him or Marco or my mom, maybe even my bandmates. How do I know? How do I know who's been lying to me?

Everett pulls in and parks in his garage, head falling to the steering wheel in exhaustion, slumping over and letting out one long sigh. Finally, *finally,* I feel the question rising in my chest and ready to be spoken.

"Everett, what the hell is going on?" My voice is neutral, but I'm screaming inside.

He turns to me and the look in his eyes is all I need to know that what he did will wound me greatly. That I might leave him tonight. Because his eyes may be full of fear, but it's the desperation in them —the somber hue in his emerald eyes that lets me know he's afraid he'll lose me tonight. Maybe he will. I'd been preparing for this possibility all day, I just thought I'd be the one pulling the trigger. But, I was too late and it was pulled for me.

"Let's get inside first." I allow him to lead me into the building and up the stairs, but I don't let him touch me. I'm afraid his touch will make my skin crawl instead of heat with pleasure like it did only a few hours ago. It already feels like a lifetime ago.

He's antsy the whole time: leaning his weight on one foot

and then the other, reaching out to me and then letting his arm fall limp, searching my face and then snapping his eyes away when I catch him. As soon as the door closes behind us, Everett begins to pace up and down his living room floor. He rips his blazer off and throws it onto the couch, yanking at his hair, and shaking his head. My numbness fades with every step Everett takes and I can feel the shock wearing off, overwhelming dread and rage taking its place.

But, he just continues to pace, lips shut, and eyes cast on the ground and my breathing grows heavy and my blood boils and panic claws up my throat at a devastating speed and—

"Everett!" I shout and he jumps in surprise, stumbling towards me in alarm. I let his hands cup my face and his forehead drop to my own. My skin doesn't crawl, but I feel nothing. His hands shake against me, but I offer him no comfort.

There's a loud pounding on the door and Marco's shout, "It's me! Open up!"

Everett curses under his breath before looking into my eyes, his wild and pleading, "do you remember what you promised me a few weeks ago? You said you'd never leave me, no matter what... Do you remember that?"

My heart sinks, I knew that would come back to bite me in the ass. "Everett, you can't—"

He shakes his head, giving me a short peck on the lips before pulling away, a somber look on his face. "I know. I know... I just... I love you, okay?"

I want to say it back, but my throat closes up and I'm much too terrified to say anything. Even if it might be the last time I get to say it. Everett simply nods in defeat before brushing by me to open the door. Marco is behind it, his tie and jacket gone, hair a wild mess, and eyes frantic as they find mine. He shoves past Everett and gives me one fleeting look before rounding on him, "we need to tell her everything. Now. This has gone on long enough."

Everett squeezes his eyes shut, closes the door behind him, and nods in agreement. I don't like this. I don't like that they know something I don't, that there is a 'we' when it comes to them. My brother and my boyfriend, both consciously hiding something from me.

"I'm going to be the one to tell her, Marco. It should be me."

"Well, it better be the truth."

Everett visibly bristles, "fuck you. What else—"

"I don't give a *fuck* who tells me, as long as someone does and does it quickly." I snap at the boys, sitting down and rubbing a shaky hand down my face. They snap their mouths shut, Marco sitting next to me and Everett plopping onto the coffee table in front so we're face-to-face. I don't want to sit anywhere near them, feeling cornered, but I force myself to be still. With each second that ticks by, the tension in the room grows more suffocating.

Just when I feel like I'm going to snap, Everett sighs and looks up to meet my eyes. "Two years ago, when I told you I saw you sing for the first time... do you remember me saying I'd been involved in some bad shit? That something terrible happened?"

I nod, the knife twisting in my gut and dread filling every inch of my body.

He breathes out a shaky sigh, "I... I'd been kicked out of my band and was completely broke, with no savings. I had bills and rent, so I... started selling drugs —pharmaceutical, prescription drugs— as a means to make money. I had a friend... David McCain, who was a pharmacist and supplied me with pills to distribute.

"But... one night, I met up with a guy named Leo Solis to sell him some Hydro. When I got there, he pulled a knife on me and tried to rob me... That was *thousands* of dollars' worth of pills and if I let him have them I was going to lose my apartment." Everett stops talking to run a hand down his face, eyes haunted, and there's a ringing in my ears that make it hard to him. "I wouldn't hand it over, so he... just *lunged* at me. He sliced my right arm pretty deep and I used the bag full of pills to hit him, knocking the knife away."

He pauses, voice shaking and eyes faraway, as if reliving the memory. He rubs at his right bicep and I gulp, staring at the puckered scar and recalling our conversation in the tub a few weeks ago. I had a feeling about that wound, but this is beyond my imagination.

“I could’ve ran then... I *should’ve*. But, I’d been drinking and I was angry and prideful and I just... I just started hitting him.” His pale face turns a concerning shade of green and I feel my own stomach churn, eyes stinging. “When the red finally cleared, I looked down and saw him... so bloody I couldn’t even make out his face. Nose broken, eyes bruised and bulging, lip busted open. The pill bottles had scattered everywhere and I was gathering them to run when I heard him rustling behind me. I turned around and... he was coming at me again with the knife, so I dodged him. I guess he was disoriented or had blood in his eyes, because he swayed and fell.

“His head slammed against a brick in the alley and that sound,” he shivers, eyes glistening and voice trembling, “that sound will haunt me the rest of my life... I ran away and heard later they found him in the alley... in a coma.”

He stops talking and his eyes are hollow and I don't dare look at Marco or say anything because my whole body is trembling and I know that I’m going to be sick if he continues. I remember now, why that name sounded so familiar.

Leo’s assault was all over the news, his name plastered on every magazine, his condition prayed over by hundreds... *Everett did that?*

Dealing drugs is one thing, but nearly beating a man to death? The thought has me lurching over, eyes swimming. Everett seems much worse off than I; eyes red and puffy, a guilt so deep there it makes my chest ache. Just relaying that chain of events, he seems to have relived it, and I fight the urge to comfort him.

"So, why is this coming out now if it's been almost two years?"

Everett is surprised to hear my voice, as if he forgot I was there. "They didn't have anything to go off of—not until Leo woke up a few months ago and identified David in a line-up. They offered David a plea deal if he named his distributers and Leo recognized me later as his attacker... But, due to the lack of witnesses, confused stories, and self-defense claims, CPS has been investigating these past few months. They weren't sure who to charge and for what crimes, but they finally made up their minds today, I guess."

I curse under my breath, squeezing my eyes shut and willing this to go away. Everett's hand twitches at his side and I know he wants to touch me, comfort me, but knows better. This doesn't seem real, doesn't seem like Everett. "Shouldn't you... wouldn't you be in jail then?"

He hesitates, looking away, "my... lawyer knew they were going to indict me for distribution and assault. She set up my bail with the judge."

Marco is frozen like a rock at my side and I feel just as stuck. My head pounds and my throat burns and this is all too *much*... Everett was dealing opiates, nearly beat someone to death over them, and could go to jail. The thought makes my stomach bottom out and my weary, love-sick heart tries to justify his actions, but I don't know what to think or how to feel. One thing he said sticks out in my mind, though, and I latch onto it, desperate for something more concrete to hold onto. "Wait, what... what do *I* have to do with any of this? Your... lawyer—"

I can't even finish the sentence before Everett's shoulders visibly deflate. "Aspen... you have to know that I love you. That everything was always real for me. That... that you—"

"*Fox*. Just tell her." Marco speaks for the first time, voice cold and harsh and Everett flinches, the shame he exuded speaking about Leo now amplified. I want to cover my ears.

"When... I heard that David was going to take the plea deal... I told Marco everything because... I knew... I knew I'd need a lawyer and—"

"Oh god," I groan, hunching over and clutching my stomach to stop from puking all over his nice wooden floors. "My mother. She's representing you for *this."* My voice wobbles and vision swims and he drops his head in shame. I brace my heart for the damage I know is to come.

"I'd already joined the band by then, for *you*... because of *you,* you know that. But, we were at each other's throats and when I found out about the plea, you and I were in this huge fight. I was venting to Marco about you and the fact that I might be going to jail and Marco mentioned your mum was a defense barrister and he came up with this—"

Marco is on his feet in seconds, "do *not* fucking lie to her! This was you! This was all you and you *know* it!"

Everett shakes his head in dismay and I'm getting really tired of the interruptions because from what little Everett has said, my mind is already piecing it together and I'm not liking the conclusion. "So... *I* came up with this idea... this *deal* with Marco," he stops to swallow and all color has drained from his face. "If... if I could get you to finally sing again in time for the competition... then... then he'd get your mom to represent me pro-bono."

My worst fear —one I've been telling myself was just paranoid delusion— has come to fruition right before my eyes. The betrayal twists into my heart like a knife, his confession sinking into every pore and engraving itself onto my very bones and if I wasn't already sitting I would've collapsed. When my dad left, when my mom rejected me, when Sam cheated... all of that pain could not even measure up to the searing agony I feel from deep within.

*It's a lie.*

*It's all been a lie.*

Every kiss, every caress, every loving word whispered into my ear have all been a part of a bigger ploy, to what? Get me to sing again so the band could win some *fucking competition*?

Marco, my own *brother* let Everett betray me like this... *helped* him orchestrate it. My mother... does she know about this deal as well? How could everyone just sit back and watch as I stupidly fell in love with a man that used me... *again*?

I suddenly feel so dirty that scrubbing my skin for hours could not wash me of this sin. I don't even realize I'm crying until I begin to heave, lungs desperate for breath when my throat is closed tight. Through blurry tears, I see Everett's own slide down his face and he places one hand on my arm, but I reel away from him in disgust. I shoot up from the couch, needing to be as far from them as possible, needing to breathe, to process everything I've just been told.

"How long?" I ask, voice unsteady and words hushed, but Everett only shakes his head desperately. He tries to move towards me, but I keep pulling away. "*How long,* Everett!?" My shout is desperate and aching and even Marco buries his face in his hands, shoulders shaking and this can't be real. This has to be a dream. They wouldn't hurt me like this. There's no *way* they would hurt me like this. It just... *can't* be real.

"Since... since before I took you to see the cherry blossoms."

This time, I really do collapse to my knees and my heart goes with them.

I thought Everett was different, he *told* me he was different than the rest of the men in my life... I thought he loved me. And maybe he did, maybe it became real for him at some point, but every intention behind those feelings were lies. How could I ever believe him again?

*Everything* was a lie.

Treachery: betrayal of trust; deceptive action or nature.

# TRAVAIL

Isn't is weird how our whole body depends on a heart?

The constant contraction and whir of our heart proves that we're alive. That we're breathing. That we're here. When you're nervous, or scared, or in love, the heart pumps faster and faster, trying to keep up with these emotions. And when you're sad, or shocked, or heart-broken the heart slows and gives you time to adjust. To let everything sink in.

It supplies blood through your veins and vital organs and flushes out toxins without any conscious effort on our parts. It keeps us breathing, it keeps us alive. The heart is the powerhouse of life.

And mine's been broken.

I felt the first crack when my dad left, the second when my boyfriend in middle school called me fat, the third when I realized my mother would never love me the same way she did Marco, the largest crack less than a year ago when Sam and I broke up.

And I thought it had given up: withered and died.

But, then Everett came along with his cheesy jokes and dimples and crude compliments and the clouds cleared and the birds were chirping again and I felt the flowers inside of me growing through those very cracks in my heart.

Everett breathed the air back into my lungs. I could feel my heart beat inside of my chest again. Strong and steady and full of love.

But, it was a lie.

The clouds have returned angrier than ever, the birds are flying into windows, and the flowers have been stomped on by his expensive boots.

My lungs turn black from the poison he breathed into me. My heart has died.

My vision blurs and I can't even breathe and Everett just keeps trying to hold me, to touch me, but every time he comes near me I scream and he flinches back as if I'd hit him. His confession won't stop ringing in my ears and all I can seem to do is go back over every word he ever said, every touch, every kiss and try to separate where the lies ended and truth started.

In these memories, Everett's gentle hands transform into devious claws and strangle me.

"Aspen, please just listen to me, okay?" Everett begins to pace the floor when he accepts that I won't let him touch me and I really should just, but my feet won't allow me to move. "I never... I never meant to hurt you. I just... I was desperate when I heard David and Leo identified me. I would've done anything to get out of that situation, but I never wanted *this*... I—"

"Stop, *God*. Please, just stop," I choke out, my plea sounding desperate and pained. "This is *exactly* what you wanted! You got me to sing again, you got my mother to be your lawyer, and you got some easy action as a bonus... this is *exactly* what you wanted!"

Everett's face scrunches in disgust and dismay and he begins to mumble 'no' over and over under his breath and he reaches out to me again, hand brushing my arm. The flesh stings as if I'd been burned and the bile rises up my throat and I never want him to touch me again. Just the thought of him kissing my skin, whispering in my ear, hands roaming my body is enough to have me doubling over and clamping a hand over my mouth in an effort to stop the urge to hurl.

He used me, just like all the people in my life do, and I let him.

"Aspen... *no!* I can't believe you'd even say that... I love you,

Aspen. I do—"

I place my hands over my ears, squeeze my eyes shut, and let out a desperate groan to get him to stop talking. I don't... I can't stomach hearing that ugly lie from his beautiful lips again. "How could I believe anything you say when you've lied to me for months? When you had an ulterior motive from the very *first day* you tried to be my friend?" I turn to face a silent Marco, growing more and more hysterical, "I bet you had a good laugh when I told Everett I loved him, that I fell for him so hard and so *easily*."

Everett falls to his knees in desperation, burying his face in his hands, and the sight makes me sick to my stomach.

Marco finally steps in, his own eyes rimmed red and frantic, "Aspen, the deal was meant to benefit *you!* You would be able to sing again, we'd win the competition, and you'd be happy!"

"So, you pimped me out to your friend? Used me as a pawn to win a *stupid* competition? Watched as I fell for every single one of his lines and thought that would make me *happy?"*

Marco rears back at the rage in my voice, realizing how royally he fucked up. That this is a situation he can't rectify easily. That everything is falling apart around him.

I wonder how that must feel.

"I told Everett not to get romantically involved with you, I just wanted him to *befriend* you." Everett's looks at Marco in a silent plea, but it's ignored, "But, when you two came out as a couple, I realized that this was a fucked-up idea, but it was too late. I should have told you, but I was afraid you'd never forgive me... Things got so out of hand so fast.... I can't even begin to explain how sorry I am. I just... wanted the old Aspen back. *My* Aspen back."

His voice cracks and he's desperately trying to hold back tears. On any other occasion, I'd do anything to comfort him, to make him feel better, but I just don't care.

"Is that supposed to make me feel better?" My voice is laced with venom and from the way Marco's face contorts, I know it infects him. "The fact that you didn't *mean* for me to fall for

Everett? That you had some twisted idea this was all for *my* benefit? That makes it *better*? You disgust me. You *both* disgust me."

Everett heaves in the corner and Marco stumbles back into the couch and the room is starting to spin. Images of Everett brushing my hair behind my ear, holding me at night and whispering he loves me, touching me so gently, and looking at me like I'm the only thing that matters flash through my mind in quick succession and I try not to let those memories crush me.

Were all those moments lies? It seemed so genuine, he can't be that good of an actor. But, how can I know? How do I know when everything else has been a lie?

*Does it even matter?*

I know I'm no saint. I can be irrational and a bit of a bitch, but what could I have possibly done to deserve this? What have I done in this life or a past one that warrants everyone I love to hurt me? To use me? To *betray* me?

Maybe I just wasn't meant to be happy.

"I need to leave."

Marco's head stays down, but Everett practically launches himself towards me, eyes widening in panic and chest heaving frantically, "no, don't leave. You can't leave, I need to... I need to fix this. Let me fix this. Aspen, please."

I round on him, the sound of his voice cracking makes my chest ache and the rage I felt upon hearing this horrible secret transitions into something much worse.

Travail: a state of great suffering of body or mind.

"*Fix* this?! You can't fix this, Everett." He flinches at the volume of my voice and it's hard to believe that we were so blissful just a few hours ago. "You lied to me! I asked you if you were hiding anything from me and you denied it. You *promised* not to hurt me. I believed in you, trusted you... You don't love me. You wouldn't hurt someone you love like this."

Everett continues to shake his head in dismay, but I can't stand another second in this room without the air being sucked from my lungs. He makes one more attempt to get me to stay, "I know... I know what I did was wrong, but think about it... I got a lawyer and we both found love and you can't tell me that doesn't mean anything because—"

My lungs burst with hollow laughter, skin heating with rage, "you can't *actually* be trying to justify this? Why even apologize, then?" Marco raises his head to look at me and I shoot them a sardonic smile. "I mean, I started to sing again in time for competition, right? And my mom will surely win your case, Everett. You both got what you wanted, I was just collateral damage."

And with that, I walk out of his apartment and slam the door behind me, trying to keep myself together when my whole world is falling apart. I swallow down my tears until I can be alone and try not to let this soul crushing revelation overwhelm me.

Everett doesn't come after me and even though I try not to want that, when my footsteps are the only ones echoing through the hall, the disappointment is crushing. I wander the streets aimlessly, the sky as gloomy as I feel, and I must look ridiculous in this formal dress with puffy eyes and a ruddy face.

Where do I go? How do I move on from this?

From the first day our friendship began, the first day I actually thought Everett was a genuinely decent person, the first day I felt my heart stir at the sight of him, he had an ulterior motive. From the cherry blossoms to now, he's been getting close to me for *this*.

That's why he was so adamant about getting me to sing recently, why he wanted me to forgive my father, why he was trying to right every wrong in my life.

To fulfill his end of the bargain so Marco would then fulfill his.

I guess he succeeded. But, at what cost?

I stop on the corner of a deserted street to lean against the cold brick and let that settle into my bones. I feel slightly delirious and dizzy, exhausted from the events of the day and trying to make sense of the senseless. Everett really fooled me, broke down my barriers, made me trust in him... only for him to turn out like all the rest. It's so pathetic and ironic that I start giggling manically in the street, passerby staring warily.

My deteriorating heart squeezes and aches and I can barely see straight. The bile I'd been pushing down since the moment we stepped out of the gala rises and I'm running to the nearest trash can to vomit. I continue to hack and heave even after I empty all the contents in my stomach, even after my vision clears.

I feel sick and I feel dirty and all I want to do is rub my skin raw.

Scrub it until all evidence of Everett ever touching me is wiped clean, until every cell in my body forgets how it felt when his lying mouth kissed me, when his devious fingers traced my skin, when his treacherous breath washed over my face as he seduced me.

Because he got what he wanted and it wasn't me.

# HOPELESS

One week passes with me in bed, cocooned in my blanket, and shutting my blinds to block out the light. I turn off my phone to avoid the incessant calls and texts, try to sleep and push away the nightmares, and eat even when I feel sick. There's a knocking on my door every day.

I know it's him. It's always him.

I feel like a flower withering away, deprived of its sun. I feel numb until I remember his radiant smile or contagious laugh, and then the pain is excruciating.

When the ache in my chest feels like an anchor, when my lungs are drowning in despair, I find myself having to count down from ten just so I can breathe again.

But, ten is the first time we met and he made a vulgar comment about my skirt. Nine is our first kiss and even though it was dirty and wrong, I felt as if I swallowed sunlight. Eight is the fight that came after and the terrible things we said. Seven is the cherry blossoms and when it began for me and something else entirely began for him. Six is the dressing room when he touched me for the first time and I felt alive. Five is Marisol and Sam. Four is the first time we made love and I found home in his arms. Three is when he told me he loved me and I believed it. Two is the secret and lies I tried to ignore. One is when they all came to light.

And counting to ten does nothing but pain me.

I've had a lot of time to think and I spend most of it worrying about Everett. Worrying about this court case and being absolutely horrified about what he did to Leo. I do understand Everett's desperation to find legal help when facing something this serious, his willingness to do whatever it took to be free. But, it doesn't matter. Because if Everett had befriended me and simply *asked* for help, both Marco and I would've done anything for him. That's what friends do.

Instead, he chose to lie, to manipulate, to hurt me. *That* cannot be forgiven.

I sometimes wonder if I'm overreacting; if I can look past this indiscretion and give Everett another chance for both of our sakes. But, then I remember Everett showing up on my doorstep that day, determined to be my friend and taking me to see the cherry blossoms. I remember how sweet he was, how attentive, how curious about my life.

Now, I know why.

My phone vibrates on the table next to me and Yoda stirs in his sleep, cuddling up to my side. Maybe because I'm so tired, maybe because it's been a week and the ache in my chest has lessened, maybe I'm just a sadist, but I pick up the phone anyway.

Avery starts to shout on the other line before I can even say hello, "Aspen! What the hell is going on? I've been calling you for days, I even showed up at your house! Everett hasn't shown up to practice since that article came out and Marco's been sulking around... Jesse told me you were taking a break? Did you and Everett run off together? Are you pregnant? Did you —"

"Avery?"

A pause, and then a slightly breathless sigh, "yes?"

"Did you know?"

She's silent on the other line and I can hear the faint strumming of a guitar and Jesse's distant voice. "Know what? As far as I'm concerned, I'm the one left in the dark here."

And I have to laugh at the irony of that, though the sound is dry and scratchy from my throat being so neglected. "Did you know that Everett only got close to me for some deal he made with Marco? That he used me for my mother?"

I hear Marco's voice in the background and I really want to hang up, but I hear a door closing, and then more silence. "I'm sorry, *what* did you just say?"

"They made a deal that if Everett could get close to me, get me to overcome my fear of singing in time for the competition, then Marco would get our mom represent him for this whole assault/drug case going on." My voice is monotone, though the feelings beneath are anything but. Saying the words out loud is a painful experience, one that rattles the cage around my heart.

"Jesus Christ. That explains why Everett isn't around and why Marco has been a total ass." she lets out a quiet gasp, cursing under her breath, "holy shit... Marco."

"What? What is it?"

There's more cursing and what sounds like her hitting something before she speaks again, voice tinged with guilt and a little bit of bashfulness, "I slept with Marco."

I jolt up in bed, an emotion other than extreme grief and rage hitting me for the first time in days. "What the fuck? *When*?"

"The... the day you told us you were dating Everett." When she hears me gasp she lets out a frustrated groan, "I swear to god I had no idea what he was doing with Everett. I was just comforting him and it kind of... happened? But, *Jesus*, I never thought he would do something like this to you... fuck, I'm so sorry. I'm so disappointed..."

And I feel my deceased heart twist at her words because now I've dragged her into this mess, a mess Marco created, and shattered her illusion of the man she's been in love with for years.

"What are... what're you going to do, Aspen?"

I don't know what it is about this question, but all of the feelings I'd been pushing down resurface in one horrifying swoop. My throat closes and my eyes sting with tears and I desperately want to swallow them back down, but I just fucking can't. Because I have no idea what I'm going to do. My family betrayed me. The love of my life used me, lied to me for months on end, and I don't even know if any of those feelings were real. If any of it was real.

Again. This happened to me *again.*

My mother, my father, Marco, Everett, Sam... everyone, almost every single person in my life has deceived me and I can't help but wonder if it's not them, but... *me?*

What is it about myself that makes it so easy for others to hurt me?

"I have no fucking idea," I choke out through my tears, the crushing weight of everything pressing on my chest and making it difficult for me to breathe.

"Oh, Aspen," her own voice cracks at the sound of mine. "Should I come over?"

"No, no... I just want... I need to be alone."

She sighs sadly, "I'm just a phone call away, Aspen... you've survived a lot of things. I know you'll survive this."

"Avery... I'm sorry about Marco."

Her breath is shaky and when she speaks her voice matches it, "me too."

I hang up then because I'm afraid the ache in my chest will consume me. When I pull my phone away and see all the missed calls and texts, I try hard not to throw it at the wall.

Like clockwork, there is a banging on my door as I stare at the call log.

Yoda instantly jumps up from the bed, running to the door and yapping in excitement. But, I stay snuggled up in the covers. He'll stop in a few minutes.

"Aspen! Please... I know you're in there!" I attempt to block out Everett's voice with my pillow, but it does very little. "Just... just let me see your face... *please.*" His words are strained and I have to blink back my tears, slowly pulling back the pillow and indulging in the way my name sounds falling from his lips.

He calls out to me again and again and like a fly to a zapper, it draws me near.

I crawl out of bed slowly, my unused joints aching. His pounding only grows louder and more desperate and Yoda sits by the door, wagging his nubby tail.

Placing my palm against the cool wood, I lean up on my tiptoes to look through the peephole. Everett lifts his head just then and looks right into the hole, making me jump back in surprise.

His emerald eyes that were once so bright have dimmed slightly; now gloomy and drooping, with dark circles beneath. His hair is greasy and mussed and his face looks gaunt, as if he hasn't had a good meal in a bit. I doubt I look any better.

Everett leans his head against the door, "Aspen... I miss you. Please let me talk to you, let me explain." The agony in his voice and the desperate plea have me choking back a sob, the sound loud enough to have Everett reeling back and looking into the peephole once again. "Aspen?! You're here, aren't you? Please let me in... please talk to me."

I squeeze my eyes shut, slumping against the door and sliding down until I'm sitting, my arms wrapped around my knees. I don't say anything, just cuddle up to my dog and listen to Everett sniffle and bang his fist against the door once more.

"I'm sorry, Aspen. You have to understand it was never just about the deal," he sighs in frustration and I hear a shuffling noise, and then a light thud next to my head. He must have sat on the floor as well. "I know we can get past this. We can go somewhere once my trial is over... we can we can get through this if—"

"How? How can you possibly think we can move on from this?" My voice is cold as ice and I have a heart to match.

But, my tone doesn't stop Everett's light, hopeful gasp through the thin wood, "Aspen? *God*... It feels so good to hear your voice again... I know what I did was wrong, but... I love you. You know I love you, right? I never once lied about that. You have to—"

"I have to what? *Believe* you? Yeah, you asked me to do that once before, and look how that turned out." I don't know why I've bothered talking to him, it's only confusing me more. Some days I'm so irate it feels like my skin is on fire. Other days I'm so miserable it feels like there's a storm inside me. But, now... now I just feel *tired.*

Tired of being treated this way, tired of *feeling* this way. Just... tired.

Everett sniffs from the other side of the door and I hear him take in a shuddering breath. His voice cracks and my heart does too. "Fuck... I know I lied, but I would never... I would never lie about *that.* Please, just open the door, baby."

"Don't call me that... Please leave."

I hear him choke out a sob, "I can't... I won't leave you."

This time, it's me who bangs my fist against the door, shouting now, "just go! I can't... I can't talk to you right now. Please... for once, just do something good for me... and *go.*"

My last words come out in a strangled sigh and Everett heaves at the request.

"I'll go... for now. But, I'm not leaving you. I'm not giving up on us... on this." He pauses, sighing lightly, "I'll leave the band. If you want me to, I'll quit. Jesse told me you haven't been showing up to rehearsal. I'll quit so that you can come back... can continue to do what you love. Don't... don't give up on that because of me. Don't let this hinder your progress."

A sob from deep within my chest wracks my body and I cover my mouth to stifle the noise, my heart burning as his footsteps fade down the hallway.

Then, I cry for him, I cry for me, I cry for us and everything we lost.

Hopeless: having no hope or chance of changing or improving.

# INDURATIZE

Induratize: to harden the heart.

It's a word I first heard from my father the summer I turned 12 and I thought it was the saddest word in the world. I prayed it was one I'd never have to experience. But, it's one I embrace now, one I let seep through my very flesh until I feel the cold locks around my heart click into place. A word I found so frightening once, I find solace in now. Tired of the pain, of the confusion, of the betrayal.

I let the numbness take over.

That detachment is what allows me to open my door when Marco knocks on it the last day of Everett's trial. He jumps when the door swings open, stuttering in shock. It's the first time I've seen him in almost a month. I haven't seen anyone besides Avery a few times and Jesse once. My absence hasn't stopped everyone from calling me multiple times a day, though: Jesse about the band, Everett to grovel, Marco to apologize, my mom about Everett, Sam about me, and Enzo about picking up the phone.

"A-Aspen, oh my god," he barges into my apartment, spinning to face me. "Do you know how long I've been trying to contact you?"

"Do you know how long I've been trying to avoid you?"

Marco rears back, pausing to gather his words and whatever nonsense is about to come out of his mouth. "I know... I know what Everett and I did was wrong, but you know we had your best interest in mind. I did it for *you,* Aspen. You can't... stay angry at me forever."

"I'm not angry."

"You clearly are."

"I'm hurt, Marco." Though my voice cracks, I still feel nothing, express nothing, "I'm hurt you lied to me, used me, had someone *else* use me for their own personal gain. And I'm not sure I want to associate with someone who can hurt me so easily and try to justify it."

His face crumples at my words and I know that he's going to start groveling, start apologizing. Though it's exactly what he should do, I don't want to hear it. I'm tired of people apologizing for shit they aren't really sorry for.

"I quit the band."

His remorseful look shifts into one of indignant disbelief and shock. I'm just surprised Jesse hasn't told the rest of the crew yet. Maybe he's hoping I'll change my mind and pull through. Maybe I would if I still had the capacity to feel guilty for leaving.

"W-What?! Aspen, no! Why?"

"I don't have any interest in it right now." I don't have much interest in anything anymore. How can I, when my heart has dimmed and dimmed throughout the years and finally burned so bright that, in a flash, it exploded and burned out?

"How can you—" he shakes his head, taking a step towards me. "Don't quit the band because of us Aspen, you can't do that... you love singing, you *started* the band..."

And I know he's right because although I'd rather die than admit it, their little plan worked. Everett helped me love singing again, love myself again, and I'd be so very grateful if the methods to get me there weren't so toxic.

If the methods to get me back to who I used to be hadn't destroy me in the process.

Marco's plan to get me singing again in time for the competition backfired majorly and now I won't be attending at all. "The deed is done," I sigh and usher him towards the door, "now, can you please go? I'm running late for something."

My last sentence makes him stop, rounding on me just as I open the door to shove him out, "Everett's trial? You're going?"

I tense at the question, "go, Marco."

He sighs deep and heavy before stepping through the doorway, "this conversation isn't over. I won't let you give up on your dreams because of a stupid mistake." I just roll my eyes, closing the door behind him, but he wedges his foot inside to stop it. His voice is gentle and his eyes are swimming with guilt when he speaks again, “I’m still angry he got involved with you that way, but he does love you, Aspen. Anyone with eyes can see the way he looks at you. If you believe nothing else, at least believe that."

Then, he removes his foot, the door shutting on him. My chest stabs, but I don't let the words settle, don't let them wrap around my bleeding heart. They bounce off my skin like rubber.

Maybe he does love me, maybe he doesn't. It doesn't really matter anymore.

* * *

The courtroom is standing room only.

Reporters, fans, friends, and family fill every seat, the whole room buzzing with gossip and the clicking of cameras. It’s a large oval chamber covered in oak and the smell of old books and justice. The carpet is green and ugly and makes my nervous nausea grow. I see my ex-band mates in the first row, but I linger towards the back. Lost in a sea of faces.

I battled with the idea to come today in the first place, but I had to know. Even if he hurt me, I need to know that Everett gets a just hearing. Need to know he’s okay. I still care for Everett regardless of how he hurt me. I think I'll always care for him, always love him because he came into my life in a time when I needed someone the most. But, I don't want him to know I came, I don't want to give him that hope. I wear a floppy hat and sunglasses to cover my tired eyes, bundled up in layers so he can't even pick my ass out in the crowd.

I've been keeping up with the proceedings over the last two weeks via Avery. I know all about the prosecution bringing forward a witness who claimed Everett initiated the brawl. I know how my mother tore apart that testimony, expertly revealing that the witness hadn't come on the scene until Leo was already on the ground. I know that my mother called Leo's roommate to the stand who confirmed that Leo told him of his plans to rob his dealer in great detail. I know that she also called character witnesses —Jesse and Avery— that attested to Everett's changed ways and pacification. I know that the prosecution painted Leo as a desperate and sick man the country had failed. I know my mother painted Everett as a man in dire need of support, who needed to defend himself against an attacker trying to steal his only source of income. I know that the prosecution showed photos of Leo's bruised and beaten face, and compared it to Everett's measly stab wound.

I know that the trial could go either way.

Everett saunters into the room just a few minutes later clad in a snug suit, hair slicked back, and face expressionless. His entrance spurs more whispers, but my mother trailing behind him in her barrister uniform of the black robe and white wig, manages to quiet the rumblings with a single look.

My mother is speaking to him in hushed tones as they make their way down the aisle, but Everett is hardly paying attention. His eyes scan every inch of the courtroom, sweeping over every face, only growing more and more distressed when he passes each one. I make sure to duck behind a tall reporter when he looks in my direction and he soon grows dejected, shoulders slumping and gaze falling to the ground when he can't find who he's looking for.

*Me.*

He stops to say hello to our friends: hugging Jesse, but getting a cold greeting from Avery. Enzo simply nods in a greeting and my brother completely ignores him.

My mother throws Marco a quick wave, but is quick to slip back into professional mode. She drags Everett to the front, through the mini gates that separate us, and into their seats at the desk. The prosecution —one main barrister that is short and stubby and looks kind of like Danny DeVito— is already in his seat and it doesn't take long for the very tall and very somber looking judge to stride in through the back doors.

The last day of trial begins with the prosecution's closing statement, painting Everett as a burnt-out rock star whose only concern is making money, no matter the cost. Not only was he furthering the opioid crisis in the UK, but also almost killed a man when his payment was threatened. Even if Leo attacked first, there were many opportunities to deescalate the situation. Everett, pride bruised, attempted to kill and almost finished the job. Irresponsible, reckless, cruel.

They paint Leo as a wayward innocent, corrupted by people like Everett, who push drugs on the vulnerable population. That Leo's desperation was the fault of the dealers who caused his dependency. Leo stabbed Everett by accident, and Everett nearly killed him to save his pills. Leo was the victim. Leo has long-term brain damage and low-motor function and Everett walked away unscathed.

And one last final blow, "this is a face loved by thousands, but it's one of a monster."

The words cut through me like glass and I can feel the rage boiling up inside of me like a kettle. Everett hangs his head low, face covered by a wall hair and my chest aches painfully when I think of how those words must have made him feel. Despite all of my precautions to keep my heart closed off, I can feel it ache for him. Call for him.

Neither Leo nor Everett are blameless, but I feel for both of them.

My mother is scribbling on a notepad furiously, shaking her head and whispering to Everett as the prosecution saunters back to his seat, more than pleased. But, Everett is unresponsive. If he was dejected when he couldn't find me in the crowd, he's positively crushed now by the prosecution's scathing words.

But, my mother isn't the #1 defense barrister in the country for nothing.

Her stride is confident as she takes the floor, facing the jury instead of the judge like the prosecution had. The room falls into a stillness that almost makes it hard to breathe. And when she does open her mouth to speak, all the air in my lungs is stolen from me. She opens with a greeting and explanation of the jury's burden of proof, but this is all a warm-up to the big show. Like her children, she's also a performer.

"My daughter has this odd fascination with definitions, with words. She probably has the biggest vocabulary of anyone you'll ever meet. So, I decided to take a page from her book before starting this trial. Assault occasioning Actual Bodily Harm under British law is defined as: the intentional or reckless unlawful force against another person that causes bodily harm. Now, let's dissect this definition in regard to the charges against my client. Firstly, 'intentional' insinuates that my client knew Mr. Solis before he approached him for narcotics. That he'd somehow knew Mr. Solis was planning to rob him and had intended to get into a scuffle, ending in Mr. Solis's injuries.

"That seems highly unlikely, doesn't it? The very first time my client met Mr. Solis was the same night this altercation occurred, clearly stated in the report. He had no way of knowing Mr. Solis' plans, therefore, 'intentional' is a false narrative. In that definition, is also the word 'unlawful' and maybe I've missed something here. Did my client attack Mr. Solis first? No, he only fought back in self-defense. Did he stab Mr. Solis? No, in fact, Mr. Solis stabbed *my* client.

"Mr. Fox simply wanted to provide a service to Mr. Solis, who in turn, tried to rob and assault him with a deadly weapon. Mr. Fox tried to leave the scene twice, but was stopped by Mr. Solis's attacks both times, resulting in my client being stabbed. My client was defending himself against those attacks, and due to his inebriation, Mr. Solis tripped and fell. My client, though guilty in other matters, was not the instigator in Mr. Solis's condition. What happened to him was a tragic accident brought on by his own poor choices. Words like assault, unlawful, and intentional don't apply in my client's case. Therefore, you must acquit on all charges."

The courtroom is stunned into silence and I feel pride swell up my chest like a balloon. I've never seen my mom in action, never seen her defend someone so passionately. Never seen her use *me* as a tactic. Although we aren't close by any means, although she was neglectful and secretive, I have to admit: she's pretty amazing.

Everett finally drags his head up, glancing up at my mom as she rounds the table to sit back down. Jesse actually begins to clap at the closing statement, wiping fake tears from his eyes, and causing Enzo to slap him hard on the back to get him to sit back down. The judge bangs his gavel and dismisses the jury to come to a verdict.

The courtroom fills with chatter and my eyes travel to the opposite end of the benches where a group of five or six men and women are huddled around each other, praying. It doesn't take a genius to know that they're the Solis family. Whatever verdict comes today, there is still a long road of recovery and healing for Leo Solis ahead. Still trauma, still pain, still addiction. There will be no victory.

Everett glances at the group many time, eyes rimmed red and mouth taut. He even tries to head their way at one point, but with a hand on his arm and a shaking head, my mother stops him. Everett remains in his chair, completely tight-lipped and depressed as if the judge had already walked in and declared him guilty on all counts.

The interval is long and I'm not exactly sure if we're supposed to wait for the jury's verdict or if they'll even come to a decision today. However, it only takes 45 minutes before they're filing back into the room and handing the judge their verdict. When the judge sits back in his chair, the loud room descends into a silence filled with tension and anticipation. He takes his sweet time fixing his robe, rubbing his bald head, and shuffling his papers. Everett is rigid in his seat, head bowed, as the room waits with bated breath.

"The jury finds the defendant, Everett Fox, on one count of possession with intent to supply Class B Drugs... guilty. An unlimited fine of £20,000, a non-custodial sentence of probation for two years, and 75 hours of community service to be completed within the year is the punishment. Any violation of these conditions will result in immediate imprisonment.

"For the charge of Assault occasioning Actual Bodily Harm, the defendant is found... not guilty."

The heavy air in the courtroom seems to disperse at once, everyone letting out a huge sigh of relief. Everett's head drops into his hands and his body relaxes instantly. I feel as if a weight has been lifted from my shoulders. As if by hearing this, by coming today, I've fulfilled my duty. I'm relieved and can finally put everything from the past few months behind me.

Everett is okay, he'll be just fine. With or without me, he'll be fine. And I'll be fine too. I just need time to heal from the lies I've told myself and the ones that have been told to me.

My mom pats Everett on the back before walking over to the prosecution —probably to shove her win in his face. The media all file out one by one, satisfied with the verdict, and our friends practically clamber over the seats to congratulate Everett. With a distant smile, I watch as Jesse pulls him into a hug and Marco goes to talk to my mother while Enzo and Avery hang back. With a deep breath, I head towards the doors in order to slip out unnoticed, but make the mistake of turning my head to glance towards my friends one last time.

I nearly choke when I lock eyes with Everett, his mouth agape and emerald eyes lighting up at the sight of me. My body stills as Everett stares, blinking rapidly as if to make sure I'm really there. I can tell he wants to greet me, to walk over, but there are too many people between us and too many feelings.

Slowly, I smile, eyes soft, and mouth a sincere *congratulations* that makes him beam like a kid in a candy store.

A matching smile curls up his lips as he mouths a quick *thank you*.

With one last lingering look at the hope in his eyes, I turn with resigned tears and stride out of the courthouse without looking back.

And when I get home that night, I pack a bag.

# CLOSURE

I've always loved the sea.

The mysteriousness of how endless and ancient it seems, the feeling of the cool sand between my toes, the calming waves, the salty air... It reminds me of simpler times. When Mom would take us to Brighton beach every weekend to try to cheer us up, to try to make us forget we'd been abandoned. Of course, we didn't forget, but we acted like we did for her sake. We built sandcastles and played footy and tried to pretend things were normal.

I can feel my pulse on my tongue. Steady and fast. Sand molds to my feet and settles between my toes as I take determined steps towards the noise barely audible over the roaring waves ahead. Laughter, music, distinct voices booming over the crowd.

It's chilly out, but only because the sea is so close and the breeze is biting —the air giving off a whiff of saltwater that you can taste when you lick your lips.

Beyond the large gathering, there's a fire just before the roaring waves, a small crowd gathered around it. I hear it there, somewhere in that group, floating towards me. The raspy and quick laughter, deep and familiar, and making my heart flutter in my chest. My brain tells me to turn back, to leave without saying anything. But, my heart knows better. My heart is what keeps me walking towards the party. My heart is telling me I need to say goodbye.

Closure: a feeling that an emotional or traumatic experience has been resolved.

So, I keep walking, the figures at Everett's ill-advised party becoming clearer and my insecurities growing as they do. The urge to turn around has never been stronger as I take note of the crop tops and summer dresses, glancing down at my boyfriend jeans and ratty sweater that keeps slipping off my shoulder.

The closer I get to the tent, the less courage I have and the higher my heartrate climbs, until I do eventually turn around, only to slam right into someone standing awfully close behind me. "Oh my, I'm so sorry, I wasn't... Aspen?!"

The voice is gratingly familiar and I finally glance up at the long dark locks, light brown eyes, soft pink dress, and feel my stomach plummet even further. "Marisol, hi."

She smiles wide and carefree, eyes slightly glazed over and drink sloshing in her hand. When she speaks, it's slightly slurred and the party is so loud I have to strain my ears to hear. "Thank god you're here! Everett's been in the worst mood all night, you'll cheer him up!"

She's obviously unaware that Everett and I aren't exactly on speaking terms and I'm not gonna break it to her. "Why is he upset? He's not guilty."

"That's exactly what I said! But, he's still sulking." She leans closer, voice jovial, "but, now you're here and we can get the party started!"

Although I still resent her for helping Everett make me jealous, I find her joyful disposition refreshing. So, I force a smile on my face and nod, "I'll try my best."

She laughs then, much too loudly for what I've said, "please! You won't even have to try! As soon as he sees your face he'll cheer up! The guy is obsessed with you."

My smile falters, "what... what do you mean?"

She takes a sip of her drink before speaking, "well, you're all he talks about. Even when we were still hooking up he was always complaining about you or laughing at something you said. *God,* he was always calling me to ask how to fix whatever fight you two got in. He drove me and himself mad with all his worrying. It was cute and kind of pathetic at the same time… but, I'm just glad you two are finally together and happy!"

My stomach churns like the waves a few dozen feet away and my heart is lodged in my throat and I feel like I might be sick with grief, so I just smile absentmindedly before walking away as quickly as possible. Although I'd like to deny it and just let the betrayal and rage consume me, I'm beginning to believe that Everett loves me. When his feelings started, though, I can't be sure. I'm not sure of anything anymore.

Anything except that it's time I work on myself and just *breathe* without all of this lying, without everyone I love hurting me. Regardless of their intentions. I just need a fucking break: to be selfish, to heal, and to learn to love myself again.

I can't do that here.

"Don't let Jesse see you," I jump when a tanned arm stretches out, holding out a red up filled with mysterious liquid. "He might burst into tears and beg you to rejoin the band."

I gingerly take the cup from his hand and glance up to see Enzo's small smile, "thanks for the heads-up… and the drink."

He nods as I look out into the sea of familiar and unfamiliar faces—Everett still remaining unseen. My hand shakes as I lift the cup to my lips and take a large swig, reveling in the burning sensation as it slides down my throat.

"I wasn't expecting to see you here." It's the first time I've spoken to Enzo since everything fell apart, but I can tell from the sympathy in his eyes that he knows what happened. Who told him is unclear, but I find myself surprisingly embarrassed that he knows. Knows that I fell for Everett's lies.

I'm guessing they've all heard the news by now if my recent missed calls are any indication. I feel vulnerable, like my heart is bleeding and bruised on the table and everyone is just watching it struggling to survive.

"Yeah, well… I'm going away for a while. So, I came to say goodbye."

If Enzo's surprised he doesn't show it, just continues to watch the people in front of us dance to some pop song and the group farther down the beach running around the bonfire. I see Marco and Avery in that group, arguing with each other, as she walks away and he pulls her back. The guilt tugs at my stomach again, but I push it down.

Enzo's husky voice cuts though the music, "should I go away with you? It would be fun."

I laugh, taking another gulp of my drink. "I'm sure it would," my smile falters and I glance back out at the sea. "But, I need to go alone. Be with myself for a bit."

He stares intently, searching the side of my face, but I refuse to face the pity in his gaze. Avery shoves Marco away, stomping over to the tent we're standing in. Marco tugs on his short hair and kicks up a wave of sand. I look away, the moment feeling too private to spy on.

"Fox is an idiot."

This makes my head snap towards Enzo, my heart plummeting at the mention. There's a softness in his eyes and tick in his jaw. "Don't, Enzo."

He lifts his hands in surrender just as Avery spots us and beelines her way through the dancers. "I'm just saying... he's an idiot. An idiot who loves you and still chose to hurt you and that's why you deserve better. That's why I'm glad you're leaving."

I open my mouth to thank him through the lump in my throat, but Avery cuts in. She rips my cup from my hand and downs what little is left. Hiccupping, she wipes some snot from her nose, face flushed an upset pink. "Your brother is such an ass."

Enzo claps me on the back and flashes me a sad smile, passing me his almost full drink.

A goodbye.

I squeeze the hand on my shoulder before it falls away and watch him disappear into the crowd, chest tight, before facing Avery. "Avery... I hope you're not... I hope you're not *not* with my brother because of me. You've... had feelings for him for so long and finally—"

She almost looks offended, "he's not who I thought he was. He basically pimped out his own sister to win our competition... even if he thought it would help you it's still wrong... I love him, I do. But, I just need time away from him right now."

*Sounds familiar.*

I nod somberly, taking a gulp of the drink Enzo gave me. It only burns a little on the way down, so I drink the rest quickly. A cough rattles my chest as the warm liquid swishes around in my otherwise empty stomach. I'm just buzzed enough for the numbness to settle in my bones.

Numb and buzzed enough to do what needs to be done.

"So, did you get everything set up?"

Avery's brows scrunch together in confusion before realization settles. She quickly shakes all depressing thoughts from her head, clapping her hands together in a way that clearly means business. "Yes, I had them turn on the electricity and gas for you. The water will be turned on when you get there. I also had the maids stock the fridge. They'll start work on the second week you're there."

"I don't need maids, Avery."

She looks so confused, I might as well have said the Earth is flat. "Yes, you do... how else would you eat? How else would the house be kept clean? How would you survive?"

My laughter reverberates around the tent, almost as loud as the music and I know it has more to do with the liquor warming my veins than Avery's (hopefully) joking manner. When my laughter dies and I look back at my beautiful friend to see a bittersweet smile on her lips, I realize that was the first time I've genuinely laughed in a long time. I'd been gradually getting better: smiling more, eating more, sleeping more. It's been a long time since I've been able to laugh without bursting into tears afterwards.

Every day, it gets easier. Every day, the pain in my chest lessens.

I clear my throat uncomfortably, not letting the sadness settle. "Thank you for letting me stay at your summer house, Avery."

"No thanks needed. I've always got your back, girl." I pull her into a hug, eyes swimming. The hug is warm and long and I use it to ask what I've been dying to know since I pulled up to this beach.

"Where's... um, where is Everett, anyway? I-I should at least tell him I'm leaving."

She turns her head to glance behind her, towards the shore, and I follow her gaze. And when I do, below the numbness, below the icy cold layers of my heart, I feel it squeeze painfully in my chest. Because he's sitting on a log just out of reach from the ocean's greedy fingers, with three girls surrounding him, and he looks nothing like Marisol described. His head is thrown back in laughter and though the music is shaking the tent and the roaring waves are even louder, I swear I can hear the deep rumble of his laugh.

And it cuts right through me.

It's then I realize how tightly I'm wrapped around his finger, how tightly the shackles at my feet are bound.

Because I should hate him, should despise him for what he did. The sight of him should disgust me and there should be no inkling of warmth towards him, even in the deepest crevice of my heart. But, somehow... just the sight of him with other girls, laughing so carelessly, while I can barely bring myself to smile nearly rips me to shreds and destroys all the progress I've made.

"I'm fine. I'm gonna go dip my feet in the water." I avoid Avery's worried gaze and comforting embrace, making my way through the throngs of sweaty bodies, towards the edge of the cliffs at the end of the beach. On the way there, I grab a bottle of whiskey from the cooler.

I've been so stupid. I was always the one to call first, the one that remembered anniversaries, the one that waited up at night for them to come home. I was always the one who loved more.

Until Everett.

He was chasing *me*, always watching, always letting me know how wanted I was. I think I let that consume me, cloud my judgment. Even when I thought he was hiding something, I trusted him. Chose to live in the sunlight instead of letting the shadows consume me.

Everett was supposed to be different. He wouldn't let me down like my dad had, wouldn't neglect me like my mom had, wouldn't betray me like Sam had. But, he was just like the rest.

I think that's what hurts the most.

The sand is cool between my toes, the drink warm as it slides down my throat, and the air crisp with the ocean breeze. The noise of the party eventually fades as I make my way down the beach until reaching the cliff, walking around to the alcove so I'm hidden from view. It's a large bluff that shields me from the crowd, but allows me to enjoy the ocean breeze and gaze out into the blackness of the waves.

It's like God loved this cliff so much he took a spoon and scooped out the edge of it, swallowing it whole, and creating this little cave.

The image of that makes me giggle and I plop to the ground with a dull thud, a bit of the whiskey spilling onto my jeans. I bring my knees to my chest and close my eyes, listening to the push and pull of the waves, completely content.

Then I think I'm the ocean and Everett is the moon, pulling me in and pushing me away.

Then I think that maybe I drank more than I should've.

A voice cuts through my peaceful silence. A raspy and slow, familiar voice that sends chills down my warm flesh.

"Mind if I sit here, Munchkin?"

# FINIFUGAL

*Everett*

I was nervous at the trial.

The type of nervous that makes bile rise up your throat and palms clam up uncontrollably. The kind that makes you feel as if you're on a rocky sea voyage because your stomach won't stop turning and you're unbelievably dizzy.

I was nervous at the trial.

But, now, standing above the woman I love and waiting for her to grant me permission to sit... I'm more nervous than I've ever been. And that thought almost makes me laugh because there's no way I should be more nervous around a girl than I was on trial for assault.

I really hadn't expected her to come to the party, hadn't even expected her to come to the hearing. But, that didn't stop me from desperately searching for her at both. When Enzo told me she was here I almost didn't believe him. But, when I actually saw her walking along the shore, I all but ran from the groupies just to catch a glimpse of her.

Now, Aspen doesn't even glance at me. She just continues to squint out at the vast ocean as if she can find the answers to the universe in the almost blackened night waves. She takes a swig of the bottle and her chestnut hair flares across her makeup-less face in the wind, but she doesn't bother to stop it. Her much-too-big olive sweater exposes her tanned shoulder and her bare feet are almost completely covered in the grainy sand.

She's never looked so gorgeous.

Her mouth remains tightly shut, but she holds the bottle up to me and I take that as an olive branch. I grab the bottle from her grasp, sitting on the sand next to her, but not too close. My heart hammers wildly in my chest and my nerves paired with the few shots I've had make me slightly dizzy. And even though the tension in the air is almost palpable, even though she hasn't spoken a word, even though I'm almost positive she hates me...

This is the happiest I've been this entire month.

"Do you wanna hear a joke?"

It's been a long time since I've gotten to tell her a joke and I really just want to hear her call me an idiot again. Out of the corner of my eye I see her lip tilt up in a small smile, "always."

"What did the hotdog say after the race?"

Finally, *finally* she glances at me. Her hazel eyes are more of a soft brown than they are green and they're slightly sad when she squints at me. "I don't know, what?"

"I'm a wiener!"

She shakes her head dramatically, though I can see her biting back a grin. "Idiot," her laugh is breathy and weak, but the word slips out in a fond and endearing tone.

And then we're quiet again. I take a sip of the whiskey, letting the harsh liquor warm my veins as I stare out into the dark abyss and try not to let on how much I'm freaking out right now. Because she isn't yelling at me and she's not crying and it's just kind of... calm? It's almost how things used to be between us before... before I fucked it all up.

*Almost* like how it used to be, but not quite.

Because if it was like before, I'd be holding her hand or brushing her hair back or kissing her neck. I'd be trying to get into her pants and she'd laugh me off, but eventually give me a dizzying kiss before pulling me back towards the cars, laughing all the way.

But now... forget about touching her, she won't even look at me.

"Are you having fun?"

Her question shocks me and I snap my head to look at her as she holds her hand out for the bottle, face expressionless. "Now I am."

"It looked like you were having plenty of fun with those girls."

My heart stutters because her words mean that she was watching me, that she was bothered I was talking to other girls. I try not to let that little bit of hope spread, but I can feel it growing along with the grin on my lips. I can tell she regrets bringing it up from the scowl on her face and pinkness in her cheeks and my chest feels a little lighter because she looks so adorable.

And *God*, do I love her.

"Those girls were just trying to get me to give them Enzo's number."

Her cheeks grow an even darker shade of scarlet and she avoids my gaze, taking an even bigger swig of the bottle. She doesn't seem drunk, but the bottle is nearly half-empty.

I want to ask her why she came to the trial or how she's doing or even what she ate for breakfast, but I have no idea what the boundaries are. I don't know how to act around someone that wants nothing to do with me when I want everything to do with them.

It feels like I've been deprived of oxygen for so long and finally, *finally* I can breathe again, but I've forgotten how.

"Aspen... I," I clear my throat, running sweaty palms against the ripped denim of my jeans, trying to calm my nerves. "I just wanted to thank you and say how much I appreciated you coming to the trial, how much it meant to me that—"

"I'm leaving, Everett."

Her voice is so abrupt, her statement so shocking, that I choke on my words and have to swallow them back up, coughing violently, "w-what?"

"I'm leaving London... going away for a while."

Her voice holds no emotion and I have to shake my head a few times to make sure I heard her right. She's sitting with her elbows on her knees and the bottle between her legs and her eyes trained on the ocean as if she hadn't said anything of importance at all. I let her words sink in, really resonate, and I swear I've never felt that kind of searing pain.

It's like my lungs forget how to function as I struggle to intake a full breath and my heart pumps erratically in my chest, suddenly feeling like I want to scream or cry or both.

"Why?" The word comes out harsher than I intended and I try to swallow down my anger, my anxiety. Try desperately to calm down.

But, like the sand I sit on, I feel her slipping through my fingers and no matter how hard I try, I can't stop it.

She doesn't answer me and takes her sweet time sipping gingerly from the bottle, staring out into the sea with furrowed brows and set jaw. I can feel my frustration growing with each second that passes, the panic clawing at my throat.

*"Why?!"* I repeat myself, almost yelling. Aspen jumps slightly at my raised voice, turning to face me in alarm. "Why are you leaving, Aspen? How can you... just *leave*?"

"I need to get away, Everett. From all of this. From..." she trails off and I want to pretend that she wasn't going to say me. "I need some time away. Some time to work on myself."

But, I'm already shaking my head, "why can't you do that here? You already quit the band and cut everyone off. You cut me off—"

She's irritated now, "I may have cut you off, but you gave me the knife."

I take deep breaths to quell my anger, to try to reign in my dread. Eyes stinging, I have to blink multiple times to get it to stop. I'm torn between letting her go and falling at her feet to beg her to stay. I'm always going to fight for her, but I'm also fighting for her happiness, and it pains me to think she'd be happier away from me.

"How long, Aspen?"

She swallows, looking away at the sound of my defeated voice. "I honestly don't know."

It feels like she just squeezed my heart in her unforgiving fist, a physical and unforgiving ache in my chest. I gasp for air because it feels as if it's been stolen from me.

"No! I can't... you can't leave me behind, Aspen, *please*." My voice cracks and I bury my head between my knees so she doesn't see my face crumpling and the tears that slipped down my cheeks. I hear her sniffle, feet shuffling in the sand.

"This isn't about you, Everett. For once... for once this is about *me*. Everything is so fucked right now and... I just need to breathe again. I need to *live* again."

"Well, what about *me*?" I look at her, let her see the tears on my splotchy face. "I can't breathe without *you*, so what about me? What am I supposed to do if you leave?"

It's selfish and pathetic, but she hasn't even left yet and it feels like a huge chunk of my heart has been ripped right out of my chest and I'm left raw and bleeding at her feet. I'm grasping at straws here because I know I'm fighting a losing battle, but I can't just do *nothing.* I can't just watch the girl I'm so madly in love with walk right out of my life without trying to stop her.

She winces and drops her face to her knees, not bothering to wipe away her own tears. "We just aren't good for each other anymore, Everett. You asked me to trust you, and all the while you were lying to me. You *knew* what you were doing would hurt me and yet you kept doing it. We just... we aren't good anymore, it's not healthy... you need to learn to breathe without me."

I choke on a sob, running a hand down my face to wipe the pitiful tears away. "I promised I'd fight for you. Even if you're gone for months... for years, I'll still be here because we *are* good together. What I did was horrible, I know. I'll regret it for the rest of my life, but everything else? Everything else we had was so... *so* good."

"Everett..."

"I love you, Aspen," my voice is hoarse and desperate and she squeezes her eyes shut against it. "I'm so in love with you, it's pathetic. You're all I think about, you're all I want. I—"

"*Please*... please don't make this any harder than it already is, Everett." And the way she says it... the desperation in her voice and the way it cracks.... I stop speaking. It's silent again; just the sound of the ocean between us and the distant party behind us. I try to let the waves calm me, try to reign in my panic at the crushing thought that this might be the last time I see Aspen... for who knows how long. That she may not even want me when she comes back.

I take this opportunity to appraise her out of the corner of my eye: her chestnut locks highlighted by pale moonlight, the arch of her brow and curl of her lash, the slope of her nose, the plump flesh of those lips I've kissed so often... I trace her features over and over again, engraining every little detail into my brain from the golden rim around her pupil to the small freckles dusted across her cheeks. I want to memorize it all.

I want her to haunt my dreams.

"Everett," I barely hear her whisper my name, her voice almost carried away in the breeze it's so small and shaky. "Will you kiss me?"

I nearly choke, coughing harshly and glancing over to see if she's serious, to see if I heard her right. But, her stare is level and sure, gauging my reaction and waiting for an answer. I almost feel as if this is a trap, but it's a trap I'd gladly fall into. I don't know her intentions or why she suddenly blurted this request out, but it's an opportunity I could never pass up.

It's an opportunity I may not have again.

"Are you sure?"

She simply nods, scooting closer, and I can feel my pulse on my tongue —heavy and fast. I meet her halfway just as she reaches out to place her palm on my cheek and I nearly weep at the touch. My eyes search hers for any trace of doubt, but they're soft and sure. My hand shakes as I reach out to cup her jaw, leaning in closer and tasting the breath between us. My eyes snap to hers one more time for permission, but they're already closed. Gently, I brush my lips against hers and they spark together almost violently, so charged up we might catch fire. Her hand buries itself in my hair as mine cups the back of her neck, applying more pressure between our lips and almost moaning at the pleasure. I feel like I'm dreaming and I never want to wake.

Our first kiss in almost a month and maybe one of our last.

I sigh into her mouth and she takes the opportunity to slide her tongue against my lip before delving into the creases and meeting mine. She tastes like whiskey and home and I never want to stop kissing her. I'm almost dizzy from her taste, her scent, the feeling of her delicate fingers tracing my neck. Dizzy with lust, with love, with grief.

I grab her face with my shaking hands and pull her onto my lap and moaning when she wraps her thighs around my hips. She nibbles on my bottom lip lightly and lets out a gentle sigh, pulling away just enough so that her lips brush against my own when she speaks.

"Make love to me, Everett."

My head rears back because there's no way those words came from her mouth, "what?"

A soft smile pulls on her swollen lips as she runs her thumb across my mouth, a gentle sadness in her eyes that makes my chest sting. "Make love to me, Everett."

I look at her closely to gauge if she drank more than I thought, but her eyes are clear and her words aren't slurred and, holy shit, she is dead fucking serious. My heart beats in my chest like a drum as I try to make sense of what she just asked me because it feels like this is her goodbye. That this is our last night together, and I refuse to believe that. She could barely look at me yesterday... and now?

"Aspen... I'm not... I can't sleep with you when you hate me, when you're leaving."

The words hurt coming out and I almost want to swallow them back up, but I don't want one more night with her. I want a hundred more nights with her, a lifetime of nights with her.

She runs her hands down my chest and I shiver under her touch, my grip tightening on her hips. Torturing me, she ducks down to graze her lips against my own, making my breath quicken and resolve weaken.

"I don't hate you, Everett. I never did," she whispers, and my heart sings at the confession, relief washing over me in a tidal wave. When she speaks again, her voice is shaky and choked with unshed tears, "I just... I want you to hold me before I go."

"I've missed you so much." The desperation is clear as the waves crash at our feet and moonlight kisses our skin, "more than you could possibly know... I don't want you to leave."

She places a chaste kiss to my lips, rubbing against my crotch and making me groan out, almost embarrassingly turned on just by having her touch me. I groan because she's on top of me and kissing me and wants me after all this time and I feel like I'm dreaming.

"Then show me." Her voice is raspy and low, but so, *so* sad. "Show me how much you missed me, Everett. Show me how much you love me. I want to feel you again, I want you to hold me before I go."

And I know that she'll be gone in the morning. I know that doing this, being with her again, will only make her goodbye hurt more. It'll destroy me. But, I'd let her destroy me. I'd do anything to feel her in my arms again, if only for a brief moment.

So, I prepare my heart for devastation.

I yank her face back to mine and slam my lips to hers, causing the most delicious moan to fall from her delicate lips and she tangles her fingers into my hair, tugging on the roots harshly.

Her lips taste like poetry and lullabies and I feel myself wanting to memorize every line, every stanza. My hands slide down her hips to grip onto the flesh of her bum tightly and she mewls, pressing herself tighter against me. She slides her hands down my neck and across my chest, leaving a trail of fire behind them, and making a guttural groan slip past my lips. The only sounds are those of the roaring waves, Aspen's soft moans, and the distant sound of partiers a mile down the beach and muffled through our little nook of stone. She pulls away, lips leaving petal-soft kisses against the stubble of my jaw, the flesh of my ear, and the crook of my neck. My breaths come out as pants and all self-control has left my body.

All I see is her, all I smell is her, all I taste is her.

Each kiss, each caress, holds a quiet desperation and pained sadness. A goodbye that neither of us want to acknowledge.

Instead we communicate in the only way we know how: our bodies.

I can't help but notice how different this time feels than the rest. My hands are less sure; they shake when I make my voyage around her body. Her lips are hungrier than ever before: kissing every inch of my jaw, my neck, as if embedding my taste on her mouth.

"Oh, fuck," I groan when Aspen grinds her hips down onto mine, nimble fingers working on the buttons of my flannel. She groans with impatience when they don't budge and grabs my collar to yank the flannel apart in her desperation, buttons popping off in every direction.

And *dear god*, is that hot.

Her nails lightly scratch down my chest and a violent shiver wracks my body as our lips collide with a ferocity that shocks even me. She slides my shirt down the length of my arms until it drops onto the sand and I'm quick to turn us and lay her down upon it as a makeshift blanket. I slow my actions now, not wanting to rush this, wanting to remember every second. I recall a word Aspen taught me after a date at the cinema and my chest pangs with the irony of it now.

Finifugal: hating endings; of someone who tries to avoid or prolong the final moment of a story, relationship, or some other journey.

My fists tangle in the bottom of her sweater before sliding it off her body, our lips separating briefly as it falls to the sand next to us. She's braless, laid completely bare against my shirt and I take this moment to look at her, *really* look at her. Her hair falls in messy waves, her cheeks are flushed a deep pink, her lips swollen, her body beautifully tanned and slightly rosy, and her hazel eyes... mournful, but full of passion.

She's never looked more beautiful.

I bring my lips down to her neck, softly grazing my teeth against her freckled flesh and loving the way her back arches, grasping my bicep, "oh god, Everett."

The sound of her moaning my name makes me bite down and I laugh lightly when she writhes beneath me. I kiss every inch of her, branding her with the evidence of my affection and burning holes into her flesh with my hot lips. Her fingers grip onto my hair desperately when I latch my teeth around a pink nipple, tugging lightly before soothing it with my tongue and kissing the puckered skin gently. I pull away only enough to undo her jeans, sliding them down with her underwear and chuckling when she kicks them off in a hurry.

But, I stop then. I stop and sit up on my knees to get a clear look at her beneath me.

I look at her like a blind man just granted sight, like a man in love, like this might be my last chance.

She watches me attentively as I drink in the sight of her: the swell of her petite breasts, curve of her hips, smoothness of her legs. My calloused fingers reach out to trace the jagged scar on her ribcage, the little white marks on her hips that signify her growth, the small freckle below her belly button. Her own personal map of life. She looks downright ethereal.

I take a mental picture of her, so that I never forget. I burn the image into my mind until I could draw her from memory. I take my time exploring her body, kissing down her breasts while my fingers dance across her ribs, delving my tongue into her belly button. Her nails leave trenches in the arm that reaches out to tweak her nipple and I kiss the skin at the top of her thigh.

Looking at her, it's the first time I have believed in a god.

I worship the curves of her lower body; my fingers write hymns against the glowing skin of her hips and I whisper prayers between her legs. I make a confession where her thigh meets her pubic bone and my tongue recites the gospel against her soft, aching flesh. She tugs at my roots and I sacrifice myself to her happily.

She writhes underneath my unforgiving tongue, cursing, and calling out to a god I've now seen.

My tongue focuses on her bundle of nerves, loving the way she calls my name, how she glows like an angel underneath the moon. I revel in her taste, fingers gripping onto the flesh of her thighs to keep her steady as her back arches and she trembles uncontrollably, coming undone.

Greedily, I lap up everything she has to offer, crawling back up her flushed and heaving body to slip my tongue between her lips, to have her taste herself.

She helps me out of my jeans, laughing at how tight they are, and it almost feels like nothing changed. Except, it's obvious this time is different from the sorrow in Aspen's eyes, the shakiness in my movements, the crushing pain in my chest. I try not to think about what happens after this, try to focus on this moment and how beautiful she is, laid bare on my shirt. I drown out the noise at the end of the beach, focusing on her heavy breaths and thundering heart.

My lips gently press against the plush of hers. *I love you.* She places her palm against my cheek, reddened lips pulling into a soft smile. *I know.*

And then, slowly, I inch my way inside of her, trembling and trying to calm myself down so I don't finish right here and now.

"Fuck, Aspen," I moan when I feel her warmth, her tightness around me. "You feel so good... always feel so good."

She moans, keening against me, and pressing her chest against mine as I slip out of her before thrusting back in deeper and harder. My face buries itself into the crook of her neck as she bites onto my shoulder, our bodies reconnecting over and over again. Her legs wrap around my waist and she shivers at the new angle, her tongue swiping up the length of my neck and causing a groan to claw up my throat. I bring my lips back to hers, sighing into her mouth as my fingers trail down the length of her body to circle her clit.

"*Everett...* oh my god," she breathes out, nails scratching down my back and yanking on my hair. I pull my other arm from her breast to grasp her hand, using it as leverage to dig into her hips sharply, enough to brand myself in her body.

*I was here.*

She meets my thrusts with equal fervor, eyes locking and communicating the words we don't have the courage to say. The only words out of her mouth are: *fuck* and *Everett.* Every moan, every plea is a language only we understand. As I watch her mouth pop open and eyes squeeze shut, I suddenly want to thank whatever god is out there for giving me these hands to caress her, giving me these lips to kiss hers, giving me these eyes to look upon her face.

I forget every girl I've ever touched, I forget every fight we've ever had, I forget that she's leaving me. By now, I've even forgotten my own name.

That is, until she moans it into my ear when I push into her again sharply.

She angles her hips in a way that almost makes me black out and my groan vibrates into the skin of her neck. She's almost screaming with pleasure now, the sound barely overshadowed by the roaring waves. I dig my toes into the sand beyond my shirt and she clings onto me desperately as I pull out of her slick warmness slowly and push back into her fast and hard.

I grasp her jaw in my hand and bring her lips to mine, delving my tongue into her mouth.

She tastes like every coffee she made me share over breakfast. She tastes like the laughter that spilled from her lips at my cheesy jokes, like getting drunk off peach schnapps and dancing to really bad music. She tastes like all our secret rendezvous and the tears we shed. She tastes like all our petty fights, like all the 'I love yous', like every kiss that ever passed between us.

She tastes like love.

"Aspen," I whine, my movements growing sloppy and shaky as I realize this is coming to an end, that this can't last forever. I feel like I'm about to lose it all, but I restrain myself until I feel her legs shaking around me, a garbled version my name slipping past her lips as she orgasms beneath me. She squeezes her eyes shut and clenches around me and I lose it.

"I love you," the words are moaned from my mouth into hers.

I tense above her and it feels as if I've been electrocuted; her touch, her kiss, her essence like being struck by lightning. And then, suddenly, the electricity short-circuits and my nerve endings that were set ablaze now burn out as I release inside of her, shouting her name, and collapsing against her. Our bodies are slick with sweat, breaths harsh as we recover, burying my face into her strawberry scented hair, and kissing the flesh of her breast as we both come down.

Everything feels so right, but so, *so* wrong.

Her fingers run through my hair and I listen to the steady thrum of her heartbeat until my breathing evens out and the fog clears and then I do something so horrifying it's unspeakable.

I begin to cry.

It happens suddenly without me even realizing it until the tears pool between the valley of her breasts and she sits up in alarm to lift my head.

"Everett..." She chokes out, and I don't even care how pathetic I look, how humiliating this is. Because she's leaving me and this may be the last time I get to hold her, get to kiss her. The thought is so crushing I don't care if I'm crying in front of her. I wrap my arms around her waist and bury my face between her breasts and cry, the sharp pain in my chest too profound to ignore.

"Please don't go... don't leave me."

At my choked-out plea I feel her own body begin to shake underneath me and I can hear her sniffling, imagining her furiously wiping at her own tears, "Everett, please." I know this is hurting her, that this is painful for us both. But, I can't stop. I hold her to me, crying silently against her soft flesh. She runs her fingers through my hair and doesn't let me see her own tears. I lean up to kiss her one last time before laying my head on her chest again.

And we just stay like that all night.

Long after the distant noises of the party die out, long after night has fallen. We both hold each other, unwilling to let go, but both knowing that it's inevitable. The world grows dark and I confess my love to her as if singing her to sleep.

My whispers could be heard through the night, echoing around in our little cave until we both inevitably fall asleep, "I love you. I love you. I love you."

But, in the morning, she is gone.

# REINVENT

*Four weeks later*

There's something about music that just makes you feel. The lyrics, the tempo, the soul has the power to move you into a depression, pull you from even the deepest of shadows, or transport you somewhere that isn't your life.

Music is the very pulse of life itself.

But, this music just... *isn't.*

The baby blue grand piano that sits in the bright and open den of Avery's beach house hasn't been played in years. Though she's a master player, Avery hasn't been here since she was a child and the piano was essentially abandoned. Neglected, it was left to rust due to the humidity of the ocean a few yards away, and is more out of tune than Jesse.

But, you can't just desert something because you have no use for it anymore, leave it isolated and unloved. It's not right.

So, it's been my mission these last four weeks to work on restoring the beautiful piano and I thought I'd made progress in replacing the strings and setting the temperament, but the off-pitch keys almost make my ears bleed. I groan in frustration and slam the lid closed, desperately wanting to give up and hire a professional, but knowing I won't. Because this little project has been the perfect distraction from where my mind constantly wants to wander.

Because even though I've officially spent four weeks in this little house by the sea... my heart is in London. Might always be in London.

I came here to get away, to recover, to learn to love myself again. But, I see his eyes in the sun and his voice is in the waves and his face is in my dreams and I can't escape him. How can I move on when his grip is still latched onto my heart, his laugh still echoes through my ears, his smile lives behind my eyes, and every breath I take manages to remind me of him.

My hands slip off the ivory and I'm immersed in silence once again. It's always silent nowadays and though it's refreshing, I miss the noise. I miss Jesse yelling at the TV, Enzo yelling at Marco, and Avery yelling at them all. I even miss Everett's awful jokes.

I never thought I'd say that.

But, these last few weeks have been the breath of fresh air I needed. My lungs had been turning blue for so long and are now pumping life.

I spent the first week here lying around without showering or brushing my hair or opening the fridge. I was walking around in Everett's old flannel and eating mangoes in a vain attempt to smell like him.

But, at some point I took a bath and put on some make-up and wiped away my tears.

Reinvent: change (something) so much that it appears to be entirely new.

I've taken this time to reinvent myself; to write songs and paint (terribly) and read books and mold myself into someone better than before. Someone I can be proud of. I take walks on the beach and try to restore the piano, and... sing.

For the first time in so long, I've been singing in the shower again and humming while doing dishes and setting free the voice that was locked away for so long.

And I know that I owe that to Everett, but I also know that gift is tainted.

And the wound is still there, aching and burning, but I slowly feel scar tissue covering it. Every night, I remember

Everett's cries on that beach, his soft voice reminding me how much he loves me, his gentle hands caressing my cheek as I pretended to be asleep. Every night, his cries get louder, his voice more persistent, and the ghost of his fingers dancing across my cheek.

He haunts me.

My phone dings and my heart leaps into my throat, the excitement I feel pitiful. I shake my sobering thoughts away and pull it out to see a text from Jesse. I curse myself for the disappointment I feel.

**Jesse:** *Please come back, Aspen. I need you. Enzo is being rebellious again and refusing to show up to practice.*

**Me:** *Just threaten to call his mom. She scares the shit out of him.*

**Jesse:** *SEE! This is why I need you back, Aspen. I'll do anything.*

**Me:** *Make me the manager and we'll talk.*

**Jesse:** *Well, it was nice knowing you, Aspen.*

**Jesse:** *Just kidding! But no, you can't have my job, you git.*

My chest aches uncomfortably in my chest just imaging the smile on Jesse's face as he texts me and what his thick Scottish accent would sound like jumbling all the words up. Almost subconsciously, I find myself exiting out of our conversation and sliding over to one I haven't replied to in months, but am always getting notifications for every few days or so.

**Everett:** *How're you liking Whitstable? I heard it's boring there.*

**Everett:** *It's supposed to rain up where you are this weekend. Do you have an umbrella?*

**Everett:** *I heard a funny joke today and even though I know you wouldn't want to hear it, you're the only one I want to tell it to... Can a kangaroo jump higher than a house?....... Of course, a house doesn't jump at al!.*

**Everett:** *Why did u leave without sying goodbye? Howw could you do that to me? I miss you adn yu don't even care you jsut left.*

**Everett:** *Aspen, I'm so sorry about all those voicemails and that text... I got drunk with the lads last night. I didn't mean any of it. Except that I miss you. I miss you and I'm sorry.*

**Everett:** *Hope you're well. xx*

The last one was sent just a few nights ago and like the rest, never received a reply. But, every single time, my thumbs hover over the keyboard, unable never do their job. There is absolutely nothing and everything to say. Each text, each call, each voicemail picks away at the ice surrounding my heart, but they also pull at the stitches over the wound he made on my heart. Each one makes me bleed a little bit more.

Once again, my thumbs glide over the keys, twitching. There are a million things I want to say, but none feel right. None make me brave enough to bring my thumbs down. And then there's a brutal knock on my door and I put my phone away altogether.

A sign from above, no doubt.

I turn towards the door, wondering if it's the maid or nosey neighbor, but it turns out to be the last person I'd ever expect in Whitstable. "Mom?"

She looks so out of place in her beige pencil skirt and blazer, a gift basket in her hand, and smile plastered onto her reddened lips. Especially when I'm dressed in a jumper and leggings with a hole in the knee. She doesn't wait for an invitation and simply steps through the threshold, heels clicking on the hardwood, and voice echoing through the small entryway.

"You have no idea how hard this place was to find. All Avery told me was that it was down the street from a petrol station. Do you know how many of those are in this Podunk town?"

I'm hardly listening to her ramblings, more focused on the fact that she's actually *here,* in my temporary home, and I'm not imagining it.

Our relationship has been at an awkward medium since our heart-to-heart about the real reason she distanced herself from me. We've spoken on the phone a few times and texted here and there, but I'm always torn between rage for her disregard and desire to repair the relationship I've been missing from my life for so long.

"Mom... what're you doing here?" She sets the large gift basket on the table next to the front door and takes the opportunity to face the mirror on the wall, pushing her russet hair back. When she turns towards me, her smile is gone.

"Well, you refused to tell me your new address and I was worried about you," She searches my face, brows furrowing, "Aspen, darling, your skin looks dry. I hope you've been moisturizing."

"I live on the beach, Mom. I get a lot of sun."

"Well, I hope you use sun block then."

It's so ridiculous that I have to laugh as I lead her down the narrow hallway, past the staircase, and to the tiny kitchen at the end of the hall. She takes a seat at the table and watches as I pull out a kettle and teabags. I feel her staring and when I turn, she has her eyebrows raised in surprise, "I thought you didn't like tea."

My cheeks heat and I hide my smile behind a wall of hair, "It's grown on me."

She remains silent as I set the kettle to boil and sit across from her at the breakfast nook. It's only when I drag my eyes up to her soft copper ones that she speaks again, "you seem different, somehow. Happier, maybe? More... *you*. The you before Sam, before your father left."

I'm surprised at her observation, surprised she remembered his name. A familiar weight presses on my chest and I look down at the tiny markings on the light color of the wooden table. I do feel more like my old self again, more confident and free. But, I feel like I'm missing something... and I know it's him.

"Why did you *really* drive two hours to get here, mom?"

This time, it's she who averts her gaze, picking at her manicured nails and working at her jaw as she tries to formulate her next sentence. "You know, I have to say that I was wrong about Everett. When Marco first approached me asking for a favor for a friend in trouble I thought—"

"Wait," I raise my hand up to stop her, the words not sitting right with me. "What do you mean Marco approached you?"

She looks as confused as I feel, "he told me Everett was in

trouble, but didn't have money to afford my services. Marco sounded very troubled by it and doing a case pro-bono would look good for me so I took it... why?"

I'd assumed my mom had known about the deal, maybe even helped Marco come up with the conditions in a twisted way to 'help' me. I wouldn't have put it past her and a lot of my hesitation in starting over with her had involved that assumption, but now...

I feel the ice around my heart crack a bit more —knowing that Everett and Marco hadn't involved my mother in their little scheme. That they hadn't tarnished an already fragile relationship with her. She was in the dark as well.

"It's... nothing. Go on." No point in telling her now, no point in opening old wounds.

She easily drops the subject, "my point is that I had prejudged Everett before getting to know him. He's... a good man, Aspen. He truly cares for you."

Her words are a match and anger sparks inside of me. Never has she taken an interest in my love life, or my life in general. Never, has she been there for me in my heartbreaks and pain. And now, she thinks she can just suddenly get involved in something she knows nothing about?

"You don't know anything about our relationship, Mom."

"Because you never even told me you were dating! I had to hear it from Everett!"

"What do you mean you heard it from Everett? You two talk about me?"

Her perfectly waxed brows furrow in confusion, "Marco brought Everett over for a family dinner last Sunday, the boys didn't tell you?"

"Everett went to a family dinner? Willingly?"

She sends me a glare, though it's half-hearted at best, "Yes, honey. He came over with a bottle of wine and baked lasagna as a thank you for the trial. He's a very sweet boy, funny too. And... well, it's plain to see that he's madly in love with you."

"Mom..." My tone of voice should be enough to warn her off

the subject, but she waves me off dismissively.

"I know it's none of my business and I've no idea why you're in this tiny house in this god-awful town or why Everett seems so depressed," she stops to glower at me, mumbling, "because you never tell me anything. But, I do know that that boy loves you and regrets whatever he did deeply. He finds any reason to bring you up in conversation: if I have any of your old report cards or tapes of you singing, if I heard from you, if you ever used the tire swing in the backyard... I'm not telling you what to do or trying to weasel my way into your life, but I thought you should know he hasn't forgotten you for a second."

I don't want to let her words settle.

I don't want to let them seep below my skin and burrow through my bone, settle in my veins, and pump through my body with their unwanted hope. But, I don't stand a chance against the warmth that melts the ice in my heart, the deep stir in my belly at Everett's affection. At the reminder that such a pure and wonderful thing was tainted by his lies and deceit.

Before I can process what's happening, my face crumples and I feel the hot burn of tears behind my eyes. I try to swallow down the lump in my throat, but the pain is so overwhelming, I feel it beginning to choke me. I gasp for breath as the first tear falls and my mom is so shocked she nearly trips, scrambling from her chair and into the one next to mine.

"Mom... I don't want to forgive him... I can't. He hurt me so badly. He asked me to trust him, believe in him, and was lying to me the whole time... I'm so confused, everything—"

I'm cut off by a violent sob wracking my chest and it only worsens when I feel my mother's dainty hand wrap around my head and bring it down, cradling it to her chest. I can't even remember the last time my mother consoled me like this. The last time she even held me.

"Shh, shh," she coos, petting my hair and swaying us back and forth. "Don't cry, Aspen. It's all right. You don't need to cry anymore." Not even the kettle's tell-tale screech can't drown out my cries. But, there's something about my mother's warm embrace and whispers of encouragement that make the storm inside of me slowly clear.

I'm tired of crying. I'm tired of feeling this way. Tired of feeling sorry for myself.

"Do you still love him?"

"I do. Of course, I do." She lifts my face from her chest, wiping away my stray tears and offering me a kind smile. I feel that deep pull of love in my chest at her sudden warmth and wonder if this is what I've been missing all these years. I wonder if I had had this version of her growing up if I would've turned out any differently. If I would've been able to forgive Everett.

"Then what's the problem, sweetheart? Even though I'm not crazy about the idea of my daughter dating a man I represented in court... you love him and he loves you, why are you torturing yourself like this?"

She wasn't there when my dad abandoned me, when Sam stomped on my spirit, when I cautiously let Everett into my heart, only to have him turn it black. She was never there, so she doesn't understand the deepness of this betrayal, the way all my fears were answered by the man I thought loved me.

How I don't know how to forgive that broken promise.

"Because it's ruined... what we had, it's been ruined."

Her brows furrow and she tucks my hair behind my ears, smile reassuring. "Then you start over, honey. If there's no going back to what you had, you just start over."

She lets go and gets up, her words echoing through the chambers of my heart. I watch as she turns off the stove and pours the water into two mugs, steeping the teabags in them. She's being so attentive, so motherly, that I'm completely thrown. My emotions are muddled, eyes tired and puffy. I'm deep in thought when she takes the seat across from me again, setting the tea down. I blow on the hot liquid, watching the steam curl away from my cool breath.

It smells like Everett.

"I only want you to be happy, Aspen. Whatever you decide

to do, do it for yourself."

"Okay, who are you and what have you done with my mother?"

She rolls her eyes, a sad smile on her face, "I've realized some things myself these last few months... and Everett may have convinced me of my mistakes with you."

My jaw drops and eyes nearly bulge out of my skull, "What're you talking about?"

But, now she decides to remain mum, shaking her head and taking a sip of tea. She looks around my kitchen, but her gaze is far away. I'm trying really hard not to let my mind run wild with the possibilities of what he could've said to her, but it hardly works.

"I didn't actually come here to talk about your love life."

She reaches into her Valentino bag and, as if it's a bomb, slowly pulls out a long white envelope. She bites on her lip, eyes glued to the parcel in her hands.

"I've been holding onto this for a while now and I know you may hate me for it, but... I wanted to give it to you when you were old enough, when the time was right. And I feel like... you need this now more than ever." And with that mysterious prelude she slides the envelope over to my side of the table, but I don't dare pick it up. My entire body freezes when I see the familiar handwriting, my name in the center, and the one attached to the return address.

*Nicolo Marino*

My heart drops to the pit of my stomach and every single shocking thing that has ever been said or done to me does not equal the disbelief I feel at being faced with this letter.

"He sent it just a year after he left and by then you'd finally begun to move on. I didn't want to re-open that wound, but I know now that wasn't my decision to make." She stands from her chair, purse in hand, "whether or not to open it, the decision is all yours."

I couldn't move if I tried. I just remain glued to my chair, heart squeezing in my chest, reading the same name over and over again. My mother walks over to my solid frame, places a short kiss to the top of my head, and leaves without another word. I listen to the clicking of her heels until they fade into the distance.

I don't know how long I sit at the table, staring at that ominous white envelope.

But, my tea grows cold and the world goes dark and I still don't move.

* * *

Right on schedule, my phone rings just before the grandfather clock in the den chimes ten o'clock.

The envelope has long been stuffed into the top drawer of my dresser and I have long been staring up at the popcorn ceiling of my bedroom with Yoda, telling myself I wasn't waiting for this phone call. The white light from my phone casts a dim glow around the room and I stare at the name on my screen as it rings twice more.

**Everett**

Every night, on the dot, he calls at this time. Every night I let it ring without so much as sparing a glance at the phone. Whether it's because my mom spoke of him so fondly, or the bomb disguised as an envelope she gave me, or because I'm simply lonely, my thumb hovers over the green button.

And for the first time in almost two months, I accept.

"Hi."

My voice sounds much too loud echoing around my empty bedroom, and I feel as though I'm doing something bad, so I lower my voice into the quietest of whispers, repeating myself. But, he remains silent on the other line.

He sucks in a sharp breath through his teeth, then there's a scuffle, before his voice is transporting through the other end. Dozens of miles away, but if I close my eyes, it's almost as if he's lying in this bed next to me.

"Aspen," he sounds shocked, like he can't quite believe I answered. "You... hi... you-you answered." My laugh is breathy, though it still sounds sad. Hollow.

"My finger slipped."

The other line is dead silent, and then a sharp laugh cuts through and I nearly collapse with relief. "God, I," he chuckles breathlessly, though the sound is slightly pained, "I really didn't expect you to pick up... I don't... I don't even know what to say."

"Then why do you call?"

His answer is quick, honest. "Because I miss the sound of your voice."

There's an ache deep in my chest and I squeeze my eyes against it. I don't know how to respond to that so I remain silent, just listening to his soft breathing. We're quiet for a long time, but neither one of us dares hang up the phone. "Do you like it in Whitstable?"

"Yeah, yeah I do. It's... quiet here."

"I never pegged you as a small-town girl."

"You and me both," I laugh, the conversation light and easy. "How's life as a free man?"

His sigh is deep and painful, "it's hard... I still feel so guilty. Tried to contact Leo, but he wanted nothing to do with me... Can't say I blame him, what I did was so fucked."

"Yes, but you both made mistakes. It was just a serious of unfortunate events that led to his injuries. He needs a lot of healing, but I think one day you'll be able to make amends. You can't blame yourself... You've grown a lot, Everett. Don't let your past define you."

I realize the irony of my statement, my inability to take my own advice. All I hear is Everett's deep breaths and I wonder if I crossed a line. Soon, though, his voice comes through small and grateful, "Thank you, Aspen. That's exactly what I needed to hear."

My heart sings at the sincerity in his voice and we're quiet again. The light tone of our conversation is gone and I just want to hear him laugh again. I want the image of him crying on the beach to vanish from behind my eyelids.

"So, how're the boys?"

Everett grumbles and I can practically picture the pinched, annoyed look on his face. "All they do is play that stupid game. If I have to hear them yelling at the tiny football players on the screen one more time I may just quit the band too."

"You're just mad because you're no good at that game."

He gasps indignantly on the other line, but I can hear the smile in his voice, "I'll have you know that I've beat Jesse!"

I hate how big my grin is, "that was *one* time and only because Enzo spilled beer on Jesse's new leather couch and distracted him."

"It still counts." I chuckle and there's a lull in conversation again. I should hang up, but the isolation is getting to me and I guess I miss the sound of his voice too. I listen to his breaths and my mind drifts to the envelope sitting a few feet away — taunting me, calling to me.

"My mom came by today."

I can hear the shock in his voice, "she did?"

"She told me you gave her a talking to?"

He nearly chokes on the other line, coughing violently, and I can picture the deep blush of his cheeks perfectly. "I did *not* do that to the woman that saved my ass from jail! I just... I didn't mean to get in between you two. But, I had to say something."

"Well, whatever you said worked. She was actually kind to me today. Almost acted like a real mom... It was incredible and heartbreaking all at once."

He sighs deep into the phone, calling my name in a way that could make the dam inside me burst again, so I stop him. "She... gave me a letter today."

His voice is sympathetic and raw, indulging my change of topic, "a letter?"

"A letter my father wrote to me a year after he left."

He exhales loudly and I don't even know why I'm telling him when I haven't even told my brother yet. "Wow, I mean...

how-how do you feel about that? Are you going to read it?"

"I... I don't know. Am I mad because she kept it from me or grateful? Burn the letter in the fireplace or frame it? I'm just... so confused all the time, about *everything.* I don't know what to feel or do anymore."

I think we both know that I'm referring to much more than the letter.

"I'm here, you know that, right? Any time of the day. I just... I wish I was there with you right now, wish I could take it all back. Wish I stopped you on that beach... I miss you, Aspen."

A part of me wants to bask in his affection, drown myself in it. But, another part of me wants to hang up before I'm sucked back in. Two months of detaching myself from him and one conversation is all it takes to have me spiraling again. "I should go."

"But—" he begins to protest, but quickly stops himself, the grief in his voice pulling at my heartstrings. "Okay."

"Okay." I don't hang up and neither does he. There's only the sounds of our breaths, of our hearts thumping —bruised and hardened, but beating in sync.

"Will you answer the phone the next time I call?"

I don't want to hear the hope in his voice, don't want to be the one to snuff it out. "I-I'm not sure."

"I'll call anyway." He doesn't sound sad, but he doesn't sound happy either.

I smile, reluctant to hang up, but knowing I need to for my own sanity, "Goodnight, Everett."

"Goodnight, Munchkin."

# DOR

*Everett*

Those sappy love songs that play on the radio never really made sense to me.

Until I fell in love with Aspen.

I was never able to connect with the heart-wrenching breakup songs my mum adored.

Until I lost Aspen.

Now I understand both much too clearly.

There is a hollowness in my heart that makes every beat sound meaningless, empty. Like the life has been sucked right out of me and my body is just going through the motions.

Keeping me alive, without really living.

I go to practice and go out with the lads and write songs and live my life like normal except that nothing is normal. Because even though it's been two months, there's still a purple toothbrush in a cup by my sink and strawberry-scented shampoo in my shower, a pair of white knickers under my bed, and a lone dangly earring on my bedside table.

Nothing touched, nothing moved, as if Aspen could walk back in my door any day now and pick up where we left off.

But, the sun rises and the sun sets and my world is still shrouded in darkness.

"Hey, Fox, you ready?"

I'm startled out of my stupor when Marco walks around the

tent to where I've been hiding out all night —sitting on a crate and watching the sun set and trying to ignore the terrible ache in my chest. Marco looks about as uncomfortable as I feel in his tight-fitted suit. In one quick motion, he's ripping off his tie and unbuttoning the first few buttons of his white dress shirt.

"Jesse isn't going to approve, Marco," I scold, but he just rolls his eyes at me.

"Jesse can fuck off," he gestures toward me with furrowed brows, "If you can have your shirt practically unbuttoned to your navel, then so can I."

And maybe it's the irritation in his tone it, the pout on his face, or the way he rolls his eyes that are just a few shades darker than Aspen's, but he's never looked more like his sister and I have to look away —the wind howling through my hollow heart.

"Have the bride and groom come down yet?"

Marco shuffles next to me, "they're on the way now," he sighs deep in his chest, and I glance up to see him frowning. "Tell me why Jesse is making us perform at a wedding? This is going to ruin our image."

I have to admit, when Jesse first suggested we perform a wedding, I thought it was a joke. Maybe even punishment for all that happened in the last few months because none of us want to be wedding singers and we need to concentrate on rehearsing for the competition next month.

But, now it makes sense.

"I saw one of the judges for the competition sitting at the bride's table. He's the uncle."

Marco's frown morphs into a surprised gape, "that sneaky little git. Genius, he is."

My chuckle is cut short by a vibration in my pocket and I whip my phone out, only to see a text from Jesse telling me to help with sound check. The flash of hope is gone just as quickly as it came; a strike of lone lightning in the otherwise endless black sky. My calls and texts remain unanswered. Except for that night last week, that wonderful night when I finally heard her voice again. Where, for just the few minutes we were on the phone, my world righted itself again. It was so easy, slipping back into that routine with her. I could almost feel her there next to me, almost taste her, she was so close. But, now she's gone again and the silence is more deafening than ever. And I can't even try to forget her, it's impossible.

I don't think I'll ever be able to get over her, I don't think I'll ever want to.

My shoulders deflate and I try to blow it off, but Marco has already seen my disappointment, "have you heard from her?" He kicks the chunk of grass at his feet and he doesn't even need to say her name.

She's like a secret thought never spoken aloud, but one we're all aware of. A constant name on the tip of everyone's tongue, the empty spot on stage.

"Have you?" I avoid his question, the answer feeling too personal to share. The conversation we had too intimate, too meaningful to me.

I let Marco in my relationship once before and paid the price.

"Nope, I've practically got frostbite from her cold shoulder." His voice is despondent and troubled and I bite back a chuckle, knowing that feeling all too well. He misses her more than he cares to let on and feels like shit that she's hours away, isolated from her friends and family.

Chattering, glasses clinking, and loud laughter all sound from the tent and I know we've got to go up soon, but all I want to do is sit here and wait for a call that may never come.

"How do I make this right?"

His sigh is almost as loud as mine, "when you find out, let me know."

I wonder, briefly, if he knows about the letter. The letter his mom gave to Aspen from their dad. I wonder if he knows his mom visited her at all. I'm just about to ask this when coiled hair, bronze skin, and red dress walk from behind the tent to stand in front of us with hands on her hips and a frown on her lips. She has that same pinched look on her face she gets every time she has to address Marco or I. Annoyance, anger, disappointment.

"The bride and groom just arrived. Get your asses in here." That's all Avery says before whipping around to make her way back inside the tent.

Marco's eyes follow her every move.

The tent is draped in white: white curtains, flowers, and china that's almost blinding. The couple is already gathered in the center of the fake wood covering the grass with guests surrounding them. The bride gave us a detailed song list and, predictably, every song is sappy and heart-wrenching.

It's gonna be a long night.

The groom smiles at his bride and takes her hand in his, spinning her into his arms as Enzo starts in on the bass line. She laughs all the way as she lands in his embrace, righting herself as they sway together. The crowd slowly joins them as I begin to sing, but my eyes are glued to the married couple. The look so in love, so happy. Spinning in a circle and goofing off until she places her head on his chest and he kisses on the top of her head. I feel the hollowness in my heart then, my voice catching a bit at the sight of them. But, it's not them I see anymore.

It's Aspen and I.

Her laughing as I dip her low to the ground and place a big kiss on her glossy lips. Swinging her back up and holding my hand out so she can spin underneath it, laughing the whole way.

So close I can almost feel it, almost taste it.

But, the song fades and we disappear and the strangers are back in our place, the effect soul crushing. I have to look down at my boots and try to swallow the lump in my throat.

I'd never imagined myself getting married, until I met her. And it was so real and clear in front of my eyes just now. My fingers just barely grazing it, everything I want almost in my grasp... only to be snatched away, the image breaking like throwing a rock into a mirror.

Shattered, just like me.

I wasted so much time. The cat and mouse game, keeping everything a secret, only kissing her behind closed doors, all the arguments... I just... I wasted *so* much time.

When we finish our set, I don't say anything to my band mates, I don't even look at them. I make my way towards the bar, but my feet feel like lead. The bartender gives me a funny look when I tell him what drink I want, but obliges me anyway. Before I can even take a sip of the bitter liquid, though, I hear an annoyingly familiar voice next to me.

"Thought you didn't like coffee." Enzo leans against the bar, blazer discarded and white sleeves rolled up to reveal an array of ink against his tanned arms.

I take slow sips, cringing at the bitter taste, but savoring the scent. Her scent.

"It grew on me."

We stand in silence, sipping at our different poisons as the guests mill about, chatting without the loud drums and thrumming guitar overpowering their voices. The judge of the contest is speaking to Jesse and even though I can't hear a word they're saying, I already know Jesse is kissing the man's pale, stuck-up ass.

"Jesse's concerned your mood is going to bring down the party and put us in bad favor with the judge." Enzo's leaning against the bar top and if I didn't know any better I'd think he's actually concerned about my well-being. But, I do know better. I know he hasn't liked me since I step foot in Jesse's apartment and hit on Aspen and I really don't blame him.

"What mood?"

He scoffs loudly, cocking an eyebrow in my direction, "please, you look like you're singing the world's most depressing song up there, for *every* song. It's pathetic man."

My face flushes because I didn't think it was obvious, I'm usually very good at putting on a persona for the crowd, good at hiding how I really feel. I clear my throat and try to play it cool, "can you blame me? My community service is exhausting and I'm not even half-way done yet."

It's partially true. Waking up at the crack of dawn three days a week to pick up trash from the motorway is not as glamorous as it sounds. Though, it's much better than the alternative. In between dreams of Aspen's smile and laugh, I'm haunted by the image of Leo bleeding in the street. Haunted with dreams the judge said 'guilty' instead of the reality.

Life has been pretty bleak, but I'm grateful to be free.

I can tell Enzo doesn't buy it from the way he shakes his head and sighs. He glances at the cup of coffee in my hand, then my face, before speaking again.

"It's her, isn't it? You miss her. That's why you walk around like a wounded puppy, why you don't come out as often, why all the songs you've been writing have been on par with Adele in the heartbreak department."

I deflect by gasping and putting a hand on my chest, completely flattered, "Adele?! I never expected such a compliment from you, Zozo!"

It doesn't get a laugh or even a smile. No sense of humor, this one. But, I don't want to talk about this with him. I don't want to talk about it at all. So, I choose to ignore his statement and down the rest of my coffee in silence. Enzo's eyes stay trained on me and he opens his mouth again to speak, but there's a sudden buzz in my pocket. My hand reaches for it lightning fast and my heart suddenly comes alive again when I read the name on the screen.

**Aspen**

"Yeah, okay, I'll work on my attitude. Thanks, Enzo. Bye." And then I'm striding away as fast as I can and Enzo is calling after me, but it doesn't matter.

All that matters is Aspen. All that matters is that *she* is finally calling *me* after months of silence, months of ignored calls. All that matters is that I get to hear her voice again.

And I press accept before I even get away from the noise and

I can barely see where I'm walking in the dark, but it's down a hill and near a tree and I have to lean against it to steady myself, "Aspen?"

Like I don't know it's her, like I'm not trying to bite down the biggest grin and calm the pounding behind my ribs. Like my whole night didn't just completely turn around with something as simple as her name lighting up my screen. God, what happened to me?

Then, hushed and low, sending shivers down my spine, "hi, Everett."

Finally, I've come up for air. Finally, I can breathe again.

"How... How are you?"

I hear the sound of the ocean in the background and remember our last night together: how soft she felt, how she moaned my name, how tragically beautiful the whole thing was. I remember waking up the next morning with swollen eyes, on top of cold sand, and how the world went dark when I realized she was gone. I didn't move from that spot for hours.

"I'm... I'm really, *really* well actually."

I can hear the smile in her voice and maybe I should feel disappointed or sad that she's happy without me, but I remember her trembling body on that beach and how the light in her eyes died when I told her the truth and even though my heart squeezes painfully in my chest...

I'm just happy that she's happy.

"What could possibly make you sound this giddy?" She laughs and the sound is music to my ears.

"I-I," and she has to take a big breath just to calm herself down and I don't even realize how large my grin is until my jaw begins to ache. "Everett, I sang tonight."

My heart stops in my chest. "Sang? Sang where? Why? For what?"

"There's this pub down here that has an open mic night every Friday and I don't know... I just walked down there for a drink and there was only about twelve people inside and I just... I got up on stage... and I sang."

Pride swells in my chest so quickly and heavily that I fear it may crush me. The fact that she can finally bring her amazing vocals into the world again has me nearly tearing up. That she can finally go back to doing what she loved so dearly makes everything that happened worth it. I'm just glad what I did didn't tarnish her gift forever. After all this time, the world can hear her voice again. I just wish I was there to see it.

"That's... that's so amazing, Aspen. I'm so incredibly happy for you."

When she speaks again, I can hear the smile in her voice, "for the first time in so long I sang in front of a crowd... and you were the first person I thought to call. Because I know I have you to thank for that."

I don't know what that means for us, what her even calling means for us and maybe one day I'll ask her, but for now I'm just ecstatic to be a part of her life again. Even a small part like this—a phone call once a week.

"You have nothing to thank me for, love. That was all you."

It's silent again after that, but I can hear the deep roar of the waves and the howling of the wind so alive on the other end. This is enough. For now, this is enough for me. I'm sure that our break is almost over and I'll have to go on again soon, but I won't be the one to end this conversation. I don't know when I'll get the chance to have it again.

When her voice interrupts the quiet it's small and intimate and I push the phone to my ear a little harder, "Everett, I just—"

"Everett? We're waiting for you. Come back to the party, you're up soon."

It's the wedding planner that walks up behind me, speaking much too loudly. I wave my hand dismissively at her and try to talk into the receiver, but it's clear that Aspen heard her too.

"Oh, you're busy," she sounds flustered and surprised and I can't even get a word in with how quickly she's talking, "I shouldn't have called so suddenly, I'm sorry. I'll let you get back to her— I... I mean the party." I yell her name into the receiver, ignoring the woman in front of me, who storms off in a huff.

"We're performing a wedding, Aspen. The wedding planner just wants me on stage."

It's silent again and I can just imagine her cheeks hot and her slapping a hand to her forehead in embarrassment. The image is so clear behind my eyelids. She tries to play it off, "did you guys have to become a wedding band after I left?"

"Don't flatter yourself," I chuckle deep in my chest, and after a few seconds of silence I take a risk and say what's on my mind, "but, there's nothing to be jealous about, Aspen."

She scoffs, though it sounds more alarmed that arrogant, "jealous?! I'm not jealous, Everett."

"Okay." I grin like an idiot, my heart functioning properly for the first time in ages.

"I'm not."

"I said okay."

"You—" she sighs, though I can hear the smile in her voice, "whatever, I'm hanging up now."

"All right, Munchkin. Can I expect to hear from you again?"

There's a shuffling on the other end before, "maybe... I have to go now."

"Okay, I love you—"

The words slip out almost on instinct, like second-nature, like they always used to. They're out before I can catch them and I hear Aspen suck in a harsh breath through her teeth. The conversation dies and I can practically feel the tension through the phone, almost palpable.

"I'm sorry... I've... I have to go."

I was expecting it: the avoidance of the subject, the rejection, but my heart still feels like it's been ripped out of my chest and Aspen is watching me bleed out in front of her. I swallow the painful lump in my throat and try not to remember how those words tasted when she would whisper them into our kiss.

She hangs up before I can say goodbye and my phone stays glued to my ear long after the beeping has stopped. I make my way back up to the tent with a heavy heart and a word on my mind that Aspen mentioned in passing once. One that I hadn't paid much attention to, one that never crossed my mind until now.

Dor: the emotional pain one feels when they're separated from the person they love.

# SAUDADE

I've always been a prideful person.

I don't like being told when I'm wrong, I don't forgive easily, and I hate being embarrassed. I'm not proud of it, but it's a fault of mine like any other. The longer I'm in Whitstable, the more I debate if it's my true anger and heartbreak holding me back from London, or if it's my pride. Maybe it's both.

I came here to heal, to find happiness, to learn to love myself and... I have, *mostly*. I'm singing again and I wake up every morning with a smile on my face and confident stride to my walk. I'm happier for the most part, my wounds carefully superglued back together again. And yet... there's still something holding me back from leaving my past behind, from really starting over.

Everett.

He physically dug himself deep into the veins and arteries of my heart a long time ago. Every pump of blood, every beat it makes is just him, him, him. There's no escape. Staying in London didn't make me happy and moving a dozen miles away didn't make me happy either.

I don't know what I want anymore.

The door slams shut behind me and encases me in the silence of my temporary home. I let go of Yoda's leash, letting him run wild after our walk, and contemplate the eerie calm of my solitude. A cruel reminder of all I've lost. My phone dings and I welcome the noise, knowing I'm not really alone. Knowing people still care.

**Marco:** *Mom gave the cook the day off. Attempted to make meatloaf herself. Please save me.*

I laugh even though I don't want to and just reply to his text with a gif of someone eating and crying. Besides Everett and my mother, I'd also been slowly welcoming Marco back into my good graces. Most of our conversations revolve around Avery, anyway. Despite what happened to me and Marco's part in it, I don't want their relationship to suffer. Avery has been pining for my brother as long as I can remember and I'm pretty sure she's the best thing to ever happen to him. If Everett and I can't be together, then at least one couple can repair the damage their little deal wrought.

So, I've been giving him some advice to win her over: where to take her on a date, what flowers to buy her, what she likes and dislikes. I believe it's been going well so far, but Avery still seems skeptical of Marco's true personality and intentions.

I don't blame her. People you think you know can blindside you.

When I make it up to my room the first thing I do is pull out the familiar, ratty gray hoodie from the back of my closet and slip it over my head. It's something I only dare take out from the depths of my closet when I'm feeling especially lonely or sad. The familiar scent of mangoes and tea wash over me and it makes my heart ache with a longing that almost tears me apart. If I could make his scent into a candle, I would have one in every room of the house.

I take a minute, eyes closed, just to bask in the warmth Everett's hoodie gives me. Allow myself just a minute to imagine what life would be like if nothing changed, if I had just let him keep this secret. To imagine Everett is in the other room, about to walk in and tell me some stupid joke before wrapping his arms around me and telling me how good I look in his clothes.

And I really can't explain what possess me to take out my

phone and snap a picture of me wrapped up in the hoodie and nothing else. I also can't quite explain what comes over me that has me sending the picture to Everett. I swear I black out for a second and wake up as the picture is being sent. Maybe I got too wrapped up in the daydream and sent that as if it was real. And then I really want to toss my phone across the room because, what the fuck? What's he going to think getting that picture? Why would I send something like that? How is he—

But, I don't get much time to panic before his name is lighting up my screen and I'm accepting his call with a shaky heart and flushed cheeks.

"Are you trying to kill me, Aspen?"

I curse under my breath because things are so awkward already and I'm sending the cruelest mixed signals known to man. "I-I didn't mean to send it."

The excuse is a feeble one, but it's really all I can think of with my brain this foggy. He's breathing hard on the other line and I envision him pacing the foyer of his apartment, running an exasperated hand through his curly mane.

The image is so clear I could almost reach out and touch him. *God,* it's been so long.

"You... you took that with you?" His voice is low and raspy and slightly hitched in awe, like he can't quite believe what I just sent him. "You... wear it?"

My cheeks actually burn from how hot they're getting and I take a seat on my bed because my knees are growing weak. There's no point in lying to him when I handed over the evidence via text, "sometimes."

He sucks in a sharp breath between his teeth and my heart is a hummingbird in my chest working overtime and overheating.

"Fuck, Aspen," the gravel in his voice makes chills trickle down my spine and he lets out a heavy sigh, shuffling on the other line. "You can't just... I'm trying really hard here not to come down there and bring you home and you aren't... you aren't making this very easy on me."

He sounds like a man who has what he wants most in the entire world right in front of him, but it sits behind impenetrable glass he can't break. He sounds frustrated and miserable and I feel awful. "I'm sorry... I don't know why I sent that."

But, I do know why. I just don't want to say it.

"I just... what do you want from me, Aspen?" His voice cracks and so does a piece of my heart. "This... talking to you like nothing changed, but not being able to see you or touch you... sending this picture like everything is fine when it so clearly isn't... this is torture."

I know he's right, it's torturing me too. I don't know if I should stay here or go home to Everett. I don't know if everything would be able to go back to normal... if it can be as easy and amazing as it was when I was so blissfully unaware. I don't know if I can trust him again.

"You think... do you think this is easy for me, Everett? I'm just as lost and confused and hurt as you are. I don't know—"

"Please, please stop... I don't want to fight with you, Aspen. I just... I just miss you is all."

His voice drips with sincerity and tugs at my heartstrings and I'm suddenly so upset I don't want to pretend anymore. "I miss you, too. All the time, every day."

He sucks in a harsh breath, "what does that mean, Aspen? Do you... forgive me?" There's that hope in his voice, still shining through the dark clouds I've cast over him.

"I-I don't know... I want to."

"Are you coming back to London?"

"I don't know that either, Everett..." The sigh out of his mouth speaks a thousand words and I can almost see his shoulders slump, see him running a palm down his face, see him biting back tears. I can see all the emotions boiling up inside of him like a volcano, ready to erupt.

This is the breaking point, I can tell.

"What can I do? What do you want me to do, Aspen? I'll do it," his voice cracks and I know that he's crying now and I know it was a mistake to say those things. "I'll do anything you want, just *please* come home. Come back to me."

"Everett..." He sniffs and I taste salt on my tongue, "stop this, please." we're both crying now, our hearts bleeding and butchered at the floor by our feet and I feel the foreign walls around me closing in, feel my resolve crumbling to the ground with every shaky breath. "Everett, I-I have to go. I'm sorry, I shouldn't have sent that photo. I'm sorry for confusing you and being confused and I'm just a mess right now and.... and I have to go."

I hang up before it gets worse. I love Everett with everything I have in me. Every cell in my body screams for him. But, my heart has taken a beating and my brain won't let me forget the months of lies, the false start, and the deal brokered at my expense to win a fucking competition. What do you do when your heart is ripped in two very different directions?

My eye catches on the top drawer of my dresser, the envelope stuffed inside calling out to me like it has been for almost two weeks now. Though it may hurt me more than I already am, I pull on leggings and open the drawer anyway, grabbing the letter.

I need my father's advice now more than ever.

With my phone left on the bed, my hoodie pulled tight, and the letter gripped in my hands, I walk out of the house and through the back door, straight into the sand.

The sun has set long ago, leaving the stars to peek out from the blanket of black above and the frosty night air to chill my skin. I can't even see the waves from the endless darkness stretched out in front of me, but the one lamppost outside my back porch provides enough light for me to take a seat on the soft beach. I sit in the cold sand with my arms wrapped around my knees, watching the stars blink in out of existence. I concentrate on listening to the soft lull of the waves as they crash against the shore and retreat again.

Offensive and then defensive. Over and over. Much like me.

When my heart has calmed to the steady beat of a drum, my nerves have settled, and a smooth tranquility has taken over,

I finally bring the envelope up to the light. The once white paper has now faded into a soft yellow, some sort of liquid spilled long ago, blurring out my name written in the familiar shaky chicken scratch of my father's.

Without further thought, I'm tearing into the top of the envelope and pulling out the parchment. It's only a few pages long, but filled with black, smudged ink. It's with a deep breath and slightly shaking hands that I unfold the crisp paper and begin to read the letter written to me all those years ago for the first time.

*My dearest daughter,*

*Reading this letter, I can imagine how confused and hurt you must feel—one year of silence and then a measly letter in the mail?*

*I'll tell you, Aspen, it has taken me these last 325 days to gather up the courage to write to you, the courage to face what I've done to our family. I've started this letter many times in the past, always too chicken to write more than a few sentences before stopping. Just ask my fireplace how many drafts of mine it has eaten.*

*But, today is your birthday.*

*The first birthday I'm spending without you and I truly hope the last.*

*I suppose I should start from the beginning. That I should tell you how the last sixteen years I've spent with your mother slowly turned sour. How we both began to change in ways the other despised. I should tell you I fell out of love with your mother many years ago. That we only stayed together for you and your brother. But, I'm sure you already knew of our resentment for one another. You've always been very intuitive.*

*What I don't want to tell you is how I fell in love with my assistant. How she was funny and kind and ambitious and everything your mother isn't. How I began to imagine a life with her —a life away from the one I had then. I shouldn't have pursued it, I know. It wasn't right or fair to you kids or your mother. As you know, I'm not a perfect man. Far, far from it.*

*I'm sure by now you've heard an entirely different story from your mother, but you have to know that I wanted to bring you along with me to this new life. I wanted you and your brother both. But, your mother is tenacious and has resources and money I could only ever dream of. I was fighting a losing battle. When she dug up indiscretions from my past and threatened to bring them to light if I filed for custody I had to stop my efforts.*

*I would've lost my job and reputation, mia figlia.*

*Of course, I know now, that losing you was a much greater tragedy.*

*Leaving the house that day, leaving you behind without even getting to say goodbye... it was the hardest thing I've ever had to do and I've regretted it every day since. I can't even begin to tell you how many times I've called the house and hung up, waited outside your school for you to come out with your friends, how much I've wanted to show myself to you, to explain.*

*But, how could I show my face to a daughter I abandoned?*

*Aspen, there's been a whole inside my chest where my heart used to be for a year now and I want it back. I want my daughter back.*

*Courtney and I are leaving England. We've decided to move back to the states, to New York, and I want you to come with us.*

*I know you don't want to leave your brother or your mom, but please, share this letter with Marco. Offer him the choice to come, I would love to have both of you in my life again. To make up for lost time. But, I know this is a lot to ask.*

*We're planning to leave a month from now. If your answer is yes, please write me back and I will set everything up. I will fight for you this time, for your custody and your brother's if that's what you both want. Please think about it. Courtney would love to meet you and I miss you, mia figlia. I miss you more than I could possibly explain. I know none of this excuses what happened last year, none of this could ever be enough for you to forgive me, but I truly hope that you're able to one day. That you won't let your hurt and resentment for me affect your judgment in the future.*

*If you decide not to join me, I understand. I won't bother you again. If you only take away one thing from this letter, let it be that I didn't leave you willingly. That I didn't* not *want you.*

*You* are *wanted.*

*You are everything. You deserve happiness.*

*Even if I can't be the one to give it to you.*

*If I don't hear from you within the next month, then I'll have my answer. Just know, that whatever you choose to do, I'll always love you and be thinking of you. And I hope that your love for words is never crushed and your thirst for discovering new ones is never quenched.*

*Saudade: a deep emotional state of nostalgic, profound melancholic longing for an absent someone that one loves.*

*Happy Birthday my beautiful daughter,*

*Papà*

# NOTORIOUS

When I was nine years old I was almost swallowed by the sea.

Despite my mother's constant nagging and my father's incessant warnings, I waded into the treacherously freezing waters on an early January morning while they were busy setting up a picnic. I was a good swimmer, quick and strong.

But, the sea was stronger.

Before I was even knee deep in the water, the riptide pulled my ankles out from under me and swept me away. I was instantly blinded by the blackness and numb from the icy water. My senses were completely cut off by the furious ocean and I had no way of pulling myself out from her tight grip. I thrashed and writhed for what felt like hours, trying to swim one way and being pulled another. My lungs ached for air that wouldn't come and everything inside of me felt like a balloon being pumped full of too much air, about to burst.

The ocean was going to eat me and use my limbs as toothpicks.

And just when I was about to give up, when the fighting had tired me and my lips turned blue, my father pulled me from the ocean and dragged me back to the shore. I was safe.

But, those few minutes spent battling for my life, trying to fight against the inevitable, against something much more powerful than I... I thought that nothing could be more terrifying.

Until now.

I can tell the cab driver is growing restless, his fingers tapping against the steering wheel to the rhythm of whatever band is playing inside the large club. He shouldn't be complaining though, the meter is still running and has been since we left Whitstable.

I already practically owe the guy my entire wallet.

My eyes glide over the scene outside the tinted window once again —taking in the abundance of nicely dressed men and women stumbling in and out of the venue, the door opening every time, allowing the rest of the world to taste the music coming from inside and then closing again, masking it slightly.

Tonight is the night of the competition. The competition Saints & Sinners has been preparing for for over a year now. The one that guarantees us —no, *them*— a recording contract with a major record label. The same competition I was supposed to sing at, had Marco's deal gone through. And somehow... I found myself in London, sitting outside the venue in a cab that smells overwhelmingly like marijuana and cologne, too afraid to go in.

I can't even fully explain the events in the past 72 hours. Everything happened so quickly, without much thought or planning, and I'm not entirely sure how I got here.

But, it all began with that letter.

That too late goddamn letter from my father asking me to move with him eight years ago.

I was livid when I finished reading that letter over for the third time. Angry at my father for taking so long to write and then never writing again and then angry at my mother for hiding this away from me, for letting the opportunity slip through my fingers.

All I could think about were the 'what ifs'. What if I took his offer and grew up in the states —would I still be singing? Would I never have felt the pain and heartache of feeling unwanted by every person in my life —all stemming from my father's rejection?

My whole life... my whole life could've turned out differently.

But, the prospect was snatched away without me ever being aware it was there in the first place. So, I ripped that letter to shreds right there on that cold beach.

And then I cried.

I cried for everything that could've been. For my father who waited desperately for my reply, for my mother who was so insecure she had to keep me from him, for Everett, and mostly, for me. For who I could've been.

And then I gathered all of the little pieces of parchment, carried them back into the house, and taped the pieces back together. Decided I had to tape the pieces of my life back together. Because I was tired of the 'what ifs', of wondering what could've been, of letting people walk out of my life. Letting fear hold me back and cage me in.

I want to be the girl that I could've been.

So, I stayed up all night restoring that *damn* piano. I refused to leave Whitstable with the piano unfixed and unloved. Didn't want to abandon it again. Through a lot of sweat, some tears, and a little bit of blood from the tools, I finally finished tuning and replacing the strings. The sense of fulfillment and finality was overwhelming. As soon as my fingers touched those ivories keys and heard the perfect, lilting music, it was like a chapter of my life had finally closed.

I could finally move on.

With my father's final words to me looping in my head like a broken record, I re-packed my bag for the last time just after the sun rose. I started making calls to my landlord about renewing the lease in my apartment in London, then to a moving company to move my things back, and my job to start teaching guitar again. The next day I ordered this cab and drove the two hours back to London, trying not to jump out of a moving car.

Now that I'm actually here, I'm having a hard time following through with my resolve. Knowing that Everett is inside the building, so close, has my stomach as angry as the waves were that day on the beach when I was nine.

"Listen, lady, my wife is going to kill me if I don't make it home for dinner tonight. Are you going inside or what?"

My nerves are so taut that his booming voice makes me jump in my seat and I have to take a few calming breaths before I pull out my wallet with shaky hands and hand him the amount the meter is blinking at me. Grabbing my backpack, I exit the cab and stand in the middle of the road as my last chance to back out of this disappears into the busy London streets.

I run across the street to stand directly in front of the building, watching as people spill out of the entrance. I feel kind of silly standing there in my leather skirt, bustier top, tall boots... and ratty backpack.

A few people give me odd looks, obviously wondering if I'm a little lost —dressed to the nines outside this club with a full backpack on my shoulders like Dora the fucking explorer, but I ignore them. I'm already prepared to spill my guts out onto the street next to me, I don't need to worry about what I look like to strangers.

The music is closer now and I'm slightly relieved when I realize it's not one of our songs. Hopefully they haven't gone on already because this whole thing would be shot to hell. I take deep breaths, filling my lungs with cigarette smoke and the familiar stench of puke —so different from the smell of salty air I'd gotten used to. I focus on the clicking sound my heels make on the concrete as I head towards the door, the big and bald bouncer already eyeing my backpack. He gives me a once over and I try to look as serious as possible, "are you on the list?"

I hesitate slightly. There's a list? For a competition? I can't just walk in? "Uh... I don't think so, but I used to be in one of the bands that's performing tonight—"

He's already looking at the people lining up behind me to get in, "that means nothing to me. If you were still in the band, you'd get in."

It's clear he's trying to dismiss me, but I've already come this far and I'll be damned if this random burly asshole is going to turn me away when I know I'll never get up enough courage to do this again. When it's clear I'm not moving until he acknowledges me, he rolls his eyes and looks at the clipboard in his hands, "let me check the list. What's your name?"

"It's Aspen Marino," I rise on my tiptoes to try to peak at the names, "I told you I'm probably not on there. But, my brother —"

"Nope," he shakes his head and my stomach drops, but then his finger points to something I can't see on the paper, "you're right here."

This stops me in my tracks. I'm on the entrance list? Did they know I was coming?

No... that's impossible, I haven't told anyone. So, did someone put me on the list in the vain hope I would show up anyway? Could it have been Everett?

My heart leaps into my throat and my body warms at the thought that he's still waiting for me. My mind tells me not to jump to conclusions, but my heart has been through a beating and demands for me to believe it. The bouncer clears his throat at me for holding up the line and pushes the door open. I smile in thanks and step through without a moment of pause.

There are well over two hundred people squeezed into the small venue, all jumping around and singing along to whatever band is rocking out on the stage situated at the end of the room. My body vibrates from the loud bass and the picture frames hanging on the walls are practically falling off at every beat. It's dark, the only light coming from the stage and red lamps that give the venue an eerie glow. Graffiti covers every inch of the Victorian wallpaper and the bar wraps around both the right wall and the little space beside the door. There's little room to sit and the amount of people, darkness, and booming music make me dizzy and nauseated. I glance up to see the judges sitting at a table on the second floor, busily scribbling notes. Even though I'm not performing, my stomach still fills with anxious nerves for my band.

"Well, well, well... look who rose from the dead."

A grin spreads across my cheeks at the familiar and thick British accent. When I spin around, I'm met with shaggy brown hair, cerulean eyes, and a mischievous smirk. "Sam."

Our hug is quick, but affectionate. My respite has provided me with a lot of clarity and a more forgiving nature. I don't want to hold grudges anymore; my chest feels heavy enough without that weight bearing down on it.

He pulls away, mussing up his hair before assessing me. When he speaks, he has to almost yell because of the volume in here, "so, where did you go?"

"Away."

He smiles, eyes brightening, "ah, that's my favorite place to be."

I grin, feeling my nerves dying down at our easy banter. Maybe the rest of my friends won't hate me for being MIA all this time. Maybe they'll be as understanding as Sam.

"Have you gone on yet?"

His mood instantly sours, light smile easily flipping into a frown, "yeah, but we completely blew it. I was too nervous to sing properly, my voice kept cracking. And Jimmy kept mucking up the notes."

"I'm sorry to hear that."

"No, you're not," he laughs, nudging me with his elbow. "You're biased though. Probably rooting for Saints & Sinners, right?" I gulp, the nerves back just at the mention and my eyes flit back over to the stage where the current band has stopped playing and started to pack up their equipment. Sam notices this and follows my gaze.

"Well, you're here just in time. They're on next."

And sure enough, Jesse's red head peeks out from behind the

curtain with a new mic and cords, starting to plug everything in. Marco also slips through the velvet, glancing out at the judges before dragging out each one of his drums and symbols from the back. Avery follows with her keyboard, their eyes catching and nervous smiles shared.

That's also something that changed rapidly in the last few days. A very giddy and —way too personal— call from Avery told me that she and Marco were working things out. Over and over again. And though I'm happy to hear that, it also makes me want to vomit.

Enzo follows the couple a few minutes later, plugging in his bass and tuning the strings. Everett is still nowhere to be seen, but that doesn't stop my heartrate from skyrocketing.

My knuckles turn white against the straps of my backpack and just when I think I may pass out from nerves, I feel Sam tap my shoulder. "It'll be okay, Aspen." Even though he has no idea what's going on, his words are enough to slightly ease the waves in my belly, "I've got to get back to my band, but... It was really nice seeing you. I'm glad you're back."

I watch him disappear into the crowd, too far away to hear my reply, "me too."

And then, all of a sudden, there he is.

The air is stolen from my lungs at the sight of him. And though it's only been six weeks since I last laid eyes on him, it feels like a lifetime. I don't know what I expected to see, how different I thought he'd look. But, I'm pleased to see familiar brown locks, deep dimples, shining emerald eyes, tattoos, and his staple black attire that is slightly wrinkled.

He steps up to the mic and squints at the crowd stretched out across the room, the mob growing wild at the sight of him. My nerves get the best of me and I find myself slipping into the shadows, hugging the wall. He clears his throat, eyes still searching the room, but coming up empty. Unlike the day of his trial, it's not bitter resentment that has me hiding away, it's fear. Fear that it might be too late, that he may hate me. Fear of what the future has in store, to take that last step.

"Hello." The familiar, slow rasp of his voice lights a fire in me and hearing it, I know I've made the right choice. I know that I'm staying. "I'm Everett. And this is Enzo, Avery, and Marco —our manager Jesse is behind the scenes. We're going to play something new for you guys and we hope you enjoy it. We are Saints & Sinners and this is *Everything Good.*

The lights dim to a soft red hue and everything quiets apart from my racing heart and its rhythmic beat. Enzo strums his bass softly, the drums following in a light trickling sound like rain and I know this is something I've never heard before, something written after I'd already left. It's soft and sultry and from the crowd's enthusiastic shouts, I can tell they love it even though Everett hasn't begun to sing yet.

But, when he does, the crowd goes wild. And so does my heart.

His voice is low and soft and though the words are pretty generic, they instantly strike a chord. His eyes are glued to the floor, but all of the emotion within him is expressed by the lyrics, by the pain and love in his voice as it trembles, rises, and falls.

*"Everything good must come to end, but baby, please don't say we're through."*

He finally looks up, completely transformed into his stage persona —sexy and unattainable. But, his voice is almost sad, the intensity in his eyes slightly dimmed. The song carries on into the chorus, his voice powerful and desperate, his mouth making love to the microphone.

*"Just give me one last night to prove that I can be your man. Let me tattoo my lips on your skin, let your tongue wash away my sins. But, please, don't say we're through."*

The screaming of the crowd fades until I don't hear them at all. There's nothing else but Everett and his haunting lyrics. Chills freckle my skin and I'm stunned into silence as I watch him perform. My whole body is alive and thrumming, fueled by the rawness of his emotions, the familiarity of the romantic lyrics.

The longer the song goes on, the more he sings about losing a love and begging her to stay —to hold onto her even if for one last night... I know the song is about me.

And that's why, right before the final surge of the song, I find myself stepping out from the shadows, walking into the crowd. Avery notices me first, just as I reach the middle of the pit, standing stock still in the midst of a swaying mass. Her eyes grow twice their actual size, and with them, so does her smile. Her eyes flit between Everett and I and I know that if they weren't performing she would call out to him. I would smile back if I didn't feel like I was going to throw up, if I wasn't waiting for Everett to look at me.

But, Avery's excitement makes Marco glance my way in curiosity, catching my eye and essentially having the same reaction she had. And when I look over to Enzo, I see his shocked gaze trained on me as well.

Still, Everett's attention is focused on the opposite wall.

Then, almost all of a sudden, they aren't. It's as if he senses me there beneath him, watching him, because his eyes shift from the wall to my spot exactly.

And then the whole world stops.

If Enzo wasn't in the midst of a solo, I'm sure Everett would've stopped singing instantly upon catching my eye because his jaw goes slack and his frame freezes completely. He blinks rapidly, as if to make sure he isn't hallucinating and because I'm an idiot, I do the only thing my body will allow me to do.

I fucking wave at him.

Despite my instant regret, it does seem to wake him up because his mouth closes, eyes grow wide, and shock immobilizes him completely. My heart bruises my ribs and my lungs are turning blue from holding my breath and I'm completely overwhelmed with emotion. Wanting to both run up on stage and kiss the life out of him and also run away and never look back.

Then, he grins at me so wide and giddy, that he resembles a

little kid on Christmas. His dimples dig deep into his cheeks and his mossy eyes grow light and I know I sport an exact replica of his smile on my own lips. And then it's his turn to sing again and the grin fades from his lips, but his gaze never leaves my face —only growing more intense as he belts out the last few lines of the song. Singing to me, about me.

*"If I may, can I say, that I'll wait. I'll wait for you… even when my skin folds together and my body grows cold, I'll still be waiting for you. So, baby, please don't say we're through."*

His voice fades along with the lights and the stage goes black, his final lyric echoing around the room. Just as quick as he appeared he's gone again, but leaves an awe in his wake. The crowd is clapping and cheering so loudly that my ears ring and even though I'm no longer a part of the band, even though I didn't get to participate —the pride that swells inside my chest almost crushes me entirely.

They did it. They *actually* did it.

And all I want is to see them, to see Everett.

So, with shaky knees and a shakier heart, I push through the crowd of people, towards the back of the club. When I walk up to this bouncer, I automatically give him my name. Much to my delight and surprise, it's also on this list.

I pass through the black door, unsure what I'm meant to do now. I really should've prepared a speech or something. Luckily, I don't have to think about it for too long because Jesse is standing just outside the door when I'm let in. "Aspen!" I'm instantly pulled into a bone-crushing hug, the Scotsman pulling away to give me a harsh peck on the cheek, "you're back!"

I'm smiling just as hard as he is, "I think so, yeah!"

"Thank god! You've no idea how hectic it's been without you keeping everyone in line."

"Isn't that you're job as manager?"

"That's beside the point," he waves me off, putting his hand on my back and turning to lead me down the hallway. "I have to go help the band take everything down, but you can wait in our dressing room if you want."

What I really want is to see Everett, but it might be better if I have some time to get myself together and figure out what I'm going to say to him. My heart still hasn't calmed down and I'm afraid that when it comes to actually talking I'm going to blubber like an idiot.

Jesse leads me to a door marked 'Saints & Sinners' and leaves me to go back on stage.

I instantly run to the mirror, huffing when I notice that my once curled hair has fallen to flat waves and that my red lipstick has bled slightly. I try tousling my hair and reapplying my lipstick, but my hand is so unsteady that I end up just making it worse.

So, I opt for pacing the room instead, trying to calm myself down for when he walks in, but knowing that I'll be anything but.

Everything used to be so easy between us and now I don't know how to act or what to say. All I know is that I don't regret leaving and I won't apologize for it. I learned so much about myself by just getting away and taking time to learn to love myself again. But, I do regret that Everett was collateral damage, even if he was the catalyst in my decision.

I hope that he doesn't hate me for it.

To keep myself busy, I set down my backpack and bend down to rifle through it for my powder, but I've only opened the zipper when I hear the door open and shut behind me.

I don't even have to turn around to know who it is.

Because as soon as he's in the room, my body begins to hum and the air fills with an oppressive static that only his presence can cause. The room suddenly feels too small, like my lungs have been filled with cotton balls; aching for air, but also clogged. And my heart... my poor heart can barely keep up with my hectic emotions and I've no idea what to say.

Thankfully, Everett finds his voice so I don't have to.

"Skirts a bit short, don't you think, Munchkin? Not that I mind, because I really, *really* don't mind."

I swear everything inside of me wakes up at his slow, raspy

drawl. My body thrums like someone just flipped on a switch. Like I was lying dormant these past two months and now my heart is fluttering in my chest and my nerves are pulled taught, my stomach wild and roaring from the storm he brings with him everywhere he goes.

A slow smile spreads on my hot cheeks as what he said sinks in—the first words he ever said to me.

It feels like a lifetime ago.

A lifetime since I first met Everett, since I called him a womanizer and kissed him in the bathroom, fought with him at a party and let him into my dressing room. A lifetime since he took me to the cherry blossoms and kissed me in an alley and took me to his apartment. A lifetime since he told me he loved me and proved it to me every day after. A lifetime since he healed my old wounds. A lifetime since he broke my heart.

Long enough, if you ask me.

When my heart feels strong and I find my courage, I turn slowly and brace myself to face him again. As soon as my eyes land on his they brighten, a grin so wide I think it might split open his face, spreads on his cheeks. He takes a hesitant step closer, gaze tracing every inch of my face as if he can't quite believe I'm standing in front of him.

As if he believes I might disappear.

We're both speechless and unsure of what our next move should be. There's an ocean of words yet to be said between us, waiting for us to wade through the dangerous waters of regret and pain and... love. I don't know what the future may hold, but I can finally see the light at the end of the tunnel. They might lose or win the competition, Avery and Marco may break up or get married, I might reconnect with my father or never see him again.

I might start over with Everett or maybe I won't. There might be doubt and mistrust and more heated arguments and lies and hurtful words and it may not even work out. But, I feel something beginning to glow from within, like I've swallowed the sun.

I can see the hope.

His voice is breathless, giddy. Smile so bright that it's blinding and eyes so wet, I fear he may start crying. It's only one word, but that single word signifies so much, stands for something much more than the two of us could ever imagine.

"Hi."

"Hi."

And then we're laughing, our stares interlocked and intense, breaths choked by tears. But, they aren't sad tears any longer.

It's time.

It's time to begin again.

Notorious: famous or well known, typically for some bad quality or deed.

When I first met Everett, I believed he was just some perverted weirdo with awful jokes, notorious for being a wild and heartless womanizer. But, through knowing and loving Everett, I've learned many things. The most important:

Definitions were meant to be applied loosely.

# EPILOGUE: EUDAIMONIA

*Three years later*

"You're going to be late."

I ignore the small voice, strumming the nylon strings of the vintage Gibson, tongue poking out in concentration. Closing my eyes, I feel the vibrations of the chords and listen to the tinny noise of the grossly out-of-tune guitar. But, I can hardly hear it due to an even more out-of-tune voice that repeats their statement as if I hadn't heard them the first ten times. I groan, opening my eyes to stare at golden irises that mirror my dad's, curly chestnut hair similar to Marco's, and freckled cheeks that look so much like mine.

"Am not."

"Are too."

"Am not."

"Are too."

A deep growl rumbles my chest and the eight-year old squeals, running off into the hallway of the fancy studio. Rolling my eyes, I ignore him and tune the guitar until the strumming sounds like silk, placing it back on the stand, and glancing up at the clock above the recording booth.

Shit, I *am* going to be late.

"Luca, get your shoes on! We—"

"You're late, you know?" A gruff voice, tilted with a slight Italian accent has me spinning around, heart stuttering in my chest. He steps into the wide, sparse entrance of the recording studio with a grin on his thin lips. His grey suit is crisp and curly salt-and-pepper hair is slicked back. The wrinkles are prominent in his olive skin and his eyes are tired, but warm.

"We're not late, Dad. We're just... making an entrance."

Luca comes racing into the room at the sound of our dad's voice and I watch with a genuine smile and slight ache as he picks Luca up and swings him around, laughing all the while.

Finding out I had a six-year old brother two years ago was... *unexpected,* to say the least. As if reuniting with my father wasn't an already tumultuous event, discovering a sibling I never knew I had only worsened our strained relationship.

Marco and I showed up on my dad's doorstep, unannounced, just a few months after Saints & Sinners won the band competition and scored a record deal. After revealing to Marco everything Mom had kept from us, he was *infuriated.* Finding out our father *did* want us, but that it was our mom's blackmailing that made him lose all hope shattered Marco's perfect illusion of our mother. He didn't speak to her for nearly four months, and I had to practically drag him with me to New York, just as upset at our dad.

When my father swung open the door, his surprise was almost comical. He stood, mouth agape, in the tiny entryway of his townhome, as the two children he left behind 10 years prior finally reappeared. Once the shock wore off he began to cry hysterically, profusely apologizing, and Marco and I could only watch as the 46-year-old man wept in front of us.

Gone was the young and virile Italian man who raised us, replaced by the worn face of someone who experienced much loss. His belly had rounded out slightly, hair had begun to grey, and he carried with him a heavy weight that dragged his shoulders down. His appearance shocked and saddened me greatly. I'd missed so much of his life. He'd missed so much of mine.

So much time had been wasted.

I couldn't even fight him off when he pulled us inside,

wrapped us in a tight hug, and fervently kissed our cheeks and foreheads, touching our faces to see if we were actually real. Marco will deny it today, but he was almost crying as much as my father.

I'd planned a big, emotional speech. A speech chastising my father for leaving without a word, for not fighting harder, for not trying to contact us when we were adults. But, all of those words died on my tongue when I saw the man I once knew fall to his knees before us.

Then, Luca came bounding toward the entryway and our hearts stopped.

Born just four years after my dad abandoned us, Luca is everything good passed down from the Marino line. Funny, charming, intelligent, and kind. But, he's also stubborn and short-tempered and everyone tells me that we're eerily similar.

I don't see it.

In the last two years since showing up on my dad's stoop, we've tried to rebuild everything lost. Weekly phone calls, visits between New York and London, and daily 'Word of the Day' messages. It's not perfect and it's not easy, but I'd rather have him in my life than out of it. After all this time, it feels as if a great weight has been lifted off my chest, that something incomplete inside me has finally been filled.

"C'mon, people! What's taking so long?" Courtney, my step-mother, waltzes in behind my father, "hi, Aspen. You're looking gorgeous as always." I shoot her a tight-lipped smile and return the compliment, not used to the idea that someone only ten years my senior is my step-mother. She's dressed in a pretty blue chiffon dress that compliments her strawberry blonde hair and seawater eyes and it's plain to see why my dad fell in love with her. It also doesn't hurt that she's everything my mother isn't: compassionate, patient, and loving.

She sits Luca down on the bench next to the door and helps him put his dress shoes on as I awkwardly hug my dad in greeting, "you do look beautiful, mia figlia."

"Thank you, Papá."

He grins with pride and it doesn't take long for Courtney to usher us out the door, holding my garment bag out to me as I lock up the studio.

The studio belongs to Jesse, who took most of the prize money from the competition to build us our own practice space so we'd finally get out of his apartment. It's where we recorded our first record with Everett and I both singing lead vocals and It's where Jesse now records and manages talent other than our band.

Our record sold really well, benefiting from the success and press surrounding the win at that competition three years ago. A few of our songs even made it into the top 50 chart for the UK. We went on a small national tour that was both exhilarating and exhausting and as soon as we got back, we began work on our second studio album —which was also fairly popular. Our mild success boosted Jesse's career and now we hardly see the lad. I'm just grateful he gave me a key so I could use one of the rooms to teach guitar and give singing lessons. I may not need the money anymore, but I enjoy teaching, and it gives me a chance to work on my voice.

It was hard for me for a while: getting back into singing. There were many, many times I got up to a mic and just *choked.* Whether it was in the recording booth alone or even up on stage in front of thousands of people. It's not easy getting over stage-fright and I still feel that anxiety sometimes now, still need to meditate just to even breathe into a mic.

But, slowly, I found my voice again, found myself again.

I lock up the studio and we rush down the hall as I try to quell the nerves in my stomach for my performance today. I'm happy my dad could make it, but I dread playing referee for him and my mom all night. We've shared a handful of holidays now and they try to be cordial, but it's a wonder how they were ever married, their relationship is so volatile.

And just as we burst through the glass doors, my phone rings.

*Speak of the devil and she shall use her cloven hooves to call you.*

"Yes, mommy dearest?" My dad grimaces as we hurry down the street to his rental car.

"Aspen, where the hell are you? I swear sometimes you—" She cuts herself off and I hear the crowd behind her over her heavy, calming breaths. I smirk, climbing into the backseat with Luca as I wait for my mom to collect herself, using the breathing technique her therapist taught her.

"Just... please at least tell me you're close, Aspen?"

My dad pulls out of the lot and I start to unzip my shorts because I really need to look presentable or I'*m* going to need therapy from the lecture my mother will give me. "Are we far, dad?" I roll my eyes at my mom's groan and recite what he tells me "it's just 30 minutes, Mom."

"If your father is driving we won't see you for another hour. Always drove like a gran—"

"Bye mom!" I hang up even though I know she'll reprimand me for that later and slip my top off, "don't look guys, I need to get this dress on."

Luca groans, shielding his eyes in disgust, and I playfully shove him as the car winds further away from the city.

The dress is a deep red silk with a dangerously-dipped cowl neck and high slit, and I'm able to remove my bra and shorts from underneath the dress just as we're entering the country. Luca holds up his phone so I can fluff my brunette bob and touch up my red lips, absentmindedly playing with the gold medallion around my neck. I catch my father's gaze in the rear-view mirror and clock his smirk, my cheeks growing as red as my dress. Clearing my throat, I remove my hand from the fox emblem necklace and focus my gaze out the window.

The venue is just outside Essex and the closer we get, the more my palms sweat and heartrate quickens. After a few turns, the trees grow thicker and the sound from the city fades, replaced by farms and fields. By the time the road widens into a roundabout in front of the large stone warehouse, the sun has begun its descent behind the grassy knolls beyond the horizon.

Predictably, my mother is waiting at the entrance, face pinched and arms crossed. My dad lets out a heavy sigh and Courtney shifts uncomfortably in the passenger seat as we shift into park. With a deep breath, I exit the car on shaky knees and walk towards the petite woman in her very expensive, powder blue dress.

Her dark eyes graze my figure, "don't know why you guys picked such a revealing dress for a wedding."

I struggle not to roll my eyes, "you look lovely mother."

She responds with a tight smile, pressing a light kiss to my cheek. My father jerkily strides towards her and compliments her dress, earning him a polite nod. Courtney says her small hello and Luca hides behind my legs, casting his eyes down. My mother would never be rude to a child, but she took the news of a new family member harder than Marco and me both.

My mother breaks the uncomfortable silence, tone impatient, "well, you've held us up enough. It's show time." She instructs Courtney and my father to head down the trail and take their seats in the clearing where the ceremony will be held, before turning to Luca and me.

"Luca, you'll be given the rings inside, so put them in your pocket and don't lose them." He nods nervously and I smile at him in reassurance. "Aspen, keep your eye on him and go line up, I have to take my seat." I nod and usher Luca through the steel door, hearing the commotion of women's voices inside.

"And Aspen?" I glance over my shoulder and nearly tip over at the sight of a warm smile on my mother's rouged lips, "You *do* look lovely... reminds me of my prom." She laughs, the sound rare and light, and I bask in its mirth, thanking her. She shoos us off before turning to wind down the cobblestone and I watch until she disappears behind the trees.

With a deep breath, I open the door and am swept away in wedding chaos as the employees work on setting up the stage and tables. The large warehouse is all oak and stone, with tall vaulted ceilings and varnished walls. The tables are round and white with black and red flower arrangements in the center. Hanging from the ceiling are metallic moons and stars that glint off the setting sun and create a romantic night-sky effect. The decorations are a compromise between Avery's rebellion and her parent's conservativism: magical and extravagant.

Luca heads to the groomsmen's room and I turn down a hallway to the right, already hearing the slightly panicked, high trill I love so dearly.

"Aspen Marino! If I didn't just pop a Xanax, I swear I'd throttle you!"

I want to respond to Avery's indignation with some excuse or witty comment, but the words get lodged in my throat and hot tears prick my eyes.

The windows lining the wall cast her in the sun's warm glow, highlighting her bronze skin and making her honey eyes shine golden. Her dark curls are pulled up and back, held there by crescent shaped pins. The dress is a perfect compromise between her personality and her parent's desires. The top is a plunging neckline made of lace, embroidered with stars and moons that showcases her full breasts. The bottom is a slim, trumpet silhouette that molds to her curves and trails behind her in a crepe satin material with matching lace trim.

She notices my emotional turbulence and frantically shakes her head, holding her hands out, "No, no, no. Don't you *dare* cry. I can't take anymore."

She jerks her head to the side and I finally take notice of Avery's younger sister, Mira. They're almost exact replicas of the other, except Mira has bleached hair pulled into box braids and is a bit heavier than Avery. Her rouged cheeks are stained with tears, dark rimmed eyes puffy, and pierced nose runny. Mira huffs and pulls me into a quick hug, "whatever, I'm just emotional because I'm *relieved* Marco is taking you off my hands."

I laugh and clear my throat of the tears, "Yeah, I'm relieved that you're taking *Marco* off my hands... And, you look... *hideous.*"

Her laugh is light and jovial and she pulls me into a hug that I revel in.

This day has been a long time coming. I've dealt with years of their squabbles and break-ups. Years of their mushy baby-talk and make-ups. Until finally, after a gig last Spring, Marco grabbed the mic, got down on one knee, and suddenly proposed to Avery in the middle of a set. It wasn't necessarily romantic, but Avery loved it, disturbingly making out with him onstage.

I don't have much time to appreciate how beautiful my future sister looks before the distraught wedding planner bursts in to start ushering us towards the exit. Avery gulps and pulls a flask from her garter belt, taking a large sip. I laugh and grab her white, red, and black bouquet as Mira, Mira's long-term girlfriend, and Avery's cousin start to line up at the door.

The soft opening notes of *La Vie en Rose* sound from beyond the door and the planner ushers the girls out one by one. The soft evening light filters through the trees as each bridesmaid disappears behind the curve of the petal lined trail. I wait a few seconds after Mira, squeezing Avery's hand before stepping into the sunset.

The trail is winding, but the fairy lights guide me as the dreamy music gets louder and the guests slowly come into view. I step out of the tree line and glance up, eyes skating over Enzo and Jesse, before focusing on the man standing next to my very nervous-looking brother.

My grin widens instinctively, heart thundering, and I try to focus on not tripping. Mossy eyes light with affection, full lips pull into his signature smirk, and recently chopped curls brush his ears. He slowly shakes his head, taking in every inch of my figure as I make my way down the aisle, blushing profusely.

Everett's eyes never leave me, even when I take my spot in front of the altar, even when the music hits the chorus, even when Avery emerges from the forest and begins her trek down the aisle. Marco's eyes well up and even though it's not conventional, as soon as she reaches him, he plants a big, wet kiss on her—earning plenty of hoots and hollers from Enzo and Jesse.

Marco and Avery trip over their lines throughout, giggling and teasing each other. I feel Everett's intense stare on me the whole time, and will myself not to indulge in his attentions. But, as the couple exchanges their vows, my eyes involuntarily drift over to catch his gaze. His smile grows and he wiggles his eyebrows at me, making me chuckle as the couple shares their sappy promises and recollections of their tumultuous romance.

Everett's eyes grow soft and sincere and I know we're both reminiscing on our own journey these last four years. How we grew from animosity to love, only to be plunged into deep hurt and betrayal. How we crawled up from that pain together and started over as friends after I came back from Whitstable. How we wrote songs together, sang together, and hung out every day, *together.* We had to learn to love each other again, to trust each other.

We had to tend to our roots before our branches could grow.

It wasn't until our album release party, six months after I came back from Whitstable, that Everett got the courage to kiss me again. Starting over was difficult and nerve-wracking, but so very worth it. We've spent the past two years making music, laughing, and learning in our shared loft with Yoda. I continued teaching and Everett volunteered at a rehab clinic and we grew together. Even though we still argue and there's still pain, we're in a stable and loving relationship. Everything is how it should be.

Though, I still don't think his jokes are funny.

I refocus my attention on the couple just as the officiator announces them married and laugh when Marco takes Avery in his arms, dipping her low to the ground, and kissing her in a way I know Avery's parents must hate. The guests stand and cheer and my heart sings in chest, eyes stinging, as they walk down the aisle. I meet Everett in the middle, looping my arm through his as we follow the couple. He grins at the cameras, lips grazing my ear "that's some dress, Munchkin... couldn't keep my eyes off you."

The hair on my neck rises and I let out a shaky breath, smile secretive, "if you like the dress, you should see what's underneath it... or what's *not* underneath it."

I feel him tense beside me and he clears his throat, picking up the pace through the trail. "Fuck, you're such a tease, gonna have a tent in my pants for all the photos." His words are accompanied by a cheeky squeeze to my bum and I squeal, smacking him with the bouquet and hoping the videographer didn't catch that.

The bridal party takes photos for much too long before Everett and I can make our way onstage to perform for the first dance. Enzo's already setting up his bass when we get there and I give him a quick hug before nodding at the fill-ins for Marco and Avery. I tune my guitar, staring out at the patiently waiting crowd as Everett adjusts his mic, shooting me a wink and reassuring nod that settles my nerves.

Enzo and I begin the opening notes of *Can't Help Falling in Love* and Everett's voice slowly trickles in, soft and electrifying. Marco twirls Avery into his arms as I harmonize with Everett, lilting and low —the perfect companion to his timbre. Our voices melt together, so powerful in their passion, that even *I* get chills. His stare is intense, my stomach fluttering and smile soft as the world fades away. The couple sways in front of us, but I can't take my eyes off of Everett as the words fall from our lips, laced with love. By the time the last chords are played and our voices fade, my eyes are stinging and my heart is full.

My attention refocuses on Avery and Marco as he spins her into his arms and kisses her, the guests rising from their seats and clapping. Half the room is wiping their eyes, including my mother and father. I can't tell if they're emotional from the first dance or our duet, but either way, my cheeks flush and I'm quick to hand my guitar to the actual hired band.

The reception carries on with more dances, cake, and

toasts. Everett's toast is riddled with awful jokes and sexual innuendos that make half the room cringe and mine is mostly trying not to cry and rambling about how happy I am my best friend is now my sister.

Jesse flaunts his newfound success to anyone who will listen, Enzo flirts with the bartender, and my mother chats with Avery's parents. But, everything is so loud, the steak dinner makes me nauseous, and the warmth of the room all cause my head to spin. I leave to get fresh air and walk until I find a small bridge crossing the river just outside the venue. Taking deep breaths to quell my rocking stomach and pounding head, it's here that Everett finds me, not five minutes later.

His face pinches with concern as he crosses the bowed bridge, "I was looking for you... are you alright?"

"I'm fine, just hot and tired." I lean my elbows against the railing and let the night breeze cool my flushed cheeks, basking in the peace of nature.

Everett matches my stance, holding out my gold clutch, "this keeps going off."

Curiously, I grab the bag from him and open it up, face instantly paling when I see who's calling. I haven't been feeling very well lately: constantly tired, dizzy easily, and frequent headaches. Honestly, I didn't think much of it, but Everett grew worried when I fainted in the shower one morning and suggested I get checked out by a doctor. Even though I assured him it was likely anemia, Everett insisted.

"Hi, Dr. Ahmed." Everett's brows raise to his hairline, but I keep my gaze focused on the dark water below, cast with an eerie pale glow from the moon.

"Ms. Marino, so sorry to bother you on a weekend, but I thought I should give you your blood results as soon as possible." I gulp, trying not to let on how nervous I am and ignoring Everett's burning gaze. The music from the venue is muffled and soft, but I'm sure my heartbeat is louder.

"Well, you were right, you are anemic," I breathe a sigh of relief, shoulders slumping, but she's not done. "But, that seems to be a symptom of your pregnancy."

I take in a sharp breath and seem to hold it there, limbs growing numb as my mind tries to rationalize what she just said. The music stops and the water stills and the insects cease chirping and my world hits pause as those words reverberate around my skull.

"What?" I blink rapidly, positive I didn't hear her correctly, and almost wanting to laugh at the absurdity of the statement.

"You're pregnant, Ms. Marino."

The breath finally leaves my lungs in a gust of air and it feels like my souls leaves too. Everett is watching me attentively, but there's no way I can face him now. Because the world went from pause to fast forward and I can't keep up with my emotions. I feel the blood rushing out of my cheeks, harsh pound of my heart, spinning of my stomach, and I have to hold onto the railing so I don't vomit or faint again, nearly dropping my phone into the river.

"Are you... you're sure?"

She must hear the tremble in my voice because when she speaks again it's much gentler and low, as if speaking to someone on the brink. "Very sure, Aspen. These tests are 99% accurate, you're definitely pregnant. About six weeks based on your hCG levels."

I try to work through exactly what she's saying, but my vision blurs and I can't catch a full breath through the lump in my throat. I've always had an irregular cycle, so it makes sense I didn't notice I was late. And even though I'm on the pill, I'm not perfect at taking it on time... It all makes sense now: the dizzy spells, the nausea... *hell*, even my breasts have been sore. I chalked it all up to anemia and just being a woman... talk about denial. I was right about the iron deficiency, but only because I have a leech growing inside me, sucking all my nutrients.

Pregnant? *Me*? A mother?

*I'm going to be sick.*

Unaware of my sudden panic and turmoil, Dr. Ahmed rambles on about pre-natal vitamins and iron supplements, but my brain is too full to take any of that information in. I say a quick goodbye and hang up the phone, fighting the urge to throw it in the river and forget the conversation ever happened. Everett remains quiet, but I feel him watching me. How the hell am I supposed to tell him? What will he think?

I don't even know what *I* think... it's not that I don't want children or don't want *Everett's* children, but I'm only 24 and we're supposed to tour next year and I'm not even married and my mom will kill me and—

And then I'm leaning over the railing and dry heaving, lungs burning and throat aching. I haven't had anything to eat or drink all day and I'm suddenly grateful for that because all that comes out of my stomach is gas and air. Everett is quick to saddle up behind me, tucking my short tendrils behind my ear and rubbing my back.

"What's wrong, Aspen? Are you okay?" Except I can't answer him because I'm still gagging, eyes swimming and stomach clenching. When Everett speaks again, I can hear the slight alarm in the tremor of his voice. "Not gonna lie, I'm kind of freaking out here."

*You have no idea.*

My headache is sharp and vision is blurred when I finally turn to face him. The moonlight casts his face in shadow, but I can still see those seawater eyes and full pink lips and dimples I love so much. His hands are stuffed in his pockets and he's rocking slightly, brows furrowed. I take a deep breath, lungs burning and hands shaking, and just decide to tell him. Better to confess it now than let this life-alerting news eat away at me.

"Well, I *am* anemic," My voice is steady, calm, and the exact opposite of how I feel. Everett's shoulders slump with relief and he shakes his head, laughing lightly. But, there's a crease between his brows, like he's waiting for more. I rip off the Band-Aid. "But, I'm also pregnant."

He's brushing his curls back when I say it and his hand freezes in his hair, body rigid except for his rapid blinking. He's silent for so long, I wonder if he even heard me, heart beating at my ribcage. Everett's hand finally leaves his hair, voice shrouded in genuine disbelief, "what?"

"I'm pregnant, Everett."

He rears back in shock, mouth agape and breaths harsh as the words settle in the air between us. I wait with bated breath as he steps towards me and then falters, pacing the creaky bridge instead. Everett and I haven't really discussed children before, either too young or too busy to think about it. I know he'll support any decision I make, but I'm nervous for his reaction and how this will change our dynamic.

"Are you—you are? I mean... you're sure? You... we... you're really pregnant?"

I groan, hands on my cheeks as I answer him, "apparently six weeks pregnant, yeah."

Suddenly, Everett strides towards me and wraps his arms around my waist. He lifts me into the air, swinging me around dramatically, and I'm so high-strung and shocked by this response, I let out a startled laugh. He doesn't stop until I tell him I'm nauseous, setting me down gently. His grin is so wide and blinding it almost hurts to look at, dimples indenting his cheeks, and mossy eyes shining with unshed tears. He keeps shaking his head, brows high and cheeks flushed. I stable myself against the railing, slightly out of breath and dizzy from the spin and surprise of the last five minutes.

"Holy shit... holy shit, *holy shit*!" He laughs manically as the gravity of my words finally dawn on him, grabbing my cold cheeks between his warm palms, "You're really pregnant?"

I can't help but giggle, grabbing his hands, "For fox sake, *yes!*"

And then he's kissing me, lips soft as he grins against my mouth. I return the kiss, but my heart is still heavy in my chest and my nerves are still pulled taut. I push him away, hands shaking against his chest, slightly stunned by his excited reaction.

"You… this is good news?"

He moves his hands to the tops of my shoulders and pulls me into his chest for a hug, "are you kidding? This is *wonderful* news! I mean… surprising and unexpected, but you're fucking *pregnant*! We're having a baby! I can't believe it…"

I feel him grinning against my neck and I start really crying. His words make my heart flutter, but my stomach twists at his elation. He pulls away to meet my gaze, grin slowly faltering and eyes growing somber, "It *is* good news, right? How do you… how do *you* feel about it?"

I swallow the lump in my throat, not wanting to rain on his parade or disappoint him. I didn't expect him to be so happy, feeling slightly thrown. I'm afraid to share my own feelings now, worried that I don't share his enthusiasm. Shouldn't I be just as excited? Just as joyful?

"I… I don't know. It's not that it's *bad* news, but it's just so unexpected. We have plans… this could change our entire careers, entire *lives*." Except, these are all minor issues. I feel the real reason I'm so hesitant to celebrate hovering over me like an ominous, dark cloud. I bite my lip, but my chin starts to wobble and I gasp for air, "I'm… I'm *scared*, Everett. I'm so scared."

He's quick to pull me back into our hug, rocking us and smoothing down my hair. I cry into his shoulders, clutching onto his expensive suit, and wondering if it's the new hormones making me so emotional.

I'm terrified to be a parent because my own tumultuous upbringing has scarred me. My father's abandonment and mother's neglect didn't leave me with good examples of what a parent should be. Although we mended bridges eventually, my parents made me distrustful and cynical for the better part of my life and I'm afraid of repeating their pattern. If I know anything, it's that a good parent does the exact opposite of what they did… but, I guess that's a good place to start.

He coos into my ear, voice gentle and sympathetic, "It's

okay… It's okay. We have a great support system who'll help us as we work on music… And, it's okay to be scared, this is a big deal. I'm scared too, honestly… Completely terrified because I know any kid we have is going to be just as stubborn as you." I smack his chest lightly, but it does succeed in replacing a sob with a laugh. I can hear the smile in his voice, "But, really, I'll support any decision you make. All I know, is that we *can* do this because we'll be doing it *together.*"

And now I'm crying for an entirely different reason, his reassuring and supportive words making my chest squeeze and shoulders slightly lighter. I still feel that trepidation and worry, but knowing I have such a wonderful and stable partner by my side makes me feel hopeful. I clutch onto him, letting his strength and calm disposition soothe me. The tears eventually stop and I'm left red-faced and sniffling, nodding at Everett's concerned gaze.

"Together."

He grins and places a light peck on my lips, resting a ring-clad hand on my stomach, eyes light with awe.

"My munchkin is having a munchkin."

My chest bursts with laughter, adoration and love fueling my veins at his silly statement. I feel my heartrate slowing, growing more stable with every supportive word and tender look from Everett. It's scary and life-changing, but Everett's right: we can do this, together. "We're gonna be parents."

Saying it out loud makes it feel more real, but my voice is still filled with disbelief. Everett wraps his hands around my waist, slipping down to grip my bum, brows waggling, "you're going to be such a MILF," I let out a sharp laugh, cheeks burning, and Everett can't stop grinning. "Six weeks, huh? That's *some* conception story."

I grow even more flustered, already making that connection, but hoping he wouldn't bring it up. Groaning, I cover my face in embarrassment, remembering the port-a-potty at the festival we were playing at and the grabby hands, greedy lips, and urgency that had us climbing inside the dingy bathroom and ravishing each other.

"Never. Say. A. Word."

He laughs jovially and I'm feeling much lighter, the fear slowly waning and being replaced with excitement at the prospect of raising a mini-Everett. We're quiet, holding each other and listening to the croaking frogs below and the dull music from the venue. Then, I feel Everett's shoulders slump, a low curse emanating from deep in his chest, "Oh no… this fucking sucks."

I rear back, shocked by the exclamation, "excuse me?"

He's quick to shake his head, holding his palms up in surrender and faltering back, "no, no, no! *This* is wonderful, I'm seriously over the moon about our lil munchkin, but… this kind of ruins my plans."

"Well, it ruins mine too, but—"

"No! *Fuck,* I'm mucking this up," he's pacing again and I frown, watching his expression grow panicked as he furiously runs his fingers through his hair. "I… was planning something big for our anniversary next month, but now I'm worried you'll think I'm only doing it because I knocked you up… But, if I do it *now,* you could still think it's because I knocked you up."

I roll my eyes at his phrasing, "Just spit it out, Curly."

He stops moving, clearing his throat and straightening his jacket, "right, okay… So, I've been planning this for a while and during Marco's bachelor party last weekend I had him help me with it." Walking towards me, he starts to unbutton his shirt, hands shaking slightly. He takes a deep breath, stare intense and eyes dark, before pulling the crisp white shirt open.

I gasp, heart stuttering, as the moonlight casts a pale glow on his tanned chest, where a new tattoo lays over his heart. It's still slightly pink and raised and I'm careful not to touch it.

It's a simple outline of a small aspen tree.

"Everett," I breathe, heart nearly bursting at the seams as I take in the beautiful tree of my namesake, everything clicking into place, "Is this why you've refused to take your shirt off around me lately?"

He laughs, but the sound is strained and I can tell he's nervous. "Yeah, it was hard to fight you off, though. Kept trying to get in my pants, you sex addict."

I lightly slap his chest, careful to avoid the fresh ink, but I'm too weak to laugh at his playfulness. I really don't want to cry again, but the gesture is so sweet and meaningful, I feel my eyes burning.

Everett isn't done though.

He pulls his shirt down further and I notice script inked underneath the roots of the tree, squinting my eyes to see it in the darkness, "mi vuoi sposare?" [will you marry me?]

My heart leaps to my throat as I read out the Italian once, twice, then three times, blinking rapidly to make sure I'm not seeing things. Everett's chest heaves under my palm and his shaky breaths fan my face. His stare is intense as he takes in my reaction, brows furrowed in worry.

"Is... Is the Italian right? Marco helped me with it, but I swear if he was pulling some kind of joke I'm gonna—"

"Everett," I cut him off, voice wobbling and heart bruising my ribcage, hairs rising on the back of my neck, "are you... asking me to marry you?"

I try to remain calm as I wait for his confirmation, but Everett digs in his pocket silently, eyes soft and cheeks pink. He pulls out a small, blue velvet box, holding it delicately and taking a deep breath. "I bought this ring the week after you came home," I choke on a sob as he finally meets my gaze, eyes light with love, but darkened by fear, "I've carried it in my pocket for three years, waiting for the right time to officially ask you to be mine.

"I wasn't expecting it to be tonight, but now seems as good a time as any," his laughter is weak and breathy, nerves making his hands shake. "I love you, Aspen. I think I have since that first night I saw you signing in that bar six years ago. Despite all the shit we've been through, these last four years have been the best of my life. You're incredibly talented and kind and witty and stubborn and you hate tea, and you mean the world to me. You make me a better man and I love you even more for it... Every day I get to wake up next to you is a good day and I want to spend the rest of my life with you by my side... So, marry me, Aspen?"

My heart squeezes painfully in my chest and I'm bringing his head down to mine in no time, kissing him fiercely and tasting the salt of tears on my tongue.

"Yes, Everett. Of course, I'll marry you."

His lips are soft and warm and send shockwaves through my system. We smile into the kiss, laughing giddily, and he pulls away to open the box, revealing the ring inside. It's a gold band with one sapphire stone in the center, surrounded by smaller diamonds. It's petite and unique and vintage and perfect. His trembling hands slide it onto my finger, the ring fitting perfectly and feeling as if it was always meant for my finger. I can't stop the tears now, trying to get a lungful of air as the world spins in front of me. He rests his forehead on mine, the giddiness fading, as his breath fans my face. "I love you, Aspen."

"I love you, Everett."

He folds me into a hug, the muffled, romantic music reaching us through the trees. We sway silently, not wanting to break this moment, to walk back into that wedding and pretend nothing happened —because no way am I going to tell Avery about the engagement or baby during her wedding.

We stay in this singular bliss a little longer, feeling both fulfilled and nervous for the future and all it holds. The ring feels foreign on my finger as I run my hand down Everett's back, trying to plant my feet firmly into the ground so I don't faint. So much has changed tonight, so many things set in motion.

I bask in the peace of the moment, the silence, until Everett breaks it.

"What should a joke have in common with a pregnancy?"

"No."

"A good delivery."

And I actually chuckle at his horrible joke, silently hoping our child has my sense of humor.

His body is warm in the cold of the night, and through the trees I can see the warm glow from the venue's window. I can just make out our bandmates at the bar, clinking their glasses and laughing, Avery and Marco looking into each other's eyes with fond smiles. Beyond them, are my estranged father and his wife, lovingly dancing and holding each other. I even see my mom, at a table near them, with a small smile on her face as Luca shows her something on his phone.

The sight brings tears to my eyes, chest squeezing painfully. At one point in my life, I felt so low, so destitute, that my whole world was shrouded in a bleak dark. But, instead of cursing that darkness and hiding in it, I chose to turn on the light, and saw all the hands of the people I love reaching out to me.

The flowers have bloomed in the darkness of my heart, my loved ones tending to them carefully and consistently, even when they threaten to wither.

I've made amends and forgiven Everett, my family, and myself. I chose to face the light.

It hasn't been easy, but it's always been worth it.

I glance up into Everett's soulful eyes and feel the warmth of his love, bask in it. His palm lowers to my stomach once again and my now ring-clad hand meets his there. His other hand caresses my cheek and mine falls against his newly-tattooed chest.

His breath fans my face and eyes reflect the moonlight, "together."

I smile, voice soft and sure, "together."

Eudaimonia: "human flourishing"; contented state of happiness, healthiness, and prosperity.

# ABOUT THE AUTHOR

## Mags Mcmillan

This is Mags McMillan's first published novel, but she has been writing in journals and on walls since she was six years old, and has poetry published in her alma mater's literary journal. She also has other stories available online and plans to continue writing between her studies. She enjoys hiking, horror movies, and bad jokes. Since this is her debut novel, she would greatly love and appreciate reviews left on Amazon or Goodreads!

Contact: magsmcmillanauthor@hotmail.com

Printed in Great Britain
by Amazon

59246075R00220